WHAT BECOMES OF THE BROKEN HEARTED

LISA HOBMAN

Boldwood

First published in 2018. This edition published in Great Britain in 2024 by Boldwood Books Ltd.

Copyright © Lisa Hobman, 2018

Cover Design by Debbie Clement Design

Cover Images: Shutterstock

Every effort has been made to obtain the necessary permissions with reference to copyright material, both illustrative and quoted. We apologise for any omissions in this respect and will be pleased to make the appropriate acknowledgements in any future edition.

A CIP catalogue record for this book is available from the British Library.

Paperback ISBN 978-1-83656-737-0

Large Print ISBN 978-1-83656-738-7

Hardback ISBN 978-1-83656-736-3

Ebook ISBN 978-1-83656-739-4

Kindle ISBN 978-1-83656-740-0

Audio CD ISBN 978-1-83656-731-8

MP3 CD ISBN 978-1-83656-732-5

Digital audio download ISBN 978-1-83656-735-6

This book is printed on certified sustainable paper. Boldwood Books is dedicated to putting sustainability at the heart of our business. For more information please visit https://www.boldwoodbooks.com/about-us/sustainability/

Boldwood Books Ltd, 23 Bowerdean Street, London, SW6 3TN

www.boldwoodbooks.com

For Grace. You continue to surprise me and I couldn't be prouder.

1

CASSIE

Cassie's life was perfect.

She wasn't one to brag aloud to others but inwardly she knew, without a doubt, that it was true. In fact, it had become a regular occurrence for her to lie in her pristine bed with its gazillion thread count, Egyptian cotton sheets, in the stunning Glasgow West End apartment and just grin like an idiot.

She had good reason though. The man sleeping to her left was none other than Seth Guthrie, the sexiest, loveliest, most handsome man she had ever met. And he loved her: boring, geeky, bookish Cassandra Montgomery. He was the clean-cut businessman who could've had any woman he wanted, whilst she was the *Big Bang Theory* watching, *Marvel* movie loving, grunge music obsessed woman who was ten years his junior. They say opposites attract, but Cassie still couldn't quite believe her luck. She knew she wasn't hideous by any stretch, but she also knew she didn't really fit into the mould you would expect the wealthy tycoon to select his partners from; although rather like Eliza Dolittle in *My Fair Lady* she had been gradually transformed from the ripped jeans, lumberjack shirt and Doc

Martens wearing young woman to a designer dress wearing sophisticate. And now, here they were, snuggled up on a Sunday morning just as they had been for the last four years.

Seth owned the apartment when they met and whilst the exterior of the Victorian building, with its sandstone frontage and bay windows, was the epitome of Cassie's dream house, the interior was quite different. Seth's taste was what you could call minimalist. Plain white walls with white and grey furnishings – all extremely modern – and very little artwork to speak of, apart from some monochrome canvases with obscure titles that Seth had picked up from a gallery in Chicago. Cassie was desperate to bring some colour and character-filled charm back to the place that had once been filled with period splendour and she had made no bones about telling him so. His reaction had been something along the lines of, 'Anything for you, darling.' But it was clearly to appease her. She figured it would all happen in good time. She had grand plans for the place and she knew how much he adored her. He wouldn't deny her this wish, she was sure. She would be marrying him soon and then she would probably feel better equipped to stake her claim on the place and make her mark.

She had her best friend, Davina, to thank for the introduction to the love of her life. Vina and Cassie had met on their first day at university when they'd walked into the same lecture theatre together.

* * *

School had never really been a joy for Cassie. The learning wasn't the issue. The other kids were. She had always been a little different to her classmates and so had few memories of true school friendships. Where the majority of her peers had both parents, she had lost her mother at a young age. And where everyone else tended to be financially comfortable, Cassie's dad had to strive extra hard for the luxuries in life, resulting in charity shop purchases that instigated mocking and derisive stares.

Confidence wasn't something she'd ever had in abundance and for the most part she tried to blend into the background – becoming part of the fixtures and fittings rather going out of her way to be noticed.

Flashbacks of the trauma she'd experienced at the beginning of a new school year taunted Cassie as she walked into her lecture on the first day at university. She was very much aware that she looked like a deer in headlights as she allowed her wide eyes to scan the student-filled auditorium searching for someone to sit beside who didn't look quite so intimidating as the rest.

A pretty dark-haired girl made a beeline for her and grabbed her hand. 'Hi, I'm Davina, although you can call me Vina as I'm pretty sure we're going to be best friends. Come on. There are two seats free over there.' The insistent stranger tugged at Cassie's hand and she followed willingly.

Once they were seated Vina looked at her expectantly.

Realising she hadn't introduced herself yet, Cassie blushed as she did so. 'Oh, sorry, I'm Cassandra Montgomery. But most people call me Cassie.'

Vina held out her hand. 'Fabulous to meet you, Cassie.' They shook hands like they had just agreed on a serious business deal, not a new friendship.

Vina began to chat to Cassie as if they had known each other for ages and Cassie's nerves started to dissipate.

'You have the most gorgeous hair, Cassie. I wish mine was

blonde.' The pretty young woman sighed. 'Black hair is so... dull.'

Cassie smoothed down her hair, surprised at the comment seeing as she had literally just dragged a brush through it before class. And add to that the surprisingly pleasant, yet unfamiliar, feeling brought about by the compliment. 'Oh... Thank you. But your hair is beautiful. So shiny.' Her words carried the conviction she felt and she was shocked that this perfect specimen of womanhood would want to change anything about herself.

Vina shrugged. 'Hmm. I guess we all want what we can't have, eh?' She followed this with a giggle. 'Good grief, maybe I should be in a Psych class instead of Business and Finance.' She rolled her eyes.

Cassie scrunched her brow as her stomach twinged. Poor Vina had clearly walked in to the wrong class. Business and Finance was in a whole other block. This was, in fact, Comparative Literature. She was about to point out Vina's mistake when she glanced towards the white board at the front of the room. To her absolute horror the words:

Business and Finance – Lecture 1

were emblazoned in black against the shiny, stark white.

Her heart leapt. Before she could stand and dash out of the auditorium a tall, slender, bespectacled man wearing a blue shirt and khaki trousers walked in, dropped his briefcase and began firing jargonistic questions at the gathered students. Hands began to fly up in eagerness all around her and Vina was frantically typing on her top-of-the-range laptop.

Cassie leaned towards her new friend. 'Vina,' she whispered in a strangled panic.

The raven-haired girl's eyes stayed focused on her screen. 'Hmm?'

'I shouldn't be here.'

Vina turned to face Cassie and patted her arm. 'Oh, don't say that, honey. We're all in the same boat. This is all a bit intense but I'm sure it'll get easier. Don't forget it's only day one. Just give it time.'

Feeling her cheeks heat to the point of near spontaneous human combustion, Cassie leaned closer still. 'No, I mean I'm in the wrong bloody lecture. I thought this was a literature class.'

Vina's green eyes widened and she stared, open-mouthed for a moment. 'You're not kidding, are you?'

Cassie cringed and shook her head, no.

'But how—? I mean— oh God, Cassie, you nutcase!' Vina proceeded to fail at hiding her amusement at Cassie's ridiculous predicament. 'Okay, we need to get you out of here with your dignity intact.'

Cassie glanced around and was greeted with scowls from the other students who were clearly unimpressed with the two new friends' lack of concentration.

'Is there a problem, ladies?' The harsh voice of the tutor broke them from their whisperings.

'Erm... yes, sir. I mean... Cassie has had an urgent email to say she needs to attend the front office immediately to sign some paperwork,' Vina informed the man who now stood, hands on hips and with a line of irritation creasing his forehead.

'Well, then, you'd better go so I can get back to teaching, hadn't you?' he snapped as he glared at Cassie.

She nodded and gathered her belongings as quickly as possible, the all too familiar feeling of all eyes on her made her skin prickle as she did so. The heat in her cheeks indicated that her face was probably now the colour of a London bus and she kept her head down as she turned to walk towards the steps.

Vina grabbed her arm and whispered, 'Coffee at one in the quad?'

Cassie grinned. 'See you there.'

It was the start of a very firm friendship, which involved many girls' nights, lots of laughs and visits to each other's homes during the holidays. And this was all before Seth entered onto the scene...

* * *

Cassie rolled over to gaze at her man as he slept; the immaculate white pillowcase formed a halo around his messed-up hair and she smiled. Seth was rarely dishevelled but it somehow suited him and she was a little saddened that he didn't often remain unshaven. The five o'clock shadow that currently graced his angular jaw increased his sexiness by several notches. He looked nothing like his usual self, she mused. And nothing at all like the smart, suited man she had met all those years ago.

Reminiscing about how they met was another favourite pastime of hers and even though Seth poked fun at her for being an eternal romantic it didn't stop her...

The Guthries were such a lovely family – very wealthy yet still down to earth for the most part. Their huge Georgian mansion house in the most exclusive, rural area on the outskirts of Glasgow, with its line of expensive cars and household staff told of a very different life to Cassie's. She'd been brought up by her father in the small Cumbrian village of Dent where the two of them lived in a small but pretty cottage with their little dog, Bilbo.

Vina Guthrie's family had sent her off to university with the best of everything, whereas Cassie's dad had scrimped and saved following the death of his wife to ensure there were funds available to further his daughter's education. He had always put Cassie first. Losing her mother at a young age had left her with an emptiness and need for security that her father had clearly sensed. He rarely left her side when she was small and often told her stories of a princess whose mother had met the same fate. But in the story the princess eventually met her Prince Charming and the couple lived happily ever after. By the time Cassie had started her university course she hadn't met a single person who matched up to the perfect man her dad insisted was the only one deserving of his darling girl. He talked of security, not only financially but emotionally. All the boys she'd known were ridiculously immature and lacking in any ambition. She was beginning to give up hope of ever meeting someone who could withstand the pedestal her father had created in her mind's eye with his ideals for her future.

It was their final year of university and Vina had informed Cassie that her elusive big brother was coming to the city on his way home from a business meeting in Asia and that he was taking her out for dinner. Cassie was delighted for her friend seeing as Seth didn't seem to get much time to socialise. He had never been present when she had accompanied Vina home for the holidays so he was the only member of the Guthrie clan that she hadn't had the pleasure of meeting. Her knowledge of the businessman was limited to the stories Vina had told her and the photos of him dotted around the Guthrie residence. What she did know back then was that he was very handsome in a dreamy music and wind machines kind of way. It sounded like he had a wicked sense of humour and could prank with the best of them in his youth but that he had always been Vina's protector and Cassie greatly admired that quality in him.

Cassie sat on Vina's bed as her best friend rummaged through her wardrobe to find a suitable outfit for the occasion. Cassie wasn't paying too much attention and was, instead, miming along to a Pearl Jam track blurting from the speaker in her room.

'Did I mention you're invited to dinner, too, Cass?' Vina asked as she selected and discarded various items from her extensive collection of designer clothes.

Horrified, Cassie sat bolt upright from her lounging position on Vina's bed. 'What? No! I can't go!' She glanced down at her jogging bottoms and scruffy old *Spiderman* T-shirt.

Vina grinned. 'Well, not dressed like that you can't. Here try this on.' She threw a pretty navy-blue dress at Cassie. 'I think it'll suit you much more than me. That colour just drains my complexion.' She sighed.

Cassie shook her head. 'But you'll want to catch up with Seth alone and I'll just be in the way.'

Vina turned to face her and placed both hands on her hips. Fixing her with a determined stare she stated, 'You're my best friend. You're coming. End of. Get dressed.'

Cassie and Vina arrived at Bella Italia in the centre of Glasgow at seven thirty and were led towards their table by the maître d'. As they approached they were greeted by a familiar, handsome, beaming face.

'Davina!' He scooped her up and swung her around, regardless of the cramped space between the tables.

Vina squealed, paying no mind to their surroundings. 'Noodle-head!'

The dark-haired man placed Vina down and turned his

attention to Cassie. 'And I'm guessing you're the best friend I've heard so much about? Cassandra, right?' he asked in his lilting, Scottish accent that had been somewhat softened by so much travelling.

Cassie felt the telltale signs of embarrassment glowing in her face as she nodded. 'Yes, that's right.'

He held out his hand. 'A pleasure to meet you, Cassandra.' His gaze locked on hers and she was momentarily transfixed by his verdant eyes as his deep, sensual voice reverberated through to her core. She was taken aback by how much he resembled Gerard Butler in real life, and was fleetingly swept away into a fantasy featuring the two of them locked in an embrace as he saved her from some mortal peril.

Oh my word, that voice. That accent. And he's incredibly good-looking. The sexiest man I've ever met. So very sexy. Hmm, sexy Seth.

Realising she was staring she slipped her hand into his where it was swallowed up and she smiled nervously. 'Lovely to m-meet you too, Sex... eth... erm... Seth.' Her eyes widened and she cringed, shaking her head in bewilderment and embarrassment as her steamy thoughts slipped out as words.

Vina burst into hysterical giggles. 'Sexeth? Well, it's the first time I've heard you called that, Noodle-head. And we know I've heard you referred to by all manner of delightful names.' She nudged Cassie who was now standing with her eyes scrunched tight and praying for the marble, mosaic tiled floor to open up and swallow her.

When she opened her eyes again, Seth was smiling and there was a distinct twinkle of humour in his eyes. 'Oh yes, she's right. I've been called much, much worse.'

Cassie swallowed hard, fighting the tears of utter mortification at her ridiculous slip-up. 'Well, I can't think why that would be,' she said forcing a smile. 'And please call me Cassie.'

'How kind you are, Cassie. Oh, and there is a story behind Vina's nickname for me, in case you're wondering.' He gave her hand a slight squeeze, which caused her heart to skip and further fuelled the inferno raging beneath her skin.

'Shall we?' Seth gestured to the table and the two friends followed closely behind.

Vina nudged Cassie again. 'Are you okay?' she asked with a grin.

'I'm fine,' Cassie lied.

'Honestly, only you could call my hulking great brother *Sexeth*. Hilarious. I don't care if it was an accident, that's definitely one to keep a mental note of for the future,' Vina teased.

Throughout the evening the conversation flowed effortlessly. Admittedly it was mostly lead by Davina as she revelled in telling her older brother of the antics she and Cassie had got up to during their time at university. He listened intently and laughed every so often. It was sonorous sound that reverberated from somewhere deep inside his broad muscular chest and Cassie found herself staring again.

Eventually Cassie plucked up the courage to speak. 'So, Vina tells me you're on the way home from a business trip to Asia. I bet that was exciting.' She had never travelled to Asia. In fact, the farthest she'd been was Greece for a girls' holiday during the last summer break from uni; the flight for which had been traumatic to say the least. Poor Vina's hands probably still held the indentations made by Cassie's nails. Now the thought of regular international flights both terrified and thrilled her.

Seth took a gulp of his red wine and smiled, revealing a set of perfect white teeth. 'It's exciting for about the first five minutes of the flight and then it gets quite monotonous to be honest. And as for the visit... I didn't really get to see much apart from the inside of meeting rooms. The flight was better than usual though. I had this little pod in first class all to myself. The flight attendants brought me champagne and I watched the latest Brad Pitt flick on my own personal screen. Very flash.' He raised his eyebrows and Cassie fought the dreamy sigh threatening to escape her.

The evening passed by in a lust-filled haze for Cassie. Seth was attentive and asked her lots of questions about her likes and dislikes. It was quite pleasant to have someone appear so interested even if it was a show for his baby sister.

He seemed to find her addiction to *Marvel* movies amusing. 'So you like a buff hero then, eh?'

Her cheeks flushed with that familiar heat again and she tucked her hair behind her ear. 'What girl doesn't? Although, I don't exactly expect my hero to be wearing a special suit or carrying an indestructible hammer.' She smiled.

Seth wiped imaginary sweat from his brow. 'Phew. I was just going to say a man has a lot to live up to where you're concerned.'

She shook her head as her heart skipped a little. 'Oh no. Not really. My dad has just encouraged me to look for the best in a man.' She inwardly cringed as she realised she was now flirting with him.

Seth nodded. 'I see. I see.' There was a hint of a smirk on his face as he smoothed his tie down with a large, tanned hand.

Vina made a snorting noise. 'Bloody hell, get a room, you two!'

Cassie turned to glare at her best friend but immediately felt guilty. Here she was hogging the brief time Vina had with her older brother. It was just so hard not to. All he was missing was the white charger and a lance.

At the end of the meal Vina excused herself and once she was out of earshot, Seth leaned across the table and fixed Cassie with an intense gaze. 'Cassie, I'd like to see you again. Can I take you out for dinner?'

Her heart flip-flopped in her chest as she let the words sink in. 'You mean... you mean like a date? Just the two of us?' *Well durr, you lemon head.*

He grinned. 'Exactly like a date. Unless you already belong to some other lucky chap?'

Belong? 'Erm... no, no, no, no, no I'm not seeing anyone.' *Stop rambling, you idiot. You sound like that old guy from The Vicar of Dibley who repeats himself, only without the comedy factor.*

He nodded and handed her a business card, lightly stroking her fingers as she took it from him. 'Great. Send me a text to this number and I'll save yours to my contacts. I'll give you a call with the details.'

She hurriedly did as he requested before Vina returned, worried at how her friend would react if she knew.

'I look forward to spending a little more time with you, Cassie, and then we'll find out if I match up to those exacting standards,' Seth informed her in that deep silky voice of his and she swallowed, her mouth suddenly rather dry.

'Me too,' she whispered in reply. 'Erm... looking forward to spending time with you, I mean.' She cringed, hoping that he didn't think she meant the standards thing.

He would go on to tell her months later that her bumbling idiocy on their first meeting was endearing and he knew from the moment she called him Sexeth that he wanted her as his own.

Wow. Just wow. A man of taste and sophistication fell for nerdy britches Montgomery. *In your faces, bullying high school peers.*

In. Your. Bloody Faces.

2

From the moment he had declared that he wanted to see her again on that fateful night, Seth had embarked upon an old-fashioned mission to woo her. She recognised the traits from the classic romance novels she loved so dearly. There were flowers, walks in the park by the Kelvingrove Gallery, small tokens of his affection such as teddy bears, chocolates and jewellery. Vina joked that she had never seen her brother behave in such a soppy way and Seth continued to insist she was wrong, that he wasn't an old romantic; even though he clearly was.

Cassie couldn't believe how lucky she was but Seth insisted *he* was the lucky one. Any time he travelled abroad for business there would be long conversations on the telephone – some that were decidedly raunchy – and he eventually insisted that she should move in so that she could be there when he arrived home. Apparently, there was nothing he hated more than getting back to an empty apartment.

From the moment she moved in everything seemed to click into place. Cassie never imagined she would ever be this happy. And never in her wildest dreams did she imagine that someone like her would end up with someone like Seth Guthrie. The reluctant-to-admit-it romantic who adored every single thing about her.

The weekend of their third anniversary of 'coupledom' had proved what a romantic Seth truly was. It was strange not to be waking up in their Glasgow apartment but the weekend in Alnwick had been a sweet surprise he had arranged especially for her. The bed was smaller than they were used to. However, a normal sized double bed meant that she was snuggled closer to him, so it wasn't at all bad. The scent of him infiltrated her nostrils and she sighed with sheer contentment.

Puffin Cottage was so beautiful with its bare stone walls and log burning stove. It was reminiscent of where she grew up, so Cassie felt right at home. Seth said he'd known instantly when he saw the photos on the booking site that she would adore it. He knew her so well.

She lay awake with her head propped on her hand, just watching him. His handsome chiselled features were relaxed in slumber and she found herself wondering what her life would have been like had she not met him. He took charge and she liked that. He was everything she imagined her dad wanted for her. If she hadn't met him she had no idea where she'd be. Realising she hated that thought she shuddered causing him to stir, so she held her breath unwilling to break the spell of watching her Prince Charming dreaming just yet.

Eventually, his eyelids fluttered open and his mouth stretched into a gorgeous smile. 'Hey, poppet. How long have you been awake?'

'Oh, not long,' she lied.

'Hmm, well are you just going to lay there or are you going to let me make love to you?'

She playfully tapped her chin. 'Oh... I don't know. Hang on; give me a minute to think.'

He launched himself at her and she squealed with delight as he scooped her from her own side of the bed and settled between her thighs.

He pouted. 'You wear too many clothes to bed,' he informed her as he tugged at her satin nightie until it was completely removed and he cast it aside.

She giggled. 'But it was really chilly last night.'

He began to feather kisses along her shoulder to just under her ear. 'That's what you get with old buildings that haven't been brought to the present century yet. Draughts, cobwebs and woodlice.'

In spite of herself, she gasped at the sensation of pleasure that spread like heat throughout her body, making every nerve ending spring to life.

'Hmm,' she moaned. 'I love old buildings though,' she sighed as he took her peaked nipple into his mouth.

With a mouthful of her flesh he mumbled. 'But you love me more.'

She pulled her lip between her teeth as he stroked his fingertips down the length of her heated body and her eyes drifted closed as he teased her.

She nodded. 'That's very true.'

'And when you marry me you'll promise to obey me in your vows, won't you?'

Wait, what? Her eyes sprang open and she gasped. 'I'm sorry?'

He pulled away and propped himself on his elbows as he sank himself into her yielding body. 'You heard me.' He grinned.

'But... but...'

He chuckled at her response. 'Cassie, darling, don't gawp at me like a deranged goldfish. What's surprised you so much? You know I'm a traditional man and I like the old vows.'

She stared up at him in shock considering this was the first time the M word had been uttered, never mind the word 'obey' being uttered in the same sentence. 'Marriage though?'

He took her mouth in a deep, lingering kiss that not only stole her breath but also the last shred of ability to form cognitive thought.

'You feel so good,' he groaned as he moved but she could no longer concentrate.

'Seth... Seth... stop,' she gasped through a confused fog of desire and frustration.

'Don't want to,' he mumbled as he nibbled at her neck.

Realising arguing at that precise moment was futile she gave in once again to the pleasure warming her blood until she cried out his name in release and he followed suit.

Once their breathing had calmed and the sated fog had cleared Seth flopped to the bed beside her and turned to face her.

She reached up and stroked his unshaven face, loving the way the spiky hairs rasped at her soft skin. 'You've never mentioned marriage before, Seth. You've completely thrown me.'

He grinned and raised his eyebrows. 'I just love the element of surprise, don't you? And anyway, it's not like I actually proposed during sex. I have more class than that. I just mentioned it in passing, that's all.' He shrugged as if it was no big deal, which irked her.

'But you could've mentioned it when you weren't sucking on my various erogenous zones. There really is a time and place for such conversations. And that wasn't it.'

He tapped her nose lightly. 'Like I said my little love muffin, it wasn't a proposal.'

He sat upright and stretched his arms above his head and the defined muscles of his back expanded and contracted and Cassie found herself thrown once again.

Realising she had a serious point to make she sat up too and pushed all thoughts of the man of her dreams' naked body aside. 'But you want me to obey you?'

He turned to face her. 'Does that really bother you so much?'

She chewed on the inside of her cheek as she contemplated the outdated words. 'Honestly? Yes. I don't know if I'm comfortable with the whole obey concept. This is the 21st century you know.'

Shaking his head, he sighed. 'My mother said those words and you don't see her being downtrodden in any way, do you?'

He had a fair point. American-born Vanessa Guthrie, née Claremont, was anything but downtrodden. She was her husband's equal in every conceivable way. In fact, it could be said that her husband worshipped the ground she walked upon, so she was probably a little more than equal.

Seth leaned forward and kissed the tip of her nose. 'Just say you'll think about it. Then when I do ask you to marry me, you'll know what I expect.' Before she could protest further he climbed out of the bed and walked towards the bathroom whilst she ogled his taut bottom.

He certainly didn't look ten years her senior. In fact, he looked better than most men her age. And he was obviously much more mature. He had real, honest to goodness life experience. And there was nothing sexier than a man in a suit. Unless it was her man out of his. And, of course, there was the smell of his cologne. It could easily turn her into a gelatinous, lustful wreck.

She waited for him to finish his shower and to shave the sexy stubble away and then she followed him in whilst he dressed and went to make coffee. Once she was ready she found him in the quaint lounge – on his phone as always. She stepped close and slipped her hands over his shoulders and down the hard plains of his chest as she inhaled his fresh clean scent. He switched off the screen and slipped the phone into his pocket.

'Did I interrupt something important?' she asked as she walked around to the front of the couch where he sat.

'Oh no, poppet, just business. You know how it is. Always in demand.' He tugged her hand and pulled her onto the seat beside him. 'Anyway, I thought we could go and visit the castle today. I know how you love draughty, old buildings so that one should be right up your street,' he teased. 'Then tonight we're booked into that lovely French bistro on the main street in Alnwick. It has really good reviews. Although I doubt it will be quite as good as the places we're used to in the cities but one can hope.'

She kissed his chin. 'It all sounds wonderful.'

He stood and tugged her hand. 'Come on then. Let's go. Lots to cram in today.' She walked towards the coat rack and he patted her bottom lightly before grabbing the keys to his sports car from the side table. 'Ooh, one sec though. I have a gift for you.'

Her heart lurched. Is this it? Is he actually going to propose? It seems odd that he brought it up when he did. There must've been a reason. Her pulse raced and she waited for him to return from the kitchen. When he arrived, he held in his arms a large box, wrapped in beautiful paper and tied with a satin ribbon. She sat on the couch and he passed it to her. Eagerly, she tore at the fancy gift-wrap and delved into the box like a child on Christmas Morning. She half expected it to be a trick – one of those box-within-a-box scenarios but instead, she pulled out a beautiful, tan leather handbag with the designer label embossed on the front.

She heard his feet shuffle and she glanced up at him. Gift giving was the only time he ever appeared nervous. 'I saw it and thought, *"Ahhh, my little poppet will just adore that,"*' he told her eagerly. 'You do like it, don't you?'

She nodded. 'Oh yes, yes it's lovely. So very me.' She smiled widely trying to fight the niggling disappointment that it wasn't actually a ring. It appeared that there was a designer bag for every single occasion. One to cheer her up on the anniversary of her mother's death, one for the day they moved in together, several for birthdays and Christmases and even one when Cassie had finalised the details of her new freelance business. And here was another to join the ever-growing collection. The problem was, she was one woman with many designer hand-bags and not enough occasions to justify their use. Okay so there were many business dinners and charity events but still, it was difficult to make use of so many. He's so thoughtful and I'm such an ungrateful cow, she thought.

She stood and flung her arms around his neck. 'It's wonder-ful. I love it, sweetie. It's so perfect, in fact, that I'm going to swap it with my other right now and take the new one with me today.'

* * *

The medieval castle at Alnwick was just fabulous; situated on a picturesque mount in the Northumberland countryside by the River Aln, the square keep struck an imposing figure. Cassie had seen it on television when it had been used as a film set so to be standing in the stunning, landscaped gardens was a dream come true and she wondered why she hadn't been before. The sun shone down on the couple as if it knew they were celebrating their three-year anniversary and Cassie wondered if her mum had put a good word in up there for them. They walked the spectacular grounds hand-in-hand, admiring the countryside views that surrounded them from the rampart walkways. They took in the splendour of the state rooms and Cassie imagined what life must've been like as a member of the Percy family all those years ago when the fourth Duke of Northumberland restored the rooms to their current glory. It had clearly been a labour of the love. The ornate carved ceilings and renaissance paintings were such a splendid sight to behold.

Every so often Cassie would glance over at Seth who would quickly squirrel his phone away and feign interest just for her. Modern architecture was more his thing and she accepted that, wholeheartedly, as one of their differences. After all, liking exactly the same things would have meant a lack of conversation and a pretty dull life.

Back in the grounds once again they watched as a group of children underwent 'broom flight training' with a *Harry Potter* lookalike and they laughed along as the youngsters ran around leaping, pretending to fly as observing parents snapped myriad photos, hoping to catch that perfect mid-air shot.

Seth squeezed her hand. 'So, how many of those do you want?' he asked as he nodded his head towards the energetic boys and girls.

She frowned at the question. 'Gosh, I don't really know. I hadn't thought that far ahead to be honest. I'm only twenty-six so I have plenty of time to decide.'

He pulled her into his side and kissed her head. 'You always forget about the age difference between us, don't you? My silly little poppet.'

He was right in a way. It wasn't something that she was

consciously aware of all of the time – well until he brought it up, which wasn't that often. Although the condescending tone he had used on that particular occasion did annoy her somewhat. But she reminded herself it was just his way and he was only being sweet, so she didn't comment on the matter.

She slapped his arm playfully. 'Oh, stop it, will you? You're thirty-six, not eighty-six.'

He pulled her into an embrace and gazed down at her, his green eyes filled with sincerity. 'Yes, but I want lots of children so I want to be planning these things now, not in ten years' time when you think you're ready. You'll be over the moon once you've got a baby inside of you. All this talk of waiting will be long forgotten, you'll see. And children are very important to my family line.'

There seemed to be little consideration for Cassie in his monologue and worry niggled at the back of her mind. 'Yes, but you're your own person, Seth. You don't need to follow everyone else's life plan. We can decide on things like kids together when we're both ready.'

He released her and held her at arm's length. 'No, I'm aware of that. But this is my life plan, Cassie. I want a large family. And don't call them kids. Kids are baby goats, darling.' She scowled at him and opened her mouth to retort but he placed a finger on her lips. 'Sorry... sorry that was snide and uncalled for. It's just that I need to have children. It's something I've always wanted and not just because of the family line. You do understand that, don't you?'

She clenched her jaw. 'Yes. Yes, of course, I understand.' The last thing she wanted was to be railroaded into being barefoot and pregnant before she was ready. But she loved him, he was the perfect man for her and she didn't want to fight on their anniversary so she decided to lighten the mood.

'Well, when you propose to me properly, Mr Guthrie, we'll discuss such matters then, hmm? In the meantime, there's no harm in practising, is there? Now are you going to get me an ice-cream or what?' She pulled away from him and took off towards the ice-cream stall where a long queue was forming and he followed behind with a handsome smile on his face.

The rest of the day was free from talk of marriage and babies and Cassie was grateful for that small mercy; feeling so much more relaxed because of it.

* * *

Later, back at the tiny cottage they made love again and then showered and dressed for dinner. Cassie wore the little black designer dress that Seth had bought her from a very exclusive Edinburgh boutique. It fit like a glove and hugged her curves perfectly. She loved the reaction it elicited from him when she wore it.

He walked up and slipped his arms around her waist. 'Well, look at you. I do know how to pick clothes, don't I?'

She shook her head. 'Do I sense a hint of arrogance there, Mr Guthrie?' she teased.

He leaned in to kiss the exposed flesh of her neck. 'Not arrogance, darling. Just the truth.' He patted her bottom before turning away. 'Now come on. Something about this country air has given me a huge appetite and I don't just mean for you, my tasty morsel.'

A taxi was waiting outside the cottage, which surprised Cassie as Seth always preferred to drive when he had the chance. Like a true gent he opened the door and allowed Cassie to climb in first and when they later pulled up outside the bistro he was out first to do the same.

With her arm linked in his they walked into the dimly lit, busy restaurant. The delicious aroma of garlic and Herbes de Provence emanating from the kitchen made Cassie's stomach growl in anticipation as a smartly dressed young man showed them to a secluded table towards the back. Seth pulled out Cassie's chair and she sat.

'We'll have a bottle of your finest Bordeaux to begin with, please,' Seth informed the waiter before taking his seat.

'Very good, sir. Here are your menus. I'll be back shortly.' He handed the leather-bound booklets to them and left.

Seth glanced around their surroundings and crumpled his nose as he regarded the wax covered wine bottle acting as a candle holder in the centre of the table. 'I didn't think people still did that,' he said with disdain.

'Oh, I think it's quite sweet. It's rustic.'

He reached across the table and took her hand. 'That's why I love you. You have this amazing ability to see beauty in ugly things.'

She paused for a moment and frowned as she let his strange words sink in. A little patronising perhaps but she knew that when it came to expressing himself outside of the business world his turn of phrase could leave a lot to be desired.

'Don't scowl, poppet. You'll get permanent lines and that would ruin your pretty face. Anyway, you know what I meant. I like modern, clean lines and fresh colours. But you... you like derelict things. Old things that people would usually discard. And I don't just mean me.' He chuckled.

And just like that his apparent arrogance had changed to self-deprecation and her heart warmed once more. 'Like I said earlier, you're not old, silly.'

The waiter arrived with the wine and poured some into Seth's glass for him to try it. He took a sip and paused with a slight grimace on his face. He glanced up and Cassie pleaded at him with her eyes not to say anything negative.

Seth placed his glass down. 'Yes, that's fine. Thank you.' Cassie breathed a sigh of relief and was sure she saw the waiter do the same.

Once the waiter had taken their orders for food he left again and Seth sighed. 'I should've taken you to Glitterati in Edinburgh like I wanted to.' He spoke quietly as if only to himself.

Cassie reached over and squeezed his hand. 'No, no this is lovely. So quaint and—'

'Dark,' he interjected.

She sighed. 'I was going to say cosy.'

'Anyway, whilst I remember I need to let you know we have a very busy week ahead. Do you have your diary?' Seth asked as he took another hesitant sip of his wine.

Cassie took a drink and placed down her glass thinking it didn't taste bad at all in her opinion. 'You want to talk about that now?'

He shrugged. 'Might as well synchronise diaries, poppet.' Reluctantly Cassie reached into her oversized new designer bag and pulled out her mobile phone at which point Seth heaved a sigh. 'Why don't you use the diary I bought you?'

Cassie frowned, wondering how to inform him that the huge Filofax was rather cumbersome. 'I prefer to put things in my phone then I can set reminders. You know how scatter-brained I can be.'

He raised his eyebrows. 'Well, I hope you never lose the damn thing then, eh?'

Her temper began to rise and she hissed, 'Bloody hell, Seth, I'm not twelve.'

He glared at her momentarily and then smiled. 'You're right, darling. I apologise. Now... Monday is dinner with Jasper and Pippa.'

Cassie looked down at her phone and secretly rolled her eyes. Jasper was such a lecherous prat – always aiming any conversation directly at her breasts. Pippa, on the other hand, was around the same age as Cassie and really quite lovely. She had to wonder what Pippa saw in Jasper. She genuinely seemed to adore him. Pippa, Vina and Cassie often met for cocktails in Glasgow City centre and Pippa always had some story to tell about her husband. It was clear she was aware of his nuances but it didn't seem to bother her. Seth called them the terrible trio and feigned annoyance whenever she arranged her girls' nights. But she knew that secretly he loved the fact that Cassie had a ready-made friendship with his younger sister.

She typed into the calendar on her phone. 'Okay. Noted.'

'Tuesday, we have dinner with my parents.' He thumbed through his slim black diary. 'Wednesday, we're going to the theatre with Maxwell and Sophia Grant. I may be working with Max in the near future so it's a good chance to meet with them and get friendly. Oh and just a heads-up – don't call him Max to his face. He hates it. Thursday I'm working late so you'll need to get dinner before I'm home. And Friday—'

'Erm... Friday I'm travelling to Cumbria to see my dad. I did tell you. I promised him I'd go for the weekend.'

Seth's eyes widened with alarm. 'The whole weekend?'

Cassie nodded. 'Yes, Seth. He's my dad. I don't get to see him that often I can hardly believe you'd begrudge me one weekend,' she pleaded knowing full well she shouldn't have to.

He huffed and closed his eyes. 'I don't begrudge it, darling. Not at all. It just messes things up, that's all.'

Cassie shook her head as annoyance began to build. 'He's my dad, for goodness' sake.'

Seth reached across the table and stroked her arm. 'Let's just leave it for now, okay? We can rearrange things. Perhaps you could visit the weekend after?' Cassie opened her mouth to protest but Seth held up his hand. 'Here comes our meal. Let's not spoil the evening.'

They ate in silence for a while and Cassie was glad that the food was so delicious that it distracted her from the anger that had begun to bubble up at her boyfriend's inconsiderate attitude. Eventually her anger began to dissipate and she placed her cutlery down at the end of the meal and rested her hand on her full tummy.

'That was wonderful but I could do with a nap now I'm so full.' She huffed.

Seth smiled. 'So you're not angry with me any more?'

She rolled her eyes, frustrated in the knowledge that staying angry at Seth Guthrie was something she just couldn't do. 'No. You're forgiven but only because I'm too stuffed to fight.'

'Well, in that case, I think we should have a toast.' He nodded over her shoulder and suddenly the waiter appeared with two champagne flutes and a bottle of Bollinger. The thought of more alcohol, especially the bubbly kind, made Cassie feel a little bilious but she smiled widely in spite of the fact.

'Oh, how lovely. Bolly, my favourite.' The truth was she had never even tasted champagne until she met Seth. But she had definitely acquired a taste for it.

The waiter poured them a glass each and left them alone yet again.

Seth smoothed his tie down and took a deep breath. 'Well, I'm hoping we'll soon have more than just our third anniversary as a couple to celebrate.'

In her overstuffed state, Cassie wondered what on earth he

was talking about. Probably another business deal in the bag. 'More?'

He fumbled inside his jacket and Cassie couldn't believe he was going to get his damn diary out again after their earlier argument. But instead when he revealed his hand he held in it a small, black velvet box and she gasped as her hands instinctively covered her heart.

He pulled his chair around so he was seated closer and he took her hand. 'Cassie Montgomery, you're the most frustratingly intriguing and beautiful, yet sometimes the most absurd, creature I've ever met. And I want to be the one to look after you. Will you let me do that?' He released her palm and opened the box causing a flash of sparkle to dazzle her. Nestled in the cushion was a very large, diamond cluster ring. She stared at it and then up at him and then back at the bling in the box.

'Cassie? Darling, will you?'

She burst into tears and lurched into his lap. 'Oh yes, Seth. I will.'

* * *

The following morning she awoke with a very fuzzy head and a mouth as dry as the Sahara. She lifted her hand to examine her ring. In the light of day, it was even bigger and more ostentatious than she remembered. It was a real statement piece. Yes, that's what it was. A statement of his undying love for her.

As Seth lay contentedly snoring beside her she replayed his proposal over and over in her mind, smiling at how perfect it had been. Until it dawned on her that he hadn't actually asked her to marry him. Not in those exact words. What he'd asked was if he could look after her. Like she was a pet or an elderly person. Or worse still, a mistress.

At least he hadn't broached the whole 'obey' situation again, nor that of babies. She knew deep down that he was just eager to get on with their life together as a married couple but that once he calmed down he would see there was no great rush. After all, she wanted to make sure she was settled in her new business venture for a couple of years, at least, before they married and started thinking about expanding their family of two. She had always loved the written word and her adoration for stories had led her to study literature at university with the ultimate goal of making a career out of her love. Becoming an editor and proofreader had seemed such a natural step for her and it was something that she could easily do freelance; an appealing prospect considering the social life she now had with Seth. Aside from movies, music and the man in her life, books were still her great passion. Becoming Mrs Seth Guthrie was also a very exciting prospect and so what if he didn't technically ask her to marry him? It was inferred by the dramatic and gigantic cluster of rocks catching the light from her finger.

Seth awoke and rolled on top of her. He began to kiss her neck. 'Good morning, future Mrs Guthrie. God, that makes you even sexier now, you know?' He mumbled as he nibbled at her sensitive flesh. He tugged at her nightie and moaned. 'Too many clothes again.'

3

Standing in Edinburgh's Glitterati restaurant the weekend following Seth's bizarre marriage proposal, things were now clearer: why he had been so frustrated about her weekend visit to Cumbria, why he had been so keen to synchronise their diaries. And why he'd talked of rearranging things. He'd had the whole engagement party planned in advance and it just made her love him more. He'd wanted to surprise her and it had certainly worked. Now, here she was in the beautiful top-notch eatery, surrounded by the people she loved who were there to help the couple celebrate their wonderful news. He had even planned the music and chosen the closest things to love songs he could find from all her favourite bands and she had to fight tears as Pearl Jam's 'Just Breathe' floated from the hidden speakers. He knew her so well.

Seth had even arranged for Cassie's father to travel from Cumbria for the event and he had come armed with new photos of Patch, his little Jack Russell crossbreed. He'd bought the cute bundle of fur to keep him company seeing as he missed Bilbo very much. Cassie flicked through the images with a giggle. He was such a cutie and she really missed having a dog around. But Seth wouldn't hear of having pets. He didn't really tolerate mess of any sort. That was just one of the foibles that Cassie had accepted and learned to deal with, although having a dog around was something that she wished he would change his mind about.

Glitterati was the most exclusive restaurant in Edinburgh and it fit Seth to a T. White walls surrounded them, overhead crystal chandeliers with modern, rectangular shards reflected rainbows of light around the large space. White leather covered the seating at the bar and at the tables, and pristine white marble floors lay underfoot. As she gazed around the place, Cassie wondered with amusement if perhaps the restaurant owner had based his décor on Seth's apartment. It was eerily similar.

Even though they usually spent their weekends in their home city of Glasgow, Seth had insisted on the best for his bride-to-be. Of course, he had the connections to save the date at short notice and their gathering had taken over the place for the whole evening. Cassie dreaded to think how much it had all cost but she knew better than to ask.

Vina and Pippa were there to congratulate her on her exciting news and Jasper had, of course, inadvertently congratulated her breasts. Lots of people from the Guthrie's property company were there, wealthy associates too and his parents seemed delighted with the news of their son's impending nuptials.

Cassie's dad was slightly bewildered, however. 'Isn't this a bit showy, eh, Cassie?' her dad asked after kissing her on the cheek. He fidgeted with the tie he was wearing and looked incredibly uncomfortable in his attire. He was more of a jeans and jumpers type.

Cassie laughed knowingly. 'Welcome to the life of the Guthries, Dad.'

He shook his head and whistled as he peered around the lavish, achromatic surroundings of the restaurant. 'I don't think I'd ever get used to it, Cassie. And in all honesty, I'm surprised you have.'

A little upset by his comment, she scrunched her brow. 'What's that supposed to mean?' She had always presumed that Seth was the epitome of the perfect man that her father had hoped for her. His money, his ambition and most of all the fact that he worshipped her were all the things that had been clear priorities to her dad. Or so she had thought.

He sighed. 'This is all just very... Seth.' He was right. Seth was a tiny bit obsessed with all things white and pristine, so Glitterati was the obvious choice of venue for him. But like her father, Cassie was more at home in Wellingtons and scruffy jeans, walking around the countryside or sitting on a beach in the rain.

In fact, when she was small that had been their favourite pastime. Her father would take her to St Bees Head, regardless of the weather and they would walk down to the bay to skim stones and eat sandwiches on the sand. Then it would be a trip to the beach café on the seafront for ice-cream cones. He had always made a big deal of quality time, especially after Cassie's mum passed away. Cassie had little to no actual memory of the woman who gave birth to her but her dad made sure that she stayed alive in conversations and stories. He had done everything he could to ensure that his daughter never went without; often meaning he would do just that himself. Yet he never complained.

She turned to face her dad and found him watching her with a look of concern creasing his brow. 'What's wrong, Dad? I thought you'd be happy that I'm going to be secure now I'm all grown up.'

He smiled but the reaction didn't reach his eyes. 'Are you happy though, sweetheart? That's my main concern. All the money in the world doesn't matter if you're not happy.'

She placed her hands firmly on his arms and fixed him with a sincere gaze. 'Ecstatically so, Dad. You have nothing to worry about on that score. It's not the money. He loves me and I love him right back. He treats me so well and has my best interests at heart in everything. You can rest assured that my happiness is as important to Seth as it is to you.'

He cupped her cheek in his rough, over-worked palm. 'That's good to hear. I just— I worry that's all.'

She smiled and shook her head. 'There really is no need. Honestly.'

He pursed his lips. 'But... don't you think he's just a bit too—'

She quickly folded her arms across her chest defensively. 'If you're going to say old then don't even go there.'

His brow crumpled again. 'Actually, I was going to say wealthy and different. He's just so... well... the opposite of you. You're sweet and funny and kind. You're down to earth. You know hardship and it's made you the person you are.'

She huffed as annoyance began to niggle at her, regardless of the fact that he was speaking the truth. 'Well you know what they say about opposites attracting, Dad.'

'Oh yes. I've heard the saying, sweetheart. I just worry that your life revolves around Seth and his friends. I worry you have nothing for you. That's all. I don't want you to lose your identity. He makes so many decisions without consulting you. Where you live, where you go on holiday, how your apartment is decorated. What about your choices?'

'I have my business now, Dad. So I'm absolutely fine. Please stop worrying. I'm very happy and very much in love and I am going to marry Seth.'

'Didn't he set you up in the business though?'

She heaved a frustrated sigh. 'No. That's not true at all. He advised me, yes, but it was all my own hard work, not his. And his friends are my friends too. I love him, Dad. Please can you accept that and be happy for me?' This wasn't a conversation she had ever anticipated having over Seth; especially not with her dad. It somewhat shattered the idea she'd had all along, that Seth was exactly who her dad would choose for her if it were up to him.

He leaned forward and kissed her cheek before pausing to take a long look at her and then he nodded. 'If you're happy then I'm happy.'

As a sense of relief flooded her veins, someone clanked a glass and a hush descended over the gathered guests. 'Where's my poppet?' Hearing his voice, Cassie rushed to Seth's side and he slipped his arm around her waist. He kissed her head and then turned his attention to the crowd of friends and family. 'Last weekend, Cassie and I celebrated our third anniversary as a couple. Although, as you already know Cassie also agreed to be my wife on the same day.' A rumble of applause travelled the room. 'We wanted to gather our nearest and dearest here to this wonderful, award-winning venue in Edinburgh to celebrate with us. And it was a good opportunity for me to check out some property too for the business, Father,' he said in a theatrical, loud whisper, held up his glass and Seth's dad followed suit as a few people good naturedly jeered him. 'Oh, come on. I'm always in business mode, guys. No one knows that better than all of you.' He laughed. 'Anyway, I hope you'll all raise your glasses with me and toast to the future Mrs Seth Guthrie.'

Everyone in the place simultaneously raised their glasses and spoke in unison. 'The future Mrs Seth Guthrie!'

Once everyone had sipped their champagne, Seth continued, 'Now you're all no doubt expecting a long, drawn-out engagement as is the trend these days but as I'm such a busy man I see no point in hanging around to start my life with my new bride and ergo, I'm happy to announce that Cassie and I will be married in just three months.'

Cassie gasped and snapped her gaze up to Seth as a raucous applause rang out around the room. She tugged on his shirt to gain his attention, but he just mouthed the word – 'Surprise' and grinned at her before scooping her into a passionate embrace to the delight of their audience.

* * *

The rest of the party was lovely. A pianist played classical music on the white Steinway by the bar, the couple were handed beautifully wrapped gifts and the food was out of this world. Thankfully there were no more shocks at the restaurant and Cassie resolved to have serious words with her fiancé later that evening for the ones he had bestowed upon her when she wasn't able to protest. Her poor dad had later pulled her to one side in a panic over the stress of affording a Guthrie style wedding in the traditional manner of the bride's father footing the bill. Although Cassie knew for certain that Seth wouldn't be asking for a single penny from him. He too was a proud man. She tried to reassure her dad as best she could but he left the restaurant early and returned to his hotel room, much to Cassie's dismay.

Back at the luxurious Balmoral Hotel, Cassie locked herself in the plush en-suite. She leaned on the vanity unit and stared at her pallid reflection in the mirror. Things were moving too fast. Yes, she loved Seth more than anything. Yes, she wanted to marry him. But after the content of the previous weekend's conversations she was filled with worry instead of excitement.

She had been looking forward to a long engagement where she would have time to talk to Seth about his determination over her 'obeying' her husband in their vows and the idea of starting a family as soon as they were wed; although she was set firm in her determination to veto both of those ideas and she wouldn't be backing down, no matter how much Seth protested. She knew, without a doubt, that he was the one. He was the stuff of dreams and she knew very well how lucky she was. But she had hoped to have some part in the planning and organisation of her own 'big day'. Instead it felt like some of what her dad had feared was, in fact, true. Seth was controlling this huge step in her life and she didn't feel 100 per cent comfortable with that.

In addition to this was the fact that her proofreading and editing business was in its infancy and she wanted to spend time building up her client base to add to the workload she already had waiting in the wings. She had sufficient work from several independent authors to take her way past the Seth-imposed three-month deadline. They had been very keen to work with her after reading testimonials from the clients she had worked with for free when setting things up, and she was looking forward to getting stuck into some honest to goodness paid work of her own. Had she known in advance of Seth's plan and that she would need to account for a four-week absence from work for their honeymoon in Australia – another of his surprises sprung on her in the taxi on the way back to the hotel – she would have made plans accordingly.

And speaking of honeymoons, she was touched that he had planned and booked the trip – he was nothing if not thoughtful – but she would have liked to have had some input on the destination. She hated flying as it was, but to fly to the other side of the world was her idea of hell. She was feeling somewhat railroaded into the whole scenario and as her heart raced and her breathing became erratic she felt sure she would pass out. She stared at her reflection willing herself calm but her attempts were futile as each time she became a little angrier, the other half of her brain reminded her of how ungrateful she was being. Talk about being stuck between a rock and a hard place.

Aaaargh!

'Cassie? Poppet? What's happened in there? Have you hurt yourself? Do I need to call a doctor?' Seth's worried voice and knocking could be heard. She hadn't realised she had made the exasperated sound aloud.

'N-no, I'm fine... stubbed my toe on the bath. Out in a minute.' She panted as she tried to control her breathing.

'Okay, well, I have some more champers out here for us. I had them deliver it. Thought we could have our own celebration.'

She clenched her jaw for a moment and then carefully replied, as lightly as possible. 'I don't really feel like drinking any more, Seth. I just need a bit of time to catch my breath.'

There was a long pause before he spoke again and when he did she discerned disappointment in his voice. 'I did it all for you, darling. To make you happy.' Her anger began to melt away as always. 'I only want what's best for us. And I can't wait to start my life as your adoring husband. That's all. I'm just eager to call you my wife. I know we've been together a while now but I want us to be official. To make that commitment.' She closed her eyes and lowered her head. Why had she been so bloody ungrateful? She didn't deserve him. 'Planning weddings is so stressful and I just wanted this to be easy for you. I wasn't trying to spoil things. I hope you know that.'

Why, oh why couldn't she stay angry at him? He was right though. Weddings were incredibly stressful things to plan. She'd watched *Bridezillas* on TV. She knew the score. Perhaps she had jumped the gun and presumed he was being controlling when in actual fact, he was being kind and considerate?

She walked over to the door and unlocked it. When she pulled it open she was greeted by a very forlorn-looking Seth, his bottom lip protruding like a sulking toddler and her heart melted completely. She could never resist those green eyes. He looked so very silly but simultaneously gorgeous with his top two buttons unfastened exposing just a tiny bit of chest.

His sleeves were rolled up and his hands were in his pockets. 'I really didn't mean to upset you, poppet. I honestly thought I was doing the right thing.' He held out his arms and like iron to a magnet she was drawn into his embrace and inhaled his wonderful, familiar scent.

'One thing though, Seth. There's something I must insist upon.'

He kissed the top of her head. 'Name it.'

'Please let me pick my own wedding dress, okay?'

There was a long pause before he said, 'Ah... erm...'

She lifted her chin and glared up at him. 'You haven't? Please tell me you haven't. Bloody hell, Seth, if I'd wanted to be on *Don't Tell the Bride* I'd have applied for the damn show.' She shoved angrily at his chest and he almost toppled over.

A wide grin spread across his features. 'Kidding. Sort of. Vina and Pippa are taking you shopping next weekend. Pippa has great taste as you know, and she has contacts in some very exclusive boutiques. I'm sure you'll find something stunning with their help.'

She rolled her eyes, realising once again that he was in control even though his heart was in the right place. 'But *I'm* picking my dress. Not them,' she insisted, sounding rather like that sulking toddler she had compared Seth to earlier.

He shrugged. 'Of course, darling. I wouldn't dare go so far as to make such a bold decision on your behalf.'

In spite of herself she giggled. 'Pfft. But you'd choose the date and venue of the wedding and the location and duration of the bloody honeymoon. The least you can do is let me have this one thing.'

'But of course. Just make sure it's easy for me to get you out of it at the end of the day, okay? Not too many buttons or laces when I want to ravish my new bride.' He raised his eyebrows lasciviously and she shook her head but couldn't fight the silly grin.

Feeling like she had won a victory, albeit a small one, she allowed Seth to pull her towards the bed and undress her.

4

The following week went by far too quickly. Cassie's feet hardly hit the ground in between dinner with Seth's clients, dinner with his parents and theatre with his rugby buddies and their wives – all the things he had rearranged from the week leading up to the surprise engagement party.

Friday evening was her first bit of free time and for once she didn't have to get dressed up or plaster her face in make-up. Six o'clock arrived and she sat on the sofa waiting for Seth to come home. She had been working on a project for a new client and her eyes were sore from staring at her laptop screen all day. It was intense work, which had taken every ounce of concentration she could muster so as she sat in the silence of her empty home she closed her eyes in the hope that doing so would ease the headache that was threatening *before* it really took hold. She was just dozing off when she heard the door to the apartment open.

'Hi, honey, I'm home!' Seth called in a silly sing-song voice that made her smile in spite of how awful she was feeling.

He walked through to the living room, planted a kiss on her head and dropped a huge bouquet of fragrant pink roses in her lap. 'Roses for my own English rose.'

Cassie gasped. 'Oh, wow, Seth they're so lovely. Thank you.' He never ceased to amaze her with his romantic gestures.

'You deserve them for putting up with me. So, how's my little poppet today?'

She sighed. 'I'm wiped out. I think all the excitement of the past couple of weeks has caught up with me.'

He straightened up. 'Hmm. Right. That's it. I've heard enough,' he stated and Cassie wondered what she had done wrong to deserve such a decisive, terse tone. Before she could ask he grabbed her hand and tugged her towards the bedroom.

Ugh, not now... She really wasn't in the mood for sex. 'Seth... I—'

'I'll sort the flowers later. Get your clothes off.'

'But Seth—' she whined and almost stamped her foot.

'I said get your clothes off. I'm going to go run you a luxurious bath. I've brought home a bottle of the best Pinot Noir I could find in that little off licence down the street. I'm ordering takeaway Chinese food in. And you, my darling girl, are going to relax and do nothing but read a book for pleasure for once, for the rest of the evening. You spend so much time working on books you don't read any more and you love to read. So, there will be foot massages, back massages... I'll even feed you if that's what it takes.'

She stood, staring open-mouthed as guilt niggled at her for her presumption. 'I... thought you wanted sex.'

He grinned as he stepped towards her, cupped her face in his palms and kissed her gently on the lips. 'Cassie, you're the most desirable woman I've ever met, and believe me, I would *never* refuse sex with you if *you* wanted it. But I can see how tired you are, poppet. And what you need is some R and R. So that's what you're going to get. Now strip.' He tapped her nose and left the room in the direction of their en-suite.

As she sat in the steamy bathroom, cocooned in the warmth of the water and the scent of Jasmine with one of her favourite classic novels in one hand and a glass of Pinot Noir in the other, she realised it was times like that when any worries about the age gap, their differences and everyone else's opinions, melted into insignificance.

Seth delivered fully on everything he had promised and as she lay in bed later that night snuggled up next to her man with a sated appetite and a relaxed warm glow thanks to the wine, the bath and the wonderful, sensual massage he had given her, she smiled to herself. She really was so very damned lucky to have him. She drifted off to sleep with his arms lovingly and protectively wrapped around her.

All too soon Saturday dawned and Cassie was faced with the prospect of wedding dress shopping. It was meant to be fun so she had no idea why she was so wound up about it all.

Vina had called to say she had booked a cab and at nine sharp Cassie saw the taxi pulling up to the curb outside her building. She grabbed her bag and called to Seth, who was taking a shower, to tell him she had no clue what time she'd be home. He was off to play rugby – a sport that she really didn't like – but even the thought of standing on a muddy field appealed more at that moment than the idea of searching for the perfect wedding dress. The fact that he would come away from the pitch all dirty and masculine added to the appeal and just the mental image alone was enough to send her lady areas into meltdown. There was something so visceral and erotic about seeing a usually clean-cut man all rugged and rough.

She hurriedly made her way downstairs and climbed into the waiting taxi. After greeting her friend, she stared out of the window and chewed on her nails.

'You know, you could look a little more excited about today.' Vina's words pulled her from her fantasy. 'I mean, I know you're marrying my control freak of a brother but come on! You're getting to wear a dress by none other than Isabella Montenegro for goodness' sake.'

Cassie scrunched her brow and turned to look at Vina. 'I'm sorry, *what?*'

Vina rolled her eyes. 'Oh, don't tell me you didn't adore her pieces at Glasgow Fashion Week. Pippa and I were drooling, don't you remember?' She giggled and fanned herself.

Fidgeting in her seat, Cassie turned more squarely towards her best friend. 'But... I thought I was choosing my *own* dress?'

Vina's eyes widened and she began to back-pedal. 'Oh... erm... well yes. Obviously. I mean *durrr.*'

Cassie was immediately suspicious about what was going on and her terse tone reflected the fact. 'Vina?'

Vina cringed. 'Pippa suggested Isabella to Seth and he agreed. It's kind of a done deal, sweetie. But there will be a few to choose from,' she enthused as if one of the most important decisions of the wedding hadn't just been ripped away from her friend.

Cassie clenched her jaw and her eyes began to sting. He couldn't let her have this one thing? This one *simple thing* for her own wedding? After the way he had looked after her the night before, putting her first, making her feel special, he had to ruin it with his overbearing, controlling alter ego. How could one man have two such different sides to his personality?

Vina slipped her arm around Cassie and squeezed her tight. 'Aww, look how happy you are. You're all teary eyed. I'm so glad you're excited now. I was worrying there for a second.'

Shaking her head, Cassie closed her eyes briefly. 'No... no, I'm *angry*, Vina. He promised. He swore that *I* would be choosing my own wedding dress. He's chosen the date, the venue *and* the honeymoon.' She counted each thing off dramatically on her fingers. 'What do I get a say in? Nothing? Well, I get a say as to whether I turn up on the day that's for certain. And the way I feel right now, I'm not so sure I want to,' she blurted in a breathless rush. 'If this is the shape of things to come then maybe I'd better think things through. He already said he wants me to *obey* him in the vows. Obey him! Like I get any other bloody choice. I want to go home. In fact, scrap that. I want to go for a drink.' Her voice hit a new pitch she'd never experienced before and as the taxi stopped at a red light she scrambled around reaching for the door handle.

Vina stared open-mouthed for a few seconds as if dumbfounded but coming to her senses grabbed Cassie's arm to stop her. 'Hey, honey, it's nine twenty-five in the morning. It's a bit early for alcohol, don't you think? And please calm down. He really does mean well, you do know that, don't you?' Panic filled her voice. 'Please don't give up on him over this. You can choose whatever dress you want.'

Cassie widened her eyes. 'Oh, really? And what if I want a...

a... Sally Swizzlestick dress, hmm? Do they do *those* in Isabella Montenegro's shop? Hmm? Do they?'

Vina pursed her lips, clearly trying not to laugh. 'I'm sorry, honey but I don't think *anywhere* sells Sally Swizzlestick dresses.'

'I think you get my point, Davina. Seth says I can choose my dress provided it's an Isabella Montenegro dress from an Isabella Montenegro boutique. But what if I don't *want* that? What if I want an off the peg dress? What if I want to have a dress made by the little old lady who does sewing repairs at that shop on Sauchiehall Street? What then?'

'But... erm...'

Cassie heaved a defeated sigh. 'My point is that this should *my* choice entirely. *I* should choose the shop. *I* should choose the style and *I* should choose the damn budget.'

Vina tilted her head. 'Is that what's really bothering you? The money?' She reached and squeezed Cassie's hand. 'You do know that Seth won't be asking your dad for a penny, don't you? So, you have no upper limit on the budget.'

'That's only part of the problem, Vina. Don't you get it? If he's controlling me this much before we're married how will it be after? I can't breathe right now, I feel so stifled. It's ridiculous,' Cassie growled in exasperation.

After a long, thoughtful pause Vina nodded slowly. 'I do understand. Totally. I'm so sorry, sweetie. I just got carried along in the excitement. And a dress by Isabella is my dream, not yours. You're right. One hundred per cent right. It should absolutely be your choice. Let me make a call.'

Cassie leaned forward and rested her head in her hands as Vina spoke to Pippa on the phone to tell her there had been a change of plans. They rearranged their meeting destination and new directions were given to the cab driver.

* * *

Ten minutes later, they pulled up outside a small vintage clothing shop off Sauchiehall Street and Cassie's heart began to race. This was *just* the type of place she would've chosen. Thank goodness Vina knew her well.

Vina smiled as she leaned to open the door. 'Come on, panicky pants. Let's go get you a dress, eh?'

Cassie grabbed for her hand. 'I'm sorry to be a drama queen. I don't mean to be ungrateful. I just—'

'Hey, you're talking to the girl who grew up thinking that the TV only had one channel and that was sports. Seth Noodlehead is a control freak. No one knows that more than I do. But he loves you fiercely, Cassie. He wants you to be happy and if that means we rebel then so be it.' She winked. 'He's just so fixated on everything being perfect, I think he's forgotten that you're involved too. Silly sod really is too much of a perfectionist.'

The friends climbed out of the cab and were greeted by Pippa who gave air kisses in true socialite style. Holding Cassie at arm's length the stunning redhead raised her eyebrows. 'Cassie Montgomery, whatever will we do with you? You get the chance to wear the best wedding dress designer in the whole of the UK and instead you decide on some old second-hand thing?'

Cassie shrugged. 'I know you both must think I'm potty, but this is just more me.'

Vina and Pippa linked an arm each with Cassie and Vina kissed the side of her head. 'Not potty. Just quirky.'

Cassie scowled. 'Gee, thanks.'

Pippa nudged her and rested her head on her shoulder. 'I think Vina means that in the nicest possible way, don't you, V?'

The raven-haired woman rolled her eyes for what felt like the millionth time. 'Well, *durr*.'

Cassie began to relax and decided that it was actually nice to have her two closest friends with her on this special day, even in spite of how it had started. Friends were something Cassie had few of. Ever since her miserable days at school she had found it difficult to trust people and so kept her circle very close-knit. Thankfully, growing up, her dad had been her best friend and she had found she didn't really need anyone else. Large groups of people made her uncomfortable but now, as part of Seth's world she was becoming more accustomed to it. However, her *real* friends remained small in number.

Once inside the shop with its rows and rows of evening gowns, flapper dresses and smoking jackets they were shown through to a room at the back, which concentrated solely on wedding dresses.

'I'm surprised at how clean it smells in here,' Pippa said as she took in her surroundings.

Cassie laughed. 'They may be vintage, Pip, but that doesn't mean they were dragged out of a skip.'

'Oh. My. Goodness. Look at this, Cassie,' Vina exclaimed from the other side of the room. 'It's you. It's just so you. Come see!' The enthusiasm Vina was feeling was audible in her high-pitched tone and Cassie's heart skipped with excitement now instead of dread.

The other two friends joined Vina who held up a long, half lace covered ivory dress with a sweetheart neckline and beaded capped sleeves. It really was stunning.

'Oh yes. You must try it on, Cassie. It's gorgeous,' Pippa agreed.

Without protestation Cassie took the frock and walked over to the fitting room in the corner – simply a curved rail with a heavy tapestry curtain hanging from it. She undressed and slipped into the dress and stared at her reflection.

It shouldn't have been this easy surely? She'd heard of people trawling around ten shops and going back to the first one in the end but this was just crazy. Not only was the dress a bargain at four hundred pounds but it fit like a glove to her curves as if it had been made especially for her. Skimming over her body, the vintage lace that reached to her knees was dotted with tiny crystals that caught the light when she moved. Underneath this were layers of chiffon that swished gently against the floor to the perfect length for a pair of two-inch heels. It flicked out slightly at the bottom with a slight train at the back but nothing too over the top. To finish it off perfectly the neckline was tasteful yet sexy. According to the label the dress had been worn by an Edinburgh bride in 1955 and that really iced the cake for her.

This was it. She was in love.

Feeling a little less like a Bridezilla, she turned around in the small space and gazed at the detailing on the back of the dress. She knew immediately that Seth would be absolutely blown away by the sight of her in it, regardless of the age or price tag on the garment. She could imagine his face as his hungry eyes devoured her.

Taking a deep breath, she stepped out of the small fitting area and was greeted by gasps from her friends.

'Oh... my... wow!'

'Bloody hell, Cassie, it's perfect!'

Tears of the happy kind stung at her eyes as she told them, 'I don't need to try any others on. This is it. It's perfect.'

Pippa clapped her hands gleefully. 'Well, in that case I say we go on a bloody shopping spree and have a stop off at a champagne bar to celebrate!'

Vina lifted the little price tag and made a very unladylike snorting noise. 'The champers is on Seth I say, considering what was going to cost you *four thousand pounds* is costing four bloody hundred!'

Cassie laughed. 'After what the swine has put me through with his controlling ways I'm inclined to agree with you on that.'

5

The champagne bar at the Grand Central Hotel was fairly quiet when they arrived; this wasn't surprising though considering it wasn't even lunchtime. It was one of the places that Cassie never tired of regardless of how many times she visited. Part of this was down to the Victorian style interior decoration of the place – a great love of hers. The black and white marble tile floor gleamed under their feet as they entered and they quickly found a table and perched on the stools beneath the huge crystal chandelier. A smartly dressed, rather handsome waiter brought a menu and they made their selections.

The conversation initially centred on wedding plans and Vina told of how excited her brother had been in her recent conversations with him. 'Honestly, you'd think he was the bride. He's such a big softy you know. Adores the bloody ground you walk on,' she told Cassie.

All of the frustration she had been feeling at the start of the day was waning rapidly and her resolve to chastise him further about his actions was diminishing by the second. The more champagne she drank, the more warm and fuzzy she became until she couldn't wait to get home and kiss Seth from head to toe. Okay, so he was a control freak but he was her gorgeous, sexy control freak. And she was soon-to-be Mrs Control Freak. Anger was replaced by excitement and her temper by a light-headed giddiness.

Pippa was gulping down the sparkling alcohol elixir as fast as the waiter could replace it and when Vina hinted that perhaps she should slow down she shook her head vehemently.

'No, no, I need this. After the way things have been going at home I deserve this.'

Vina giggled. 'Pips you've had enough, sweetie. You're whirring your *slurds*.'

Cassie burst into hysterical laughter. 'Vina, you said "whirring your *slurds*."'

Vina paused and a look of confusion appeared on her face. 'Oh yeah. I did. I did say that.'

'You girls are so fucking lucky. You know that?' Pippa interjected, her lower lip protruding like a toddler who'd been told there was no more chocolate.

Vina frowned and patted her arm. 'Why do you say that, *schweetie*? Why?' She leaned her chin precariously on her hand.

'Because... Vina you don't have to worry about a man seeing as you don't have one.' Vina's indignant expression spoke volumes. Then she turned her attention to Cassie. 'And Cassie, you have Seth. And Seth is just so bloody wonderful. You both make me sick.'

Cassie raised her eyebrows. 'Gee... thanks, I think.'

Vina attempted to roll her eyes but almost fell off her stool in the process. 'Pippa, whatever is the matter? You have Jasper and he adores you.'

Pippa huffed and finished off the contents of yet another glass. 'Does he? Does he really?'

Cassie and Vina shared a worried glance. 'Has something happened, Pippa?'

Her lip began to tremble. 'I think he's having an affair with his secretary. I mean could he be any more of a damned bloody cliché?'

Vina opened and closed her mouth, clearly unable to find suitable words so Cassie spoke instead. 'Whatever gives you that idea?'

Pippa sniffed and picked up a napkin from the table to dab at her eyes. 'Oh, you know, the usual. Working late. Smelling of someone else's perfume. Oh, and the fact that there was a text from her on his phone thanking him for a very special time with a fucking winky face emoji after it. A winky fucking face. How much more obvious could she have been? Can you believe that bitch?'

'B-but that could mean anything, honey. Don't jump to conclusions, eh? You should speak to him,' Vina suggested.

Pippa's eyes widened and she wagged her finger at her friends. 'Or spy on them. I could spy on them and see if I'm right.'

Cassie glared at Vina in desperation. 'Oh, I think speaking to him would be best, Pips. Like Vina says. It could be something very innocent.'

Pippa regarded Cassie with incredulity. 'Look, just because the grass on your side of the fence is bloody emerald green and littered with diamonds it doesn't mean everyone else's men are perfect. He's cheated before. He could do it again just as easily.'

Trying to ignore her friend's acerbic tone, Cassie gasped. 'He's cheated before?'

Pippa's face coloured bright fuchsia pink and she lowered her eyes. 'He was... erm... married when he met me.'

Cassie formed an 'o' with her mouth and suddenly felt very

sad for her friend. What had started off as a lie had come full circle by the sound of it. She was grateful that she and Seth were based on a solid foundation of trust and no secrets.

* * *

When Cassie arrived at home she found Seth lounging on the sofa with his laptop. With all her anger from the start of the day forgotten she leaned over and smoothed her hands down his chest, planting a kiss on the side of his head.

He closed his laptop and covered her arms with his. 'Good day, poppet?'

She shrugged and nuzzled his neck. 'Well, I got a dress,' she mumbled into his warm skin.

'You don't sound too happy about it. But from what Davina said in her text you looked stunning.'

She began to kiss him just underneath his ear, a place she knew he liked to be kissed. 'No, I'm happy with the dress. But... would you take me to bed and make love to me? I need to be close to you.'

He tugged her over the back of the sofa so that she landed in his lap. 'Happy to oblige you there, darling. But let's stay here, hmm?'

* * *

The next morning Cassie was looking forward to a lazy day with Seth. There was no dress to search for, no rugby matches to attend and the Sunday papers had already been delivered. Seth had brought fresh coffee through to the bedroom for them and they lay snuggled together reading.

A text messaged pinged through to Cassie's phone and she reached across to find out who it was.

The message was from Pippa.

> Hi. Can we meet? I think we need to talk. Well I know I do. Thanks. P x

Bang goes a relaxing Sunday, Cassie thought as she remembered the tense conversation about her friend's marriage the day before. It wasn't unheard of for Pippa and Cassie to meet without Vina but it was rare. The three were usually found together and it struck Cassie as strange that Vina wasn't mentioned; after all she too had witnessed Pippa's meltdown the night before.

Niggled with curiosity and never one to let a friend down she hit reply.

> Hi Pip. Of course. Where and when? C x

Another reply came rapidly.

> Jake's café on Sauchiehall Street. Eleven?

She replied right away.

> Sure. See you there x

Seth huffed. 'What was all that about so early on a Sunday?'

Being careful how she responded she said, 'Oh... it was Pippa. She wants me to meet her for coffee.'

'But you saw her yesterday. I thought we were having some *us* time today?'

'We are. I won't be long, promise. I'm just going to jump in the shower. But I'll be back as soon as possible.'

He placed his newspaper down on his lap. 'What's wrong with her?'

Forcing a smile and reluctant to divulge any details until she knew the facts – especially seeing as Jasper and Seth were close friends – she told him, 'Oh. Nothing. We just said we'd meet up again to chat about the wedding and stuff. You know how it is.'

He pulled her into his arms. 'Oh, I do. Once you ladies get wedding stuff in your heads there's no stopping you. But hurry home, okay? I want you all to myself later.'

She planted a kiss on his forehead. 'Don't worry. I'll be all yours. No distractions.'

As she clambered from the bed he gave her bottom a swift smack causing her to yelp and scowl at him. But the grin on his face soon made a grin appear on her own.

'You're incorrigible, Seth Guthrie.'

He breathed on his knuckles and rubbed them on his bare chest. 'I pride myself on the fact.'

Sauchiehall Street was always busy regardless of the day or time and this Sunday was no different. It was one of Cassie's favourite streets in the city with its cheery shops painted in an array of bright colours and its mixture of modern and nineteenth century architecture sitting comfortably side by side. Her favourite building of all was The Willow Tea Rooms. Designed in 1903 by none other than Charles Rennie Mackintosh, it still displayed many of its renowned design elements after its current owners had lovingly restored it. Cassie wondered why

Pippa had chosen to meet her at Jake's trendy coffee bar instead of the beautiful old building that they usually frequented.

She arrived at the sage green painted café bang on time and found Pippa already waiting for her towards the back of the main room. It all seemed a little cloak and dagger and as she arrived at Pippa's table her friend stood and gave a teary-eyed hug.

'Thanks so much for coming. I was worried I had upset you yesterday. And I'm sorry we're not meeting at the Willow Tea Room but Jasper's friends often stop in there and I'd really rather not bump into any of them.' The two friends sat. 'And I hope Seth wasn't annoyed at you coming out. I know you said you were having a day just the two of you.'

Cassie reached and squeezed her friend's hand. 'Oh no, he doesn't mind at all,' she lied. 'Is Vina joining us?'

Pippa shook her head. 'No, she's gone to her parents for the day, remember? They want to introduce her to that wealthy, young bachelor they've met. Sounds like a trap if you ask me. Poor V.' Cassie racked her brains and vaguely recalled a conversation the previous evening about the man Vina's parents wanted her to meet. He had a very long and posh double-barrelled name and owned lots of property, including a Highland estate. There had been lots of laughter about the prospect of mono-brows and buck teeth. And Vina had repeatedly insisted she was a woman of the 21st century and no parent was going to tell her who to marry. Yet she had obviously backed down and had gone after all. 'Anyway, I feel I owe you an apology. I was a total bitch yesterday. I hate to think I ruined your special day, sweetie.'

Cassie smiled and shook her head. 'No, no. Don't be silly, of course, you didn't.'

A young, smiley woman with tattoos and dreadlocks appeared to take their order and soon left them to talk.

Once the waitress was out of earshot Cassie addressed her friend. 'So... how are you today?'

'Apart from hungover?' She smiled. 'Oh... I honestly don't know any more, Cassie. I think my marriage is over.'

'Is it really that bad?'

Pippa's lip began to tremble. 'I think so. I confronted him last night. He says I'm being ridiculous but I could see it in his eyes, Cassie. He stormed out and refused to talk to me because apparently I was too pissed.'

'And today?'

'Today he's giving me the silent treatment. Says his secretary is flirty but that he would *never* do anything about it.' Her tone was mocking and tinged with disbelief.

But Cassie grasped on to the tiny shred of hope her friend had. 'Well, there you go. He'd never do anything.'

Pippa shook her head slowly and grimaced. 'I messaged the bitch. She says they kissed. That she wants *more* but he's not sure what he wants. Well, he needs to make up his damned mind. The bastard won't put one over on me. Not on me.'

Oh, shitty shit. What could Cassie say to that? The secretary had admitted the infidelity with Pippa's husband. And even a kiss is a betrayal of trust. She reached for Pippa's arm and placed her hand gently upon it. 'I'm so sorry. What will you do?'

Pippa shrugged. 'Well... they say revenge is a dish best served cold... so let's just say I'm biding my time. But if he thinks he's getting away with it he's sadly mistaken.' She sighed and then fixed Cassie with a stony gaze. 'It just shows you though. It shows you that even the *best* men are bastards, Cassie. We can't trust *any* of them. They're all the same. *All* of them.' The emphasis she placed on the word 'all' sent a disconcerting shiver down Cassie's spine but thankfully it was fleeting. She didn't say so but she knew that Seth was nothing like that. *Her* man was faithful to the core. And she was incredibly fortunate to know that with a marked certainty. Okay, so he was a control freak and a perfectionist but he was loyal to a fault. And she was at the centre of his world. This she knew without a doubt.

The cheery waitress returned and placed the drinks on their table and left them. Cassie took a sip of her coffee and pondered on what Pippa had said.

Choosing to ignore the blanket comment she made about men she tentatively asked, 'Do you think you'll leave him?'

Pippa burst out laughing, a reaction that shocked Cassie to the core. 'You're joking, aren't you? I'm financially invested in this damned marriage. Why should I lose out just because he can't keep it in his pants?'

Cassie frowned. 'But... how will you trust him? And... God forbid what if he leaves *you*? I know that's a horrid thing to suggest but it's possible. This... fling might be something more.'

Pippa leaned forward conspiratorially and after a quick glance around her she said, 'He wouldn't dare. I know his business dealings. I know absolutely *everything*, Cassie, and I could ruin him if I chose to. He knows this. He's scared. And anyway, what is it they say? If you can't beat 'em... join 'em.'

Horrified, Cassie opened her mouth to speak but struggled to find the words initially. Mirroring her friends manoeuvre she leaned forward too. 'You're going to have a... a... *threesome* with them?' The thought made her feel a little nauseated and she failed to see how anyone would benefit from that particular situation.

Pippa almost choked on her mouthful of coffee as she descended into a fit of giggles once again. 'I don't mean *literally* join them, you daft cow. Oh, come on, Cassie, darling, surely you're not that naïve?'

Completely and utterly confused by the entire conversation, Cassie shook her head. 'Honestly? I have absolutely no clue what you're talking about. I think you've lost your marbles, Pips.'

Pippa grinned and rolled her eyes and reached across the table to squeeze Cassie's arm. 'God, I love you. You know that? You're hilarious. And I mean that in the nicest possible way. You're so sweet, Cassie. And your relationship is so bloody perfect you can't see beyond your rose-tinted specs.'

Slightly affronted at her friend's patronisation, she huffed. 'Look, I think we've ascertained that you think I'm an idiot so just get to the point, okay?'

Pippa pouted. 'Oh, I'm sorry, sweetie. I didn't mean to offend you. Please don't be cross? What I mean is... I'll have my own affair. Then we're even.' She held out her hands as if she had just stated the most obvious solution to her problem.

Cassie shook her head vehemently. 'Pippa, that's not the way to deal with this. You need to talk to Jasper. Work things through. And if things don't improve, you should leave him. You know as well as I do that you will both end up hurt if you go down that route.' She couldn't believe her friend's ridiculous logic. She adored Pippa but she clearly had some crazy ideas when it came to relationships.

'Oh, fuck, now you're judging me, aren't you? You're not going to tell Seth, are you?' Her eyes widened.

Cassie sighed and shook her head. 'No, you're one of my closest friends, Pippa, I won't breathe a word. I just think you're making a huge mistake. That's all.'

Pippa smiled and tilted her head to the side. 'I love that you're so concerned about me, Cassie but I'm a grown woman. And divorce just isn't an option. But while he's dipping his wick in the work ink I'm letting him nowhere near me. And I'm a woman in my prime. I need sex.'

Wishing she was at home right now, Cassie asked the one question she didn't really want the answer to. 'Have you already met someone? Or are you intending on trawling the bars? Because I'll tell you now, I draw the line at accompanying you on *those* nights out.'

'No, I haven't met anyone... *yet*. But I don't need a wingman, sweetie. I'm bold enough to find my own boy-toy.' She winked and Cassie's stomach rolled.

'Pippa, please be careful, okay? I mean there's unwanted preg—'

Pippa held up her hand in a halting motion. 'I'm thirty-one. I'm well versed in all things STD and I have no intention of letting anyone but Jasper impregnate me. But only once he's got this bimbette out of his system. Ooh, I know, why don't we have carrot cake whilst we're here? I've heard it's divine.' And just like that their bizarre conversation was over.

* * *

Later on, once she was back at their apartment, Cassie found Seth surrounded by the Sunday papers, his glasses perched on his nose. He looked up as she walked in to the lounge and dropped her bag on the sofa.

'Oh, there you are. I was wondering if I should send a search party. How was Pippa?' He rolled his eyes dramatically as he asked.

She climbed into his lap and kissed him long and hard before answering. 'She was... erm... fine. But I missed you so I said we had plans and I came home.'

He smiled lovingly at her. 'Ah, well, you're home now. How

about we head back to bed for a while?' He feigned a yawn. 'I could do with a nap.'

She smiled. 'Oh, really?'

He raised his eyebrows. 'Really. Anyway, what was all the drama about with her? Jasper says she's been accusing him of all sorts lately.'

Thinking on her feet but hating to lie she clambered off his lap and stood. She began to undress and she backed away. 'Oh, I don't think we need to talk about them, do we? Surely we have other things to occupy ourselves with?'

Seth didn't need any further encouragement. Jumping to his feet he gave chase and Cassie squealed with delight as she ran towards the bedroom.

6

Mondays always came around too soon, especially when Seth was leaving on business. This time he was heading to the USA, to Seattle – a place Cassie had always wanted to visit. After all, it was the city that had sparked the era of grunge music. And even though many would gasp at discovering it, Cassie was a huge fan of some of the bands that made up the genre.

Her musical tastes were very eclectic and whilst she loved to listen to Debussy and Mozart with Seth, she adored bands such as Pearl Jam and Soundgarden. Seth wasn't at all keen on what he called 'that noise' whenever she was cheeky enough to put it on. Then he would make some joke about being an old man and Cassie would tell him how she loved their differences as it gave them so much to talk about. Although music wasn't a topic they covered very often. Unless it was a trip to the opera and Seth was telling her about the first time he'd heard a particular piece. She often wished he would give *her* favourite bands as much kudos as she gave the orchestras he loved but it wasn't something that worried her too much.

As he gathered the things he needed, she begged him to

make a trip to see some of the places she wanted to visit and to take lots of photos, places such as the Crocodile Café and Neumos where some of her favourite bands had played. And the Terminal Sales Building where the Sub Pop record label began. And although she wasn't particularly keen on modern art she managed to convince Seth to visit Isamu Noguchi's *Black Sun* sculpture seeing as she wouldn't get to see it herself. After all, Seth hadn't invited her along much to her disappointment.

He was going to be away most of the week and although she knew she'd miss him like crazy, it was a great opportunity for her to get through some of the work from new clients that had been piling up since Seth's proposal had tipped her world on its axis – but in the best possible way, obviously.

Determined to make a go of her new proofreading and editing business she had told Seth that working was what she'd be doing when he was meeting clients and taking in some of her suggested sights.

'You know you don't *need* to work don't you, poppet? I want to look after you, remember?' he told her as she sat on the vanity beside him where he fixed his tie.

'I'm aware of that and I really do appreciate the sentiment but I actually like my work and business is really taking off, so I want to stick with it. And I don't need you to look after me. I'm an adult, remember?' She made a face at him.

He grinned. 'Oh yes, very adult behaviour.' He tapped her nose and then kissed her on it. 'Well, maybe when I get home we could go away for a few days?' he said with his concentration now focused on his reflection.

She cringed. 'Oh, I don't think I have the time just now. What with the wedding on the horizon and work...' Her words faded as she watched his expression change to one of disappointment. She noted a few extra wrinkles around his eyes and flecks of grey in his hair. All making him far more distin-guished-looking and sexy.

A line appeared between his eyebrows and he turned to face her. 'It sounds a little like you're putting your hobby before our relationship, Cassie.'

Her anger spiked within her. 'Hobby? It's not a hobby, Seth. It's my business.'

He huffed. 'Okay so bring your *work* with you.'

She flared her nostrils. 'Did you just stress the word work like you meant it in air quotes?'

He chuckled and stepped towards her, nudging her thighs apart so he could step into the space they created. 'Oooh, I love it when you get all shirty. You're sexy as hell when you're annoyed.'

Not wanting him to leave under a cloud she rolled her eyes and bit back her annoyance. 'I'm sure you say these things to wind me up.'

He leaned forward and kissed the tip of her nose. 'Perhaps I do. Maybe when I get home you can *work* on me?'

'Well, you certainly need work, Mr Guthrie. Anyway, I'd better go get ready if I'm coming to the airport.'

'Oh, I wouldn't bother, poppet. You said you have work to do so why not make a start? No time like the present, eh?'

He made a very good point so she pushed down the disap-pointment at not waving him off. 'Okay. If you're sure. I do have lots to do.'

He stepped away and walked towards the bedroom. 'By the way, mark your diary, next week we're going wedding cake tast-ing. My mother insisted. I'll email you the details.'

'Oh? Is your mum coming too?' She didn't manage to hide the hint of disappointment tinging her voice.

'Yes. She's far better at these things than I am.'

'But I'm good at eating cake,' Cassie told him playfully.

'Ah yes, but this needs a discerning palate, darling. Not one that enjoys blueberry muffins from takeout venues.'

Cassie huffed and was on the verge of a sarcastic retort about his comments when he appeared in front of her again in his full suit and almost took her breath away.

'You're staring, poppet,' he told her as he bent to kiss her lips.

'I'm not... okay I am but... I was hoping we could choose a cake between us. Just me and you.'

'Aww, my sweet Cassie. My mum wants to be involved. Let's just give her this one, hmm?'

In her mind Cassie screamed, *I want to be involved too but you don't seem to be bothered about that, do you?* But instead she nodded and let him hug her tight.

'Now, you behave whilst I'm gone, okay?' He winked and she smiled in response.

'As if I would ever do anything else.' A thought sprang to her mind and she blurted it out without giving it any thought. 'Ooh, I forgot to mention, I have a two-day course in Edinburgh the week after next.'

He scowled as he gathered up his case and passport. 'And you're choosing to tell me this *now*? Look, we'll discuss it when I return.'

Cassie folded her arms defiantly and tried to ignore the regret niggling at her for the outburst. 'Nothing to discuss. It's all paid for. I'm going. End of discussion.'

'You're so bloody stubborn, Cassie. The sooner we get those marriage vows sorted the better as far as I'm concerned. See you soon.' He kissed her swiftly and headed for the door.

'Love you!' she shouted. 'And I'm still not saying I'll obey you!' she continued, realising that the door had already closed so he couldn't hear.

Two days of Seth's absence had seen Cassie plough through a huge pile of work. Her favourite so far had been a novel about a time-travelling soldier who had fought in many wars but had chosen to stay in the present day when he'd fallen in love with a nurse in a 21st century war zone. On top of that, she'd received some excellent feedback from a potential new client who had informed her that some work would be forthcoming soon. She was buzzing and ready to celebrate so when Vina called and invited her out for drinks with her and some friends she jumped at the chance.

When they arrived at their favourite champagne bar they were met by a large group of Vina's colleagues but there was no sign of Pippa. Cassie immediately regretted coming out. The last thing she wanted was to spend an evening with a group of people she didn't know when she could've stayed home and read a book in peace. As she searched the group trying to spot a familiar face she absently wondered if Pippa was off with her new lover or out hunting for one.

Vina ordered their drinks and they all congregated at one end of the bar.

'Have you heard from Pippa recently, V?' Cassie asked as discreetly as possible.

She took a sip of her bubbling beverage and shook her head. 'I was going to ask you the same question. I haven't heard from her since we went dress shopping. I texted her to check she was okay the day after and she said everything was fine but I haven't heard from her since. I messaged and invited her to meet us but she didn't reply.'

Cassie sighed. 'I'm a bit worried about her. She's been acting... well... she doesn't seem herself.'

Vina shook her head. 'I'm not surprised with what she told us though. Are you?'

Cassie didn't want to divulge the details of the conversation she'd had with Pippa so she simply shrugged and changed the subject. 'So, how did it go with Mister Framlington-Smythe? You've avoided answering me by text and now I have you as a captive audience.' She giggled.

Vina's cheeks coloured pink. 'His name is Harry Heathcote-Thurlow, you daft bat.' She pulled her lips between her teeth. 'And oh my God, Cassie, he's gorgeous!'

Cassie widened her eyes and gasped. 'You've been holding out on me!'

Vina leaned closer. 'I don't want to jinx it, Cassie. He's just about the most perfect man I've ever met. And I've got some pretty bloody amazing men in my life to compare him to.'

Cassie flung her arms around her friend. 'I'm so happy for you. When are you seeing him again?'

'I've actually had a sneaky date with him this week already. And before you get cross, I didn't tell you because I wanted to be sure he liked me too.'

Cassie decided to forgo the telling off she would normally give Vina for keeping things so quiet. 'And?'

'And... the way he kissed me the other night tells me he's as smitten as I am.' The girls simultaneously squealed like they would have done in their university days and jumped up and down on the spot, while hugging.

* * *

Later in the evening they walked along the bustling city streets of Glasgow, which were alive with groups of singing party-goers and the aroma of food concessions selling burgers and kebabs to drunken passers-by. They eventually arrived at an exclusive nightclub down an alleyway. Smartly clothed bouncers assessed everyone closely before letting anyone inside. It seemed the more money you appeared to have and the more beautiful you were assisted access greatly. Cassie was relieved to be with Vina who underwent less scrutiny than others and even knew the bouncers by name. The two burly men looked Cassie up and down but didn't pay much mind to her really. Clearly Vina's seal of approval was all that was needed.

Cassie was a little tipsy by this time and whilst Vina shouted over the music that she was going to order a jug of Sex on the Beach, Cassie gestured towards the ladies. Once in through the door she was taken aback by how luxurious the room was. Gilt mirrors faced her as she approached the stalls and the sinks themselves seemed to disappear into the walls somehow, *like those infinity pools you see on TV*, she thought. There wasn't a single paper towel in sight. Instead there was a neatly folded pile of what appeared to be the best Egyptian cotton towelettes, which were placed in a discreet linen bin after use. Crikey, how the other half live, she mused, only realising moments later that she was soon to be part of that so called *other half*.

She walked into a stall and closed the door behind her and, staring at the marble floor, she tried to decide just how drunk she was. Maybe she should switch to soft drinks?

'So you really think he sleeps around? I thought he adored the bloody ground she walked on.' Cassie held her breath, feeling a touch guilty for listening in on the gossip coming from outside her stall. She recognised the voices of two of Vina's colleagues.

'You've seen her, haven't you? She's so bloody demure it's sickening. I've heard that he's only with her because he likes a challenge. It's like something out of *My Fair Lady*. But I'm sure she loves his money.' The two women cackled like witches stirring up mischief in a cauldron.

'I think you're right though. I wouldn't have put them together. She's just too...' There was a pause.

'NICE!' the two voices announced in unison and then descended into a fit of giggles.

Cassie remained silent but felt a little sorry for whomever they were discussing. There was nothing wrong with being a decent human, after all. Someone shouldn't be hated for that.

'Yeah, I heard that he's had a fling with his secretary.'

'Oh yeah, I heard that too.'

Shit, Cassie thought. *They're talking about Pippa and Jasper.* Her eyes widened and she tried hard not to move and give away her presence.

Voice number one spoke again. 'I bet all these so-called late nights and business trips are excuses so he can go get his rocks off with someone who has a bit more about her.'

'Oh yeah. Fancy the job, do you?'

Voice one laughed. 'Oh, God yes! I'd ride him like a—'

The door swung open and someone walked in, forcing the girls to stop berating Cassie's friend. Although she was a bit surprised to hear them referring to Jasper as someone they'd pounce on. He wasn't exactly male model material.

'Hey, ladies. Have either of you seen Cassie? I seem to have lost her.'

Cassie recognised Vina's voice and was on the verge of shouting out but the next words from the gossip bitches stopped her mid-inhale. 'Cassie?'

Voice one giggled. 'Yeah, you know, Cassie the really *nice* girl who came out with Vina tonight.'

'Oh yes, of course,' voice two chimed in. 'Cassie, the *nice* girl. Really *nice*.' The two girls sniggered and Cassie's heart plummeted like she was on the sharp descent of a roller-coaster.

'Hey, I don't know what you're finding funny about my friend but have you seen her or not?' The annoyance was evident in Vina's voice.

'Nah. Maybe she went home. Probably can't handle her drink. Usually happens to nice girls.'

'Hey. Stop it. Whatever your inside joke is about. Stop it right now. Cassie is my best friend and my brother's fiancée, so you might want to think twice before mocking her. He does run the bloody company after all.'

Voice number one laughed again. 'Oh come on, V, we're only having a giggle. And we were just talking about how Lena here would like to ride—'

'A taxi home!' the voice now known to be Lena interjected. 'Yeah, work tomorrow and all that. Home time for us, right, Tanya?'

'Probably a good idea. We wouldn't want you turning up for work hungover, now would we? What would Seth think to that? Hmm?' Vina's acidic tone cut through the atmosphere like a cheese wire.

Cassie waited until she heard the ladies room door close and silence had descended before she unlocked the stall door and made her way to the sink. She washed her hands and then, with the burden of everything she had overheard weighing her down, she dried her teary eyes.

7

Standing in the little shop surrounded by hundreds of images of pretty, elaborate, and mostly over the top wedding cake designs Cassie wanted to scream, '*Cake is cake for Pete's sake! Can we just go home now?*' But instead, like the dutiful wife-to-be she was, Cassie smiled sweetly as Mrs Guthrie and Seth chatted to the designer about the perfect cake for *her* wedding. *Cassie's* wedding. Not the current Mrs Guthrie's – even though you'd have been forgiven for thinking otherwise.

Seth stood there nodding in agreement with his mother and making all the right, affirmative noises as she talked *at* the designer about colours and flavours. Cassie watched her fiancé, knowing full well that this is exactly what he must do in his boring business meetings. Every so often he would turn and smile at Cassie or kiss her head. She knew there was something not quite right seeing as he was never overly affectionate in public. Although, there was the distinct possibility she was being paranoid after the conversation she had overheard earlier in the week. *They were just jealous*, she repeatedly told herself. Clearly they both fancied him. One of them admitted as much to the other. But after hearing Pippa talk about Jasper having an affair she couldn't help the doubt that niggled at her.

Once the meeting had come to an end and Cassie had sampled so much cake that each one melded into the other and she had no clue which was her favourite, they agreed on one. Cassie had all but given up on having an opinion about *her* wedding. What was the point? So long as she married the man of her dreams it would all be perfect in the end. Or at least she hoped it would.

Cassie and Seth walked his mother out to her car where her driver was patiently reading a newspaper waiting for her return. After air kisses they waved her goodbye and decided to walk home seeing as the sweet cake shop wasn't far from their apartment.

The sun had begun its lazy descent and as they passed the Kelvingrove Art Gallery it was lit up with the orange glow of the early evening sun. The many windows glistening like mirrors as the light hit. They sauntered hand-in-hand in contented silence, through the park that surrounded the gallery and Cassie inhaled the fresh breeze. Living here was wonderful. It was easy to pretend that you were out in the middle of the countryside instead of on the edges of one of the busiest cities in the country. A squirrel leapt from a tree to their left and paused in the centre of the path as if to assess them, before taking off and scurrying up the opposite tree.

'I love being surrounded by all this green,' Cassie said, absentmindedly as they walked.

Seth squeezed her hand. 'Yes, it's pretty to look at but you can't beat the hustle and bustle of the city to prove you're alive.'

'Don't you ever imagine yourself leaving the city? Even when you retire?' Cassie *couldn't* imagine living in the city forever.

He frowned. 'Leave Glasgow? Never. It's what I thrive on,

poppet. This place. The pace of life. I'll sleep when I'm dead, darling.' He chuckled.

Cassie couldn't help the sinking feeling that knotted her stomach. She had visions of them maybe moving to the seaside when he retired; long walks on the beach, maybe getting a dog – even though that idea would horrify Mr Clean. But the city was what he loved so maybe she could make do with visits to the seaside and countryside. Kelvingrove Park was a great compromise after all. And to have it practically on her doorstep was great.

'Come on. Out with it. I know you have something on your mind.'

She glanced up at him and sighed. 'Oh, nothing I'm fine.' The expression on his face told her he wasn't buying it. 'I'm just a wee bit overwhelmed I guess. All this wedding stuff—'

'See this is why I wanted to sort it all out. It's stressful enough without you having to arrange everything too.'

'But that's what a bride is supposed to do; get stressed about the decisions *she's* making. Not those being made around her, Seth. I know you want to save me from it all but like I've said before; I'm not some damsel in distress. It's not like *My Fair Lady* and I'm some project you have to work on.' She echoed the horrible conversation she had overheard and a shiver travelled her spine as she did so. 'I'm your equal and I need to be treated that way.'

'Cassie, where's all this coming from? I've never thought of you as some *project*. And, of course, you're my equal. Who has planted such nonsense in your head, sweetheart?'

'No one,' she lied. 'Oh, I don't know... I just feel a little bamboozled.'

He pulled her into his side. 'Darling, this is the last thing I wanted. Just say the word if there's anything you want to change about the wedding and I promise it's done.'

Guilt niggled at her and knotted her stomach simultaneously. Was she blowing things out of proportion? Was this just a normal bride thing?

She nuzzled into his embrace. 'Just forget it. It's fine. I'll be fine.' A heavy silence fell between them and Cassie searched for something to fill the void.

Eventually Seth beat her to it. 'Vina says you had a nice girls' night out whilst I was away. Although from what I gather you had rather a lot to drink and got all emotional,' he teased. 'Why didn't you tell me about it?'

His use of the word 'nice' made her shiver again. 'There was nothing to tell. I guess I'm just behaving like a typical bride.' She shrugged and grinned in the hope he would let it go.

He didn't. He stopped walking and turned to face her, placing his hands on her arms. 'Cassie, be honest. Are you getting cold feet?'

She shook her head. 'Oh no, Seth, not at all. Are... are *you*?'

He laughed. 'Why on earth would you ask me that? Haven't I been the one making all the arrangements as quickly as possible?'

Fair point. 'Well... yes... but...'

He huffed and let his head loll backwards. 'Oh, for goodness' sake, Cassie, just spit it out. If you need to say something, just say it.' His sudden change of mood irritated her.

Taking a deep breath to bolster her confidence she looked him square in the eyes. 'Am I too nice for you?'

His eyes narrowed and he tilted his head. 'Nice? Why do you make that sound like an insult?'

She shrugged. 'I just wonder what your colleagues and staff

think of me. The age gap. The fact that you're wealthy and I'm quite the opposite.'

He tugged her hand and began walking again. 'Cassie, you really are being absurd. No, I don't think you're too nice. I think you're marriage material or I wouldn't have bloody proposed, would I?' Annoyance edged his clipped words now. He was clearly exasperated.

Cassie stopped this time. 'That's the thing though. You didn't actually ask me to marry you.'

He crumpled his face and made a snorting sound. 'What the hell are you talking about? You *do* remember that night at dinner, don't you?'

'Yes, of course, I do. But... what you actually said was that you wanted to look after me. Then you asked if I would let you. To which I said yes.'

He lifted his arms in exasperation and let them fall to his sides again. 'And your point is? Bloody hell, Cassie, it was obvious what I was asking of you. I gave you a damned ring, didn't I?'

Her lip began to tremble. 'Why are you angry with me?' Although she was angry at herself for getting upset and appearing like some neurotic little woman. 'And I love my ring. But... do you actually want to marry me, Seth?'

He huffed and stepped closer, enveloping her in his arms. 'I gave you a ring. I booked a drafty old cottage in that tiny godforsaken town. I sent you wedding dress shopping. We've picked a cake. I've booked the church. What do *you* think?'

Tears escaped Cassie's eyes and left heated trails down her cheeks and she internally cursed herself for letting her emotions run so freely. 'I think I need to know for sure. I need the words, Seth. But more than that I need to know that I'm the right girl for you. That I'm who you really want.'

He swiped at the moisture on her face with his thumbs and kissed her nose. 'Cassie, I want you and I *need* you. So, can we please stop this ridiculous conversation? And just to clarify, Cassandra Montgomery, will you please still marry me?'

She sniffed as a smile spread across her face and she nodded fervently. 'Yes, yes I will.' She leapt into his arms and he hugged her tightly.

'Thank goodness. Now can we go home? It's getting bloody chilly now the sun's gone.'

And just like that the overheard gossip was forgotten and left exactly where it belonged – in the toilet – and her mind was eased. Seth Guthrie not only wanted her, he needed her. And that counted for so much. To top it off she had her official proposal.

Everything was wonderful again.

'So, what does one do on an editing masterclass course that one can't simply do online? And don't you already know it all anyway?' Seth asked from their bed as Cassie packed her modest wheelie suitcase. 'I mean you *do* sell your services as such.'

'It's a refresher really. But I think it's better to be more hands on. You know?'

'Hey, you'd better not be putting your hands on anyone but me,' he replied.

She giggled like a silly schoolgirl at his response. 'You know what I mean. It's better to actually speak to people directly when you're learning. And it's good to meet others in the same field. Swap ideas and such.'

'You mean like networking?'

She lifted her head and nodded at him. 'Yes. Like networking. You catch on fast,' she teased.

As she passed the bed he made a grab for her and pulled her down on top of him. 'Well, don't you be getting too friendly with any of the men on this *master*class. I'm the only master you need in your life,' he told her as he swatted her bottom.

'Ouch! And I hope that was a joke, Mr Guthrie.'

He rolled his eyes and freed her from his grasp. 'You take things far too seriously, soon-to-be Mrs Guthrie.'

She stood beside the bed, hands on hips. 'Hmm, well after the whole "obey" thing I wouldn't put anything past you.'

He growled and flung himself back into the pillows like a moody teen. 'Ugh, I thought we'd moved on from that now? I admitted defeat on it, didn't I? Let it go, will you?'

She bent to kiss his head. 'Now who's taking things too seriously? I appreciate you compromising on the vows. No woman in this day and age wants to say they'll obey anything except the law of the land.'

'Yes, and you made your point. Anyway, when will you be back? And why are you going on a weekend? Seems a waste to me.'

'Because, my darling fiancé, it was the time slot that worked for the course organisers. It's summer so we're using the college out of term time, meaning we have to take it when it's available. And I'll be home Sunday evening just like I told you before.'

He huffed. 'It's only bloody Edinburgh. I don't know why you won't let me drive you. I could've booked us a suite at the Balmoral instead of you staying in some dirty student hovel.' She opened her mouth to respond but he held up his hand. 'Don't bother, Miss Independence. I get it. You're capable of getting across the country under your own steam... or that of a train… or rather, I know it's not *actually* a steam train… You get my point.'

She burst into fits of laughter at his bumbling. He didn't give in easily and she loved that he was beginning to relax a little. Things had been so much better since they cleared the air.

Seth stuck out his bottom lip. 'Hey, you're laughing at me.'

She bent to kiss him once more. 'But only because you're funny in the best possible way. Now I have to go. Behave yourself whilst I'm gone!' she repeated his own parting words from the Seattle trip at him as she grabbed her jacket and made for the door.

'I wouldn't dare do anything else, Mrs Bossy Bottom!' he called back.

8

On arrival in Edinburgh, Cassie walked for twenty minutes from Waverley Station, passing the National Museum of Scotland – one of her favourite places – en-route. She was carried along by Chris Cornell's dulcet tones as he sang to her in French through her earbuds about someone trying to change him. *Hmm, I know that feeling*, she thought, rolling her eyes. But the negative thought evaporated as quickly as it had appeared. A smile stretched her face as she inhaled the warm summer air and headed towards the campus.

Edinburgh's Old Town, where the campus was located, was a mixture of Victorian, Edwardian and neo-classical architecture with some more modern structures dotted around for good measure. The imposing buildings lined the roads like sentries on guard to protect the cities multi-cultured residents. The modern red brick university building in Lauriston Place seemed a little out of character with the majority of the period structures. Its black-framed windows appeared like arrow slits in fortifications, but of course Cassie was thankful that no archers would be firing on her as she walked into the main entrance.

The college was eerily quiet; its corridors void of the usual chatter and myriad students milling around. But then again it was a Friday afternoon during the summer vacation; a time when janitors and maintenance staff were the only people walking the halls in preparation for the next semester to begin.

Once she had located the lecture theatre noted on her letter, she entered and settled herself in a seat, taking out her notebook in readiness. She was momentarily taken back to the day she'd met Vina under similar circumstances – although at least this time she was in the right place.

* * *

As courses go it was quite a relaxed affair. The other people seemed nice and they were from a mixture of career backgrounds, from authors to copy editors, to scriptwriters. After the first afternoon of study the cohort went to the local pub for drinks and a bite to eat. They chatted about their own work lives and shared pointers with each other about some of the more intricate practices.

The conversation quickly moved on to relationships and Cassie proudly announced that she was getting married soon. She was showered with congratulations and asked to share the details of her dress, the cake, etc. When asked about her fiancé she told her fellow gathered students about Seth and this sparked many shared, knowing glances.

'Okay, I'll say what everyone's thinking,' Tim, the freelance proofreader said as he leaned forward. 'You're marrying Seth Guthrie? *The* Seth Guthrie? Property mogul, wealthy businessman, et cetera, et cetera?' He frowned in what appeared to be disbelief.

Unease at his attitude prickled at her skin and she rubbed her arms. 'Yes, that's right.'

'And you're doing this poxy course?' Many of the group gasped and chuntered at his insulting choice of words but he held up his hand. 'All right, all right, what I mean is, you're *still* working? When you're marrying one of the richest blokes in Scotland? Are you mad? Shouldn't you be a kept woman? I mean, what's the guy playing at?' He sat upright again as he laughed and glanced around at his peers, clearly expecting the same reaction from them.

Sarah, the indie author, interjected, 'Tim, that's none of your business. I think you owe Cassie an apology.'

He held up both hands now and shrugged. 'Aye, aye, I'm sorry. I tend to speak my mind. I just find it a bit strange that someone would still *need* to work if—'

'The fact is I don't *need* to work, Tim. I *choose* to work. I don't want to be a kept woman. I want something for myself and that's why I run my own business. A successful one, too, I might add. And as Sarah said this is none of your damn business. You don't know Seth personally and you've only just met me. So you can keep your opinions to yourself.' Cassie stood from the table and placed down her half-finished drink. 'I think I'm going to head to bed, guys. Thanks for a lovely evening.'

The rest of the group bid her a goodnight and once she had walked away she heard them begin to chastise the errant Tim for his arrogance and ignorant, unfounded observations. Cassie smiled to herself as she walked out of the pub. But as she made her way back to the dorm block, worry niggled at her. Why were people so judgemental? Just because she was a young woman marrying an older, wealthy man didn't mean she was some kind of gold digger. She hoped this wasn't how the world – well, Seth's world anyway – viewed her.

The following day was an intense, full Saturday. Tim stayed out of her way and she was relieved for that fact alone. She found the work useful and regardless of the arse she had encountered, she was glad she had attended. During the day she discovered that an amendment had been made to the schedule and that they would be finished by mid-morning on Sunday – more than half a day earlier than originally stated – meaning she would be home to Seth just after lunch. To say this was a relief was an understatement.

That evening, after a long day of studies she made her way to the local supermarket, choosing a take-out bowl of salad and mini bottle of wine over another meal and drinks session with the likes of opinionated Tim and she was curled up in bed by ten thirty.

* * *

The final morning of the course was light-hearted and fun. And the moments ticked by rapidly until it was time for Cassie to head back to her room to gather her belongings. She shoved her possessions into her case and after applying lip gloss and combing her hair she left. The morning was cooler than the previous day and she considered texting Seth to tell him she was looking forward to letting him warm her up. *Although on second thought, I'll leave my early return as a nice surprise.* She smiled at the thought.

On the walk to the station she came across a pretty lingerie boutique and paused to peruse the window display. In a moment of impulsiveness she pushed open the door and walked in. Before her were rails filled with lace garments and tastefully dressed mannequins displaying the sexy yet classy underwear. She selected something she had a feeling Seth would love to see her in – and quickly get her out of – and with a little shyness she took it to the desk and handed over her payment.

Once she had recovered from her embarrassment she set off again towards Waverley Train Station, making sure to call in at the mini supermarket to collect wine and chocolates. She grinned to herself as the plans for her afternoon and evening ahead formed in her mind. Seth would no doubt be out when she arrived home, giving her plenty of time to reapply her make-up and tidy up her hair so that she could be waiting for him in bed when he returned. *Maybe I should be impulsive more often*, she thought as a shiver of excitement sent goosebumps across her skin.

The train journey, typically, seemed to take forever and to make matters worse Cassie had to stand for the majority of it. At one point she narrowly escaped landing in the lap of a poor elderly chap as the train jerked out of one station. When the train eventually pulled into Glasgow she grabbed her newly acquired goody bags and tugged her case along behind her as she left the hot metal tin that had been her torturous transport for the last hour.

The Glasgow that greeted her was a wet and dreary one and she flagged down a cab as quickly as she could. Once safely ensconced in the warm vehicle she stuck in her earbuds and rifled through her playlists. She was determined to listen to something that she hoped would lighten the mood and get her ready for her evening of passion. A little Kings of Leon would do the trick.

She pulled out her compact from her handbag and assessed her flat hair and pale face. Thanks to the crappy weather she would have to take extra time in the bathroom in preparation for her 'Seduce Seth Guthrie' mission. If he was home she would simply demand that he wait, naked in the bedroom. She giggled as she thought back to being called *Miss Bossy Bottom*. Well, maybe that needed to be the shape of things to come. It was about time her too often subdued assertive side took more of the limelight.

The cab pulled up outside her building and she paid the driver. As she looked through the bars of the underground car park she spotted Seth's car. *Dammit.* Determined to continue with her plans she made her way up to their apartment in the lift and as quietly as possible she inserted the key in the lock and turned it. Another shudder of giddy excitement rippled through her and she had to stifle a nervous laugh. *Good grief, Cassie, get a grip. You're engaged to the man.*

There was no sign of Seth in the living room or kitchen so she figured he must be in the bedroom already. *Perfect!* She placed the wine and chocolates on the counter top in the kitchen and made her way into the main bathroom. She fluffed up her hair, reapplied her make-up and quickly undressed and slipped her sexy lingerie on before redressing. He'd no doubt want to unwrap her like the gift she was offering herself as. On the way back past the kitchen she uncorked the wine and grabbed a couple of glasses – the chocolates could wait until later.

Softly she tiptoed towards the bedroom and smiled as she heard the sound of Seth's favourite opera drifting through the air. Taking a deep breath and adjusting her hold on the wine and the glasses she opened the bedroom door.

9

As the door swung open Cassie gasped and the items she was holding slipped from her grasp. The glasses and the wine bottle crashed to the floor shattering on impact into tiny fragments on the oak boarding and sending pools of red in splatters up the wall and the door; a blood crimson contrast to the stark white that surrounded her. A horrified cry left her throat and her hands instinctively came to cover her mouth.

'Cassie! Darling, I can explain!' her panic-stricken fiancé exclaimed in assurance as he jumped up and grappled for the nearest item of clothing he could find. Then he hopped from foot to foot as he tugged it, absent-mindedly onto his bare legs.

It just so happened that what he had grabbed was a pair of Cassie's best floral pyjama bottoms in a size twelve. He was a six-foot-two man who played rugby for fun. His thighs were like tree trunks and if she hadn't just found him in bed with one of her closest friends the whole scene before her would have been hilarious. His long, muscular lower half squeezed into Cassie's Marks and Spencer's PJs was one of the most surreal images she had ever seen and she simply didn't know how to react.

How could she?

The bizarre urge to laugh began to bubble up from somewhere twisted, deep within her. A place where clearly the news that Seth Guthrie was a cheating bastard hadn't quite registered yet. As she stood there, gawping at the scene before her featuring her fiancé and Pippa, one of her best friends – two people she thought she knew – she wondered exactly how this supposed explanation would go. Would it be like one of those ridiculous insurance claims you read on Facebook memes where the driver insists that the tree came out of nowhere and hit *them*, not the other way around?

Thankfully the anger that should have manifested immediately began to make its way to the surface in a kind of delayed reaction; her heart hammered a beat all of its own against her rib cage and her stomach knotted so tightly she feared she may throw up.

She snorted in a very unladylike manner. 'Oh, you can *explain*? This should be good.' Holding her hands up to halt Seth's imminent interruption she continued, 'Wait! Let me guess, eh? This should be fun. Okay... so...' She tapped her chin in mock concentration, her hands shaking and the rest of her body juddering in unison.

'Cassie, I—'

Her voice was loud and wavering. 'No, no, I said I wanted to guess,' she barked. 'Okay, so here's my theory... you were using our bed as a trampoline... no... no you were conducting research into the strength of the mattress we've had for three years, you know to make sure it's up to scratch. When all of a sudden, you bounced too vigorously, and all your clothes fell off causing you trip over your boxers and... and it was at *that* precise moment that your penis accidentally slipped into Pippa's vagina repeatedly until the mattress stopped moving.

Am I close?' Her wide-eyed stare fixed on her fiancé for a moment. But then she shifted her attention to Pippa who had gathered the Egyptian cotton sheets and tugged them to cover her fake breasts.

Cassie's nostrils flared. 'And you! You *bitch*! You were supposed to be my friend. I listened to you talk about your husband being unfaithful and how heartbroken you were. I tried to talk you out of having your own affair. But if I'd even *guessed* for a second that you were going to choose *my* fiancé to have that affair with I would have blacked your eyes right then and there. You betraying piece of shit. How could you do this to me? Were you trying to tell me on that day, huh? In some twisted way were you trying to tell me you were intent on shagging *my* future husband?' She stepped towards Pippa with her fists balled at her sides.

Pippa sat there, her red lipstick smeared around her face and her watery eyes flitting between Seth and Cassie, it was evident she had no clue how to respond. She backed up closer to the headboard of the ironically virginal white, designer bed and opened and closed her mouth like a dying goldfish before eventually finding words. 'It... it wasn't like that. I swear it wasn't. I had no intention of having sex with Seth. It wasn't like that,' she stuttered, her voice wavering with either fear or emotion, it didn't much matter which.

Cassie sneered like a rabid animal. 'Yeah, you already said so. Are you going to tell me this is the first time you've had your little romp session?'

The two guilty parties shouted out simultaneously, but didn't agree in their responses.

'Yes, it's the first time,' was Seth's reply.

Whilst Pippa blurted, 'No, it's not, I wouldn't lie to you.'

Seth slapped his hand over his eyes. 'For fuck's sake, Pippa.'

Pippa snapped at him, 'Well, Seth, she deserves to know about us.'

Seth lifted his arms and let them flop to his sides in exasperation. 'Pippa, there *is* no *us*. Jesus! We agreed it was just sex.'

Cassie observed this exchange with no small amount of incredulity. 'Oh, don't mind me, you two just carry on. Let me know when you've got your stories straight, won't you?'

'Cassie, poppet—' Seth stepped towards her with his arms outstretched.

She jabbed her finger in his direction. 'Don't you *dare* come near me, you lying bastard. And I'm *not* your fucking poppet, you patronising shit. I've always hated that stupid pet name. I'm a grown woman for fuck's sake. And you are *literally* a pair of lying fuckers!'

'Cassie, please stop swearing, darling. It's not ladylike,' Seth pleaded.

Cassie made a derisive scoffing sound. 'Oh fuck off, you fucking arsehole.'

He sighed and plastered on a condescending smile. 'Come on. Let's all calm down. I'll clean up this mess, Pippa can leave and you and I can talk, hmm? What do you say pop— erm... Cassie?'

Cassie's blood raged beneath her skin as her heart pushed it around her body a lot faster than usual and she quivered as she gritted her teeth. 'I'll tell you what. You get your tart to help you clean it up, hmm? We wouldn't want the oak to get stained, now, would we? I mean, it's much more important than our relationship.'

Seth gave a weak laugh. 'Cassie, don't you think you're overreacting? Me and you... *that's* what's important. We can fix this. I know we can,' he told her softly as he stepped towards her as if she was a cornered animal. 'It was just sex. Just a release. Just

once. That's all. I don't *love* Pippa. I *love* you. I'm *marrying* you.'
He reached out to tuck a strand of hair behind her ear but she
stepped back before he made contact.

Suddenly wondering why the hell she was even still there,
she scrunched her brow. 'Seth, you're not only a cheating
bastard, you're a condescending, self-centred shit-head too. And
yes, that's a fair bit of swearing right there. Now, ask me if I care.
And in case you weren't paying attention, your bit on the side
has already admitted that this *isn't* a one-time thing. So, stop
trying to brush it off like it was a spur-of-the-moment occurrence. I think my reaction is perfectly justified. We're over. I'll
have my things collected.'

She turned and walked away only stopping to grab her coat
and unpacked case from the living room and then headed for
the door but he followed, still wearing her pyjama bottoms
which were now stretched beyond recognition. *Well, they're
bloody ruined*, she thought as she looked him up and down with
disdain.

'Look, we— that is Pippa and I, met to talk about the
wedding. We got chatting about her and Jasper. One thing led to
another...' Cassie's blank expression was no deterrent to his
monologue. 'She was more adventurous, that's all— in bed I
mean.'

Cassie dropped her jacket, drew her hand back and
launched it full pelt at his face. There was a loud crack that
echoed off the walls and she contorted her face. 'Oh my God,
what the hell makes you think I want to know the sordid
details? You sick little man!'

Seth stood open-mouthed holding his bright red cheek for a
moment then he reached out to touch her shoulder again and
she flinched. 'Cassie, you can't leave. Don't forget you have
nowhere to go. Your *life* is here with me. *I'm* your life. In fact,

without me you don't even *have* a life,' he stated as if she should already know this; like it was common knowledge.

She inhaled a deep calming breath and lifted her chin defiantly. 'Really? Well then, I can assure you that I'll be on a mission from this moment to prove that there *is life after Seth*.'

And with that she pulled the door open and left.

10

Sitting alone in the first coffee shop she had come across whilst wondering aimlessly along Argyle Street, she stared into her mug playing over the awful scene that had greeted her at home. Seth's words repeated over and over in her head like a stuck record. '*Without me you don't even have a life... without me you don't even have a life...*' The terrible thing was she realised there was a very distinct possibility he was right.

When, exactly, *had* her life begun to revolve around Seth Guthrie?

Her dad had pointed out the same at her engagement party, albeit with a little more subtlety. But she knew deep down that she was to blame. *She* had facilitated Seth becoming the centre of her universe. She didn't feel she needed anyone else. When she was growing up it was just her and her dad. And then along came Seth and she felt complete. And her dad had wanted a man like Seth for her, hadn't he? Hadn't he always talked about someone to protect her and care for her when he was no longer around? Wasn't that what he'd meant? Why hadn't she realised that he would never intend for her to lose her sense of self?

She'd been so busy trying not to be the usual clumsy, haphazard Cassie Montgomery that she had, in fact, changed almost everything about her personality; her dress sense, her musical tastes, her free will as if doing so would make Seth love her more.

She'd been so damned spineless. When she looked back over the decisions that had been made for her she realised that she'd rolled over and shown her belly. She'd submitted to him like a dog to its alpha. Since meeting him she had apparently lost the ability to think for herself *and* to stand up for herself. But not only that, she'd lost the will to even try. And why *was* that? She surmised, on further analysis of her mind-set, that deep down she held onto an inherent fear that she would lose him if she asserted herself. Yet she'd lost him anyway. And perhaps ultimately it had been her fault. Perhaps in being so weak-willed and insipid, she'd posed no challenge for Seth. Clearly she lacked excitement for him, causing him to stray. But surely that said more about him than it did about her? She'd kept her moral compass intact. The same couldn't be said for her former fiancé.

As if a bright light had suddenly switched on in her mind she gasped at her train of thought and slammed her cup down onto the table as the word, 'No!' fell loudly from her mouth. She cringed and glanced up to find the other patrons staring in her direction and she raised her hand in apology before turning her attention back to her coffee. Why the hell was she questioning and blaming herself? *Seth* was the one who'd been unfaithful. If he was unhappy he should have told her and *left* her before putting his penis in another woman for goodness' sake. Yes, *he* was the bastard here. *He* was the one who couldn't keep it in his pants for a weekend whilst she was away studying. He must have a serious sex addiction if he couldn't even wait two bloody days. And what exactly did he mean about Pippa being more adventurous? It's not as if she'd walked in to find him hanging from the ceiling being bloody whipped. They were just having sex to bloody opera music. What was adventurous about that? It was pathetic really. Yet it obviously held something of interest for him to make him unfaithful.

Her stomach roiled as that word rattle around her brain. Unfaithful. He had cheated. He had taken something precious and sullied it. Like Cassie meant nothing to him. But to make matters even worse, he had done so with someone Cassie had considered a close friend.

The waitress appeared and placed another latte and a chocolate chip cookie on the table before her. She hadn't ordered either and looked up to explain that to her but the woman slipped into the booth opposite her and held up her hand. 'Before you say anything, they're on me. You've been sitting here nursing that one for ages now so it must be cold. And to be honest you look like you need cheering up.'

Cassie's eyed welled up at the considerate gesture. 'Thank you so much.' *What is it about the kindness of complete strangers that touches us so deeply?* Something as simple as coffee and a biscuit almost restored her faith in humanity. *Almost.*

Tilting her head to one side the waitress whose name badge read 'Jean' said, 'Now judging by the look on your face I'm guessing you've either been dumped or cheated on. Sadly, I know the look all too well. But let me tell you this, love, whatever he or she has done to you, you didn't deserve the heartache. So, whatever you do, don't blame yourself. Now, you give me a shout if you need anything else, okay?' She stood to leave but waited for a response.

Cassie nodded and tried her best to smile at the woman. She was around fifteen years older than her with an accent that wasn't local although Cassie couldn't quite place it. She watched as the waitress walked over to an elderly gent sitting at the counter and began to chat to him. She was clearly a very kind soul.

The coffee shop wasn't one she had been in before. It wasn't sleek enough for Seth to even consider setting foot inside. Shame considering the coffee was excellent and the staff were lovely. But with its outdated eighties décor and scribbled chalkboard menu she knew very well that Seth would never have given the place a second glance. She had happened upon the place by accident but was glad she had. Seth, she decided, was a bloody snob. How was she just realising this now?

After leaving the apartment she had stood on the pavement outside with her designer wheelie suitcase not knowing what to do or where to go. She couldn't call Vina because Seth was her brother and it would crush her already broken heart to hear her best friend take his side. Cumbria was an option as her dad worried enough as it was and he would no doubt want to kill Seth once he found out what had happened. The temptation to head straight to Jasper's house to tell him his wife was a cheating whore, was almost too hard to resist but she had a feeling he wouldn't care. It would give him the perfect out if he was indeed looking for it and judging by the fact that he was having an affair already it would probably ease any guilt he was feeling. So, she had meandered along past the Kelvingrove and had taken a turn up Argyle Street.

After eating half the cookie and draining the latte mug she stood to go and pay. The waitress, Jean, smiled as she approached. 'You've nothing to pay. It was on me remember?'

'Thank you again. What you've done has— I mean...' Cassie couldn't find the words of gratitude she was searching for in her foggy mind.

'It's fine. Honestly. Are you okay?'

Cassie nodded. 'I will be. Once I figure out my next move.'

Jean nodded knowingly. 'Well, doll, all I can say is time may be a healer but distance. Distance is the key. Get away if you can. Just leave the heartbreaker behind. I did it. Came here from Skye ten years ago after finding my husband in bed with our neighbour. I left and haven't looked back. Best thing I ever did.'

Cassie scrunched her brow. 'But is that not giving in and running away?' She winced after hearing her own words. 'Sorry, I didn't mean to sound judgemental.'

The waitress smiled warmly. 'I think it's only running away if it's you that's done the wrong. If it's been done *to* you then you're simply making a fresh start.'

Cassie nodded seeing that Jean spoke a lot of sense. And although it sounded pretty scary maybe getting away for a holiday would be good. Some time to clear her head; decide what to do with the rest of her life now it had changed so irrevocably.

She turned to leave the café but stopped as a thought sprung to mind. 'Erm... H-how did you choose where to go?'

Jean grinned. 'You'll think I'm crazy but I took a map of the UK off the shelf in my husband's study, opened it up, closed my eyes and plonked my finger down.'

Cassie's eyes widened at the prospect of giving up total control of her destination to fate. But what did she have to lose? She thanked the waitress for what was possibly the hundredth time and left.

As Cassie walked she took out her phone and searched for a reasonably priced hotel to stay in. The next time she looked up she narrowly missed a head on collision with a lamp post. *Ugh,*

Cassie you really need to stop texting and walking, idiot. She spotted a WHSmith across the road and when the traffic cleared she headed over there.

The map section was vast. But all she needed really was a map of Scotland. A tourist map would suffice. She didn't think she wanted to go to England. And Scotland was her home now. She located the map she needed and paid for it.

Her next stop was the hotel she had found. The reviews said it was clean and tidy and it was definitely somewhere Seth wouldn't think of looking – if he chose to look at all. The receptionist was pleasant but wanted to make small talk, asking questions about whether she was there for business or pleasure. She mumbled an incoherent reply in the hope that the young blonde would get the hint and once she was in possession of her key card she made her way to the second floor.

She opened the door and let it slam closed behind her. And then it hit her. Her relationship was over. She leaned against the door and slid down it as the tears came. Hot tears that trailed down her cheeks and into her open mouth. She sobbed in physical pain at the knowledge that everything she had dreamed about was gone. There would be no wedding. She wouldn't become Mrs Guthrie. She would no longer lay awake in bed with that silly smile on her face thinking about how lucky she was. Because it was all gone. Her life was no longer perfect. The man she loved more than anyone in the world had not only broken her trust but he had smashed her heart, her hopes and her dreams to a million tiny, irreparable pieces. And for what? Sex? A quick thrill with someone unfamiliar? Well, she hoped to hell it was worth it for him. Because from that moment onwards she would trust no one. She would *never* make the mistake of giving her fractured heart away so readily again. And she would be sure to build walls around what was left of her dignity to protect her from so-called friends like Pippa.

* * *

When the tears had subsided she pulled herself to her feet once again and stripped out of her clothes. She scrunched up the sexy underwear she was wearing before unceremoniously throwing it in the bathroom waste bin.

After making herself a coffee with the provisions that had been left in her room she stuck in her earbuds, took the map out of its packaging and opened it out. With a sigh she shook her head. *I can't do this. It's bloody crazy. I can't just pick a random place and go there... Can I?*

She lifted her phone and flicked through searching for a particular track; an angry track that seemed to fit her situation in sentiment and rage. She located it and hit play, then yanked open the huge bag of chocolates she had purchase along with the map and shoved a handful in her mouth. As the venomous lyrics to Pearl Jam's 'State of Love and Trust' blanked out all other thoughts she took a deep breath. *Oh, sod it. Let's do this.*

She closed her eyes, tilted her head back and with her index finger poised and ready she lowered it to the map.

11

CASSIE

One month later...

With more than a little trepidation, Cassie walked up the stone path to the front door of Rose Brae in the small Eastern Scotland seaside village of Coldingham and sighed. First impressions of the location were very positive. On a scale of one to ten for prettiness, the village was a twelve but she was still unsure of the crazy leap she had taken on the advice of a complete stranger in a café. However, fears and worries aside and as arranged by telephone, she was due to meet a Mr Mackenzie – the owner of the cottage – at ten that morning to receive the keys. And then her new life could finally begin.

Her dad had been so lovely and understanding when she had declined his offer to move back home to Cumbria. But a short stay with him had been a sad enough affair. He took the news about Seth's infidelity very hard and his attitude – especially the expletives she had never heard him utter before – told her that moving home would've been too difficult. Her dad would've wanted to talk about it and she just wanted to let it go and try to forget – something her dad wouldn't be able to do easily when someone had hurt his precious little girl. He would want to analyse everything and he would probably want to pay Seth a visit. She definitely didn't want that to happen.

So for a few days she'd revisited the places of her childhood and walked the beach at St Bees Bay with Patch and her father, laughing as the cute dog repeatedly ran towards the water and then retreated as soon as the tide appeared to be chasing him. She enjoyed the salty air and the dramatic views of the red sandstone cliffs that created an imposing backdrop to the Irish Sea as it whispered, lazily up the shingle to form rock pools. It was this break away from the city that cemented in her mind that she wanted to be close to the sea again. But just not on *this* coastline. It held too many memories and she surmised it was time to make some new ones.

Rose Brae had stood out for her immediately. It looked like such a happy place; a whitewashed stone building with cheery blue painted windows and door. It wasn't big but there was only one of her. Whilst she waited outside a sense of melancholy washed over her as she remembered the cottage Seth had taken her to on the weekend he proposed. The garish diamond ring he had given her on that trip was now banished to a keepsake box along with every scrap of evidence that they had ever been associated. She hadn't the heart to throw the box away. Not yet. She had tried on several occasions in the recent weeks but each time something tugged at her heart strings and she placed the box down and walked away. It was all quite sad really. To think she had given years of her life to someone only to discover that her original fears were founded – she really was never enough for him.

Sometimes being proved right isn't all it's cracked up to be.

Looking back – as she had been wont to do since her life

imploded – she decided it was strange how she'd somehow managed to shoehorn herself into a life she had no business encroaching upon. The modern penthouse for starters with its high ceilings and white painted walls simply screamed wealth. But then again so did the whole of Glasgow's West End. It was a far cry from the modest little cottage she had grown up in *and* from what she actually considered beautiful. But it was Seth's home and it was where *he* thrived so who had she been to argue? After all he was the major breadwinner in their relationship. That was why she had been the one to leave after finding him in the midst of his indiscretion; that and the fact that he had slept with *her* friend in *their* bed.

Now was the time to rebuild. And she would have to do that from the ground up because she discovered on walking out of the Seth's plush million-pound apartment that she pretty much had nothing. Well nothing of significance like furniture, electrical goods, and the like. She had managed to retrieve her designer handbags that Seth had gifted and they had been sold on eBay so that she had the funds to at least get by for a while. And she had withdrawn the savings from her bank account – minimal though they were. But she was at that moment rather grateful for Seth's insistence on paying for everything. Her dad had managed to surprise her with a cheque that would cover her first three months' rent – it was as if he had expected something like this. And maybe he had.

Not only had she lost physical items in the split but it appeared their so-called friends had been quick to take sides. Any friends she'd had when she met Seth had gradually been manipulated out of her life by him. And his comments about them not being that bothered if they couldn't fit around her schedule had really seemed genuine. What she hadn't realised at the time was that he was deliberately changing their plans to clash with any that had cropped up with people she had known before.

The only friend that seemed to still care was Vina. She had been disgusted at both Seth *and* Pippa and said she hated him for how he'd treated her. She had apologised so many times that Cassie had lost count. 'If it wasn't for me...' and 'If only I hadn't introduced you...' being the two phrases she repeated as she sobbed. The problem, however, was the fact that blood is thicker than the water under the bridge between Cassie and Seth and nothing would tear apart the Guthrie family. The matriarch herself would make sure of that. Vina's relationship with Harry was blossoming and their telephone conversations now comprised of her excited friend telling her all the juicy details of her love life and then profusely apologising because she didn't want to upset Cassie with the talk of relationships. Cassie, on the other hand, was actually glad that Vina was so happy. She deserved it. And it was good that one of them was.

Back in her present-day version of reality Cassie continued to wait for Mr Mackenzie. The cottage was cute and the end one of a row that sat away from the main road of the Scottish Borders seaside village. The window boxes were a little overgrown but she was looking forward to planting something colourful in them as soon as she got the chance. Although she wasn't sure what would grow now that autumn was fast approaching.

Someone cleared his throat behind her, causing her to almost jump out of her skin and she swung round to face the culprit. A scruffy-looking man stood there, a furrow in his brow. If this was Mr Mackenzie, he was younger than she had expected and he had the most piercing blue eyes she'd ever seen. His black T-shirt seemed too tight as it clung to the contours of his chest and abdomen, although on second glance she realised it was the top half of a wet suit; the bottom half was covered with khaki board shorts that just reached his knees.

He scratched his head. 'Are you Miss Montgomery by any chance?' The strong Scottish accent surprised her as she had expected an American twang like that of Patrick Swayze in the movie *Point Break*. He was most definitely the epitome of the stereotypical 'surfer dude'. And he was incredibly handsome under all that exterior untidiness. She berated herself mentally for thinking so. *Cassie Montgomery, you are steering clear of all men, remember?*

Shoving aside all thoughts of how attractive this surfer was she nodded. 'Yes, that's me.'

He shrugged and shook his head. 'Oh, right. I thought you'd be older.'

She recoiled a little at his personal remark. 'Well I thought *you'd* be older. Assuming you *are* Mr Mackenzie.'

'I am, but I'm not *the* Mr Mackenzie.'

Cassie was losing patience now. 'So you *are* Mr Mackenzie but you're *not*?'

He swiped his hand back through his dirty-blond hair and grinned. 'Okay, so you dealt with Mr *Rab* Mackenzie, yeah? I'm Tadhg Mackenzie, his nephew.'

'Oh, right. Well, then why are you here... erm... Tiger?'

He burst into hysterical laughter, throwing his head back as he guffawed. 'Tiger, ha! That's a new one on me.' She crossed her arms over her chest and he pulled his lips between his teeth to try and control his amusement. 'My name's Tadhg,' he repeated slowly as if she was stupid and her skin prickled with annoyance. After all, it was *his* name that was silly, not her she decided. It was so silly in fact, that she'd already forgotten it.

She scowled. 'I heard you the first time,' she lied. 'So, Tyj—Targ— oh, *whatever. Mr* Mackenzie.' She placed her hands on her hips. 'Do you or do you *not* have my keys? I'm suspecting not or you'd no doubt have started with that important snippet.'

'Oh aye, I do. Maybe I should have said, eh?' He chuckled.

She rolled her eyes and huffed; he was really getting on her last nerve now. 'Right. Can you hand them over then? Please?'

He rubbed at the scruff on his chin. 'Ah, no can do. My Uncle Rab said I'd to show you the ropes, as it were.'

'Well, then can you open the door and show me? I've been waiting for more than ten minutes. You were late.'

'Aye, sorry about that. Rab's away to Edinburgh and I totally forgot until I was down at the beach then I thought. "*Shit I'm meant to be up at Rose Brae with that spinster woman.*"'

Cassie gasped. 'Spinster woman?'

He cringed and his cheeks coloured. 'Well, your name... You know, Miss Montgomery,' he said in a pseudo posh old lady voice. 'Sounds all school ma'am-ish. Expected you to be around sixty if truth be told.'

'Well, I can assure you I'm neither a school ma'am nor am I sixty.'

He chuckled and shook his head as he waggled a long finger at her. 'Aye, but you *are* one of those that says neither and nor,' he said in that stupid mocking voice again. 'That's kind of school ma'am-ish.'

He wasn't helping her level of irritation and she tapped her foot. 'Look, are you going to let me in? I have a million and one things to do to get organised. The last thing I need to be doing is standing out here with someone who takes himself for some kind of Billy Connolly.'

The young man scrunched his brow. 'Who?'

Shit. I really am old. Or maybe it's just Seth's influence on me. 'You... you don't know who Billy Connolly is?'

He burst into laughter again. 'Jeez you're so easy to wind up. Of course I know of the Big Yin. Who *doesnae*?'

Realising she was literally getting nowhere fast she wondered if she had made a colossal mistake in coming to Coldingham and she hoped that this man wasn't a sample of what to expect from everyone else. 'Please, Mr Mackenzie, could you please just let me into the cottage?' She sighed.

The surfer nodded and stepped in front of her to open the cottage door. 'So, what brings you to Coldingham, Miss Montgomery?'

Hearing him call her that after insinuating she was an old woman made her cringe. 'Please, call me Cassandra.'

He turned and grinned. 'Okay. In that case you can call me Mac seeing as you don't seem to be able to remember my *actual* name.'

'Mac? Okay, Mac. And I *can* remember your name. I just didn't quite catch it.' She felt the flush of embarrassment heat her cheeks. 'I mean what kind of name is *Tiger* for a grown man?'

'It's Tadhg. Like tie but with a "g" on the end. There's no r. And it's Irish. Well, I like to consider it as Gaelic, really. My mum was Irish and my dad was a Scot. Best of both beautiful words.' He smiled and she smiled in response. He had a very cheery face and as much she hated to admit it, even though he annoyed her he seemed okay-*ish*. 'So, why *are* you here, *Cassandra*?'

She followed him inside the house. It appeared smaller than she remembered when the letting agent showed her around two weeks earlier but she reminded herself, again, that she was only one person.

Remembering that Tiger, or whatever his name was, had

asked a question, she shrugged. 'Needed a change of scenery, I suppose. The city was feeling a little claustrophobic.'

'Rab says you lived in *Glasgow*. How can somewhere like that be claustrophobic?'

Shaking her head she tried to find words to explain without *actually* explaining. 'Just... I don't know... maybe impersonal is the right word,' she said, not wishing to bombard him with the inner workings of her mind.

He nodded emphatically. 'Oh, shit, yeah, I *totally* get that. Ignorant arses, all up themselves in the city if you ask me. Give me the beach or the Highlands any day of the week.'

'I don't think you can tar everyone in the city with the same brush, Tiger. It's a bit mean.'

He turned to face her with a grin and a questioning look in his eyes. 'So, you're sticking with *Tiger*?'

She froze and her eyes widened. 'I meant, Mac. *Mac*.'

'Aye well, anyway you're best out of that place. All those bloody arrogant sods in their penthouse apartments with their high-flying careers.'

She glared at him. 'I lived in a penthouse.'

It was his turn to freeze now. 'I mean— I— oh feck, I didn't mean any offence.' He held up his hands.

'Hmm, well maybe you should just tell me what I need to know and let me get on with unpacking.' She was aware that she sounded terse but she was very tired and anyway, he didn't seem to notice.

'Right, sure. Okay so the place is furnished as you know. It hasn't really changed since the agent showed you around. Living room that way, kitchen through there.' He gestured. 'There are two bedrooms. One is upstairs with a side window that looks towards the sea and the other is next to the lounge. Some use it as a dining room and some as an office. I suppose it depends on what you'll be doing whilst you're here, eh? Right, I'll be on my way.'

He hadn't told her anything about the heating, the boiler, the oil deliveries, et cetera. 'Whoa, hang on. You need to tell me about all the other bits. How things work and such.'

He huffed and rolled his eyes. His customer service skills left a lot to be desired. He gestured to her again and she followed him in to the kitchen. 'Boiler's there on the wall. Pretty obvious really. Rab will sort the oil when it runs low but there should be enough there for now. These things here. These are called taps. You turn the top of them and water comes *oot*.'

Sarcastic pig. 'Oh, really? I'd never have guessed,' she responded dryly.

He winked. 'Oh aye, we have all mod cons here in Coldingham, you know.' He glanced around and rubbed his chin. 'Oh, and here, follow me.'

They walked down a short corridor and arrived in the lounge. 'That black box over there, you flick the switch on the wall and it lights up.' He widened his eyes and waved his arms and fingers around like a lunatic. 'Moving pictures and all manner of amazing stuff like talking and music comes *oot*. Grand, eh?'

She folded her arms across her chest. 'Thank you, Mr Mackenzie but I do know what a television is.'

He shrugged and feigned innocence. 'Just making sure I tell you *how things work and such*, Miss Montgomery. Oh, I should ask though, do you have any pets? Because if you do, and they cause damage, you'll immediately forfeit your bond. As per my uncle's contract. Thought it best to let you know in *your* situation.'

She frowned wondering what her situation was. 'I don't have any pets.'

He gasped campy and placed his hand on his chest. 'What? No cats?'

Heaving an exasperated sigh, she told him, 'Okay, Mr Mackenzie, I get your point. But I'm not an old spinster cat lady. And I think we're done here.'

He started with his deep belly laugh again and Cassie was once again annoyed that he was poking fun at her. He turned to walk towards the door. 'I think I preferred being called Tiger. And you really should lighten up. I bet you're quite a looker when you smile. You know, for an old lassie.'

Before she could muster up a suitable, scathing retort he had walked out and let the door slam behind him laughing loudly as he went.

12

MAC

Tadhg Mackenzie or Mac was ready to curse his uncle.

After all, a cat-loving spinster wasn't really who he'd hoped Rose Brae would be rented to. But seeing as Rab had failed to convince his nephew to move in, he figured it was all he could do. Rab had told him the woman was from out of town. Glasgow to be exact. *Just what we need. More bloody interlopers*, Mac thought as he trudged towards the cottage with the keys in his pocket. He'd been looking forward to a day at the beach until he realised he'd almost forgotten his duty. He was under strict instructions to be nice to the woman. As if he could be anything else! And he wouldn't ever be disrespectful to an older lady. What did his uncle take him for?

Rab thought Mac was crazy for living in his drafty old static caravan but the truth was it suited him. And he owned the land it was on so it was up to him what he did with it. The van was screened from the road by a line of trees so Mac couldn't really see the problem. Okay, so it was unconventional, but so was Mac. The plot was situated in Coldingham Bay right next to his

Uncle Rab's house and now his parents were gone, it was Mac's to do with as he chose – within reason obviously. But he had the best view of the sea and so he had no intention of moving from there.

His parents had come to own the plot thanks to his dad inheriting it from his Grandpa who he had known as Papa. Land in Coldingham was a bit like hen's teeth and so when Papa died Mac's folks took the decision to sell their modest cottage in the village and demolish Papa's ramshackle old place to build their dream home. Sadly it never came to pass. Iain and Ailish Mackenzie were killed in a tragic boating accident in the South of France when Mac was just twelve. It had been a second honeymoon of sorts that the inheritance and sale of their house had afforded them. Mac was staying with Rab, Iain's older brother at the time the accident occurred and there he stayed as Rab took on the role of guardian. The land and proceeds of the house sale had remained in trust for Mac until he reached eighteen and then it was his. Most people thought he would sell the land and relocate with the vast amount of money he would no doubt make. They were wrong. He purchased a static caravan and moved right on in. That had been six years ago.

Since he had taken up residence on the land he had been inundated regularly with ridiculously excessive offers from building companies, desperate to get their hands on the prime real estate land but he had no intention of selling. Ever.

And so, since the age of eighteen, he had been on a long camping trip. By choice. He didn't need to work thanks to life insurance that was bestowed upon him after his parents' demise so he wasn't beholden to anyone. Although he was by no means lazy. He taught surfing in the summer months and he helped his Uncle Rab out with the holiday cottages he owned.

Rab had gone up to Edinburgh on some undisclosed business and he had, therefore, entrusted Mac with the task of handing over the keys to Rose Brae's new tenant. When he arrived, he spotted the woman already there, standing outside the cottage with her back towards him. He guessed he would be about to get a roasting from the middle-aged spinster seeing as he was late. And from what Rab had said, middle-aged women could be stroppy – hence his bachelor lifestyle.

When the woman turned to face him he got the shock of his life. She certainly didn't look middle-aged. Nor was there any sign of a cat. She had beautiful, vivid blue eyes – although he noticed a distinct hint of sadness in them. Her blonde hair was scraped back from her face in a ponytail, revealing delicate features and pretty, full lips. She wore skinny jeans and a long-sleeved white top with little, pale blue spots on. He realised it wasn't at all like him to take so much notice of what someone was wearing. But she was bloody gorgeous. That is until she opened her mouth and almost bit his head off. Although it was no doubt deserved due to his tardiness. He insinuated that she was a bit like a headmistress and she didn't take that too well at all.

At the end of his visit, he came to the conclusion she'd had a sense of humour bypass. She didn't laugh at any of his jokes and women usually did. In fact women were usually falling at his feet. But not this one. He decided that there was a good chance she had still been in the *good looks* queue when it was time for the issuing of *sense of humour* because she certainly was beautiful. Evidently looks could be deceiving.

He couldn't help noticing that behind her terse attitude and mask of annoyance she oozed a kind of melancholy usually seen in Film Noir heroines. And he wondered what misfortune had brought her to Coldingham. Especially when Rab said she was from Glasgow and she was clearly an English lass. Why choose somewhere so far out in the sticks? Why not go home to England? He presumed time would tell, although thanks to her attitude he doubted that he would be the one to do the discovering.

13

CASSIE

Once she was alone in her new surroundings, Cassie wandered around the cottage. The small entrance way led through to a shaker style kitchen diner with stairs off to one side and then a short corridor led through to the downstairs bedroom and cute little weather boarded bathroom. It was clean and tidy but lacking personality. The décor was the typical magnolia of holiday lets and the walls were bare.

She wasn't sure where to start. The only time she had lived alone had been during the first year of university and that was in halls so it didn't really count. The prospect of being self-sufficient both terrified and excited her but there was so much to do before she could relax. She didn't exactly have much to bring in from the car, but what she really wanted to do was sit down with a cup of tea and get used to the idea that she was finally there. She had only driven for two and a half hours but thanks to her lack of sleep in the previous few weeks it might as well have been *twenty*-two. There was no real wonder the arrogant man had called her an 'old lassie'. She felt as though she had aged ten years in the past month with all the heartache and tears shed.

She walked back into the kitchen and searched through all of the rustic cream units to look for a kettle but there wasn't one. It was just as well she had purchased one to bring with her; although that would mean emptying the boxes from her car first. The kettle was underneath the dinner service, mugs, glasses and cutlery she had purchased. She hadn't wanted to wrestle with Seth over the designer set they had been bought as an engagement gift by his parents. Quite frankly, she's never seen the point in expensive plates anyway. She was inherently clumsy so they would only have ended up broken like the wine bottle and glasses from that fateful day at the apartment. Seth had always insisted on the best of everything – or at least the most expensive. He equated splashing his money to success and happiness; she could see that with a little distance.

She took the car keys from her pocket and walked outside to the narrow lane where she had parked. The boot was crammed but it was only a small hatchback so it didn't take much to fill it up. She began to carry her possessions into her new home and tried to ignore the niggling sadness tugging at her heart. The last thing she wanted to be was lonely. But that's precisely what she was now.

Once the car was emptied she rifled through the bag of food she had bought on the way over and realised, to her dismay, that she had somehow forgotten tea bags and milk. How the hell could she have forgotten the most *obvious* things? It was the straw that broke the proverbial camel's back and she began to sob uncontrollably. Leaning on the wooden work surface, her body shuddered as tears dripped from her nose and chin and formed little dark pools where they landed. Her heart squeezed in her chest as memories of her time with Seth played in her mind like a heartbreaking movie. If only there was a pill that you could take that would wipe away only the memories you didn't want to keep. All the pent-up emotion and devastation of the betrayal caused by two people she thought cared about her, poured out leaving its mark on the wood.

How could they have done it? And more importantly, *why?* What had she ever done to deserve such evil deception from people she had cared for? The scene she had walked in on now made her feel nauseated. Seeing the man she loved, naked and between the thighs of one of her closest friends had been something she could *never* unsee. And the fact that neither had apologised – not that it would've helped if they had – just made the pain so much harder to bear.

The bed they had shared, made love in, laughed in, was tainted; the bed where he had comforted her as she cried on the anniversary of her mother's death; the bed where he had held her and told her how important she was to him and how much he loved her and needed her; the bed where they had planned their future, their wedding, their married life... their *family*. All marred along with the memories of those precious times. Stained by betrayal of the worst possible kind.

She clutched her stomach as it knotted and clenched, causing her to drop to her knees. She had given him everything. All of herself. She had all but lost her own identity because she was willing to sacrifice *anything* to be with him. She couldn't stand the pain of it. The bitterness was eating her up inside and she was powerless to stop it. It had all been for nothing. All the years they had spent building trust, falling in love. All wasted.

Every. Single. Second.

She sat there on the kitchen floor with a heavy heart and the weight of loneliness she felt pushing her into the tiled floor.

* * *

Cassie wasn't sure how long she remained there but
eventually she pulled herself to her feet. *I must forget him. I
must move on,* she repeated over and over in her mind. It
would become her mantra, she decided. It would take time
but that was something she had in abundance now. She
walked through to the bathroom and regarded her blotchy
face and reddened, swollen eyes in the mirror. *I need to be
stronger. I need to stop loving Seth-Bastard-Guthrie.* She splashed
her face with cold water and she wiped herself dry with the
sleeves of her top thanks to the unpacked towels sitting in
a box.

'Come on, Cassie, tea is what you need. The great British
cure-all. Or maybe wine... and chocolate,' she told her reflection. She knew there was a little Spar at the top of the street so
she went back through to the kitchen and grabbed her handbag,
checking to make sure she had a foldaway shopping bag inside.
She slipped on her sunglasses to disguise the fact she had spent
goodness knows how long crying and, making sure to collect the
keys from the door, she pulled it closed behind her and set off.

The high street was quite narrow but lined either side with a
selection of quaint shops and houses. People drove by her on
the way to the beach with surfboards strapped to the roofs of
their cars and she decided that she would definitely make the
most of living so close to the sea. She stopped to peer in the
window of a small antiques shop and knew she would be
visiting there to buy some treasures for her home. In only a few
minutes she located the Spar and made her way inside. She
grabbed a wire basket and headed towards the chiller cabinets.

But no sooner had she found the milk than she came face to
face with a familiar surfer. 'Ah, we meet again, Miss Mont-

gomery.' The Sean Connery impersonation was quite amusing but unfortunately, she wasn't in the mood to laugh.

Great. 'Oh hi, Tiger.'

'Ah, I'm back to Tiger again, eh? *Roar.*' He chuckled, making a claw with his hand.

'Oh yeah. Funny.' She knew her lack of enthusiasm was loud and clear in her tone and immediately felt guilty for her reaction. When she glanced up at him she found him scowling in what appeared to be disappointment.

He huffed and tilted his head as he assessed her quizzically. 'So, you know when you left Glasgow?'

She nodded. 'Yes. I remember it well.' And then she mumbled, 'Beginning to wonder if I did the right thing actually,' under her breath.

Not taking the hint he carried on, 'Did you not remember to pack your sense of humour or are you sending for it once you're settled?'

She gasped at his cruel remark and scrambled around her brain to find a witty and scathing retort but was only able to watch his back retreat as he headed for the checkout with his six-pack of beer. She was desperate to find the strength to follow him and give him a piece of her mind but instead her eyes began to sting once more. *Oh God, I'm becoming one of those pathetic women who cry at the slightest bloody thing.*

Yes, his words were kind of mean and harsh but in all honesty, she knew she hadn't exactly made a great first impression. And to be fair he had no idea why she had run away from the city. She knew she'd have to try to refrain from being a grumpy bitch or she would be forever lonely by the seaside.

She pulled herself together long enough to finish her shopping and took her basket to the checkout. Her purchases included everything a girl recovering from heartache could possibly need – wine, chocolate, tea, tissues and a ready meal lasagne for one. That item alone was enough to make her eyes threaten tears again. She sure knew how to live the high life.

She placed her basket on the counter and the elderly lady behind the cash register smiled at her. 'Hello, dear. Are you on holiday?'

Cassie smiled in response to her cheery disposition. This was more like it. 'Oh no, I'm going to be living here actually. I'm not sure how long for but...' She wasn't really sure how to finish her sentence.

The lady's eyebrows lifted. 'Oh, are you the lady who's renting Rose Brae?'

She nodded. 'Yes, that's me. I'm Cassie Montgomery.' She held out her hand.

She shook it and said, 'Ah, lovely to meet you, Miss Montgomery. I'm Morag. It's funny, you know, I thought you'd be older.'

Good grief.

14

After a much-needed cup of tea, Cassie began the arduous task of unpacking the boxes she had brought in from the car earlier. Most of them were filled with books she couldn't bear to part with so they were quite heavy. And anyway, she would need all the help she could get to escape her current predicament, so she intended to live vicariously through the romance novels of Jane Austen and the Brontë Sisters. With tear-fogged eyes she recalled the day she had returned to Seth's apartment with the intention of packing up all her worldly goods in old newspaper...

* * *

Seth wasn't supposed to be home so Cassie had confidently refused the offer of help from Vina, insisting she would be absolutely fine – and in all honesty not wanting to cause a rift between siblings. With mounting trepidation, she ventured to her former home, armed with flattened cardboard boxes and rolls of tape, in the hope she would be finished and have vacated by the time her ex-fiancé returned.

She unlocked the door and nervously stepped inside, pausing for a deep calming breath before closing the door behind her. A heavy silence hung in the air of what had always been a place buzzing with laughter, opera music and intellectual conversation. But being there at that precise moment was strange and filled her with a bone-deep sadness.

She quickly bypassed the room where she had discovered Seth *in flagrante delicto* with someone she had considered a good person and better friend, making sure not to even glance in its direction. The room wasn't at fault but the contents therein reminded her of that awful day and she had vowed that whatever belongings remained in there would need to be replaced. She had no intention of collecting anything from that room because she simply didn't want to relive that gut-wrenching moment when her world collapsed around her ears.

Struggling with her boxes she walked along the corridor that met the open plan living area and momentarily cursed herself for declining the offer of help. The apartment looked even bigger now that she had been away from it for a short while and it had felt *huge* when she was blissfully unaware of Seth's infidelity. But now it seemed cavernous and austere and lifeless. She felt totally out of place standing there in her high street jeans and hooded sweater.

'So, this is it then?' Seth's voice startled her and she dropped the folded cardboard to the floor as she swung around to see him standing there, hair unkempt, skin pale. He was wearing scratty old lounge pants that she didn't ever remember seeing before and a stained T-shirt that evidently hadn't been washed in a very long time. He looked nothing like the Seth Guthrie she had fallen head over heels in love with and for a split second, she felt sorry for him. In fact, the urge to hold him was almost overpowering.

Almost.

But instead she reminded herself of the reason for his suffering and her pity was quickly replaced by disdain. 'You weren't supposed to be here.'

He huffed. 'I had to be here. Someone has to make you see sense. Do you realise how crazy it's become?'

Pulling herself to her full height she nodded defiantly, determined to show no emotion. 'You knew it was coming to this, Seth. Don't pretend it's a shock.'

He shook his head and rubbed his hands over his unshaven face. 'I still can't believe you're throwing it all away, Cassie. Seriously, it's ridiculous.'

Anger spiked within her and she clenched her fists at her sides, sticking her nails into the palms of her hands. '*I'm* throwing this away? Don't you think *you* had a hand... or other appendages, in it?' She scoffed. 'What I can't believe is that you thought it could go any other way. You slept with one of my closest friends, Seth. I caught you in the act. What else am I supposed to do? Brush it under the carpet and hope we both learn to avoid the giant lump of infidelity sitting in the room?'

He huffed and stepped towards her. 'In all honesty, yes. That's what we *both* need to do. We *all* make mistakes, Cassandra. *All* of us. And that's all it was. *One* mistake. I don't love Pippa. It was just lust. Just sex. But I do love you and if you're honest you still love me too. You're the one I want to marry, surely that must count for something, hmm?'

She stood there open-mouthed and completely aghast that she had even listened to his pitiful, self-centred, vacuous monologue. 'Am I supposed to be grateful?' she shouted. 'You. Were. Unfaithful. You didn't buy the wrong toilet paper or break my favourite bloody vase, for Pete's sake. *This* is not a mistake I can forgive. And what's more I don't *want* to forgive you for what you've done. I deserve so much better. You ruined a perfectly happy relationship simply because you put your dick in my friend, Seth. *That's* the problem. I can't believe I have to spell it out for you. Surely even *you're* not so obtuse that you're somehow not seeing the reality here. We were supposed to be getting married. We were supposed to be in a monogamous relationship. But it turns out only one of us saw things that way.'

He made a noise like a growling angry bear. 'Jesus, Cassie, it's not like I bloody killed someone!'

Her voice cracked as she replied, 'No. You killed some*thing*. You killed the love I had for you. And you killed the trust I placed in you.' Her lip trembled and she jammed her nails harder into her palms trying not to cry in front of the cheating arsehole.

He shook his head and grimaced at her. 'Always my little drama queen.'

She gasped. 'You condescending prick. I'm not *your* anything. Not any more. And I'm not playing the melodramatic little woman here. I'm hurt beyond repair because my life has just fallen apart around me. This is *not* acting.' She took a breath, her heart pounded at her ribs. 'And I may never trust anyone again thanks to you.'

He stepped closer still. 'It was just sex,' he whispered as if doing so would make it less appalling to her. 'Just a couple of times. Three... four maximum. That's all.'

She knew it happened more than once but this unwanted news compounded the anger inside of her. She instinctively covered her mouth as bile rose in her gullet.

Shaking her head, she simultaneously backed away from him and gritted her teeth. 'Oh well, that's good to know. Had it been five or six times things would've been so much worse.' Her voice dripped with sarcasm. 'Knowing it was "four maximum" really eases the pain of betrayal. Thank you so much.' Her calm voice belied the tumult of emotions raging beneath her skin. 'Look, maybe I should go and come back when you're actually out. Clearly this isn't going to work.' She bent to collect her boxes from the floor.

Seth was not going to give up. 'Can't we just talk? Figure out a way through this? We've been through tough times before, Cassie, and I'm lost without you. Please?'

She straightened again and he was standing only a couple of feet away; much too close for comfort. At this proximity she could see the dark circles around his eyes and the way his greying, matted hair had evidently not been washed for days. He smelled of beer, bad breath and body odour – the complete antithesis of Seth Guthrie a month before.

She halted inhalation through her nose and glared at him. 'No, Seth. There's no time for talking now. That should have happened before you had sex with Pippa four times. It should have happened as soon as you realised I wasn't enough for you. But, sadly, I had to find out the hard way. No pun intended. Let me know when you'll be out and I'll come back.'

She tried to pass him but he held up his hands and with a trembling lip he reached out and smoothed his hand down her arm. A shiver of disgust travelled her spine and she watched as tears escaped the corners of his bloodshot eyes.

He forced a sad smile. 'No, no, it's fine. You're here now. You may as well get your things. I need this to be over with. I need to... to move on.'

Once again incredulity niggled at Cassie and although she tried not to retort the words flew from her mouth before she could stop them. '*You* need to move on? Didn't you already do that? You see I'm taking the more traditional path of moving on after my fiancé has shit all over my life. You may want to take a leaf out of my book in future. You seem to have forgotten how these things work.'

He winced. 'So bitter. It doesn't suit you. Bitterness, I mean. You're such a nice person usually.' He gave a snide laugh. 'I felt sure you'd fall for my injured puppy-dog look. Clearly you're not the person I thought you were.'

She gasped. 'You're trying to tell me your appearance today is fake?' *The bastard! The cruel, conniving, manipulative bastard.*

He scoffed. 'Well, it was worth a try. You know I don't like to lose. It's a weakness to give in, poppet. And I'm not weak. Haven't you learned that about me? I get my way, regardless of how it happens.'

His pet name for her grated on her last nerve and she rolled her eyes as she shoved past him where his large muscular frame almost filled the space between the walls. She knew he was ruthless in the boardroom, but to speak of *her* as if she was some prize; some business deal he wasn't prepared to miss out on, was sickening. Had she ever really known him?

Without looking up at him she demanded. 'Can you just let me get on with packing?'

He stepped aside but as she walked by him he reached out and grabbed her shoulder, squeezing hard to the point of pain and in a strained voice he pleaded, 'We can make this right, Cassie. Wipe the slate clean and move forwards. Let's go to bed and I can remind you of how good we were. We can forge ahead with the wedding and no one has to know. But I won't let you make a fool of me, Cassie. I simply won't allow it. You will not walk out on me.'

She managed to free herself from his vice-like grip and swung around, her hand connecting with his face in a crack.

Angry tears clouded her vision and her jaw ached from being so tightly clenched. 'Forge ahead? No one has to know? *I* know Seth. I know everything. And I am walking out on you. I'm not some commodity. I'm a human being. I deserved your respect but instead you treated me like something you could pick up and drop whenever you saw fit. You may be able to do that in your work life but I certainly won't let you do that to me. I deserve so much better. And my God, I don't want you anywhere near me. You disgust me and I am warning you to never touch me again.' Her heart pounded in her chest and for the first time ever she felt afraid of him.

He sneered and held his hands up as he backed away. 'Okay, okay. Have it your way for now. But just remember this when you end up regretting your decision. Because you *will* regret it. Mark my words. And then it'll be too late.'

A shiver consumed her and she physically juddered. 'It's already too late. And I don't appreciate you threatening me just because for *once* you're not getting your own way. I think I'll leave now. I'll ask Vina to collect my things. Goodbye, Seth.'

She dashed for the door, leaving her boxes and packing tape behind and prayed he didn't come after her.

He didn't follow but he did manage to have the final word. 'You'll be back, Cassie! I'll make sure of it. I never lose. I get my way by whatever means necessary. You'll do well to remember that!'

His words filled her with an uncomfortable uneasiness but she carried on regardless, determined not to look back.

* * *

Back in her enforced new existence she cut the tape on the final box and flattened it ready to take it out to where the others had been deposited beside the recycling bin. She pulled the fresh early evening air into her lungs and for the first time in weeks a wave of excited anticipation flipped her stomach. The sun had already begun its descent and the sky was an array of reds, oranges and purples. If she closed her eyes she could hear the sea down in the little bay as it meandered towards the beach. Such a peaceful sound. She had always loved the sea and her dad had often joked that she was a pebble in a former life. It became her dad's nickname for her when she was small and had stuck for many years. Although recently he had resorted to calling her Cassie after Seth had commented that Pebble was a silly name for a grown woman – and poppet was so much better?

She still had the polished pebble necklace her dad had bought for her when she was twelve and they were on a camping trip to Dhoon Beach in Dumfries and Galloway. She hadn't worn it for a very long time but she vowed she would do just that as soon as she had her jewellery box set out. Seth had preferred her to wear the diamond pendant he had bought her but that was now banished to the box along with her engagement ring.

Reminiscing about happier times set her mind in motion and she stepped inside to grab the keys to the cottage. Once the door was locked behind her she set off on the walk to the beach. Before she moved to the village she had calculated it would probably take around fifteen to twenty minutes to walk there from her new home which meant that she would be able to enjoy the view before the sun disappeared completely.

15

There was a distinct nip to the coastal air but Cassie was still warm from unpacking so the breeze was a welcome relief. With the sea on her horizon she aimed in its direction which took her down the high street lined with a variety of pretty buildings of all shapes and sizes and then along a country lane to her right. On one side were vivid green fields and on the other a holiday camp from which the smell of barbecue food wafted and made her stomach growl. Eventually she reached the slope that led down to the sand and by the time she reached her destination she was quite out of breath so she found a comfortable spot to sit down. She tucked her knees up to her chin and wrapped her arms around them as she took in the stunning small cove that encompassed her.

There were only a couple of dog walkers off towards the sea and a few surfers making the most of the early evening sunshine, bobbing about on their boards seeing as there wasn't enough breeze to create strong waves. A man was teaching a child how to balance on a smaller than usual board as a woman stood by watching and cheering him on. It was such a sweet family image and Cassie smiled in spite of her current situation. Seth had been keen to start a family and Cassie had felt she had ages to wait before it became a priority. Yet here she was, newly single and reluctant to even think of starting over, never mind having children. But watching this cute family unit saddened her a little.

A row of colourful, quirky beach huts spread out to her left, each expressing its owner's individual stamp – and beyond them stood a beautiful modern house built almost entirely out of glass. *The view of the sea must be wonderful from up there*, she thought as she watched the sunlight glinting on the windows. To the right, there rose a large grassy hill with rock pools skirting its edges where a few people were exploring with nets.

The vista was enough to take her breath away and cause a mixture of emotions to swell up from deep within. Memories of her happy childhood when it was just Cassie, her dad and Bilbo, running around the beach at Dhoon, playing catch or throwing bits of driftwood for Bilbo to chase. They would search the rock pools and try to stop Bilbo from jumping in them as they examined the tiny sea creatures captured by the tide. Then there was the memory of walking along the vast beach at Bamburgh with Seth, the lofty castle creating a dramatic backdrop that was the stuff of historical romance novels. She had so many things to look *back* on but at that moment she had no clue what lay ahead for her; it was quite a disconcerting feeling.

Steeling herself she kicked off her slip-on shoes and scrunched her toes in the soft grains beneath her feet. She inhaled deeply and relished the salty air as it filled her lungs and refreshed her weary senses. It was a far cry from the smog of Glasgow city and it was good to smell something other than exhaust fumes for once. Exhaling a relieved sigh, she gazed towards the small waves as they lurched towards the shore with determination only to crash down and disappear.

The man teaching the boy was now jogging towards where she sat and she realised it was Mac. 'Beautiful, isn't it?' The unexpected interruption dragged her from her thoughts and she looked up shielding her eyes from the setting sun.

'Oh, hi *again*. Yes, yes, it's very beautiful indeed.'

The young Mr Mackenzie smiled warmly and she briefly tilted her mouth in response but after their earlier encounter she wasn't in the mood to entertain him.

The wetsuit he wore was now pulled down and his bare chest was glinting with droplets of sea water. She swallowed hard as she trailed her gaze down his toned, muscular physique. Tattoos encircled his arms and she tried not to stare in fascination. She flared her nostrils when she realised she was taking notice of these silly little details about a man she found irritating at best.

He lowered himself to the sand only a short distance away and Cassie huffed the air from her lungs. She wanted to be alone and couldn't understand – with the entire available beach before them – why he'd chosen to sit so close.

He cleared his throat. 'Erm... look Cassandra... I think I owe you an apology.'

She glanced over at him to find his gaze fixed on her. Feigning ignorance she shook her head. 'For what?'

He cringed and leaned to grab a small round pebble from the sand. 'I was a bit of a shit earlier when I saw you at the Spar. I'm not usually such an arse. Honestly, I'm not. So anyway, I hope you can forgive me and we can maybe start over?'

Cassie was a little taken back by his honesty and the apology, which seemed sincere. She allowed herself to smile. 'Thank you. And it's okay. I know I haven't exactly been a poster girl for happy-go-lucky since I arrived. In fact, I've been rather a grumpy cow. It's... it's with fairly good reason but you weren't to know the circumstances. It's fine though. And for the record, I'm not usually such an arse either. And you can call me Cassie.'

He grinned, revealing a row of white but crooked teeth that really suited him. 'Great. That's great. I mean... not the part where you said you had good reason to be grumpy... but well, you get my meaning.'

'I was watching you teach your little boy to surf. He's got good balance.'

Mac laughed lightly. 'Oh, he's not mine. He's the doctor's son. I'm just the teacher.'

'Ah, right. Looks like he loves his lessons.'

'Oh aye, he's a lively wee bundle that one. I reckon he was a fish in a former life.' Mac grinned.

She nodded and smiled before turning her focus back on the sea before them and secretly hoping that he would leave her to her melancholy now.

He didn't.

'So, what *did* happen in Glasgow? And why the heck would you come to the edge of nowhere when you had the whole world at your disposal?'

Good grief. 'Oh, it's a long story. I don't want to bore you with the minutiae of my life.'

In her peripheral vision she saw him shrug. 'I'm in no rush to be any place.'

She turned to face him again. 'Look, I don't mean to be rude or offensive, really I don't, but it will probably sound that way... I really don't feel like talking just now. I hope you can respect that. I need a break from thinking about it all. I just need to *be* for a while. You know?'

He nodded again. 'Aye, I totally get that.'

She sighed with a smile and nodded. 'Thank you.' And once again she peered out at the view before her, watching as the colour palette of the sky changed yet again.

'Have you ever surfed?' Mac asked.

So the subtle thing didn't work and neither did the direct approach. 'No, Tiggy, I've never tried it.' She huffed.

He chuckled. 'Look, I thought we'd agreed you'd call me Mac? Or Tiger... I quite like Tiger, but Tiggy? Not so much. Makes me feel like a character *oot* a kid's story.'

To begin with she'd been determined to get his damned silly name right but now, purely as a mechanism to show him he was forgettable – although who was she trying to kid? – she chose to get it wrong on purpose.

She wagged a finger and nodded. 'Right, yes, Mac... Mac it is.' Waving a dismissive hand now she told him, 'Anyway, don't let me keep you from anything.' *Ooh, harsh, Montgomery, a bit harsh.*

Once again, he appeared oblivious to her invite to leave. 'I reckon surfing would be good for you. I reckon it'd help. It helped me after— Well, it just helps, you know? There's something to be said for being on your board, focusing on your balance and catching the right wave at the right moment.'

She turned slightly to watch him speaking animatedly about something that clearly held his heart and her own softened a little. A faint smile graced his features but sadness emanated from him briefly too and she wondered what heartache had been eased for him by his love of surfing.

She tucked her hair behind her ears. 'Oh, I don't think it's really my thing. I'm more of a *sitting-on-my-bum-observing* type.'

She felt her cheeks flame at her admission which showed her as the unadventurous wuss she was.

He turned his face towards her and grinned again. 'Ah, don't knock it 'til you've tried it, Cassie. Live a little, eh?' And with that final comment he pushed himself to his feet and headed off in the direction of the grassy hill without a backward glance.

16

After the first week of her new life in Coldingham, Cassie was beginning to feel a bit more settled. The village felt a bit like a comfy old sweater – familiar and cosy but not something she envisaged hanging on to long term. After all, the last time she thought she was in for the long haul she got stabbed in the heart by the excruciating sting of betrayal. She decided, therefore, to take each day as it came.

Connection to the internet had taken a little longer than she would've liked but once it was up and running she threw herself in to her work; the first local task, proofreading a website for a new Scottish Borders pet care company. Seeing all the photos of cute, furry companions made her nostalgic all over again. Bilbo, the Labrador had pretty much grown with her and he'd been such an affectionate, sensitive fellow. He was great to snuggle up to and he had this amazing way of sensing when she'd had a bad day at school. He'd sit and place his paw on her leg and tilt his head in a way that almost said 'Tell me what's wrong and let me help.' Bilbo had died of old age when Cassie was in her final year at uni and she had sobbed for three days straight.

Losing Bilbo had broken her heart but Seth, in his own typical way had bought her a designer handbag to help her get over it and that was before they were officially a couple. It was definitely his go-to solution for any problem. He had never been particularly good at expressing himself outside of the board-room and bedroom, choosing to do so with gifts instead. She knew he meant well to begin with, but as time went on and it was *still* his answer to everything she did wonder why he felt that gifts were better than words or a simple hug. His *one-size-fits-all* approach was lacklustre when it came to situations involving powerful emotions that didn't involve winning some-thing. She laughed to herself without humour as she wondered why he hadn't sent her a designer bag after she had found him in bed with Pippa.

At the end of the week her dad surprised her with a visit. To her delight he brought Patch with him and when he realised she wasn't exactly equipped for a sleepover he even took her on a trip up to a well-known furniture store near Edinburgh and purchased a new flat pack bed, mattress, bedside table and lamp. Luckily, she had decided when she moved in that it would never be an office seeing as she loved working at the kitchen table so much. She could spread out there and be near the kettle, the fire and the fridge. And seeing the new furniture in situ confirmed that the room was perfect for her dad when he chose to come and visit.

They took Patch to the beach and laughed as he chased seagulls, barking in his high-pitched yip; his tail wagging at a hundred miles an hour.

'This place is stunning, Pebble.' Her dad sighed contentedly as they stood looking out to sea.

She smiled at the return of her nickname. 'It really is, isn't it?'

He put his arm around her shoulder. 'It's just... so *you*. I think it'll do you so much good to be here. To be independent. And it's not so far for me and Patch to come and visit... if you'll have us.'

She nudged him playfully. 'Oooh, I don't know. I'll have to think about it.'

He laughed and she realised it was a sound that she had rarely heard in recent years. 'I'm proud of you, you know.'

She turned to face him. 'For what?'

'For leaving. It took guts. So many women in your position would've just brushed it under the carpet and believed him when he said it meant nothing. But not my Pebble. I'm just glad I brought you up to believe in yourself. To know that you deserve more.'

A lump lodged in her throat. He was right. If she had been another man's daughter she may have gone running back to Seth. But Michael Montgomery's daughter was made of tougher stuff – even if she hadn't realised it until very recently. Until fate forced her hand.

'You know, I thought Seth was the type of man you wanted for me: someone to look after me, someone with status, security and such. I guess I was wrong.'

Her dad sighed and shook his head. 'Cassie, if I know anything about you it's that you don't need a man to look after you. You're a strong woman. You just lost a bit of yourself when you were with Seth. But what I want for you is happiness. I don't care if you live in a bloody caravan so long as you're happy and you're *you*.'

'Morning, Cassie!' A voice from behind called out and she turned to see Mac jogging along the sand in his tight T-shirt and board shorts.

'Oh... hi, there.' She waved, hoping he would just pass on by. But of course, he didn't.

He jogged over and stopped in front of them. 'Hi, there. I'm Tadhg Mackenzie, though you can call me Mac. My uncle owns Rose Brae.' The younger Mackenzie held out his hand towards Cassie's dad.

Michael gripped it and shook it firmly. 'Good to meet you. Michael Montgomery. Cassie's father.'

'Ahhh, yes, I see the family resemblance. Although you've a little less stubble than Miss Montgomery.' Mac guffawed and much to Cassie's surprise her dad joined in. She rolled her eyes at the pair of them.

'Haha! Yes! Very funny. Very funny. So, you're my daughter's first friend here I take it?'

Mac scrunched his brow and cringed. 'Oh... well I wouldn't know about that.' He held up his hand and spoke behind it in mock secrecy. 'Not sure I've endeared myself to your lassie.'

Michael grinned. 'Oh, she'll come around.' He winked at the young man.

'Aye, well, time will tell, eh? Right, best be off. This beer belly won't flatten itsel', eh?' He set off jogging again.

Michael, still grinning, shook his head. 'Beer belly? I wish I had a bloody beer belly like that. Six-pack – yes. But not of beer that's for sure. He seems like a grand lad. You were a bit off with him.' Her dad frowned.

'He's just a bit... I don't know... intense. Full on. Irritating.'

Michael shook his head. 'Well, I liked him.'

Rolling her eyes again she said, 'You would.'

* * *

Her dad's visit was over too soon but he really did seem taken with the place and she was relieved. He seemed to relax in the knowledge that she wasn't living in some godforsaken slum. He commented over and over again that the place suited her and he called her Pebble as if it was the most natural thing in the world without Seth Guthrie to frown upon it.

Once her father had gone she continued to work on the website for the pet care company and her mind drifted and she imagined a little cuddly ball of fluff sitting by her feet as she worked; nuzzling her when it was time for walkies or dinner. Having Patch around had been wonderful and now he was gone and even though she had only been in her new place a short time, she was struggling to get used to the quiet. When she had lived with Seth there had always been something going on whether it was a dinner to dress for, or music on the stereo system. But here in Coldingham, she was weighed down by the silence. She stopped what she was doing as a pair of friendly, big brown eyes smiled out of her laptop screen at her. The tiny fellow had his head tilted to one side just how Bilbo used to sit.

Maybe a dog was the answer?

Without stopping to think things through and without writing her 'for and against' list – a method highly favoured by her ex – she quickly opened another tab and began to search for local animal adoption centres. Her heart skipped when she came across a website for a rehoming centre called BARK based in Berwick-Upon-Tweed, only a few miles away across the border into England. She decided to have a more detailed look and began to rifle through the photographs of dogs waiting to be rehomed. Her heart lurched as she regarded each bearded face and lolloping tongue, wishing she could simply take them all. She landed on a page that was titled 'Cliff' and the photo was a cute little Border Terrier with his head tilted to one side and sparkling brown eyes staring back at her. That was it.

She was in love.

Cliff was a ridiculously named, honey brown terrier with a coarse coat and an expression-filled face. He was two years old and had been taken in by BARK when his previous owners didn't want him any more. Knowing this fact about him created a feeling of empathy within Cassie. *Deceived by those he loved and trusted too. Perhaps Cliff and I could be each other's lifeline?*

She made a call to Mr Rab Mackenzie to confirm that she was allowed to have a pet at the cottage and was filled with relief when he confirmed that she was, so long as she paid for any damage that may occur as a result of the canine. But, of course, she knew this would be the case and it didn't deter her. Next, she made a quick call to the rehoming centre and arranged a visit after checking that Cliff was still waiting for his forever home. Excitement built within her and she knew that this was going to change everything but in the best possible way.

* * *

Two days later a woman from the rehoming centre made a visit to Cassie's new home to ensure that her environment was suitable and that she was home enough to take care of a pet. Once all the relevant checks were made she arranged a visit to meet Cliff the following weekend.

With a nervous excitement Cassie arrived for the very first blind date of her life – it just happened to be with a four-legged chap called Cliff. The centre was filled with the sound of barking dogs and people bustled around cleaning, playing and bringing out animals to meet their new owners. Cassie's stomach knotted and she desperately hoped that Cliff would like her – after all it was the dog that really did the choosing if the truth was known. She approached the reception desk and was greeted by a smiling young woman who took her details.

'Oh yes, our system says you're here to meet Cliff. Is that right?' The woman whose name badge read 'Maddy' asked.

Cassie nodded. 'Yes, I can't wait. I think it was love at first sight.' She giggled.

'Aww, that's great. He's a little sweetie. If you'd like to wait a moment I will get Tessa who came to do your home visit and she'll make the introductions.'

Maddy disappeared through a door and returned moments later accompanied by Tessa.

'Hi, Cassie. Good to see you again. Come on through.' She gestured to the door beside the reception desk and Cassie did as instructed. She walked into the small room which had a door out on to a small enclosed grassed area. Her palms were sweating and her heart fluttering in her chest as if butterflies had taken flight in there.

She didn't have to wait long until Tessa opened the door but this time she wasn't alone. 'Cassie, I'd like to introduce you to Cliff. Cliff, this is Cassie,' the smiling woman said as she handed the lead over.

Cassie crouched on her haunches and the small dog, yipping with excitement, leapt into her lap, almost knocking her from her feet. He began licking her face and almost climbing onto her shoulder and she squirmed and laughed as he did. It was as if Cassie was his long-lost best friend and he was relieved for her return. He couldn't seem to get close enough and Cassie closed her eyes as tears began to threaten. He was perfect and she was done for. Her heart was his immediately.

'Hello, little friend. Hello,' she cooed in her best dog-friendly tone and he lapped it up, his whole body wriggling as his tiny tail wagged frantically.

'Come on, Cliff, let's show Cassie the garden, eh?' Tessa laughed.

Cassie scrambled to her feet and the skipping dog rushed towards the outside space. Tessa unclipped his lead and he ran to the other end of the patch of grass to fetch a ball. He darted back to Cassie and dropped it at her feet.

Tessa grinned and shook her head. 'Well, I'd say that's a pretty good sign, Cassie.'

Cassie stooped to pick up the ball and Cliff skipped around in circles waiting for her to throw it. As soon as she did he went dashing after it and brought it back once again. She watched in awe as he jumped around and played but always came back to her, almost as if to check that she was still there.

It was evident from that first meeting that Cliff had already made the decision for both of them. She was his and that was that.

By the end of Cassie's third week in Coldingham, she had a new partner in crime in the fuzzy shape of Cliff the dog. She had toyed with the idea of changing his name but considering he was already two years old she figured it would only confuse him so the name stuck. In a bizarre way it suited him. She had already spoiled him rotten with toys and treats, along with a new bed that looked like a tiny couch, a blanket and a shiny new collar.

Cliff curled up at her feet when she was working and just as she hoped, he pawed at her when he was ready for attention. Funnily enough it always coincided with the time that Cassie needed to take a break from the screen. It was a match made in heaven. And apart from food and walks, he expected nothing from her. His love was unconditional. It was the perfect relationship and she couldn't believe she had waited so long to get a dog. Seth was such a clean freak. Nothing could mess up his pristine monochrome world. Well now she had her own world and Cliff was welcome to mess it up as much as he liked – within reason of course. Luckily, he was house trained and walked really well on his lead. Just perfect.

17

MAC

Mac guessed early on that the new tenant at Rose Brae wasn't looking to make friends right away and so he kept out of her way as much as possible. Her dad had seemed nice and friendly when they had met briefly at the beach but Cassie not so much. After she had been there for around three weeks he spotted her on the beach with a Border Terrier dog. His uncle had said she had called to ask if she was okay to get one and had apparently sounded ecstatic when Rab had said yes. She clearly adored the fluff ball as she ran around the sand chasing it and being chased, throwing a little red ring and drying the dog off when it had been jumping around in the shallows. She was smiling and that was a very positive step. But still he kept his distance. She'd made it quite clear that she wanted to be alone – or maybe she wanted to be left alone by *him*. Whatever the reason he watched her from afar. Not in a stalkery, creepy way. Just as an inquisitive observer.

She had never said why she was in Coldingham but he recognised the forlorn look of a love lost, in her eyes. He'd seen it on his own reflection after his parents' death and he wondered if someone she loved had also died. Or maybe her heart had been broken and she was grieving the loss of *love* itself. Both countenances would no doubt appear the same. Whatever it was, she was clearly escaping from some*thing* or some*one*. But he wasn't going to pry.

Sunday evening arrived and Mac was standing, beer in hand watching as his Uncle Rab chopped wood for his stove. It was fairly warm out and they had eaten barbecue, alfresco for dinner. Seagulls called overhead and Mac smiled up at their familiar song – a sound that made him feel at home.

'So, I see the woman at Rose Brae has a new little friend,' Mac said as he sipped on his beer.

'Aye, I checked in on the lassie. She seems settled. The wee *dug* is a cutie. Daft name though.' Rab shook his balding head and frowned. '*Cannae* remember what it is but I remember thinking "*what kind o' dog's name is that?*" when she told it to me.'

Mac laughed. 'Daft name, eh? She doesn't seem the type. Too straight-laced. So... does she seem happy here? You know with the village and all? Miss Montgomery, I mean.' He failed miserably at his attempts to sound nonchalant.

Rab stopped chopping and straightened, bending backwards slightly and huffing. 'I'm getting too old for this. You should be doing it.' He winked and pointed his axe at his nephew. 'And yes, she seems happy enough. She's a lass of few words though. A wee bit bookish if you get my meaning? Are you interested then, eh?' He winked again.

Mac shrugged. 'Only in a neighbourly way. Nothing more. I mean she lives in *your* house so I guess we're *kind* of neighbours.'

Rab chuckled and continued with his chopping. 'Aye. She

seems fine. Maybe you should call on her sometime? You know just to be *neighbourly* and all.'

Mac thought back to the responses he'd had from Cassie since she'd arrived. 'Erm... nah... I think I'll leave her be. She seemed a wee bit disgruntled when I first met her. How did she seem when you went round? In hersel', I mean?'

Rab stopped chopping again and eyed Mac with suspicion. 'Why would you want to know? You didn't go upsetting the lassie, did you?' He raised his eyebrows.

Mac scrunched his brow. 'Why would you even ask that, Uncle Rab?'

Rab rolled his eyes. 'Well, Tadhg Mackenzie, you're not known for your tact. What you think of as funny others find downright offensive.'

Mac huffed and shook his head. 'Aye well, like I said I was just asking to be neighbourly. Nothing more.'

Rab pursed his lips. 'She seems... I don't know... like she's got the weight of the world on her shoulders. And... kind of insular. But she's happy enough with that wee *dug*. She doesn't like to make small talk so don't be getting any ideas about trying to be her friend if you've already upset her once. I get the feeling she'll make friends when she's good and ready.'

Mac snorted and gave Rab a mock salute. 'Okay, *boss*. Jeez, you don't know her any better than I do and you're making all those assumptions. I mean, she must be lonely. I don't think she's met anyone else around here yet.'

Rab glared momentarily. 'Well, don't say I *didnae* warn you. And think on, I haven't had a good long-term tenant in a while so don't you go scaring her off, lad.'

Mac sighed at his uncle's warning but chose not to fuel the fire by responding. He supped the rest of his beer and decided to take himself off for a wee walk along the beach. And regardless of what Rab had said, he wasn't about to ignore the woman completely. How would it look if he did?

After all, people inherently need people. Don't they?

18

CASSIE

Thankfully it appeared that Tiger, Mac or whatever the heck he was called had got the message as Cassie hadn't seen him for a while. His uncle had popped in to see how she was settling in and to meet Cliff but there had been no mention of the floppy-haired *surfer dude*. She had almost got to the point where she had forgotten about her several unpleasant encounters with the younger of the Misters Mackenzie. Although that all changed on what had been a peaceful Sunday evening stroll when she was at the beach with Cliff.

The sun was descending and this was fast becoming her favourite part of the day. The pastel colours of the sky cast an ethereal glow over the picturesque cove and she always made a point of coming to the beach to see it happen. The air was a little chilled but she wrapped her fleece jacket tighter around herself and watched Cliff as he skipped along the edge of the water trying to catch the thin stream of bubbles created as the tide met the sand. It was peaceful. Serene. Something she had almost forgotten the feeling of.

There was a group of locals sitting outside one of the beach huts along to the left and they had strung fairy lights outside. They were cooking on a small barbecue and the smell of sausages wafted through the air along with the sound of acoustic guitar as one of the group sang 'God Only Knows' by the Beach Boys. She smiled as she hummed along to one of her favourite love songs, thankful that it held no memories of her ex to taunt her with.

Cliff stopped as he caught the tantalising aroma and stuck his nose in the air, followed by his tongue as though he thought he'd be able to taste the smell too. Cassie laughed and bent to scratch him behind the ear as she listened right to the end of the song.

Once the song ended she set off again and in between observing the ever-changing palette of the sky, Cassie threw the red rubber ring that Cliff had become quite fond of. He dashed off to collect it, bring it back and wag his tail as he waited for the whole exercise to begin again.

'Ah, so you went for a dog. That's novel.' The male voice startled her and she turned to see the younger Mr Mackenzie walking towards her on the beach. He had his board tucked under his arm and his wet hair was glistening in the evening light as a few strands fell onto his face.

She stood and folded her arms across her chest. 'And what's that supposed to mean?'

He chuckled and pushed the stray strands back from his forehead as he arrived a few feet away. 'Oh, you know, I thought crazy cat lady was going to be your MO,' he teased.

There was a cheeky glint in his eye and she smiled in spite of herself. 'You know there's a saying... if you can't find anything nice to say, keep your trap shut. Or words to that effect.'

He shrugged and grinned. 'Aye, but where's the fun in that?' He stuck the board into the sand. 'So are you going to introduce me to your wee pal?' He crouched and Cliff came barrelling up to him for a fuss.

Cassie fidgeted on the spot realising she was going to have to admit to the dog's name – an exercise that would do little to quell his thoughts of her craziness.

She straightened her back. 'Erm... sure... this is... erm... Cliff, actually.'

Mac gazed up at her for a moment, his head tilted and his lip curled in disbelief as if she had just told him the dog was an Iguana. 'Cliff? You do know he's a dog, right? Dogs are usually Patch or Rover or Deefer.' He laughed.

She scoffed. 'Well, I didn't name him! He had the name when I collected him and I thought it'd be a bit mean to change it when he's so used to it.'

Cliff rolled onto his back to encourage Mac to scratch his belly. 'Aye, fair point. Well, he's a widdle cutie pie aren't you Cliffy-wiffy. Yes, you are... yes, you are.' The dog evidently loved his silly tone of voice and wagged his tail frantically.

Cassie cleared her throat and shrugged with a shake of her head. 'Erm... it's just Cliff. Not Cliffy-wiffy. Not Cliffy-boy. J-just Cliff. His name's daft enough as it is, don't you think?'

Mac peered up at her and rolled his eyes. 'All right, aye, all right. Anyway, it's kind of fitting if you think about it.'

Cassie scrunched her brow. 'Fitting how?'

He gestured around them. 'Well, look where you're living. By the sea. Cliff... sea... get it?'

She giggled. 'Oh yeah. I hadn't thought of that.'

He paused and smiled up at her now. 'So how are you doing, Cassie? You know... with whatever it was you were running away from.'

And just like that he overstepped the mark again and her smile disappeared. 'Oh... erm... I'm fine. Thanks for asking. Anyway, better be getting back. Come on, Cliff. Come on boy.'

She turned and began to walk away, closely followed by her obedient dog but before she was out of earshot she heard Mac mutter, 'Poor lass. He must've really done a total fucking number on you.'

She chose to behave as though she hadn't heard – after all his voice had been low when he spoke so she wasn't sure she was supposed to have caught what he said.

As she walked she heard footsteps pounding the sand and he arrived beside her once again. 'Hey, look, I can introduce you to some folks if you like? Make it less... you know... lonely?'

She stopped in her tracks and turned to face Mac. 'That's sweet of you, but I'm okay. Really.'

'I'm not buying it. Something big happened to you in Glasgow. But you're out of it now. Make some friends. Plant some roots.' He shrugged.

She sighed heavily. 'Look, having friends isn't all it's cracked up to be. So, I think I'd rather be by myself, thank you.' Her tone was terse, even though she knew he meant well.

She started walking again but he was persistent. 'But you can't just live like a hermit. Even if you're a hermit with a wee dog. People need people, Cassie. You've been here three weeks and you've only met me. And I know you're not impressed on that front. So, I could introduce you to some females. What do you say?'

She stopped once again and turned to him with a huff. 'I don't want friends, Mac. Friends betray you. You think they care about you. You care about them after all.' She lifted her arms and let them drop with a loud slap to her sides. 'And you think you know them and that you can trust them and then you come home early from a training course and find one of them in bed with your fucking fiancé between their thighs. So, like I said, I'm fine!' Her words came out as an angry tirade and when she stopped she was suddenly out of breath.

'Aw, fuck. Really? The bastard. That's a totally shitty thing to do to someone. And I'm genuinely sorry you went through it, Cassie. Really I am. But like I said, people need people. And you can't tar everyone with the same brush.' His voice softened. 'I'm sure you know that deep down. I get that you wanted to escape. Truly I do. But staying by yoursel' the whole time... it's not good for you.' His kindness took her off guard and the fact that it made her warm to him angered her. She didn't need some irritating surfer to look out for her. She was done letting people look out for her. It hadn't done her any good before. And it didn't exactly help that he was so good-looking. It made her dislike him even more. How dare he be so nice *and* attractive? It just wasn't fair!

Her defences flew up and she frowned. 'How the hell can you stand there and tell me what's good for me? You've known me two minutes in the great scheme of things. And in that time you've insulted me, made jokes about me and generally made a nuisance of yourself. I don't need you. Nor do I need you to matchmake for me with your girlfriends. So please just leave me the hell alone!' Her voice cracked as her anger and sorrow erupted again. But she wasn't angry at the man before her. She was angry at the one who broke her heart.

Mac clenched his jaw and nodded. 'Aye... message received loud and clear, Miss Montgomery. I'll not be bothering you again.' There was a pained look in his eyes as he lowered his head and turned away.

Guilt knotted her stomach and she almost shouted him

back. But she knew it was too late for that. She'd made it clear she neither liked him nor wanted his help.

How to burn bridges in one easy step, a self-help guide by Cassandra Montgomery. She called to Cliff and headed for home.

19

Monday was one of those days when Cassie just couldn't focus. The words on the screen before her all melded into one big black blob on a white background. She kept on reading the same paragraph over and over as if her eyes were stuck in some kind of magnetic field. It had been this way all day and no amount of breaks and walks with Cliff had helped. At just after five she gave up – hating to be defeated but knowing full well that she couldn't present a half hashed proofread to her client. She resolved to try again in the morning.

Her head was pounding and she realised she hadn't eaten since breakfast. She decided to have a wander up to the Spar to find something tempting for dinner and maybe a bottle of wine too. Rain was lashing at the windows and Cliff was asleep under the kitchen table so she left him to snooze, grabbed her waterproof jacket and slipped her feet into her Wellingtons before heading off to the shop armed with a fold away shopping bag.

The high street was all but deserted apart from a few cars driving away from the beach, sloshing through the puddles forming at the edges of the road. The shop window lights reflected in the water and she kept her head down against the biting chill of the almost horizontal downpour.

As soon as she pushed through the door of the Spar she flipped her hood back and breathed a sigh of relief. She grabbed a basket and aimed first for the alcohol section. Too busy concentrating on what to buy she didn't notice that she had company.

She walked, slap bang into a hard wall of muscle. 'Whoops, I'm sorry about that. Not watching where I was... Oh... Hi, Mac. H-how are you?'

'Fine, thanks.' His short response was deserved after the way she had shouted at him on the beach.

'Look... I want to apologise. I was out of line yesterday. I know you were only trying to help and I shouldn't have gone off at you like that.'

He shrugged. 'Yeah. Whatever.' He turned his back towards her.

Tears of guilt stung at her eyes and she blinked to stop them manifesting. 'Mac, please? I really am sorry. I just... I have trust issues right now. I'm finding the prospect of making friends a difficult one to comprehend. But I do appreciate your kindness.'

'Aye. Right.' He continued selecting bottles of beer, pretending to read the labels and then placing them down again.

Ugh, he's not making this easy. But I can't really blame him. 'I don't suppose there's any chance you might forgive me at all?'

He turned to her. 'For what? For being a *crabbit,* moody cow? Aye... so long as you can forgive me for being a nosy bastard.' He smiled.

She smiled in response and nodded with relief. 'Oh, I think I can.'

He nodded. 'Great. And for what it's worth, I think you're well shot of them. *The Glasgow two* I mean.'

She thought how sweet it was of him to say so. '*The Glasgow two*. Hmm, has a kind of criminal element ring to it.'

A strange silence descended between them and Cassie wondered if she should invite him round for a drink, by way of an apology.

But before she could speak he broke the silence. 'Hey, you should let me teach you to surf.' His voice was filled with the excitement of a child on Christmas morning and she scrunched her face.

'Are you joking?'

'No! It'd be a great way to de-stress after a long day of... whatever it is you do that makes you look all frowny.' He pointed at her face for effect. 'And it'd be a laugh.'

It's you that makes me 'frowny', she thought. 'Oh yeah. *You*'d be the one laughing at *my* expense no doubt. I think I'll give it a miss. Thanks though.'

'Well, if you change your mind come and find me. I think you'd love it. Could even teach Cliff to stand on a board. It's do-able. I've seen videos.'

She giggled and shook her head. 'I think I'll stick to looking after him in a *safe* environment if it's all the same to you.'

He shrugged. 'Aye, well maybe the next pet you get then?'

'There won't be any more pets. I'm just sticking with Cliff.'

'Aye but just think; *now* you can fill your house with all manner of stray cats and dogs and be crazy animal lady. Then you'll be surrounded by friends that won't *ever* betray you.'

Her smile disappeared. *Why is it that he can be so nice one minute and then so bloody tactless the next?*

Suddenly he threw his head back and guffawed loudly. 'Your

face! Honestly, it's a picture. You're so easy to wind up, you know. I'm messing with you, Crabbit McGrumpy Arse. The whole cat lady thing is just a wind up.' He shook his head and held his stomach. After a few moments, when he realised she wasn't laughing along he cleared his throat and calmed down. 'I didn't mean to offend you again. It's just that you have to look on the bright side of shit like this or it'll eat you alive, Cassie. Trust me. I know.' He calmed down and stepped closer. 'Don't let your grief over what happened begin to define who you are, Cassie. Lighten up and live a little. And please make some friends. But if not get some surfing lessons. Surfing will do you so much good. I mean it. It helped me. Anyway, I'll see you around the village no doubt.' He patted her on the shoulder and walked towards the cash desk.

She once again watched him walk away, leaving her in a rather bewildered state. He irked her. That was the only way to express her feelings for the man. She didn't hate him, nor was she his biggest fan. He was just irksome.

Once she had found something for dinner she paid the cashier and began to walk home. The rain had subsided slightly – a fact she was grateful for. As she walked she pulled out her phone and googled 'learning to surf'. She was greeted with a list of dos and don'ts and began to read, lifting her head and narrowly missing walking into the lamp post at the end of her street.

'Well, if that's not fate telling me to avoid injury, I don't know what is.' She huffed and stuck her phone back in her coat pocket.

But Mac had got her thinking. Maybe a new hobby would be good for her. Maybe she should try something she never had before. Horse riding perhaps? Rock climbing? She had always favoured the path of least resistance in almost every area of her life. But where had that got her? Absolutely bloody nowhere. Well, perhaps it was time to have a little adventure.

Perhaps she would take Mac up on his offer to teach her to surf. Well, she'd certainly *think* about it and that was a start.

Thankfully for Cassie the issue with her focus was a very small blip and in the days that followed she faced her daily tasks with a renewed vigour. In fact, she could finally admit to herself that she was proud of her achievement. Feedback from clients had been excellent and work was filing in nicely. It was a far cry from the life she had left behind where she had been a very lowly planet revolving around the huge sun that was Seth Guthrie. Now she had something for herself.

People in the village were friendly and she guessed that since they had seen her around regularly they realised she wasn't a holidaymaker but a resident. There had been an increase in greetings from people as they passed her out walking with Cliff and she had taken to not walking along looking down at her phone. She was certainly feeling a little more relaxed about being there. And the prospect of making friends wasn't quite so scary. After all, Mac was right when he said she couldn't tar everyone with the same brush of deceit that Pippa and Seth had been swiped with. People deserved a chance.

She was just leaving the shop after picking up some milk when a young woman with an empty stroller stopped her. 'Cassie, right?'

Cassie felt her cheeks heating as she nodded. 'Yes, that's right.'

'I've been meaning to call on you. I'm Sally Cairns. Doctor

Cairns' wife.' She held out her hand and Cassie shook it, realising she recognised her from the surf lesson on the beach. 'I was going to pop in and invite you to our coffee morning. It's on Wednesdays and the mums in the village all gather for a coffee and a chat.'

Cassie cringed. 'Oh... erm I'm afraid I don't have children.'

'Oh, that's no problem. We chat about all sorts. Movies we've seen, books we've read.' She leaned in conspiratorially. 'Oh, and it's a great opportunity to moan about the men in our lives too.'

'I currently don't have a man either, I'm afraid.'

Sally shrugged. 'Like I said it's not a problem, honestly. You'll be the envy of the group. Anyway, we may be able to help you on the man front. Lots of eligible bachelors around these parts, you know.'

Cassie shivered at the thought. 'Ugh, no thanks. I'm fine on my own. Looking for a man is way down on my list of priorities after the last one.'

'Ooh, that sounds ominous. Maybe you can tell me about it over that coffee on Wednesday? I have to get back to collect Jack from nursery now. But honestly, you'll be more than welcome. We just live by the surgery and we meet at our house at ten. I really hope you can make it, Cassie.'

Cassie nodded. 'Thank you for inviting me. I'll try to make it.'

She appreciated the offer and kind hand of friendship from Sally but in all honesty, she wasn't sure she wanted to be the spare wheel – the childless, single woman in a room full of married mums. She decided to think about it closer to the day.

20

Cassie stood in the wetsuit and surfboard rental shop by the beach staring at rack upon rack of neoprene garments and wondering if there was a shop for lost marbles close by. If there was one, she would no doubt locate hers in there because she had definitely misplaced them.

A pretty, dark-haired young woman with a nose piercing appeared beside her. 'Hi, there. You look a little lost.'

Cassie sighed. 'You could say that. Someone has offered to teach me to surf and I think I may be crazy because I've taken him up on it. The trouble is I've no idea which wetsuit to get.'

'Oh, right. Is it Mac by any chance?'

Cassie chewed on her bottom lip. 'Yes. That's him. I saw him last night when I was out with my dog and he said he'd had a cancellation this afternoon. Am I crazy?'

The woman laughed out loud. 'Absolutely not! Mac is the best teacher around here. He's a nice guy too. Heart of gold. And surfing is awesome. You'll love it, I promise.'

A wave of relief washed over Cassie and she knew she was

going to be in safe hands. 'That's good to hear. Now... please can you help me because all these suits look the same.'

'Of course.' She assessed her for a moment. 'Okay, you're a beginner, which means you'll probably be better with a full suit. And I'd suggest maybe a 4/5 because the water can be very cold even at this time of year. Here you go.' She pulled a black and purple suit from the rack. 'Try this. Give me a shout if you need any help. Changing room is over that way.'

An hour later, as agreed, Cassie was changed and standing beside Mac on the beach. His wetsuit clung to the contours of his body and she tried hard not to look. Of course, this also meant she was self-conscious because of her own curves. Mac didn't seem to notice, or if he did he chose this moment to show some tact. He talked her through some warm-up exercises and then it was time to get in the water.

Or so Cassie thought.

'You can swim, eh?' he asked. She gave him a *what do you think* stare accompanied by raised eyebrows. 'Right, I'll take that as "shut the fuck up, Mac". Okay, so, lay your board flat on the sand.'

She scrunched her brow. 'On the sand? I won't catch any waves down there.'

He smiled and rolled his eyes. 'Oh, you're going to be one of *those* students, are you?' He took her board and placed it down. 'Before you can go in the water, you have to learn how to lie on a board. If you don't know the basics, you can't go in the water.'

She mock saluted. 'Yes, boss.'

'That's more like it. Now on you go and lie down on your belly. Or what you have of one anyway.'

She glanced down at her stomach. Life after Seth had meant a lack of appetite. She guessed it was showing.

For the next hour she followed instruction after instruction about how to hold her arms like chicken wings. How to keep her toes on the tail of the board. She was the model student and was surprised at how much she had enjoyed learning the so-called basics.

'Right, time for you to get into the sea.' Mac grinned.

She clapped her hands together. 'About time!'

Before she knew what was happening she was flung up in the air and was then dangling down Mac's rather hard back as he carried her towards the waves. Suddenly she met the water with a slap and found herself sitting in the shallows, gasping and squealing like a teenager being chased with seaweed.

'Mac! You utter shit! It's freezing!'

Mac doubled over in a hysterical fit of laughter. 'Ah, I wish I had my camera!' She stood and began to chase him but he laughed louder and ran. 'You said you wanted to be in the sea. So you got your wish, Montgomery!' Luckily for Mac he was fast and managed to dodge her at every turn until she eventually gave up and collapsed in a panting, giggling heap on the sand.

Once they'd dried off, they sat on the sand watching as the sun descended and the people on the beach, lit lanterns and barbecues.

'So, what made you want to teach surfing?' Cassie asked, genuinely intrigued.

Mac shrugged. 'It's in my blood, I guess. The sea, the outdoors. It's where I belong. I've always felt that way. I suppose surfing is part and parcel of all that.' She listened intently as he spoke. Passion oozed from him as an almost tangible entity. 'There's something so vital about the sea. The way it moves. The way it sounds. It calls to me. It's part of me.' He shrugged. 'God! I must sound like a total tube.'

She wasn't familiar with the turn of phrase but understood

its meaning. 'Not at all. You clearly love it here. By the sea. I understand that. It's always been a part of my life too.'

He nudged her with his shoulder. 'See, we have something in common.'

She lifted her chin and for a moment she was caught in his gaze. Electricity crackled in the air between them. But she couldn't have that. So she doused it.

'Well, I'd better be getting back. Cliff needs his walk.' She stood and gathered up her bag from the sand. 'Thanks for today. I had fun.' She smiled down at him where he remained.

'Aye, I can tell. We'll have to stop that, eh? You'll not be used to it.' He winked and instead of getting annoyed, for once she shook her head and grinned.

'Goodnight, Mac.'

'Goodnight, Montgomery.' He saluted her and she turned to make her way home.

* * *

The following day Cliff was in his favourite spot, curled up in front of the fire on his blanket snoozing and Cassie was sitting on the couch with her computer on her lap. She was working on a business eBook manuscript for another new client in London when her phone bleeped to indicate a new message.

She picked it up and hit read.

> Cassie it's getting bad. I'm away in France with Harry but Seth keeps calling and messaging. He's determined to find you and come to see you. He keeps saying things about winning. I hate to see him like this when it's you he's speaking of. So angry and determined. He's behaving like he does at work and that's not right.

I'm really worried, Cassie. Please be careful,
okay? I don't think he'd hurt you or anything
silly like that. But he's just not prepared to
admit defeat. I haven't told him where you are
but I'm sure he'll find out. He has so many
contacts. He keeps saying I should be taking
his side because we're family. But you're my
family too. I hate this. V x

Oh great. That's all I need. Why can't he just let me go?

The last thing she needed was a scorned Seth Guthrie
turning up on her doorstep uninvited. She was settling in so
well and she didn't want him here in Coldingham to remind her
of the reasons she'd left Glasgow behind so readily.

She chose not to reply right away, she had work to do and
quite frankly didn't have the energy to have this conversation
right now. She turned her phone to silent so she wouldn't be
disturbed again.

The next time she glanced at her phone it was six o'clock
and Cliff was padding around her feet wanting attention. 'Are
you hungry, little guy? Do you want dinner?' The responding
excited bark and frantic tail wagging gave her the answer she
needed so she closed her laptop and went to the pantry. Once
Cliff's bowl was topped up with Coldstream Crunch she opened
the fridge to see what delights lay therein for her own dinner.

With a deep sigh she closed the door. 'I really need to start
shopping properly, Cliff. I feel like Mother Hubbard just now. I
don't think I can conjure up a meal out of two eggs and a half a
tub of pâté.' Cliff stopped munching long enough to give her a
head tilted glance that almost looked like pity. 'Right, well whilst
you're eating, I'll nip to the shop. Honestly it's a good job it's
there or I may starve.' Cliff was already back to crunching his
food.

She grabbed her bag, scratched her occupied dog behind

the ear and left the house. It was funny how she remembered to order Cliff's food online from the pet shop in Coldstream but completely neglected to make similar arrangements for herself. As she walked she realised she hadn't replied to Vina's text so took out her phone from her back pocket and sure enough there were more messages.

> Are you okay, Cassie? You're awfully quiet and I'm worried about you. Text or call please. V x

And then...

> Are you angry with me? I didn't mean to weigh you down with my problems. He's just getting on at me and you're the person I usually talk to when I need someone. I suppose it's difficult when he's your problem too. V x

And finally...

> Cassie, I tried calling but it went to voicemail. I just wanted you to know that Seth knows where you are. But it wasn't through me. I swear. I've begged him to leave you in peace but he won't listen. You should expect a visit although you didn't hear that from me! He's determined to get you back Cass, even though I've repeatedly told him it's over. He says he will make sure you hear him out. I've never seen him like this. Love V x

Oh, shitty, shitty shit.

Anger knotted her stomach. How the hell could she be expected to hear him out? Vina knew exactly what Seth had done and she had been so angry with him. Cassie was shocked that she had refused to give in and tell him where his ex-fiancée was hiding – after all blood was supposedly thicker than water –

but Vina had proved the type of friend she was and Cassie was so grateful for it. It must have been heartbreaking to discover the brother she had always idolised was an expert at lying and cheating. How the mighty fall hard from their pedestals. She hit reply and began to type back an angry response when her foot slipped off the curb, and she yelped before there was a screeching of tyres, a loud scream and then nothing.

Cassie's eyes fluttered open and the smell of disinfectant assaulted her olfactory senses. She glanced around and discovered she was lying on a bed in a cubicle surrounded by a closed blue curtain. *What the hell?* Her head throbbed and she raised her hand to find a plaster on a very tender spot on her forehead. She lifted the blanket that covered her to discover her jeans were gone and there was a sizeable gash on her knee which appeared to have been stitched. In addition to all of that her ankle was swollen and had turned a rather sickly shade of purple.

'Oh, hi. You've re-joined the land of the living, eh?'

She glanced over to find Mac's head poking through the curtain. 'Erm... what happened? Where am I?'

He stepped inside. 'You had a very rapid introduction to the Tarmac road of the high street. Knocked yoursel' clean out too. Too busy looking at your phone to watch where you were heading. Thankfully, I was coming out of the shop and witnessed the whole sorry affair, so I was able to look after you.'

Cassie gasped. 'Oh God. How long was I unconscious?'

He chuckled. 'Don't worry, it's not weeks or anything. You've been out for just a couple of hours. But I called an ambulance and followed you here to A & E in my car as a precaution.'

A man in dark blue scrubs with a stethoscope around his neck pushed into the cubicle and Mac nodded before leaving them alone.

'Ah, Miss Montgomery. It's good to see you awake. How are you feeling?' He bent and shined a light in her eyes and asked her to look up and down.

'A little stupid. And a lot sore,' she replied as she felt her cheeks colouring.

'Well, you'll be glad to know there are no broken bones. Just a mild concussion, a stitched knee and a badly sprained ankle. Oh, and by the sound of it a little wounded pride too.' He smiled. 'But if you feel up to it in an hour or so you should be okay to go home. Provided you get someone else to look after the cats for a few days.'

She scrunched her brow. 'Cats?'

'Yes, your boyfriend says you're a cat sitter?'

She decided maybe it was the concussion because she didn't understand what the hell he was talking about. 'Erm... I don't have a boyfriend. Nor do I have any cats at home. I don't under—'

'Ah, don't worry yourself, Miss Montgomery. You may be a bit confused for a couple of hours. You did suffer a blow to your head.' He picked up the clipboard with her notes attached and began to write.

'Excuse me, Doctor, I... I don't know how I'll get home. Can I borrow a phone to call a taxi or something?'

'It's fine, your boyfriend is still here and he assures me he will get you home safe.'

'But I don't have a boyf—' It suddenly dawned on her that Mac was the mysterious boyfriend she didn't have. And he must've been the one who told the doctor she was a cat sitter. *I'll bloody kill him!* 'Oh, you mean Mr Mackenzie. He's not my boyfriend. I hardly know him, in fact. And he was wrong about my occupation too. I'm a proofreader and editor. I run my own business.'

The doctor was still busy making notes and didn't look up. 'Ah well, that's grand. You won't need a doctor's note to excuse you from work seeing as your boss is no doubt a little easier on you than most.' He grinned at his own joke. 'But you will need someone to sort out your own cat for a while maybe. Can't have you chasing it around the streets on that ankle. Not for a while anyway.'

'Cliff is a dog,' she stated plainly as she mentally planned her revenge on Mac.

The doctor looked up from the clipboard and frowned. 'Miss Montgomery, there's no need to be so hard on him. I think he was only trying to help and it's understandable if he got your job wrong with not knowing you that well. But he cared enough to follow you to the hospital.'

She shook her head but it hurt to do so. 'No, I wasn't talking about Mr Mackenzie being a dog. His name isn't Cliff it's... well, anyway, Cliff is my dog. I don't have a cat. I have Cliff, the dog. But... oh, never mind.' She didn't have the energy to explain further. But she did have enough energy to give Tiger a piece of her mind on the way home.

Once the doctor had instructed her to get dressed and had left her to it she sat up slowly and the throbbing in her head kicked up a notch. Thankfully, the doctor had left a prescription for pain killers so she knew she would soon be feeling better.

Feeling a little out of breath and a lot pissed off she sat in the chair beside the bed and waited for Mac to return. She was beginning to think he had left her there when he appeared once again.

'Your chariot awaits m'lady,' he said with a flourish and a small bow. He was grinning like an idiot.

She pursed her lips and narrowed her eyes. 'Oh, thank you, *darling*. Better get home to all my cats, eh?' Her voice dripped with so much sarcasm it was a wonder she didn't have to swim out of the cubicle.

His cheeks turned pink and he cringed. 'Ah, shit. The doc told you. In my defence I didn't tell him I was your boyfriend. He just presumed.'

Her scowl deepened. 'And you didn't think to correct him?'

He scratched his head. 'Erm… It didn't seem important in the great scheme of things. You were unconscious and they were firing questions at me. And I have no clue what you actually do for a living so I had to think on *ma* feet.'

She folded her arms across her chest. 'Well, your feet haven't got enough brains to knock your socks off, Mr Mackenzie. They clearly can't be trusted.'

He curled his lip, à la Billy Idol. 'I was right about you having a sense of humour bypass. Do you *ever* see the funny side of stuff?'

She huffed and flared her nostrils. 'When there's a funny side to *be* seen, I do. Look, I appreciate you waiting for me. But could you please just take me home? I'm tired and feel like shit.'

'Yeah, well, you look like shit too,' he replied like a sulky teen. 'And we wouldn't be in this predicament if you hadn't been texting and walking, would we?'

She held up her hands. 'Okay, that's it. I've had enough. You can go. Just please can you call someone to get me a cab first?'

He growled in exasperation. 'Jeez! I can see why you're single, you bloody stubborn woman.'

His words stung but she realised right then that she had been an absolute bitch to the one person who had been considerate enough to follow her to the hospital in the first place. In fact, she had been an absolute bitch from day one in Coldingham where Mac was concerned. There was no other reason for it than he was male and she had recently discovered that *that* particular strain of humanity was not to be trusted. But as an individual human being, irrespective of his gender, he'd been a fairly decent person all along – aside from his ridiculous jokes that weren't funny and his ability to push her buttons and get her back up.

Her lip trembled and her eyes began to sting with that all too familiar pre-crying sensation. *Ugh, this is all I bloody need, the waterworks again. I really am pathetic.*

He had either not noticed her emotional state or he had chosen to ignore it. Whatever the case she was relieved.

'Come on, bloody hop-along, let's get you home. No surfing lessons for a while you'll be happy to know. And let's hope the pills they've prescribed are happy ones, eh?' He thrust a pair of crutches at her and helped her to stand.

She grabbed the crutches and leaned on them. 'Look, I'm sorry... again.' Her voice wobbled and she chewed the inside of her cheek to try and stem the tears. 'It's been a rough couple of months and it's resulted in me being suspicious of everyone – deserving or not. I'm angry and I'm heartbroken but none of that is your doing, so I'm really very sorry for how I've acted towards you since I came here. I'm doing my best to push people away to try and protect myself but... I want you to know that I really do appreciate you calling the ambulance *and* following me here. *And* taking me home. And for generally being friendly when I've given you no reason to keep trying. I don't deserve your kindness, Mac...' Her voice trailed off into a sad and defeated whisper.

He said nothing for a few moments. He just stared at her like a rabbit trapped in the glare of oncoming traffic, a deep furrow to his brow.

Eventually he gave a small smile. 'I still preferred it when you called me Tiger.' In spite of the tears leaving warm trails down her face she burst out laughing and his small smile turned in to a full-on grin. 'Ah, see, I might drive you mad but I make you smile too. Now come on, apology accepted. And maybe, I don't know, give that brush a wee wash out, eh?'

She pulled her brows in. 'What brush?'

He leaned in and nudged her with his shoulder. 'The one you keep tarring everyone with.'

She rolled her eyes. 'Oh, I see.'

'Come along then crazy crutch lady, or they'll think you're moving in.'

'Crazy crutch lady?' She began to hobble towards the exit.

He shrugged as he walked beside her. 'Well, you didn't like crazy cat lady.'

21

Once they arrived at Mac's car, he opened the door for Cassie and helped her inside the ancient four by four, lifting her as if she weighed nothing. Once she was strapped in, he jogged around to the driver's side and climbed in, slamming the door.

He turned the key in the ignition and as the engine roared to life the car was suddenly filled with a pounding bass beat and electric guitars. Mac cringed and reached quickly for the off button. 'Shit, sorry about that. I'm guessing it wasn't your cup of tea, eh?'

She pursed her lips and widened her eyes. 'Maybe *you* should stop judging books by their covers, eh?' It felt good to serve him a dose of his own medicine and she couldn't help the grin on her face when surprise took over his. She continued, 'And I liked it actually. Who was it?'

He nodded, evidently impressed. 'That, my friend, was the LaFontaines. I've seen them live at Belladrum. They were bloody awesome. Shall I put it back on?' he asked excitedly.

'I think you should.'

'All righty then.' He leaned across and hit the button and they were once again surrounded by the catchy tune, voices singing about sharks in the water and a talented guy rapping in a familiar Glaswegian accent.

All the way back to Coldingham, Cassie found herself tapping along on her unharmed leg in time with the music. Every so often she would catch Mac singing and then grinning at her. His smile was infectious – although it could've been the pain meds – and she found herself grinning too.

Once they arrived back at Rose Brae, Mac helped Cassie into the cottage. The poor little dog was so excited to see them that he peed on the kitchen floor whilst making high-pitched yipping noises.

'Oh no! Cliff!' Cassie tried to bend but Mac stopped her before she face-planted onto the tiles.

'Whoah, you go sit. I'll sort this wee fella out. He's probably been fretting.'

Cassie did as instructed for once and she watched as Mac gathered cleaning products and some paper kitchen towels to clean up the small puddle of excitement. 'Thanks again, Mac. It's getting really late; I totally understand if you need to leave.'

'Hey, it's really no bother. Once I've got this sorted, I'll take him for a walk. If that's okay with you?'

Once again floored by his undeserved kindness she nodded. 'Thanks again. For everything. I... I really don't deserve it.'

From his position kneeling on the floor he rested his elbow on his knee and fixed her with a stony glare. 'So what do you deserve, eh? To be left to fend for yourself and struggle? Look, what's done is done, okay? I'm not one to hold grudges so just leave the past where it belongs, eh? Fresh start. Friends?' He smiled kindly.

She didn't know whether it was his kindness or her tiredness but her lip began to tremble once again so he rushed over to crouch before her. 'Oh feck, I didn't mean to make you cry. I'm so sorry, Cassie, you were right; I do speak without thinking sometimes. But I didn't mean to sound awful. I was actually being nice for once.'

She shook her head and laughed through her tears. 'No, it's fine. I seem to be doing this a lot lately.' She rolled her eyes as she wiped moisture from her face. 'It's becoming a habit and I don't like it. I guess this whole break-up and relocation thing has caught up with me. I'm shattered and you being so nice isn't helping my emotional state.'

He laughed. 'Jeez, so when I'm a shit I piss you off and when I'm nice I make you cry? There's no hope for me, woman.' She laughed again and he responded with that handsome crooked grin of his. 'Look, I'll take the wee man out and you have a breather, eh? It's almost eleven o'clock and I'm guessing the trauma of today has taken its toll. My mum always used to say, "You'll be right as the rain tomorrow." And I reckon she was onto something there. But one last thing...'

Cassie sniffed. 'What's that?'

He stood and grabbed Cliff's lead before turning to face her again. 'No more thanks and definitely no more tears, okay?'

Cassie agreed, her cheeks flushing in embarrassment for her emotional outburst. She reached for her bag to find some tissues and her hand landed on her phone. She pulled it out and gasped. 'Oh no! It's ruined!'

Mac stopped by the door and turned. He cringed. 'Oh yes, sorry about that. A car ran over it when you fell head first into the road. I could rescue you or it. I chose you.' With that final comment he closed the door behind him.

As she stared at the mangled plastic and glass it dawned on

her. Seth had located her via the phone. He had bought her the top of the range thing and was paying for the contract. How the hell could she have forgotten that? All he needed to do was put some kind of trace on it. *Bastard.* Well at least this meant that her life after Seth could start properly when this final tie was severed. She would purchase a new phone and in doing so get a new number.

She threw the wrecked item on the table. 'Blessing in disguise really,' she mumbled.

With a lot of effort she made her way to living room and lowered herself steadily to the couch. It was freezing now but she didn't have the energy to build a fire. In spite of the drop in temperature, she drifted off as the exhaustion of the day's events took over and she succumbed to much needed sleep.

'Hey, sleepy head. You can't stay there all night, you'll crick your neck. Come on sleepy head, wake up.'

A gentle voice whispered into her dream and she fluttered her eyes open. Mac was crouched beside her and Cliff was sitting on the couch to her left, his tail wagging in that crazy way she loved.

She rubbed her sore eyes. 'What time is it?'

Mac glanced at his watch. 'It's after one. Do you want me to help you up the stairs? Or I could bring you a blanket down here?'

'No, no, I'll be fine. Don't worry.'

He nodded. 'Okay, well I've put my number on the pad by your landline. Just in case you need anything. And don't hesitate to call me okay?'

She sighed. 'Thanks again for today, Mac. Really.'

He scrunched his brow. 'Erm... I thought we weren't doing that whole thanks thing again.'

She cringed and smiled. 'Whoops. Forgot.'

'Right, well, I'll be off. Get some sleep but make sure you get comfy first, eh? Goodnight.'

'I will. Bye, Mac.'

22

MAC

He pulled the door to Rose Brae closed behind him and walked back over to the Jeep where he had parked it on the little lane beside the row of cottages. The drive home took a few minutes meaning he was back at his chilly caravan quickly.

Watching Cassie fall into the road had been bloody awful. The fact that a hulking great four-wheel drive had narrowly missed her had made his heart almost leap from his chest. It was a good thing he'd been there. *Right place, right time.*

Luckily, she weighed next to nothing and he had managed to carry her unconscious, limp body onto the pavement where he'd called for an ambulance. The whole time he was waiting with her he was willing her to wake up and be okay. He'd teased her something chronic since she'd arrived and she clearly couldn't stand him. She had been nothing but stroppy and evasive since that first meeting – a city slicker looking down her nose at his unkempt ways. But he'd seen a totally different side to her on their surfing lesson. She'd smiled and laughed and he was the cause of that too. She had such a beautiful smile that lit up her whole face. And she shared his affinity with the beach.

He still wondered why the hell she'd chosen Coldingham to relocate to. What on earth was there here for someone like her when she was so used to the city? Surely the beach wasn't that much of a draw for her? It had been a strange evening. Seeing tears in her eyes as she repeatedly thanked him for helping her when she felt she didn't deserve it was so sad and it made him wonder what kind of shit her boyfriend had been. Okay so he cheated on her with her friend – that was bad enough. But to feel so undeserving of care? He must have been a complete arse. Although it had been good to see a tiny chink in her icy façade. He hoped that maybe they could be friends, after all. Even if it was so he could prove to her that not all friends betray you like hers had.

The morning after all the drama he rose early even though he had no surfing lessons planned. He took the opportunity to go for a run on the beach and was out the door before seven. There was a sea mist hanging over the sand giving the appearance of a horror movie set and there was no one around apart from a couple of his hardened surfer buddies who he waved to as he jogged. Those guys would be out there regardless of time, tide and weather. It was a wonder they hadn't sprouted fins and gills. For a split second he envied them and almost considered returning to the van to get his board but then he remembered Cliff would be needing his morning constitutional.

The coastal breeze refreshed and cooled Mac's heated skin as his feet pounded the sand and he glanced up the hill towards home where the rest of the villagers were beginning to wake. He smiled to himself as he ran. Of all the places in the world he could be there really was no place like home, *his* home. His roots were in Coldingham and the roads, pavements and beach were ingrained in his heart like the veins in his body. The people were like an extended family and he knew he could never live long enough to repay their kindness following the death of his parents even though he had taken it hard and rebelled there for a while. They just understood and accepted that the pain was what was causing him to behave so negatively. Perhaps that was why he had somehow gravitated towards Cassie. He recognised her grief and knew that her attitude to begin with was as a result of what she had been through. He had been given a chance so he would do the same for her.

Some people might find it dull living in such a provincial little place but for Mac that wasn't the case. He loved to travel – especially to the Highlands – but he always looked forward to returning to his caravan in his Scottish seaside village. He knew he would always call Coldingham home.

He jogged up to Cassie's cottage, knocked on the door and waited. After a few minutes a panting, frustrated, red-faced woman greeted him. 'Ugh! I officially hate crutches,' she growled.

Mac chuckled and shook his head. 'And here I was thinking they were a fabulous fashion accessory.' She rolled her eyes but smiled at the same time. 'Anyway, I've come to take the Cliffmeister for his walk.'

Her eyes widened. 'Really? But... why?'

He scrunched his brow and wondered why it wasn't obvious after her complaint about the crutches. 'Well... in case you've forgotten, you're a teensy bit incapacitated right now. And a dog's gotta do what a wee dog's gotta do, you know?' He whispered behind his hand and gestured towards Cliff, who was standing beside Cassie wagging his stubby little tail.

Cassie's cheeks flamed. 'Well, that's brilliant. Thanks, Mac. Come on in.' She hobbled inside and Mac followed.

'So, how did you get on last night? Manage the stairs okay?'

She slumped onto a kitchen chair. 'Well, put it this way, my bottom is sore and Cliff thinks I'm insane.' She laughed and he liked the musical sound. 'He watched my every move and followed me cautiously. Oh, and he tried to run off with one of my crutches when I was in the loo.'

Mac burst into laughter at the ridiculous image this all conjured up. 'Probably thought it was a huge shiny stick and all his Christmas and birthdays had come at once.'

She joined in with his merriment. 'Yes, luckily, he got stuck in the bathroom doorway.'

She really was pretty when she smiled and quite stunning when she laughed. He was definitely beginning to think there was a decent human being under all the angst.

She tucked her blonde hair behind her ears. 'I know you said I wasn't to say thank you any more but... well, I really am grateful for your help with Cliff. He really likes you. I know I haven't been the easiest person to get along with since I moved here.'

He shrugged and reached for Cliff's lead. 'Hey, it's *nae* bother. I know you've been through some shit and no one trusts easily after that. Especially when it's those you think you know the best who've done the trust breaking. But we can't all be as perfect as me, eh?' He joked trying to lighten the mood.

She shook her head and smiled. 'You're modest, too, then?'

'To a fault. Now can I get you anything while I'm out?' he asked as he clipped Cliff's lead onto his collar.

'Maybe some milk and bread? But unless they stock new legs in the Spar that's all.'

He trailed his gaze downwards to where she had her damaged limb extended. 'Nothing wrong with yours that a bit of rest won't cure.' When he lifted his head once again he found her blushing – but then he had just been openly ogling her.

He cleared his throat. 'Ahem... right then, we'll be off. I'll call for milk and bread although you maybe should sign up with Peter. He's the local milk man. It'll save you loads of hassle in the long run. He's a top guy. Oh, and he sells other stuff around Christmas time too. I always think it's important to support local business. But then I see you get your dog food from Rob at Coldstream which is great.'

'I totally agree. Use them or lose them.'

'Aye. Indeed. Right well, we'll see you later.' He walked towards the door with his new best friend.

'See you later, Mac. Bye, Cliff.' She was smiling again and Mac wondered if maybe she had turned a corner. Maybe she was settling better now? And maybe she was realising that not all men were arseholes. He certainly hoped so.

23

CASSIE

Cassie managed to make herself a bowl of porridge in the microwave and, after realising that getting it to the table was virtually impossible, she was standing at the kitchen work surface to eat it when there was a loud, thunderous pounding at the door. She almost jumped out of her skin and placed her spoon down, frowning. *Crikey, that was a quick walk, I hope Cliff has behaved himself 'cause Mac sounds pissed off if that knock is anything to go by,* she thought as she grabbed her crutches and headed to the door.

'How come you're back so qu—' she gasped as she opened the door and saw the man at the other side of it *wasn't* Mac after all.

'Hello, Cassandra. I thought I'd stop by and say hello seeing as I'm in the area.'

'S-Seth? Why— how— I mean— what are you doing here?' He looked exactly how he had when she'd first met him. A crisp, designer suit hanging from his well-toned frame and his greying hair neatly styled to frame his clean-shaven face. No signs at all of the heartbroken, dishevelled mess she had witnessed when she tried to collect her belongings, but then again she remembered that had been a failed ploy to manipulate her sympathy.

He smiled but the gesture was void of any feeling. 'Oh, I'm looking at some property in the area. Nothing definite yet but you never know, we could be neighbours.' He laughed without humour. 'Well, you could be neighbours with whoever moves in, that is. *I* obviously won't be moving to this provincial place. A little too hum drum for me. Now, aren't you going to invite me in?'

She sighed. 'It's not a good time, Seth. It's probably best if you just go.'

He stepped towards her and glanced down, his eyes widening when he saw the crutches. 'What have we here? Someone been harming you, have they? Who do I need to kill?' He grinned but his words sent a tingle of unease down her spine.

She scrunched her face. 'Good grief, Seth. I had a fall that's all. And it's just a sprain. I'm fine. Look, you should leave. I'm eating breakfast at the moment.'

'Nonsense. I'll just come in for a while.' He managed to push past her and walked into the cottage uninvited.

Reluctantly she followed him and found him in the kitchen. He was peering around his surroundings with a look of disdain contorting his face. 'How long are you planning on keeping up this charade then, Cassie?'

She lowered herself to a chair, suddenly void of her appetite and feeling somewhat defeated. 'What charade?'

He smiled that same emotionless grimace again. 'The little game of independence you've got going on. As admirable as it is and as much as you've proved you're capable of living alone, I need to know when you're planning on coming back. You know, so I can get the wedding plans back on track. We'll have to delay a couple of months now after your wobble but that's not a problem. Not with my connections.'

Her heart began to hammer at her chest. 'It wasn't a little wobble, Seth, I'm not coming back. We broke up.' *Had he gone insane? Why was he acting this way?*

He shook his head. 'Ah, poppet. You don't seem to realise yet that you're nothing without me. But you will. I can assure you of that.' It almost sounded like a threat.

She swallowed a lump of worry that had dried her throat and glanced towards the door, fearful that Mac would return with Cliff and Seth would be angry and get the wrong end of the stick.

He tilted his head inquisitively. 'Are you expecting someone, poppet?'

'Erm... n-no. I just think you should be leaving that's all. I'm not coming back to you, Seth. And you're acting strange. I don't like it.' She immediately regretted making herself vulnerable by admitting her concern like that.

He chuckled. 'Strange? Me? Don't be absurd. I think we both know it's *you* that's lost a few marbles, darling. But it's fine. We'll sort it all out. Once you're back in Glasgow. And you *will* be back in Glasgow. Oh, and you'll be glad to know I'm selling the apartment so we can make a fresh start. I'm buying us a beautiful old villa. You'll love it. Lots of *character*, just how you like things.'

She sighed as a combination of frustration, fear and annoyance caused her heart rate to pick up. 'Look, Seth, you can keep the bloody apartment. I'm *not* coming back. It's over. You cheated on me and I'm not prepared to forgive that. Please just leave.' She raised her voice and he scowled at her.

His lip curled. 'There's no need to *shout,* Cassandra. I'm neither deaf nor a child.'

'Well then stop acting like one and leave. This isn't a game, Seth. There's no prize for you to win. Just go!'

'Hey, Cassie, is this bloke bothering you?'

Her gaze snapped in the direction of the kitchen door. *Shit!* 'Hi, Mac, no, Seth's just leaving aren't you, Seth?' The words fell from her lips in a panicked rush. The last thing she needed was confrontation between Seth and Mac. Even though she knew Seth would have already jumped to the wrong conclusion.

Seth held out his hand to Mac. 'And you are?'

Mac glanced at Cassie, concern creasing his brow but he shook the proffered hand. 'Mackenzie. Tadhg Mackenzie.'

'Good to meet you, Mr Mackenzie. How do you know my fiancée?'

Mac's gaze flitted to Cassie once more, this time with a hidden question. Cassie shrugged and cringed apologetically. 'I'm helping her out with Cliff 'til she's back on her feet.'

Seth turned to Cassie. 'Mr Mackenzie *and* Cliff? My, we are making new friends, aren't we?'

'Cliff is my dog. Goodbye, Seth,' Cassie replied.

'Well, I must be off anyway. Lots to do. No rest for the wicked, hmm? I've properties to see so I'll love you and leave you,' Seth said, totally glossing over the fact that Cassie had told him to leave several times.

Mac chucked his chin. 'Aye well, don't let us stop you.'

Mac

The suited man paused in front of Mac and gave him a snide grin filled with disdain before leaving the cottage and slamming the door behind him.

Mac huffed air from his lungs through puffed cheeks and shook his head. 'Well, he was a barrel of laughs,' he said as he stared at the door to be sure the unwanted guest had definitely gone.

In his periphery, he saw Cassie rub her hands over her face and when he turned around she met his gaze briefly but quickly lowered her head as if ashamed. 'I've never known him to be like that. So... *menacing*. He's changed. I felt quite intimidated and a bit scared to be honest. I was worried about you coming back and him seeing you, but also relieved when you did. I have no clue how to even categorise his behaviour. But he's definitely in some kind of denial.'

Mac raised his eyebrows. 'Aye, I thought so, seeing as he still called you his fiancée. He's kind of a sinister guy, eh?'

'But he didn't used to be. At least not with me. He's a ruthless businessman and doesn't like to lose where that's concerned but this side of him is unnerving.'

Mac knew very well people like *that* didn't tend to change, they just showed their true colours eventually. 'What was he doing here anyway?'

She lifted her chin once again and her countenance was filled with a mixture of emotions but the overriding one was certainly anxiety. 'To find out how long I was staying here. He was acting like I'm going back to him. Like this is all a game he's waiting for me to finish. And it seems he hasn't accepted that we're over. It was... *weird*. And he says *I'm* being absurd. That I'm *playing* at being independent.'

Mac sat opposite her at the table and unclipped Cliff's lead. 'What was he saying about looking at property around here?'

She shrugged but worry creased her forehead. 'Oh, it's probably nothing. He's always buying and selling property. It's what he does. But why he's interested in *this* area I have no idea. It's totally outside the usual portfolio location.'

Mac raised his eyebrows. 'Really? You have *no* idea? I can tell you exactly why, Cassie. You said you felt intimidated and that's *it*. Mission accomplished. He thinks he can manipulate you into going back to Glasgow. Men like that don't give up once they've set their minds to it no matter what it is they want. And it sounds like he's going to keep trying. But he'll have to find another way to do it 'cause unfortunately for him there's no land or property for sale around here at the moment.'

Cassie smiled weakly. 'Yes, let's hope he buggers off back home and realises he's wasting company time and money.' She sighed and stared blankly. 'Although, he does have a lot of connections. Maybe he knows something we don't.'

Mac was determined to ease her worry. 'Nah. I'd know if there was property for sale, Cassie. I've lived here my whole life. I know *everyone*. And things like that spread like wildfire around here. Anyway, forget it. If you dwell on it, he's winning.'

'Yes, you're right.' She shook her head as if to dislodge the negative thoughts. 'So, did Cliff enjoy his walk? He looks worn out, poor thing.' She gestured over to where her little dog was curled up in a ball fast asleep.

'Oh aye, he did. He made a new friend too.'

Cassie beamed. 'He did?'

'Aye. Sally's boy, Jack. They seem to be big fans of one another those two. They've probably got the same amount of boundless energy – unlike us adult humans, eh? In fact, whilst I remember Sally's invited you to dinner on Friday night. She asked me to pass the message on. She thinks it'd do you good to have a change of scene by then.'

'Oh, that's sweet. And she's probably right. I imagine I'll be stir-crazy by Friday if I can't go out. She seems really lovely. I met her in the shop a few days ago.'

Mac nodded. 'She's a great lass. Very thoughtful. In fact, they're a great family. She's like *ma* big sister. Likes to make sure I have at least one home cooked meal a month.' He chuckled. 'She thinks I can't cook properly in my van.'

'Van?' Cassie looked bemused.

Mac's cheeks heated a little. 'Aye, I live in a caravan on my folks' land. Never got around to building the house they had planned. And now I'm just used to living in the van. I do have a cooker and I *do* use it in spite of what Sally thinks. Anyway, shall I call for you on Friday? I'm guessing you might need a chaperone if you're still on crutches and it's easy enough for me to stop by.'

Cassie's eyebrows rose. 'Oh, *you're* going too?'

He opened his hands as if it was obvious. 'I sure am. She's making lasagne and I *never* miss that.'

'Ah, right. Okay, well, yes then. That would be good, thanks.'

He nodded. 'Great, that's settled then. Right, well I'll be off but I'll call back later to take Cliff out again. And you have my number if you need anything in the meantime; especially if you get another unwanted visit from Mr Happiness.' He leaned in conspiratorially. 'Although maybe we should knock off the *hap* bit, eh?' he said through the side of his mouth and winked, immediately regretting it. He wasn't usually a winker and she'd no doubt think he was even more of an idiot, seeing as he had just intimated her ex was *Mr Penis*.

She pursed her lips, clearly trying to stifle a laugh which was a relief. 'Thanks, Mac. I do have your number but let's hope I don't need it, eh?'

Mac stood from the table and fixed his gaze on Cassie,

suddenly reluctant to leave after what he had encountered earlier but knowing he should. They had only just built bridges and he didn't want to outstay his welcome.

'See you later then.'

She raised her hand. 'Bye, Mac and thanks again.'

24
_____

CASSIE

The shock of Seth appearing on her doorstep began to dissipate and was soon replaced by anger. How _dare_ he turn up unannounced at her new home like that? What the hell did he think he was going to achieve? She had made it perfectly clear on more than one occasion that she was not going back to him but yet again he had ignored her and had stomped his way back into her life to make demands on her _and_ insult her to her face about the choices she had made. Well, he could sod off. She wasn't going to give in.

The talk of purchasing property or land in Coldingham was clearly a rouse to rile her and make her feel like he had eyes everywhere, that she couldn't escape him. All of which was manipulative and creepy and she was so relieved when Mac turned up when he did. Once again, he had rescued her from a shitty situation that she hadn't intended to find herself in and had no desire for. She got the feeling the real reason he was helping her was either pity or the fact that he adored Cliff. Mac had certainly grown quite fond of her little dog that much was obvious. But whatever the reasons she was grateful and indebted to him once again. She would have to figure out a way to repay him for his undeserved kindness.

* * *

As the week wore on, the swelling in her ankle decreased and a house call from Doctor Cairns encouraged her that she was healing fast. Getting around was still a bit tricky and Mac had called in twice a day to take Cliff for walks and check if she needed provisions. His visits had been brief and conversation had been minimal but Cassie had managed to get plenty of work done as a result. At least there was something positive about being immobile.

On Friday morning she managed to shower a little easier and blasted her hair with the dryer before carefully descending the stairs to make tea and toast. Mac arrived at the usual time and knocked twice as he had been doing, before letting himself into the cottage to announce his arrival. As always, he was greeted by the excited dog's yips and frantic tail wagging.

'Morning, Cassie, how are you today? Still up for our big night out?'

Thanks to a full work schedule, Cassie had forgotten about the dinner arrangements. 'Oh, gosh, yes. It had totally slipped my mind. But yes. Erm... should I bring something? Dessert maybe? I could bake a cake.'

Mac stopped to clip Cliff's lead on. 'Oh no, I'm pretty sure just yourself will be sufficient. She always cooks enough to feed an army. Although I can pick you up a bottle of wine if you like?'

Cassie reached into her bag on the back of the kitchen chair and fumbled around for her purse. 'That'd be great if you don't mind?'

He shook his head. 'It's *nae* bother, really. Red or white?'

'I prefer red but get whatever you think Sally will like.'

He took the offered ten-pound note and saluted her before leaving the cottage with his furry friend leading the way.

* * *

It was almost time for Mac to call for her and Cassie's stomach was knotted with nerves. *Good grief, Cassie, it's not like it's a date,* she told herself as she flicked through the clothes in her wardrobe. At least she *hoped* Mac didn't think of it as a date. No... he wouldn't... they were just friends. And they were barely even that. There hadn't been a single hint of any chemistry between them so she knew deep down that she was safe. Yes, he was a good-looking guy if you liked that laid-back, floppy haired thing. But she didn't. She liked the clean-cut, suited look – *when* she was looking. Which she absolutely wasn't. A memory of Seth in his favourite, navy-blue designer suit sprang to mind and she shook her head to dislodge the unwelcome intrusion.

She pulled out a deep red top with cut outs at the shoulders, black jeans and the only boots she could fasten comfortably at the moment. They weren't exactly dressy but they'd have to do. She hobbled around her room spraying perfume, fluffing her hair and applying lip-gloss. She hooked her red feather earrings into her ears and stepped back to assess her appearance in the mirror. She wondered if she'd made *too much* of an effort. But as she stood there, hands on hips wondering if she should change, she heard Mac's voice.

'Hi, Cassie, you nearly ready?'

'Hi, Mac, yes, down in a minute.'

After one last glance in the mirror she made her way down the stairs to find Mac standing in the kitchen. He wore black jeans and a grey, long-sleeved T-shirt that moulded to his torso, showing just how toned he was beneath. His hair was just as shaggy as usual but it suited him and there was the usual stubble gracing his strong jaw. He held a bottle of wine in one hand and a bunch of flowers in the other.

Oh, shit. He does think it's a bloody date. 'Oh, Mac they're lovely but you really didn't have to do that.'

He frowned and then glanced down in the direction of Cassie's gaze. 'Oh! No, these aren't for you. They're for Sally. I didn't want to bring wine seeing as you were. Didn't want to duplicate, you know?'

You could have fried an egg in the heat radiating from Cassie's cheeks when the embarrassment at her mistake kicked in.

She rolled her eyes. 'Oh yes, of course. I knew that.'

He trailed his gaze down her body and then back up to meet her eyes again. 'You look... wow... I mean... you look great, Cassie.'

She tucked a strand of hair behind her ear. 'Thanks. You scrub up well too.'

'For a scruffy surfing lout?' He chuckled. 'Anyway, are we off?'

She nodded and grabbed her jacket, bag and keys. 'Be a good boy, Cliffy. See you soon.'

'Oh, so you can call him Cliffy?' Mac teased.

'Shut up, Tiger,' she giggled.

* * *

Sally greeted them at the door with hugs and kisses. 'So good to see you both. Come on in. Derek is just putting the kids to bed.'

She stepped aside, and the two friends walked into the hallway of the old, beamed cottage. Mac handed Sally the flowers and Cassie, in turn, handed her the wine that Mac had picked up for her.

'You two are so kind. You shouldn't have. But thank you. What can I get you to drink?'

'Beer would be good,' Mac replied.

'Whatever you have open in the wine department will do nicely,' Cassie said as Sally led them through to the living room.

'Take a seat and I'll be back in a sec,' Sally told them.

'Wow, what a gorgeous house,' Cassie said as she took in her surroundings. The cottage was sympathetically decorated in a combination of modern and period style. And it was surprisingly tidy considering she had a toddler and a baby.

'Oh aye. She'd like you to think she's house proud. But the truth is she'll have spent today having a mad tidy up.' Mac laughed.

'Sadly, he speaks the truth but don't tell Sal I said so,' Doctor Cairns whispered as he appeared in the room. 'How's the ankle, Cassie?'

'It's getting better every day, thank you, Doctor Cairns,' she replied without thinking about where she was.

He grinned. 'You can call me Derek if you like. It's not so formal.'

Cassie's cheeks heated again. She seemed to be making a habit of embarrassing herself. 'Good grief, sorry.' She shook her head. 'You and Sally do have a lovely home, Derek.'

'Ah, thank you. Mostly down to Sally I have to say. I just decorate how I'm told.'

They laughed and were joined once more by Sally. 'What's he saying about me?' she asked as she narrowed her eyes at her husband.

'Oh, just that you're a wonderful cook.' Derek laughed.

'Yeah, I bet. And I hope you haven't built this food up into something amazing, Mac. I can do without the pressure.' She whacked him lightly on the arm.

'Too late. Cassie knows it's the best lasagne she'll ever taste this side of the border.' Mac grinned.

* * *

They sat at the dining table and Sally served up the lasagne; steam rose from within the layers of pasta, meat and melted cheese. Mac's eyes were wide like a kid in candy store and Cassie couldn't help giggling at him.

He held his hands up innocently. 'What? I'm a growing lad, eh, Sal?'

Sally tilted her head to one side and raised her eyebrows. 'Oh yeah, growing outwards if you're not careful.'

The food was delicious and the conversation easy as the four adults enjoyed their evening. There was one brief interruption when Jack appeared in the doorway asking if Mac had brought Cliff along. But he was ushered back to bed quickly by his father.

'So, Cassie, how long do you think you'll stay in Coldingham? Is it a permanent move?' Sally asked as they all tucked in to Eton Mess.

'Oh... I don't know really. I do like it here though. It's so... peaceful.' She smiled wistfully.

Mac interjected. 'Oh aye, it was until that ex of yours showed up.'

Cassie cringed. 'Oh yes, there was that incident that shattered the peace briefly. Hopefully he got the message.'

A furrow of concern etched Sally's brow. 'Oh dear. I gather you weren't expecting him?'

Cassie glanced at Mac and then slowly shook her head. 'Not

exactly. I just want him to let me go. But he seems incapable of taking no for an answer.'

'And there's no chance of you taking him back?' Derek enquired.

'After what the bast— idiot did to her she'd be bloody mad to take him back.' Mac's voice was filled with incredulity at the thought.

Sally covered her mouth. 'Oh, gosh, Cassie was he... you know... abusive?'

Cassie's eyes widened. 'Oh no, nothing like that. Let's just say he made a mistake of epic proportions with my so-called friend and I walked in on it.' She lowered her head in embarrassment at her sordid admission.

Sally sighed sympathetically. 'Oh my goodness, Cassie there's no wonder you won't take the rat back. He doesn't deserve you.'

Cassie gave a small smile. 'That's sweet of you, thank you. But anyway, can we change the subject? You don't want my disastrous love life to bring down such a lovely evening.'

Mac nudged her and grinned. 'At least you *had* a love life.'

'Now then, Tadhg Mackenzie, you've had plenty of opportunity. You're just far too picky.' Sally laughed.

'He's right to be so. I mean, he could end up with someone who makes terrible lasagne if he's not careful,' Derek said as he leaned over to kiss his wife's cheek.

Mac turned to Cassie and pointed at the couple opposite with his spoon. 'Relationship goals, right there.'

'Well, I think I'll be giving relationships a wide berth from now on,' Cassie confessed.

'Oh no, Cassie, I think that's such a shame. But I do understand your reasoning. Although you may just meet someone who changes all that,' Sally said with a sweet smile at her husband.

* * *

After the meal and several glasses of wine, Mac and Cassie said their goodbyes and set off to walk towards Rose Brae – or hobble in Cassie's case.

'Well, that was a grand evening. What did I tell you about Sal's lasagne, eh?'

'Gosh, yes, it was divine. Trouble is I'm stuffed now. I could do with a wheelbarrow to go home in.' They laughed and Cassie smiled to herself, thankful for how relaxed everything felt.

She inhaled the cool breeze travelling into the village from the direction of the sea. The salty air refreshing her senses. She glanced skyward to where there were a million tiny dots of light strewn across the deep navy canopy. The skies in Coldingham were vastly different to the ones she had witnessed back in Glasgow, thanks to the myriad sources of light pollution. Here, however, you could almost count each of the minuscule twinkles and every so often a shooting star would streak a glittering path across her line of sight.

'You're a star gazer too then?' Mac asked as they approached the turning for Rose Brae.

'The night sky here takes my breath away. It's something I don't think I'll ever tire of.'

He shrugged. 'Well, then, maybe you should just stay here in Coldingham permanently.'

When she turned her attention to him he was standing before her, a handsome smile turning his lips up at one side and the gentle evening breeze causing a few strands of his hair to flit about his face and suddenly she was caught up in the moment.

The alcohol, the lovely evening, the sky all playing their part in the magic and making her feel like she somehow belonged. All she wanted was to belong somewhere again.

Mac lowered his face towards her and her eyes fluttered closed as his lips met hers softly. It was a sweet kiss that made her heart skip and she almost yielded to him. That wonderful sensation of stubble lightly grazing her chin as his mouth moved over hers and the taste of wine on his lips.

Suddenly coming to her senses, she stepped back and gasped. 'No!' She scowled at Mac whose expression was now filled with a mixture of confusion and regret.

'Shit, Cassie I'm so sorry. I didn't mean... I just kind of... I got caught up... I'm so sorry.'

'I'd better be getting inside. Cliff will be wondering where I am. G-goodnight, Tadhg.'

'Hey, you got my name right.' He smiled, desperately trying to lighten the dark mood that had rapidly descended on them.

Distractedly Cassie shook her head. 'Did I? Goodnight.' She hurriedly unlocked the door.

'Shall I call for Cliff in the morning as normal?' He sounded hopeful.

'Oh no, thank you. I think I'll be fine. I need to get walking again soon. Might as well try. Thanks though.' She forced a smile as she stepped inside her cottage and without saying another word she slammed the door behind her and leaned against it. Cliff did his usual merry, tail wagging dance to greet her and she slid down the door to collect him up and nuzzle his fur.

'Oh, Cliff. What the hell just happened? What've I done? I think we may have to leave, little buddy,' she told the excitable dog who understood nothing of her admission. Only Cassie knew that Mac unsettled her in ways she didn't want to admit.

Her attraction to him had been increasing in spite of her efforts to quell it. The way she had felt when his lips had met hers was another problem. She had liked it. She had wanted it. But she absolutely couldn't allow it. She needed him as a friend and nothing more. She wasn't prepared to give her heart again. Not so soon after having it broken. And anyway, this was lust. Nothing more. Yes, he was attractive if you liked that sort of thing. But, Cassie told herself, she didn't. She absolutely didn't.

Did she?

25

MAC

Mac sat outside his caravan on the morning after the incident that had probably ruined his burgeoning friendship with Cassie. Every time he replayed the kiss over in his mind he clenched his jaw and growled out loud at his stupidity, slamming his balled fist onto the wooden arm of his garden chair. She wasn't interested. She had made that abundantly clear so why the *feck* had he kissed her like that? *Idiot.* All he'd done was succeed in proving that men are all the same, just as Cassie had presumed. He had confirmed that all men *do* think with their pricks. Okay, so he knew he didn't *actually* fit into that category but he had just made himself appear that way. And for what? Because he'd had wine and the sky looked pretty? *Fuck!* He should've stuck to beer. At least he could bloody control himself when he'd had beer.

'You all right, lad?' Rab's voice pulled him back from his self-deprecating imaginings. 'You're looking deep in thought there. And if you clench your jaw any harder, you'll bite your own head off.'

Mac glanced up to see his uncle standing there, car keys in

hand, squinting against the sun. 'Aye, Uncle Rab, I'm okay. It's nothing that a pair of bricks and a swift crack wouldn't sort.'

Rab hissed in through his teeth. 'I don't know if you mean what I *think* you mean but if you do then I won't ask any more questions. Anyway, I'm away off to the hospital for a check-up.' Rab closed his eyes and pulled his lips between his teeth as if realising he had just slipped up.

Mac straightened up, suddenly worried. 'What check-up?'

Rab waved a dismissive hand. 'It's nothing. Just a check-up. *Dinna* you worry yoursel'. Anyway, can you go and tell Cassie that I've got her heating oil on order? I tried ringing but her line is constantly engaged. I'm guessing she's working hard and *doesnae* want to be disturbed. But seeing as you're big pals now, you can pass it on. I'll see you later.' Before Mac could protest his uncle was gone.

Alone once more, he stared at the vista spread out before him, wondering what Rab was needing to go to the hospital for. Worry niggled at the back of his mind. His uncle had been looking pale recently. And he'd asked on more than one occasion for Mac's help opening jars, chopping wood, et cetera. Weakness – neither physical nor emotional – was something unheard of for the father figure. And he now wondered how many of these trips to the hospital there had been without Mac knowing. He decided he'd confront him when he got home. Rab was the only real family he had and if there was something wrong he wanted to know so he could help.

The plot of land he'd inherited from his parents had a fantastic view of the sea. The gated side that would've been a driveway, opened out on to the paved hill that led down to the beach, which was good seeing as *that* was the place he spent most of his time. Talk about work being on his doorstep. Rab's adjacent land had an equally stunning vista although he had a house with an upstairs which meant he could see even further than Mac.

There was nothing better than lying in bed at night with the sound of the waves lulling him to sleep. Sometimes he would try to visualise what it would've been like if his parents had got around to building their dream house before they were killed. He'd kept the blueprints and often tried to imagine how different things could have been if they'd lived. It was a modest building they had planned; double fronted with a storm porch covering the front door and two dormer windows that looked out to sea – each creating an ever-changing piece of living artwork every single day as the seasons changed.

'Mr Mackenzie. Good to see you. Do you have a moment to talk?' A voice once again interrupted his thoughts and he swung around realising it was a familiar one that set his hair on end.

His presumption confirmed, Mac chucked his chin. 'What do you want?'

Seth Guthrie smirked as he stepped through the gate into the plot of land as if he owned it himself. 'Oh, come on now be sociable, Mr Mackenzie... or should I call you Mac?'

Mac stood and sneered at his unwelcome guest. 'That name is reserved for friends. And you're *not* one. I'll ask again. What. Do. You. Want?'

The man glanced around Mac's garden as if appraising his surroundings. 'I thought we could have a little chat. I have a rather amazing business proposal for you.'

Mac shook his head. 'Nothing you could offer would be of interest to me.'

Guthrie, suited and slick-looking, held out his arms, grinning. 'At least give me a chance, hmm? Hear me out.'

'Why waste your time and mine? The answer will be no.' Mac turned to walk away towards his van.

Guthrie followed. 'Beautiful spot you have here. How come you've never built a house on the land? Surely living in the caravan is cold in winter?'

'I manage.'

The intruder was persistent. 'I reckon you could fit two maybe three on a plot this size. Think of the cash. City folks would jump at the chance to buy a little seaside escape in such a spot. It's my guess that you haven't built on here because you can't afford to do so. Am I right?'

Mac snorted. 'That's none of your business. You can *go* now.'

'Look, I'll be straight with you. I want to buy the land and I tend to get what I want. I'll give you double the value. Then you can go buy yourself a *proper* house with real windows and doors. What do you say?'

Patronising bastard. 'I say no.'

Guthrie laughed out loud. 'Ooh, you're a tricky one. But you should at least think about it. You know the value of the land in the current market, no doubt. Which means you can figure out what I'm offering.'

Mac turned to face him. 'And why would you want to buy the land? Cassie has made it very clear she doesn't want to come back to you. How is buying my land going to improve on that? Oh, that's right, it *isn't*. Now I suggest you run along back to Glasgow.' He made running leg gestures with his fingers before turning and walking into the van and closing the door.

'I'll leave you to think about it. I'll be back in a couple of days,' Guthrie shouted from his position outside the kitchen area window.

Mac opened the door again, anger building inside of him, his jaw clenched tight. 'I said the answer would be no. And guess what? I was right. My land is *not* for sale. Cassie doesn't want you here either. Go home.'

Guthrie's nostrils flared. 'But she wants *you* does she?' His voice dripped with derision. 'A long haired, scruffy-looking, layabout who lives in a fucking caravan? How her standards have fallen.'

Mac dashed down the steps towards him, fist raised. 'Get off my land, you arrogant arse. You know nothing about me or my life.'

His face now beet-red Guthrie shouted, 'I know enough. I know you kissed my fucking fiancée last night!'

Mac scrunched his face and lowered his fist, bewildered. 'What? How the fuck?'

Guthrie stepped towards him, jabbing a pointed finger towards his face. 'I saw you putting your hands and your mouth on her. She's not *yours*. Do you hear me?'

Mac shrugged. 'Last I heard she wasn't *yours* either. *She's* not a bloody plot of land, mate. You don't own her.'

Guthrie sneered. 'Is that what you think? How very modern. Your mother must be so proud. Oh, but wait...' He tapped his chin and Mac seethed at the cruel point he was making. The unwelcome intruder bared his teeth like a rabid dog. 'Touch her again, Mackenzie and you'll be *very* sorry. I won't be losing this fight. Certainly not to the likes of you.' Saliva shot through his clenched teeth.

Mac shook his head and gave a humourless, coarse laugh. 'Oh, so you're threatening *me* now? Just like you threatened Cassie, eh? Well, I hate to disappoint you, *pal,* but I'm not scared of a suited-up Jessie who can't even drive his own car. Oh yeah, I saw your chauffeur. Ponsy tosser. Get your driver to take you back to your penthouse flat with your housekeeper and bloody chef. Wouldn't surprise me if you've someone to wipe your arse too. We've no need for the *likes of you* here.' Deciding Guthrie wasn't worth the energy he turned and walked back to his van.

'I'll be back, Mackenzie. And you *will* consider my offer. Because you and I both know that if you don't you'll regret it.'

Mac chose to be the adult and ignored what he considered to be a pathetic, idle threat and things finally fell silent outside.

So the weirdo had been spying on Cassie? Guthrie could now add stalker to his list of talents and Mac really did wonder how he could've ever had a relationship with someone as sweet and... normal as Cassie Montgomery. How the hell had he hidden this sinister side of himself from her for so long? Because Cassie was clearly an intelligent woman and had she seen this side of him before she would've run for the hills – or the beach – earlier, surely?

Mac realised he was faced with a dilemma – to tell Cassie or not to tell her? If he told her she would freak out if she actually listened to him at all that is. If he *didn't* tell her and something happened he would *never* forgive himself. It really wasn't a great situation to be in. He decided he would call at Rose Brae and deliver his uncle's message about the oil and see how the land lay. Perhaps the decision would be made for him.

As he was standing at the kettle making himself a coffee a terrible thought dawned on him. What if Guthrie had been to Cassie's house after leaving his? He would've been angry. After all, Mac had told Guthrie that Cassie wasn't his to own. And the last thing Cassie needed was that psycho turning up in a rage on her doorstep. He switched the kettle off and left the van, locking the door for once, and headed to Rose Brae.

26

CASSIE

Cassie was quite excited at the prospect of working on a romance novel for a local author. The sample piece she had looked at was intriguing and she knew straight away that she would enjoy the job. She enjoyed a good romance read and being caught up in the imaginary world of passionate love. Maybe she could live vicariously through the pages – at a safe distance from the real thing. The author clearly had talent and the vivid descriptions of the sunny island where the story took place made her long for a holiday abroad – something she was never that bothered about normally.

In need of refreshment and a break, she closed her laptop and got up to make herself a coffee. Her ankle was getting easier by the day and she looked forward to the day when she could walk around without giving it a second thought. She had just filled the kettle when there was a knock at the door. She flicked the 'on' switch and went to answer it.

Mac stood there, stepping from one foot to the other and she simply said, 'Oh, it's you.' It wasn't the warmest of welcomes she was very much aware, but in all honesty, she had no clue how to act around Mac after that kiss.

He looked understandably sheepish, hunched over with his hands sunk into the pockets of his jeans. 'Erm… hi. I won't keep you. I have a message for you from Rab. He says to tell you the heating oil is ordered and he'll let you know about delivery.'

She nodded. 'Okay, thanks. Bye.' She began to close the door but Mac held out his hand.

'Hang on. Have you… had any unwanted visitors today?'

She frowned, not quite sure what he was asking. 'In what respect?'

'In the form of your ex?'

'No. I haven't. Why? Is he here again?' She shoved past Mac and stepped outside the cottage. Thankfully there was no sign of Seth.

'Okay, no that's fine.' He shrugged. 'I, erm… just wondered that's all. You know after he turned up the other day.'

'Ah well, no. I think he got the message, finally.'

Mac nodded and raised his hand. 'I'll be seeing you then.'

The look of disappointment in his eyes tugged at the decent person within her and she spoke before she could stop herself. 'Wait, do you want to come in for a coffee?'

His eyes widened and he scratched at the stubble on his chin. 'Oh, I don't want to trouble you. I know you're working.'

'Actually, I was just about to take a break.'

A wide smile appeared on his face and his cheeks coloured. 'Aye, that'd be grand then. Thanks.'

Mac sat at the kitchen table and Cliff immediately launched himself onto his lap, his little tail wagging so fast it was causing his whole body to jiggle.

Cassie laughed out loud as she watched Mac trying to avoid the dog's kisses. 'I think he's missed you.'

'No... really?' Mac chuckled. 'You daft wee dog, get your tongue *oot ma* nose.'

She stirred milk into the two mugs. 'Look, I want to apologise about last night. I overreacted. I think the evening just got away with us. I mean, there'd been a lot of wine.' She widened her eyes as she remembered the empty bottles piling up.

'Aye, there was a lot. And I should apologise too. I don't know what came over me. But if it helps I've been beating myself up ever since.'

Cassie cringed as she placed two mugs of freshly brewed filter coffee on the table. 'Oh no, don't be so hard on yourself. It was just a silly thing. But... I'd really like to get past it, if we can?'

He nodded. 'Me too. Me too.'

Cassie heaved a sigh of relief. 'Great. So... friends?'

'Friends.'

'Good. So, what are your plans for today?'

He shrugged and frowned. 'I'm waiting on Rab getting back from the hospital. I need to know what's going on.'

Concern caused her stomach to tighten. 'The hospital? When...? What...?'

'I wish I knew. He's been acting a wee bit strange lately. And he's seemed more tired than usual. Plus I think the day he asked me to hand over your keys he was going there too. The hospital, I mean.'

'Oh dear. I really hope it's all okay. He's such a sweet guy. I'd hate for him to be ill.'

Mac dropped his gaze to his mug. 'He's the only real family I have left. I don't know what I'd do if... Oh God, listen to me – all doom and gloom. It's probably nothing.' He waved a dismissive hand. 'So, what are you working on at the moment? Any more tool manuals?' He sniggered.

'Hey, that was a gripping read, I'll have you know.' She laughed as she remembered her last job.

'Aye, I bet. So, what's the latest?'

She straightened her back, quite proud of her news. 'Well, I've just been asked to edit a romance novel as a matter of fact.'

'Ooh, sounds very exciting. Well, definitely more exciting than an instruction manual for power tools.'

She grinned. 'Yes, I'm looking forward to getting stuck in to be honest.'

He raised his eyebrows. 'Oh aye, I bet you're a real bodice ripping type, eh?'

She felt her cheeks heat to furnace-like temperatures. 'I couldn't possibly comment.'

They chatted for a while longer and Cassie was quite relieved at how easy it was. Thankfully 'kiss-gate' had been all but forgotten and they managed to laugh and joke with each other as they had prior to the lip smooshing incident of the night before.

Mac lifted Cliff to the floor. 'Well, I suppose I'd better be off. I have a surf lesson at four and no doubt you're keen to get back to your handsome, shirtless hero and his muscles.' He winked and then his own cheeks flamed.

Cassie smiled. 'Well, those hunks won't edit themselves now, will they?' She enjoyed watching him squirm even though she wasn't sure why he was.

He placed his empty mug in the sink and left.

* * *

Mac

As he got the top of the lane, out of sight of Rose Brae, Mac hit himself in the head. *Why the hell did I wink at her? She'll think me a total prick now. I must've looked like some bloody 1970s sitcom actor. All nudge-nudge, wink-wink. Idiot.* He went straight home and changed into his wetsuit, grabbed his board and made his way to the beach. He figured he might as well get some surfing in before his pupil was due.

The fact that he had chosen not to tell Cassie about his visit from Seth was also on his mind. Had he made the right decision? He certainly hoped so. But what she didn't know couldn't worry her. Maybe the creep would just get sick of hanging around and give up? He could hope. Although judging by the 'I tend to get what I want' comment he doubted it.

Today's lesson was a couple of teenage kids whose parents he knew well from the village. It was evident the girl was crushing on him as her brother kept teasing her about it. They'd had several lessons now and the girl blushed every time he looked at her. Mac remained ever the professional and continued with his talk about beach safety and what to do if they or anyone else got into difficulty out on their board. The sea had stolen his parents but he refused to let that happen to any of his trainees. Their safety was paramount.

At the end of the lesson, he watched the kids walking back to their dad who was waiting up the beach. The boy was teasing his sister again. *Poor kid*, he thought with a smile as the girl shoved her brother away in a bid to avoid his mocking. Then he laughed out loud as the girl whacked her brother who was now making kissy faces at her and reciting something about her and Mac sitting in a tree.

'Daaaaad! Sophie just hit me!' the boy wailed. But Mac knew the kid had it coming.

* * *

Rab's car was back at his house when Mac returned home later that afternoon. He showered and changed into shorts and a T-shirt and jogged around to see his uncle.

Without knocking he let himself in. 'Uncle Rab? You home?'

'In the lounge, son,' Rab replied and Mac smiled at the term of endearment. He wandered through the house and found Rab sitting on his favourite chair by the window.

Trying to sound nonchalant in spite of the worry knotting his insides, Mac breezily asked, 'Now then. How did you get on today?'

Rab glanced up and smiled. 'Oh, absolutely fine. Like I said, nothing to worry about.'

Mac wasn't convinced. 'Look, you know you can tell me if there's something wrong, don't you? I mean I'm an adult now. No need to protect me and all that.'

'Nothing to tell, son. Now go and make us a brew, eh?'

Mac shook his head and sat on the sofa opposite. 'Come on. Tell me why you've been going up to the hospital.'

Rab sighed. 'I've told you, it's nothing. But I might die of thirst.'

Assuming that his uncle would tell him when he was ready he huffed and shook his head and left the room to make his uncle a cuppa as requested.

* * *

The following day Mac rose early and jogged down the beach. The sun was just starting to rise and the sky looked aflame as the glowing ball of light slowly peeped out from behind a grey cloud. Seagulls were taking it in turns to dive at the water, breaking the surface and seconds later returning to the sky, gripping morsels of food in their beaks. Some were sitting on the water as it bobbed and lapped at the shoreline and some were strolling along the sand in the hope of finding scraps that hadn't been washed away by the tide. As he travelled along the beach he slipped his sunglasses on to shield his eyes against the increasing brightness of the morning; the sun's ray reflecting on the water and dazzling him as he ran.

He approached the little closed down café that was right on the beach and paused for a few moments – the boarded-up windows and broken sign appeared sad and unloved. It was such a shame. It had been a thriving business until the owner had passed away. Thanks to the financial climate no one had taken it on yet. Luckily it wasn't the kind of building Seth Guthrie would be interested in – that was one saving grace. Mac would hate to see such a sweet little business fall into the wrong hands. It needed someone to come along and make a go of it again, to love it back to life. If only he was brave enough, Mac would be tempted to take it on. He would absolutely love to. He had often thought that when he ran by there but hadn't the guts to really consider it seriously.

Regardless of his fear, he could picture it all in his mind's eye. He'd put solar panels on the roof to make the most of the power he could generate from the free sunshine. He'd surround the place with troughs of pretty grasses that he'd water with the rain he'd collect in water butts. There'd be no plastic cups or straws – he'd watched the TV coverage on what plastic was doing to the oceans and he would in no way want to contribute to the problem. Everything would be biodegradable. There'd be recycling bins for cans placed outside, possibly by the picnic tables that would, of course, be made of drift wood or wood cut from sustainable sources. He'd hand paint the sign for the front and hang coloured bunting around the building with strings of solar lights that would illuminate the place at night.

He sighed and shook his head. 'Maybe one day, Mackenzie. When you get brave, eh?' After one last glance he resumed his run.

Further along the beach, a figure stood with a tripod and an expensive-looking camera fixed in place, ready to capture as much of the breaking day as possible before the beach was overrun with people. Mac could totally understand why so many people loved the place. It was his home but he never took it for granted. Grateful for every sunrise and sunset he got to see – and sad that his parents hadn't had the same opportunity.

He passed the little beach hut that belonged to his family and vowed that he would make use of it. It needed some TLC now as the paint around the shutters was flaking and the hinges of the door were rusty. It stuck out amongst all the others for the wrong reasons. He had found it hard to visit there. It held too many memories of his mum and dad. It was a weekly ritual come rain or shine when he was a kid – Sunday tea at the beach hut. Packs of sandwiches and flasks of tea followed by whatever cake his mum had rustled up. His uncle Rab would play footy with him and chase him around the sand when he invariably won – although he knew that his uncle had let him. So many happy memories linked him to the place but so many were hard to remember without getting misty-eyed.

The beach hut was blue and white striped but Rab had been saying for months that he would rather paint it a nice sage green. He hadn't gotten around to it yet, but maybe Mac would paint it as a surprise for him.

Eventually he made his way back up the narrow beach road and vaulted the gate into his land before climbing back into the van to shower and get ready for his day. He had decided he would take a trip into Galashiels to the big DIY place and get the paint for the beach hut. Rab would be so pleased when he saw it finally finished.

27

CASSIE

The sun was up and Cliff was doing his usual giddy dance around Cassie's feet. Her ankle was still sore but she decided to drive down to the beach and let him have a run seeing as there was no way she would make the walk down the slope unaided just yet.

She showered and dressed and made herself a coffee in her travel mug before loading Cliff into the car. She'd purchased a special seatbelt for him that meant he could sit on the seat rather than in the boot and he loved to gaze out of the window at the passing trees and sky that were visible to him from his viewpoint.

Once they arrived at the beach she clipped on Cliff's lead and he skipped out of the car, raring to go. There were already a few people setting up for the day. It seemed that in this location people would come to the picturesque beach regardless of the weather.

As she hobbled along the sand, she realised that perhaps it wasn't the best surface for a not-quite-healed sprained ankle and she had to take regular breaks to ease the discomfort. Over at the beach huts she spotted a familiar-looking figure on a stepladder wielding a paintbrush. The cute little hut was being transformed from a blue and white striped candy cane to a serene green pad. The colour surprised her. But it looked so lovely and she wished *she* could get her hands on one of the huts – but if the talk in the town was true there was a ridiculously long waiting list for the beach huts and many of them were handed down from generation to generation.

There was something magical about beach huts. She had always thought so. And often as a child she had wished she could live in one – to be close to the sea and have her own little shack were her life goals back then. So simple. Oh, how times had changed.

She absent-mindedly found herself gravitating towards the man on the stepladder and was right – it was Mac.

'Hi, there. I didn't know you owned a beach hut. It's lovely,' she told him before he had a chance to turn around.

'Oh hi, Cassie. It's my uncle Rab's actually. He's been talking about giving it a lick of paint for a while now and with him being... well... whatever it is, I figured I'd help out as a surprise for him.'

Oh, how sweet. He does surprise me. 'That's really kind of you, Mac.'

He shrugged. 'He's been good to me over the years. It's the least I can do. What do you think of the colour?'

'I love it. It's so calming and fresh. I think I would do the shutters in a pale cream though.' She cringed as soon as her words had fallen from her lips. He probably didn't want her opinion.

'Aye, I was thinking the very same thing. Nice contrast.'

Phew! 'Can I help at all?'

He shook his head. 'Nah, thanks though. The only thing I

could do with right now is a coffee. It's a shame the café up the way is closed down. It used to be great when it was open. Did a roaring trade.'

She glanced in the direction of his gaze and agreed it was a shame that the café was all closed up. She could imagine lots of people making good use of the place.

She reached towards him with her insulated mug. 'Here, you can have this. I made it at home, but I'm not too bothered. I can get one back at the cottage and I think you need it more than I do.'

He smiled and climbed down from the ladder. 'Really? Cheers, that's grand.' He flicked open the lid and took a tentative sip to assess the heat of the drink before taking a bigger drink.

Glancing back towards the boarded-up café she asked, 'Has no one expressed an interest in the building then?'

He sighed. 'Sadly, no. I think there's probably too much risk attached these days. Shame though. I'd love to get my hands on it. Although I *cannae* cook much more than beans on toast.'

She smiled at his self-deprecation. 'Oh? I seem to remember you saying that you *could* cook.'

He grinned. 'Aye, I can cook for me but I'm not sure I'd want to subject anyone else to it.'

She laughed and shook her head. 'Oh well. Let's hope that someone decides to take it on, eh?'

His expression changed. 'So long as it's not that bloody Guthrie trying to get his hands on *more* of the village.'

Cassie's hair stood on end. 'What do you mean?'

His eyes widened and he turned back, pretending to examine his painting. 'Oh, erm, nothing. I just meant with him being a developer type, you know?'

She narrowed her eyes. There was something he wasn't saying. 'No, you said getting his hands on *more* of the village.

What parts of the village has he already tried to get his hands on?' Mac fell silent with his back still towards her. 'Mac?'

He placed his paintbrush down on top of the tin of paint and turned to face her with evident reluctance. He huffed the air from his lungs out through puffed cheeks and then gazed out to sea. 'He came to see me. Offered to buy my land.'

Her heart skipped and began to race. 'He did *what*?'

'Don't worry, I said no. My land isn't for sale and I would never sell it to him. You've nothing to worry about.'

She scrambled around her brain trying to make sense of this news. 'But— why? I mean... this isn't the type of place he usually goes for. I presumed his talk of buying around here was just bravado.'

Mac turned his focus on Cassie. 'He's trying to wind you up. He likes to intimidate. But he can't intimidate me.'

She swept the long strands of her hair back from her face and sighed in exasperation. 'I can't believe him. Why can't he just accept that it's over and move on?'

It was a rhetorical question but Mac offered his opinion anyway. 'I'm guessing it's because you're hard to get over, Cassie.'

She gasped silently as he locked his gaze on her. *What the hell do I say in response to that?* Her mind whirred but Mac broke whatever spell had temporarily been cast.

'Anyway, can't a guy get his work done? Get on with you; you've a dog to walk.' He forced a laugh; clearly realising he had made the situation awkward for her.

'Erm... look, I'd like to help with the beach hut. How about I go and get some solar lights and... I don't know... cushions or something? Maybe a nice chair? There's the antique shop on the main street. There was a lovely old deck chair in there. I think it was blue and white stripes, but maybe it could still work.'

Mac's brow crumpled. 'You'd do that?'

'Absolutely. I love a bit of interior design. And to be honest, I've been desperate for a beach hut my whole life so this is probably as close as it gets.'

A handsome smile spread across Mac's bearded face. 'I think he'd be absolutely over the moon if you did that for him. You're so thoughtful. Thank you.'

His eyes glinted and the crinkles at the corners spoke of a real fondness for his uncle – his last remaining relative.

* * *

'So, you're the lassie who lives in Rab's place, eh?' the kindly, white-haired gentleman in the antique shop asked as she handed over the cash for the chair.

She smiled widely. 'That's right, yes. My name's Cassie.' She held out her hand and the gent took it.

'Lovely to finally meet you. I'm Gordon Baird, the owner of this fine establishment. I heard you had a wee spill out in the road a while ago. So apart from that, how are you liking our wee village?'

'Yes, clumsy thing I am. The ankle's almost healed now thankfully, can't say the same for my bruised pride though. But anyway, Coldingham is wonderful. So peaceful and pretty.'

He laughed lightly. 'Aye, but not in the height of summer, let me tell you that. So you're going to be sitting out in your garden now, eh?' He nodded to the chair.

'Ah, this is actually a gift for someone. But I can't tell as it's part of a secret.'

He tapped his nose. 'Fair's fair. Well I hope the recipient likes it. Now do you want me to carry it out for you? We don't want any more trouble with that ankle.'

'Oh no, it's fine honestly. It's only across the way. But thank you. Lovely to meet you.'

'And you too. Bye just now.'

She tucked the folded chair under her arm and made her way home. She had already been in to Dunbar and purchased some beach-themed cushions, fairy lights and a couple of seat pads for the little bistro set she spotted inside the hut. A buzz of excitement travelled through her veins at the thought of helping Mac to surprise his beloved uncle.

* * *

The surprise was in full force. Cassie had met Mac at the beach hut which he'd finished painting and she handed over the things she had bought. Mac put up the solar fairy lights and Cassie placed the cushions on the chairs and a glass jar with some wild flowers on the table. The deck chair was placed aptly on the front decking and when they had finished they stepped back to admire their handiwork.

Mac folded his arms across his chest as he stood beside Cassie. 'What a team we make, eh? Look at that. It's like something *oot* a magazine. Rab's going to think we replaced his old hut with a new one when he sees this.'

He was right. And it looked as magical as she had hoped. The extra solar lights had been placed inside with the solar panel fed through a gap in the wood and attached to the roof so they would illuminate as the sun descended. She had also brought some little battery candles from home to finish the place off. It looked like somewhere you'd find a couple in love having a cosy romantic evening.

'Right, you stay here and hide and I'll go get him. The sun's going down so it's perfect timing. Won't be long,' Mac told her as he jogged towards the slope that stretched away from the beach.

* * *

Cassie sat on the sand and waited, watching the sky going through a rainbow transition as the sun began to set.

Within half an hour she glanced to her right and saw Mac leading his uncle towards the hut. He had a hand held over his uncle's eyes and a huge grin on his face. She couldn't tell who was more excited, Mac or the man whose surprise this was.

'No peeking, Uncle, we're nearly there. Just mind your step,' Mac said as Cassie stood ready for the reveal, butterflies flitting around inside her.

'What are you up to, lad? You've been gone all bloody day. I knew you were up to something. I just knew it. You've not bought me a surfboard, have you? If you have, you've wasted your money. I've told you I'm no interested in surfing, son,' Rab insisted as they arrived.

'*Haud yer weesht,* Rab, eh? Now... open your eyes.' He lowered his hand from his uncle's face. 'Tadaaaa!'

Rab's jaw fell open and he placed both hands on the side of his face. Cassie's eyes welled with tears as she watched the same happen to the older man. The beach hut was completely trans-formed and just as they had hoped, the fairy lights had all illu-minated in perfect timing. It looked wonderful. Enchanting even.

Rab shook his head. 'What the...? I... oh my word... I can't even...'

Mac laughed and put his arm around his uncle's shoulders, kissing the side of his head. 'We wanted to do something special for you, Uncle Rab. Do you like it?' His voice trembled as he spoke and this triggered an overspill of tears from Cassie's eyes.

'Like it? It's... it's bloody wonderful, son. You've done me proud. Both of you.' He wiped his eyes and shook his head. 'Me and your dad used to come here with your granny and papa. We'd spend hours playing on the beach whilst they sat here reading the papers. Your granny used to pack us a picnic even though we only lived up in the village.' He laughed lightly at the memories, his eyes filled with affection for his passed parents. 'It was better to have a picnic down here than go home. Then your mum and dad used to bring you here when you were wee. I've so many happy memories of being here with you all. You in your swimming trunks chasing your mum wi' seaweed. Your dad trying to teach you to play Frisbee. Where does the time go, eh? I've been meaning to do some work on it. I can't thank you enough, son. It's beautiful. Absolutely beautiful. Your granny and papa would be overjoyed and so would your mum and dad. And Cassie, bless your heart. You're a lovely lass. And I appreciate this more than you know.' His voice cracked and he pulled first his nephew in for a hug and then Cassie who tried to wipe away the relentless tears now cascading down her face.

28

Coldingham was feeling more and more like home as the days passed. All thoughts of leaving and moving somewhere else were pushed to the back of her mind. She had Sally to chat with and they had become quite close since Sally hosted her and Mac for dinner. She had shared coffee and cake with Gordon from the antiques shop who turned out to be a novelist in his spare time. And she and Mac had settled into a nice routine of platonic friendship – all thoughts of kisses long forgotten. All was right with the world.

Although it was Saturday she was sitting at her laptop reading Gordon's latest historical fiction and had been completely sucked into the plot about the Border Reivers and their antics. There was a knock on her door and she glanced at the clock as Cliff skipped about barking excitedly at the prospect of visitors. Mac wasn't due for another hour. He had finally managed to convince her it was time for her second surfing lesson. She was a combination of terrified and excited about the prospect of actually getting out on the board this time. She stood from her seat and went to open the door. But when she did she sighed heavily. Seth stood there in jeans and a sweater, looking casual and handsome. His square jaw line was graced with a hint of stubble. His hands were behind his back and he smiled when he saw her.

'Hey. Sorry to turn up unannounced. I just thought it might be nice to see you. I was right. You look radiant, darling. Oh... I brought you these.' He held out the huge bouquet of roses he had been secreting behind his back. 'I know how you love old-fashioned flowers.'

How could a flower be old-fashioned, she wondered. 'Seth, why are you here?'

'I was just tying up some business in the area and thought I would come and take you for lunch.'

'I'm not free. I have plans.' The elderly couple who lived further down the lane passed by and waved at her. She waved back and smiled. *Such lovely people.*

He sighed and clenched his jaw as he glanced over his shoulder. 'Are you going to make me stand out here like some door-to-door salesman?'

'You can come in for five minutes, Seth, but that's it. Whatever you have planned is pointless. I've told you I don't know how many times now that we're through.'

She reluctantly stepped aside and he walked into the kitchen and as he glanced around in the same displeased way as the last time he said, 'Vina says you like me looking more casual and unshaven. So I thought I would come and show you that *one* of us is making an effort to get things back on track.'

She snorted with incredulity. 'I don't think I have any need to make any effort to get something back on track that's permanently derailed, Seth. Look, just go.'

'Aren't you interested to know why I'm in the area? What business I'm finalising?'

She shook her head. 'Not really.'

'That bit on the side of yours is interested in selling his plot. He's demanding three times the market value. Cheeky swine. But I figured it's worth it. I can build us our dream home seeing as you seem to love it here so much.'

Her skin prickled. She was pretty sure that Mac was willing to do no such thing. But she was equally worried about why Seth was pushing it. 'He's not my *bit on the side*. He's my friend. Not that it's any of your business. Look, you need to go. You can take the flowers too. Give them to your mother. Or Vina. Or, hey, maybe give them to your bit on the side, hmm? I'm sure Pippa will be over the moon.'

Ignoring the mention of his dalliance he sighed. 'She misses you. They both do. Neither can believe you're dragging this whole thing out. But I've told them I'll do whatever it takes, Cassie. You belong with me. You'll realise that soon.'

A shiver of unease travelled her spine. Was he having some sort of mental breakdown? Was he delusional? She knew Vina's feelings on their collapsed relationship as she was in constant contact by text message from wherever Harry had whisked her off to. She had expressed concern again over her brother's strange behaviour and had made it clear that even their mother was beginning to worry and had tried to fix him up with no end of eligible young women who were from his family's own circles. But he would hear none of it. According to Vina he was constantly talking as if things were normal between them. They were anything but! And the more she looked at him standing in her home with a wild look in his eyes, the more she questioned her own sanity for allowing him in.

'Please, Seth, just go. There's nothing between us any more. I just want you to carrying on with your life and let me carry on with mine.'

He stepped closer to her until she was backed against the kitchen work surface and she swallowed hard, wishing that Mac would turn up in that inimitable way he had to save the day. 'Seth... don't.'

He reached up and cupped her cheek in his palm. 'We'll be together soon, poppet. Just you and me. No interruptions. Nothing to stand between us. You'll see.' He leaned closer and she clenched her eyes closed and turned her face away, forcing the inevitable kiss to land wetly on her cheek.

Her stomach roiled with a combination of fear and repulsion. And in a low voice she whispered, 'Either you move or I'll kick you in your family jewels.'

'I'd choose the former if I were you. She's a feisty one that lassie,' came a voice from over by the door.

Seth stepped away and turned to see who the intruder was. 'And who might you be?' he growled.

'Rab Mackenzie. This here is my house and I'd appreciate it if you'd get out right now. The lady asked nicely, but I'm not so polite.'

Cassie's heart pounded in her chest and gratitude swelled from deep within her. She wanted to hug Rab and thank him for saving her from this deluded idiot.

Seth sniggered. 'I was just about to leave so there's no need to get your incontinence pants in a knot, old man.' He turned back to face Cassie with a strange hunger visible in his stare. 'I'll see you soon, darling. Don't forget me, hmm?' *The chance would be a fine thing*, Cassie thought.

The unwelcome guest walked away and passed Rab without so much as a second glance. Cassie breathed a sigh of relief.

'I'm guessing he was the ex that Mac told me about?' Rab said as he watched Seth leaving.

Cassie nodded and rubbed her hands over her face. 'He can't keep turning up like that. It's not fair. He's scaring me.'

'If he does it again you need to go to the police and get a restraining order. He's got a slate loose that one.'

'Thank you so much for turning up when you did. It seems to be a habit of mine now, being rescued by your family.'

He smiled. 'Aye well, you're becoming like family anyway so we're just looking out for our own.'

Cassie's eyes welled with tears. 'That's so sweet, Rab.'

He walked into the kitchen, closer to where she stood. 'I should apologise though, I don't make a habit of just walking in on my tenants. I just recognised the chauffeur-driven car from Mac's description and I got worried.'

Cassie held up her hands. 'Oh gosh, don't apologise. I'm so grateful.'

His cheeks tinged with a little pink and in that moment she saw the striking family resemblance between Rab and his nephew. He cleared his throat. 'Anyway, I came to say that dinner is at the beach hut tonight. It's a thank you on me. Wear something warm and be there for eight, okay?'

She grinned. 'Ooh, that sounds lovely. Thank you. I'll definitely be there.'

29

MAC

Standing before the tiny mirror in the caravan's bathroom, Mac ran his fingers through his shaggy hair and examined his beard, which was probably too long now really. He shrugged, figuring it was only dinner with his uncle. He pulled on his jeans and a long-sleeved T-shirt, grabbed his fleece hoodie and left the van just before eight.

The sky was a stunning array of purples and oranges and there was a nip to the air, but he was used to being out on the surf in winter so it didn't bother him – in fact, it made him feel alive and vital. Some of his surfing buddies were just leaving the beach with boards tucked under their arms, their jovial chatter carrying on the breeze.

One of the group spotted him and waved. 'Hey, Mac. Where've you been, mate? Not seen you for ages. Got a new woman?' Jack McMurray asked as he walked towards him on the slope.

Mac reached out and gripped the offered hand, shaking it vigorously. 'Hi, mate. Nah. Just been busy, you know? Had a few lessons down here but been helping Rab out too. He's been a wee bit off it lately.'

'Oh no, I hope he's on the mend now? Look, the rest of us are having a gathering here next Saturday night. Beers and a bonfire – the usual. You'd better make it. Nine sharp, buddy.' Jack slapped him on the back and the rest of the group voiced their agreement.

Mac grinned, liking the sound of a beach party. 'Sounds good. All being well, I'll be there. Laters, guys.' He waved as the group carried on in the opposite direction to his destination.

As he stepped onto the beach and looked to his left he caught sight of the fairy lights illuminated around the hut. It looked like something out of a romance movie. Not that that was a bad thing, but he *was* having dinner with a sixty-two-year-old man, not some blonde bombshell.

As he approached he saw that the door was open and someone was inside, candles flickered in the dim light of the evening. In the amber glow he could see it wasn't Rab sitting there after all. The closer he got he recognised the petite blonde. *Cassie? He invited her too? Well, I suppose she did help with the hut and he thinks highly of her.*

She looked pretty in her chunky Aran sweater and scarf with cartoon dogs printed on it. Her hair was loose and fell in soft waves around her shoulders. He tried to stop noticing things like that about her and instead cleared his throat, gruffly asking, 'Hi, Cassie. Where's my uncle?' He sat down opposite her at the little bistro table.

She cringed. 'I... erm... think we've been set up.'

He shook his head as he glanced out the door behind him for signs of Rab. 'What do you mean?'

'Well, when I arrived a few minutes ago, I found this card and these pizza boxes.' She gestured to the items on the table that he hadn't noticed until now. 'Oh, and a bottle of fizz chilling in a sand castle bucket full of ice.' She handed the card over to Mac.

'Sand castle bucket? Original.' He frowned as he slipped the card from its envelope. He opened it and squinted to read:

Mac and Cassie,

    You made my day by doing the hut. But I think you should enjoy it too. So I arranged for some pizzas and wine to be delivered. Consider this a thank you from me and a chance for you to get to know each other a bit better.

    Enjoy! Rab

Mac chuckled and shook his head. 'The bloody cheeky... Hey, are you okay with this? We can just call it off if you prefer?'

Cassie feigned horror. 'And waste good pizza and wine? *No way*. Get pouring, mister.'

He reached over to the side shelf and picked up the bucket and the two glasses that Rab had left there. 'I had nothing to do with this, just so you know.'

'Mac, I didn't think *you* planned it. You don't strike me as the romantic evening type.'

Affronted by her comments Mac scowled. 'Hey, I can be very romantic, actually.'

'Okay, so what's the most romantic thing you've ever done for a woman?' She held her glass out as Mac fired the cork from the bottle out onto the sand.

He poured the bubbling liquid in to the two glasses. 'I once had a sea glass necklace made for my mum. And I was only eight. Admittedly my uncle Rab helped but...'

She pursed her lips. 'As sweet as that is, your mum doesn't

count when it comes to romantic gestures, you dufus.' She laughed.

He fell silent for a while, remembering back to Sally's words at the dinner party, '*You've had plenty of opportunity. You're just far too picky.*' He huffed. 'Okay, so I've never really had a serious girlfriend. But that doesn't mean I don't have romantic *ideas*.'

Cassie gasped. 'You've never had a serious girlfriend? Really?'

He scrubbed at his beard. 'I've just never... I don't know... met anyone I wanted to put that much effort in with. I want something special. Not some throwaway fling. I want what my folks had. Something real, you know?'

Her gaze softened and the flickering flames of the candles reflected in her eyes. 'I totally understand that.'

He sat up straighter. 'I'm not a virgin though. Don't be thinking that.' He took a huge gulp of his drink and almost choked on his own blunt words and the bubbles.

She burst out laughing. 'I never even asked!'

'Aye well, I don't want any rumours starting.' He grinned.

'Oh, is that what you think of me then? That I'm now the local rumour mill?'

He laughed too. 'Well, you *do* go for coffee at the antiques shop. And Gordon *is* the biggest gossip of them all.' He opened the boxes of pizza and the smell of melted cheese and herbs wafted through the air causing his stomach to growl. 'Bloody hell! These smell amazing.'

Cassie reached across and picked up the paper plates and napkins left in the hut by Rab, before grabbing a slice from the box. 'You're so right.'

Mac paused with his slice halfway to his mouth and tilted his head. 'About the pizza or Gordon?'

She tried not to laugh but failed. 'Both.'

Once their laughter had subsided they sat in silence for a while just munching, drinking and enjoying the sound of the waves swooshing towards the sand. It was a comfortable, companionable silence and Mac realised how easy Cassie was to just *be* with. Maybe this friends lark was a good thing after all.

'What was it that drew you to Seth? If that's not being too nosy?' Mac eventually asked, intrigued to know the truth.

She sighed and placed her pizza back on its plate and looked thoughtful for a moment. 'I think it was the fact that he was so totally different to me. I was timid and quite shy. A bit of a loner as well as being clumsy. Whereas, he was so confident and knew exactly what he wanted. And he tends to get what he wants too.'

Mac huffed. 'Aye, I remember him saying something similar about my land. Shame he's finally wrong.'

'Yes, he can be very demanding. And to be honest I was so flattered that someone like him could like someone like me. I just didn't seem his type.'

'So you weren't pretentious and snobby, it's not a bad thing, Cassie.'

'I didn't see that about him back then. And honestly, he did have a sweet side. Not many people saw that aspect of him and for a while I felt very privileged to be someone who did. I guess he became arrogant though.'

Mac leaned forward and fixed her with a determined gaze. 'My guess is he was always arrogant and you were just blinded by love.'

She smiled softly. 'You're probably right. I still can't believe he thinks I'll go back to him. Did Rab tell you what happened this morning?'

He nodded slowly and pursed his lips. 'Aye. I'm glad my uncle showed up when he did.'

'Me too. I'm seeing a side to Seth now that I wish I wasn't privy to. To be honest he's… *scaring* me.'

Mac reached across the table and placed his hand over Cassie's. 'We won't let him harm you. You have my word on that. Just ask and I'll be there, Cassie. I mean it. Any time of day. Just call me and I'll literally run to your house if I have to. I won't have someone like him scaring my friend. I won't have it.'

'Thank you,' she whispered. 'I really appreciate that.'

Realising his hand was still on top of hers he quickly pulled it back and sat up again. 'Aye well, we don't need that kind of arrogant shit coming around here and spoiling the place,' he said, trying not to sound like he had any feelings other than neighbourly ones for her. He knew he had failed.

* * *

At the end of the evening, Mac walked Cassie back up to Rose Brae. She was still limping a little, but didn't complain about the pain she must have been in. He presumed she'd refuse a piggyback so just kept a watchful eye on her for any winces.

'Thanks for walking me home, Mac, I really appreciate it.'

'I really miss the days when you called me Tiger.' He chuckled.

She rolled her eyes. 'I can't help it if you have an impossible to pronounce name.'

'Guilty as charged. Well, actually my folks were.'

'Well, I suppose it's better than being the same as everyone else, eh?'

'Aye, there is that.' They arrived at the gate. 'Well, I hope you've had a nice evening. Regardless of the fact that Rab set us up. He's keen to marry me off and he really likes you so I guess he put two and two together and made five, eh?'

'It's been a lovely evening. And I feel I know you better now. You're a good friend, Tiger.' She punched his arm lightly.

'Assault! Did anyone see that?' He grinned as he looked around him and pointed at Cassie.

She giggled and placed a finger over her lips. 'Shh, you'll wake the neighbours.'

He waved his hand dismissively. 'Nah, they all know me of old.'

Cassie looked thoughtful for a moment. 'It must be nice to know that you really belong somewhere.' She stared wistfully at nothing in particular.

He reached out and squeezed her arm, hoping that it came across as a friendly gesture. 'Well you should know, eh?'

She turned her attention back to him, locking her gaze on his. 'How's that?'

'Cassie, you belong *here*. You have from day one. You just have to realise what everyone else here already knows. Goodnight.' He turned to walk away.

'Goodnight,' she called after him.

30

CASSIE

Cassie lay in bed replaying the night before in her mind and giggling at the best bits. It had been such fun and she had found herself relaxing and thoroughly enjoying Mac's company. It was a little sad that she wasn't willing to give her heart to anyone again because not only was Mac fun to be around but he was pretty gorgeous too. She had found herself transfixed on his face as he enthused about all manner of subjects. His eyes had that sparkle that had somehow been missing from Seth's although she had never realised that until last night. Mac's teeth weren't straight but they wouldn't suit him if they were. And his mop of unruly hair just added to that 'boy-next-door' charm that had begun to grow on her. He was the total opposite to Seth in every conceivable way, which was a very good thing.

Mac's wicked sense of humour had her in hysterics to the point where she had snorted fizzy wine out of her nose on one occasion, something he had found highly amusing. They had covered so many different topics and she felt as though Rab's mission had certainly been accomplished. She definitely knew Mac – or Tiger as he'd now become known to her – much better, which meant she understood him now more than she had before. His lack of tact was something he had apparently inherited from his dad who sounded like a hilariously funny guy – she was sad that she wouldn't get to meet him.

His mother was just beautiful. Mac had shown her a photo he kept in his wallet. She'd had auburn hair that fell in long waves and her green eyes were friendly, her expression warm. Sure enough around her neck had hung the little piece of green sea glass on a silver chain, commissioned for her by her doting son. He had a distant look of melancholy when he spoke of his parents and it was clear that they had been an incredibly close-knit family. She knew of the sadness of losing a parent but in a way, was grateful to not have the vivid memories that plagued poor Mac. She could only listen and reach out to offer his arm a gentle squeeze when he became emotional. Although he quickly changed the subject and began to bombard her with questions about her job – *classic deflection*, she had thought.

She climbed out of bed and tested her ankle as she had done every morning since it had started to feel better. Today was evidently a very good day – perhaps laughter was a good healer after all, and there had been plenty of it the night before.

Cliff was waiting in the kitchen for her when she had showered and dressed; his little tail performing like helicopter blades. She clipped on his lead and set out towards the beach for their morning walk. She had a mountain of work to get through when she arrived back so it was going to have to be a quick one.

As she walked she saw Sally pushing her pram back from the direction she was going in – a look of deep sadness on her face. Her eyes were puffy and red, her face showing all the tell-tale signs of wrought emotion.

As she reached her friend she stopped. 'Hey, Sally. Is everything okay?'

Sally's lip trembled and tears overspilled her eyes. 'Oh gosh, Cassie you won't know yet.'

Cassie shook her head as her heart began to pound at her ribs. 'Know what? What's happened?'

Sally swiped the dampness from her face. 'It's Rab. He's... he's—' She shook her head. 'He's gone.'

Cassie gasped and clutched her chest. 'Gone where? What do you mean? Sally what are you saying?'

Sally threw her arms around Cassie's neck and hugged her hard, mumbling, 'Heart attack. In the night. Tadhg found him in bed this morning.'

Her own heart plummeted to her stomach and her eyes stung with tears. 'Oh God. Poor Mac. Where is he?'

Sally stepped back again and nodded in the direction of Mac's home. 'Derek's at the van with him now. He's in bits, Cassie. I've never seen him like this.'

Cassie wiped at her eyes. 'Do you think he would mind if I went to see him?'

Sally smiled through her sadness. 'I think he needs his friends just now.'

'Th... Thank you. I'll take Cliff home first.'

'Why don't you let me take Cliff? I'm just going to pick up Jack from nursery and he'd love to see him.'

Cassie nodded and handed out the lead towards Sally. 'Thank you. I'll see you later.'

Sally reached out and squeezed her arm before taking hold of the lead. She nodded but didn't speak again.

With apprehension Cassie hurriedly made her way to Mac's caravan. She knew exactly where it was but had, as yet, not made it there and now she was making her first visit. She wished it was under happier circumstances.

The large gate was open slightly as she arrived and she walked through and towards the temporary structure. *She* considered it temporary, but she knew from their conversations that Mac had a completely different viewpoint on the polyurethane and aluminium box he called home.

She could hear subdued conversation as she closed in on the open door and paused. Maybe he wouldn't want her there. They weren't exactly close as such. Although the night at the beach had felt like they'd known each other longer than mere weeks. She sighed, unsure what to do for the best when a figure appeared at the doorway.

'Ah, hi, Cassie. Come to see Tadhg?' Derek's gaze was filled with compassion.

'Yes. Although... maybe he wants to be alone?' She hoped that Derek knew Mac well enough to advise her as she stood twisting her hands nervously before her.

He walked towards her and glanced over his shoulder towards the van before lowering his voice. 'To be honest, I think being alone is that last thing he needs right now. It's hit him pretty hard. He tried to revive Rab but after seeing his body it was clear to me that he'd been gone a few hours. Died in his sleep. Poor Mac. His last remaining relative gone. No... alone is something he *doesn't* need to be right now. I'm only leaving because I have patients booked in. Even if you just go sit with him...' He reached out and patted her arm. 'Thanks for being a good friend to him, Cassie.' He smiled and then made his way towards the gate.

Taking a deep breath, Cassie walked up the steps and into the van. It was surprisingly clean, she thought as she slowly stepped in the direction of the lounge end of the structure, not only was it tidy, but it was bigger than she expected.

Mac sat on the sofa with his head in his hands. 'Cassie? What are you doing here?' he asked as she approached.

'I... I wanted to check on you. I heard about Rab.' Her voice trembled as she spoke. 'I'm *so* sorry, Mac. I really am.'

He lifted his head and she had to fight a gasp. He looked dreadful. His eyes were bloodshot and rimmed with red, his face was pale and his hair was a dishevelled mess.

He stared blankly as if in a trance. 'I tried to revive him,' he whispered. 'I did all the things you're supposed to do... but... I couldn't save him. I couldn't bring him around.' He gritted his teeth and lifted his shaking hands to tug at his hair. 'I'm fucking *useless*.'

Cassie rushed to his side and gripped his arm. 'Hey, stop that. You're not useless at all. Do you hear me? You tried your best. You did everything you could but he was already gone, Mac. It wasn't your fault.'

He shook his head. 'If I'd been there, Cassie. If I'd gone around sooner...'

She spoke softly, 'It wouldn't have made any difference. *Please* stop blaming yourself.'

He scrunched his brow and stared at nothing again. 'I knew something was wrong as soon as I walked into his house. Everything was still... you know? Lifeless. He lights a fire first thing in the morning no matter what the weather's like. There wasn't one. I think I knew then...' He cleared his throat and shook his head. 'I called out to him, "Come on, you lazy beggar! You've not even got the coffee on." But there was no answer. I figured he might not have heard me so I jogged up the stairs shouting to him again. Then I spotted his bedroom door was ajar and he was still in bed.

I... I tried to rouse him again but when I went to shake him he was... so cold.' He lifted his face and met Cassie's gaze with his own pain-filled expression. 'I knew he'd been ill with him going up to the hospital a couple times but... I had no idea it was so serious. I should've known. Why didn't he tell me? I should've figured it out. I'm so *stupid.* There were heart pills by his bed. Derek says it was a heart attack that killed him. But if I'd have known. If he'd told me... maybe...' His anger and frustration at himself was evident in his self-deprecating tone but he let his words trail off.

'Mac, you couldn't have helped his condition. He probably didn't want to worry you. Just being there for him was all you could do and you did that so, *so* much. It was clear to everyone how much you loved him and how much he loved you back.'

He closed his eyes and swallowed hard. 'He was like my dad, Cassie. He was my best friend. We looked out for each other. Who's going to look out for me now? I don't *have* anyone else.'

Her heart ached for him and she felt tears slip from her own eyes but made no effort to wipe them away. 'You have Sally and Derek. You have every single person in this village. You will *not* be alone, Mac. And... and for what it's worth you have *me.*'

A pained sob left his chest and he crumpled forward as if he didn't have the strength to hold himself up any longer. She pulled him so his head rested in her lap and he clung onto her for dear life.

She closed her eyes and bowed her head as she stroked his hair and let him cry. This poor man who had lost everyone he loved to tragedy was going to have a battle on his hands to get through this, but Cassie was determined to make sure he didn't have to face the future alone.

31

Cassie eventually left Mac's van when two of his surfing buddies arrived with beer. They engulfed him in hugs and Cassie felt a sense of relief that he wasn't going to be alone all night. She walked towards the door and turned back one last time to see him lift his chin and mouth the words '*Thank you*' in her direction. She smiled and nodded before leaving him in the care of his friends.

They had sat in silent contemplation for most of the time she had been there apart from when she had insisted on making him a drink and a sandwich, which he had reluctantly consumed. Mac had talked a little about Rab and Cassie had simply been a willing ear, laughing at some of the stories and hugging Mac again when his emotions got the better of him.

She hadn't got any work done at all but in the great scheme of things it didn't matter. She couldn't focus after eventually arriving home from having a coffee at Sally's and collecting Cliff and so decided to open a bottle of wine and light the fire. She stared at the flames for a while as they danced up towards the chimney and licked around the logs that she had placed in

there; the only audible sounds were the snoring of her Border
Terrier and the crackling of the wood as it expanded with the
heat.

She walked over to her bookshelf and pulled out the photo
album that her dad had compiled for her when she was
younger. It contained every photograph that had ever been
taken of her with her mum. Having only been three years old
when her mother passed away, all she knew of her were the
stories and images provided by her dad. Any memories she
managed to conjure up herself were fuzzy and nothing exact –
maybe a smell, or a sound, a piece of music, a taste or a familiar
feeling that she couldn't quite grasp. But when they occurred
she latched onto them for as long as possible.

Flicking through the photographs now, she could understand – to a certain extent – the pain Mac was going through
and she too mourned the loss of the special and kind man
who she had grown very fond of since her arrival in
Coldingham.

The following morning was dull, which matched the cloud of
melancholy that had descended over her since she had heard
about Rab's death. She took Cliff for a walk and stopped by the
shop to collect a tub of hot chocolate powder. It felt like hot
chocolate weather and the comforting taste of melting marshmallows was bound to help – it always had when she'd been
a kid.

Once she was ensconced back in her cosy home, hot chocolate made and the fire roaring, she set to work on the tasks she
hadn't had a chance to complete the day before. She had been
working for around three hours when there was a knock at her

front door. Cliff was too comfortable in his spot in front of the fire to even bother raising his head.

She opened the door to find a pale-faced Mac standing there. The hood on his jacket was pulled up to hide most of his face but she could see that he hadn't slept much.

'Hi, Mac. Come on in.' She stepped aside and he walked by her and into the cottage. 'Do you fancy a hot chocolate with marshmallows?'

He flipped his hood down and shook his head. 'Oh... no, no it's fine. I won't keep you. I know you're busy. I just came with some news.'

She nodded. 'Okay, well come and sit by the fire.'

They walked over the lounge area and both sat, side by side on the couch. Cliff immediately leapt onto Mac's lap and Mac began to scratch the dog's offered belly. 'I... erm... I found a letter amongst my uncle's things. It was right at the top of his drawer. He can have only written it a couple of weeks ago.'

Cassie scrunched her brow. 'Oh? What was it about?'

He swallowed hard and rubbed his eyes. 'The... erm... the beach hut.'

She was intrigued as to why it had anything to do with her. 'Oh, right. What did it say?'

'He wants us to share it. Part-ownership I mean. You and me.'

She gasped and covered her mouth with her hand. 'What? But... but he hardly knew me.'

Mac smiled. 'Aye well, he knows how you've always wanted one.'

She shook her head. 'But how did he know that? I never told him.'

'Nah, but I did. And he knows how hard they are to come by so he wants us to get the use out of it. He thought the world of you, Cassie. I know you hadn't known him long but you made an impression. He doesn't openly... *didn't* openly take to people often but you... he liked you.'

Her lip trembled and her eyes blurred with tears. 'I don't know what to say. I can't accept such a big gift, Mac. It wouldn't feel right. It should be yours.'

Mac turned to face her on the couch and took her hand. 'Look, Cassie, Rab was quite insistent in his letter. Half-owner-ship each. He's added it in to his will too to make it official. As he's gone to so much trouble his wishes should be granted, don't you think? And anyway, I'm more than happy to share it with you. You helped me to get it looking just right so it's only fair. And I know how much you've always wanted one. I remember your face when you told me that. So now Rab is granting that wish.' He shrugged as he spoke so matter-of-factly like it was a done deal.

How could she refuse now? 'But what if I leave Coldingham? I never said this was permanent.'

'Well, maybe now you should seriously consider that. You fit in here, Cassie. It's your home. I own the cottage now and I have no intention of making you leave. I don't *want* you to. I like you being here.' He scrunched his brow and cleared his throat. 'As my friend I mean.'

She wiped the escaped tears from her flushed cheeks and smiled. 'I'll give it some thought. And... thank you so much. I honestly don't know what to say.'

He nodded curtly. 'Aye well, just don't go painting it pink and filling it with flowery shit, okay?'

She giggled. 'I will be sure to consult you before I purchase anything flowery for the hut.'

'And pink. Remember? No pink.'

'Yes, Mac. No flowers and no pink. Noted.'

He gestured to Cliff who reluctantly jumped down and he stood. 'Right, well, I'll be off then. I just wanted you to know... about the hut I mean. Oh, and the funeral is next Thursday at the priory. You're obviously invited. And... I'd really like it if you'd come.' His voice trembled as he finished off his sentence but he cleared his throat, evidently determined not to cry and Cassie stood to hug him.

'Of course I'll be there, Mac.' He hugged her back and she told him, 'You'll be fine, you know, Mac.'

He pushed away from her and quickly straightened up. 'Yeah... yeah. Right. See you later.' He raised his hand in a swift wave, pulled up his hood and left as quickly as he could.

32

MAC

Mac stood at the door of the priory as people left the building in solemn silence. He shook so many hands he lost count. Not only did the fact make him sad, but it simultaneously lifted him up knowing that so many people had cared for Rab.

The funeral had been an emotional event for the most part but Mac had made sure his eulogy encapsulated *everything* good about his guardian, best friend and uncle – including the funny parts too. Like the way he used to get song lyrics completely wrong when singing along to Radio Borders. The example he gave was the one where he had walked in on his uncle singing along to 'Stayin' Alive' by the Bee Gees. The lyric *Rab* sang was something to do with wearing a wig and owning shoes, when clearly that wasn't at *all* what the brothers Gibb had written. Thankfully the congregation found it just as hilarious as Mac had on the day it had happened, and for the first time in a long while he had found himself laughing out loud at the memory.

'Hey, how are you holding up?' Cassie asked as she reached him. She was the last one to leave the church and he was so grateful for her being there.

He shrugged and tried to smile. 'Oh, you know... I think Rab would've laughed at us all sitting there in suits. Especially me. The last time I wore one was Sally and Derek's wedding and he took the piss out of me something chronic.' He shook his head. 'He said I looked like I'd had a collision with a shop window mannequin and our clothes had got mixed up. Do you think he meant that suits don't actually *suit* me?' The low chuckle vibrated through his chest.

Cassie smiled and smoothed his lapels down. 'Oh, I don't know, I think you look very smart.'

He rolled his eyes. 'Oh, yeah. Now I know you're only bloody saying that 'cos you feel sorry for me. The only bloke I know who looks like they were born in a suit is your ex.' Her smile disappeared and he knew he'd said the wrong thing. 'Shit. Me and my big mouth.' He closed his eyes briefly. When he opened them her gaze was fixed on him.

'Oh, don't worry about it. You're right. He looks out of place in anything *but* a suit.' She linked her arm with his. 'Now, everyone else is heading to the New Inn, but I know you aren't that bothered about going. If you like we could go and collect Cliff and go for a walk?'

He had no idea what he had done to deserve a friend like Cassie Montgomery but he sure as hell didn't have a clue what he would have done without her since Rab had died. She had been the bearer of food, the keeper away of visitors, the deliverer of beer and the shoulder he had cried on more than once. He owed her a great debt and he would have to figure out a way to repay her kindness.

'Do you know what, Cassie, that sounds amazing. In fact, I have a bottle of champagne at the van. Maybe we could play some music down in the beach hut and drink a toast to Rab's memory?'

A beautiful, warm smile slowly took over Cassie's face. 'I'd be honoured to do that with you.'

'Awesome. Now let's go so I can get out of this bloody suit. I feel like a penguin.'

They called in at Cassie's to collect Cliff and so that she could change out of her fitted black dress that clung to her curves the way a dress is meant to – Mac inwardly cursed himself for noticing such a thing at his uncle's funeral – and when she came down the stairs she had slipped on jogging pants and a long-sleeved sweater along with a hoodie and a scarf for later. She looked great even in those clothes. And obviously Mac was noticing this as a *friend*, he reminded himself.

They headed off to Mac's van and as they walked he noticed a black car across the road that looked out of place with a bald-headed man at the wheel who he didn't recognise. Perhaps it was someone he had forgotten to invite to the funeral and they had come along to visit the grave and pay their respects. They carried on and Cassie unclipped Cliff's lead so he could run around Mac's huge garden as he loved to do these days. He quickly found a stick that was far too big for him and insisted on dragging it around, growling as he did so. Cassie and Mac watched in amusement for a while.

'Right, I'll go grab that champers and get changed. Feel free to wait inside if you're getting chilly.'

* * *

Cassie

'Come on, Cliff, you daft thing. Let's wait inside,' Cassie called out to the dog as if he understood every word. Amazingly enough he obediently dropped the stick and followed her up the steps into the van.

She walked in and although she purposefully sat at the lounge end, when she glanced to the left she could see into Mac's bedroom where the door had clicked off the latch and fallen open slightly. He had already taken off his jacket and tie and she watched as he unbuttoned his shirt and slipped it from his shoulders. She swallowed hard as she saw the muscles of his back working when he reached up for a coat hanger; his shaggy hair reaching just to the bottom of his neck and flicking out at all angles and she found herself wondering what it would feel like if she ran her hands through it. She had stroked his hair when he had been crying but it had been such a platonic act that she hadn't thought to memorise it. There was no wonder he was so defined – after all he was a very physical man. She felt her heart rate pick up as he bent to slip his black, tailored trousers from his legs. His thick thighs stretching up to his tight...

Oh my God, what the hell is wrong with me? The man is grieving for goodness' sake. The urge to slap herself was almost over-whelming but instead she immediately turned away and trained her focus on Cliff. The crazy terrier was rolling around the floor on his back making silly noises and growling at himself.

'Right, let's go,' Mac's voice pulled her from wherever the hell her lewd mind had descended to moments before she'd started watching Cliff.

She stood decisively and Cliff followed suit. 'Great. Got the bottle?' Mac held up the champagne. 'Glasses.' He lifted his other hand.

'We're good to go,' he told her.

They left the van and headed down the slope to the sand.

Cassie slipped off her shoes, loving the feel of the grains between her toes.

'You really love the beach, don't you?' Mac observed with a smile.

'I do. My dad used to call me Pebble. He used to say I was one in a former life. I don't think there's anywhere I'm happier than by the sea,' she told him wistfully.

'Pebble?'

She felt her cheeks warming. 'Yes, I know it's silly.' She was reminded briefly of Seth's opinion of her father's nickname and the sting of embarrassment caused her to cringe.

Mac shook his head. 'Not at all. I was going to say how cute it was. I can just imagine you running around on the beach with your blonde curls bouncing and your swimming cossie on. But enough about last year...' he chuckled.

Cassie couldn't help but laugh. 'Well, that only makes three of us that think it's cute. Dad used to call me Pebble right up to the year I started dating Seth. But Seth used to tell me it was a ridiculous name to give a grown woman, I think I mentioned it in passing and dad stopped calling me it. I miss it to be honest.'

Mac nudged her shoulder. 'I'll call you Pebble if you call me Tiger.' She lifted her chin and saw him wiggling his eyebrows.

'You're a nutter, you know that?'

He frowned and held his arms out to the sides. 'Well, durrr... All the best folks are. Take Rab for example, he was the life and soul of any party. Could've had any woman he wanted and he wasn't the best-looking bloke in the world. But his sense of humour was what got the ladies falling at his feet.'

'So how come he never married?'

They reached the hut and Mac placed the bottle and glasses down as he took the key from his pocket and unfastened the padlock on the door. 'Ah, well, therein lies a tale. His life was a story of the one who got away, I'm afraid. He met a lassie when he was twenty-one. Fell head over heels in love apparently. They were inseparable.'

They stepped inside the hut and sat at the table. Mac flicked on his phone and attached the little bubble-like speaker. He silently rifled through his albums until he located a tracklist simply titled 'Rab', hit shuffle and the intro to ELO's 'Mr Blue Sky' began.

Mac grinned. 'Rab loved this bloody song. He had it on vinyl and he'd play it and play it. Drove me mad as a kid.' He laughed. 'Funny because it reminds me of him now so I love it too. Sorry, what was I saying?'

Cassie was intrigued to know more about Rab and his *one that got away*. 'You were telling me what happened with Rab and the girl he loved.'

Mac sighed. 'Oh aye. Well, she wanted him to move to Wick with her. That's where her dad was buying a farm. He couldn't bring himself to leave this place. And that was the end of that.'

Cassie furrowed her brow. 'He wouldn't relocate for love then?'

Mac shook his head. 'No. His heart was always here.' He shrugged. 'Leaving just wasn't an option for him.' He leaned forwards and fixed her with an earnest gaze. 'This place... it gets under your skin and it nestles in your heart. You might leave but you'll always long to return,' he told her. 'You'll see what I mean if you ever do decide to go... I just hope you don't.' As if coming out of a trance he straightened up and shook his head. 'Anyway, it's a good thing he didn't leave. After what happened to mum and dad, I guess I would've ended up in the care system or maybe I'd have had to move to Wick if he'd have agreed to have me there. So I was lucky he chose this place. Or that this place chose him.'

She understood exactly what he meant as she peered out of the open door of the beach hut and towards the waves lapping at the shoreline as if they too were desperate to set down roots. She realised in that moment that there really was no reason for her to leave Coldingham. All the things Mac had said were true. It was already under her skin and in her heart.

And as soon as that thought entered her mind she turned to Mac and smiled widely. 'You're right, Mac. I think I do belong here.'

He popped the champagne cork. 'I'll drink to that.'

* * *

The night air was chilled when they locked up the hut. It had been a lovely evening filled with talk of Rab; Mac had shared more memories of his uncle's incorrect song lyrics, jokes and stories. He certainly sounded like a wonderful man who had managed to keep the memory of Mac's parents alive for him.

Cassie was a little tipsy as they walked up the hill but champagne always did that to her. She shivered and pulled her hoodie closer around her body.

'Hey, do you want my hoodie too? You look freezing,' Mac said as they walked back in the light of his phone torch.

She shook her head. 'Oh no, don't worry. The cold will sober me up.'

He draped his arm loosely around her shoulders. 'You can't be drunk, Pebble. You've hardly had anything to drink.'

She smiled at the use of her dad's nickname for her and after the evening they had shared she took the arm around her shoulder as a friendly gesture and didn't ask him to remove it. 'Oh, I *can* be drunk, believe me. I'm a lightweight. You ask any of the girls from my friendship group back in Glasgow and they'll confirm it.'

'Oh aye? When are they coming to visit then?'

She thought about it but didn't answer. His question was the sobering factor she needed. The fact was that apart from Vina, there wasn't really anyone to come to see her. Not now that Pippa was out of her life. Another hint that Seth had been right. Her Glasgow life really had revolved around him and his friends.

They arrived at Mac's gate and Cassie nodded towards the van. 'Look, it's been a rough day. Why don't you just go on in? My place isn't far and I'm capable of walking home myself.'

He shook his head. 'Nope. Rab brought me up to be a gentleman so I'll be walking you right to your door.'

Rab did an amazing job, she thought as they passed by Mac's gate and headed along the road towards Rose Brae. She glanced up as a black car drove by them slowly and she lifted her chin just as the driver became level with her. A balding man in a black suit stared back and nodded as if he knew her and so she smiled. *He must've been one of the mourners at the funeral*, she surmised as he picked up speed and drove away. *Perhaps the night at the New Inn has gone on longer than expected if people are only just leaving.* There were so many people who wanted to celebrate Rab's life. She knew they had all done him proud.

33

MAC

Someone was banging on the door of the van so hard that Mac woke with a start thinking it was coming off its hinges.

'What the fuck?' he yelled as he climbed out of bed and yanked the bedroom door open. He could see the shape of a man through the obscured glass of the main door and when he tugged it open, he clenched his teeth and growled, 'What the fuck are you doing here again?'

Seth Guthrie smiled in that sinister way he had perfected. 'I think you know, Mr Mackenzie. Now I suggest you let me come in so we can discuss business.'

Standing there in his underwear, Mac folded his arms across his chest. 'I told you the last time I *have* no business with you and that fact won't be changing.' He reached for the door and pushed it but Seth, persistent bastard that he was, stopped the door with his hand.

'Things have changed from what I understand, Mackenzie. I hear that you've come into *more* property since last we spoke.'

Mac chucked his chin. 'Oh yeah? And who did you hear that from?'

Seth smiled knowingly. 'Oh, I think you know. Cassie and I are still in touch of course. *Very much* in touch if you get my meaning.' He pulled his lip between his teeth and grinned. Mac wanted to slug him in the jaw. 'And she tells me that she could easily convince you to sell, but I said I could manage that task by myself. Although I know that you're quite partial to my fiancée and her... *assets*.'

Mac curled his lip and snarled. 'Leave her out of this. You haven't been in touch with her. I'd know if you had.'

Seth chuckled and shook his head. 'Oh, you *think* you know her, Mackenzie. But believe me, you really don't. She's quite the vixen – our Cassie. After your little beach rendezvous last night who do you think she was greeted by in her *bed*?'

Anger blazed beneath Mac's skin. *She wouldn't. Would she?* In spite of the fact he wished she *was* his, she wasn't and Mac knew he had no right to be jealous; but if she'd lied to him all along... 'Just go. I'm not selling my land *or* Rab's. So you've had a wasted journey... *again*.'

'Has she told you that your land is the only reason she came here? Has she told you she's a spy for me? Hmm? Has she? Did she tell you we came up with that whole "cheated on" story to make you sympathise? You see, I knew you'd been approached before about selling. And I knew how difficult you could be. So my little poppet offered to help. Clever thing that she is. Although I drew the line at her sleeping with you. I mean, who wants sloppy seconds, eh?' Seth laughed. 'Oh, that's right, you do.' Mac lurched for him and Guthrie staggered back off the step, almost collapsing backwards onto the ground. He managed to right himself at the last minute. 'What's up, Mackenzie? Hit a nerve, have I?'

It was evident in the man's cruel demeanour that he was taking great pleasure in winding him up so Mac grabbed the suited man by the scruff of the neck. 'You're a liar *and* a cheat, Guthrie. I *know* the truth. And I know that it kills you to not have the one thing you want for a change. And guess what? I'm not only talking about my land. I'm talking about Cassie. It kills you that she's making something for herself here. And that you can't control her any more,' he shouted through gritted teeth.

Seth's eyes widened, making him appear insane and he jabbed his finger in Mac's face. 'You are so very wrong. I bet she conned your uncle into giving her the beach hut, eh? She wanted a prize for herself, you see. I thought it was a bit callous, but hey, what my poppet wants my poppet gets. What can you do? The girl has me wound around her little finger. Oh, and did she tell you what other parts she likes me to be wrapped around?'

Mac lost it. He pulled back his clenched fist and flung it forward, connecting to Seth's face with a resounding crack. Blood splattered outwards and covered his chest and he pulled his fist back again, but suddenly he snapped out of his trance-like state and he stared into the wild-eyed, grinning features of the mad man before him and shoved him, releasing his hold on the man's collar. *How the hell was he still grimacing like a crazed lunatic?*

Seth laughed, a loud, head-thrown-back, blood-curdling laugh like some horror movie villain. 'Oh, you've done it now, Mackenzie. You've played right into my hands, my friend. I *will* be pressing charges unless you see sense and seriously consider my offer. I have the best lawyers and you're going to need every penny you can get your hands on.' And with his final threatening words he backed away, still smirking.

Mac's chest heaved and he glanced down at his bloodied chest, shaking. What the hell had come over him? He was the least violent person ever. *What the hell?* Seth Guthrie was right.

He'd played into the bastard's hands. His knuckles began to swell and he staggered back into the van to shower away the remnants of his heinous act of aggression.

* * *

Cassie

'Doesn't anyone knock any more, Cliff?' Cassie asked the little dog who was growling at the front door as it vibrated with the force of whoever was at the other side.

She pulled the door open and gasped. 'What the hell happened to you?'

Seth staggered in through the door and across to the kitchen table where he lowered himself onto a chair. 'That... that *lunatic*...! All I did was call to pay my respects and he attacked me, Cassie. He attacked me for no reason.'

Cassie shook her head in disbelief. 'Mac? No... no you must have provoked him. In fact what the hell are you doing in Coldingham again? You were told he wasn't going to sell.'

He shook his head vigorously. 'No, you're wrong. He'd called the office. He said that now he'd inherited his uncle's property he would be interested in talking. Said he didn't need both places. I asked when would be the best time to call and he said his uncle's funeral was yesterday, so I simply called there to offer my condolences, bury the hatchet and make a fresh start, Cassie. He's obviously grieving, but I mean... there's no excuse for his behaviour. None whatsoever.'

Cassie walked to the sink and soaked some paper kitchen towels in cold water before handing them to Seth. 'Here, do I need to take you to a doctor... or I could call Doctor Cairns to come here if—'

'No, thank you, all I want to do is get the hell out of here. I won't be making *any* kind of deal with a man who behaves in such a preposterous manner. That's *not* how I do business, Cassie. Maybe you should think twice about who you befriend. He's a vicious animal. And vicious animals deserve only one fate.'

Cassie gasped and clutched her chest. 'Hey, stop that. I'm sorry he hit you but you can't say things like that.'

Seth snorted. 'Oh, for goodness' sake, Cassie. I'm talking about *suing* the bastard not having him put down. God, what do you take me for? How could you even think such a thing? Don't you know me at all? After all the time we—' His voice was strained with distress.

Cassie dropped to her knees before him. 'Okay, it was uncalled for. I... I misunderstood. I'm sorry. Now are you sure you're okay? I can't believe he did this to you. He's just not like that. I don't—'

Seth reached out and cupped her face with his blood-spattered hand. 'My sweet poppet. You always did try to see the best in people.' He sighed. 'Please, Cassie. Just come home to me. It's been long enough. Can't you forgive me? I know I made a stupid mistake. But you're all I want,' he whispered. 'You're all I need. I promise you that.' He pulled her closer and the familiar smell of his cologne infiltrated her nostrils; for a moment she was carried away to a time in the past when she adored the man before her; when she would've done anything, *given* anything to him. He lowered his head and gently touched his lips to hers, slipping his hand around her head and forcing her nearer, trying to increase the ardour of the exchange.

She gasped and struggled to get away. 'No! Seth, let go. Stop!' He freed her from his grip and she scrambled to her feet.

'Stop teasing me then!' he shouted. 'I can't cope with the mixed messages, Cassie. It's not fair!'

She shook her head. 'What mixed messages? I told you ages ago that we were over.'

'And yet today you kiss me! There's no wonder I'm confused, Cassie. It's your damn fault. But I should've guessed you'd take his side.'

'That wasn't a kiss. It was... it was a reminiscence. A momentary lapse in my sanity. And it won't be happening again. Regardless of what's happened between you and Mac, you and I are *over*.' Her chest heaved and she felt the conflict roll like a tumult inside of her. *Why had Mac hit Seth? Had it been provocation? Were Seth's words true? Had Mac agreed to sell the land?* She gripped her hair and closed her eyes. 'Please, just leave. And please don't come back, Seth. I need to be left alone now. Enough is enough.' She opened her eyes and fixed him with a determined stare.

Seth rose from the chair and shook his head. 'Maybe you should try telling the same thing to your lover. Unless you want to become his next victim,' he spat the words viciously and threw the wad of bloody tissue into the rubbish bin beside her fridge. With heavy footsteps he walked out, slamming the door hard behind him.

Once Seth was gone Cassie locked the door, walked over to the couch and sat. She lowered her head and heaved a sigh. *When did life get so damned complicated? What did Seth have against Mac? And why the hell had Mac hit Seth?* So many bloody questions that she wanted answers to but didn't at the same time. Maybe staying in Coldingham wasn't the best idea after all. Maybe she needed a completely fresh start somewhere new where no one knew her. Where Seth wouldn't find her and where she wouldn't be confronted with growing feelings and attraction for a man who could potentially be violent.

34

MAC

Sleep evaded Mac in the hours after his altercation with Seth Guthrie. His behaviour had been so out of character that it had completely unnerved him. He was angry for lowering himself to such a despicable level. He had even struggled to look at his own reflection in the bathroom. Rab would've been so ashamed of him and that's what hurt more than anything. Although... surely Rab would've defended Cassie too? But maybe he would have handled it differently. God he wished Rab was here.

Through the night, every noise he heard made him flinch. He was anticipating a visit from the police or a court official to come and issue a subpoena. When nothing happened he still didn't relax, knowing that Guthrie was the type to strike with his venomous revenge when his prey had been lulled into a false sense of security. As misplaced as his revenge was. He had never once told Guthrie that he and Cassie were an item. But then again, he hadn't tried to correct his presumptions.

After a fitful night of dozing and fighting with the duvet, he'd risen early and gone around to Rab's empty house. Walking through the front door for the first time since his uncle's funeral was difficult. He still expected the man to shout through from the lounge for Mac to get the kettle on. But instead he was greeted with an eerie silence and heaviness in his heart when he realised that everything appeared exactly the same as it had been on that awful day. Not that he really thought that things would look different. He just didn't know what to feel or expect if the truth be told. All he knew was that he missed the man more than he could express. There was a hole inside of him now that would take some healing. Rab had helped that healing process so much after his parents' death but *this* time the healing would be down to him. He would have to get through this by himself.

Rab's glasses sat on top of the book he was reading. The book lay on the little side table beside his favourite chair. The familiar, comforting smell of home was still detectable and as he closed his eyes he could imagine Rab walking through from the kitchen with a tray full of sandwiches – his favourite food. A lump formed in Mac's throat as he opened his eyes and walked over to the wall of photographs, proudly displayed for any visitor to see; every one of Mac's achievements was there from school awards to a photo of him holding his Surf Instructors' certificate that he had travelled to the south of England to achieve.

One thing was clear, Rab had been very proud of the boy he considered a son. And not a day went by that the man didn't tell him that. After the tragedy of his parents' deaths Mac could have gone off the rails, become some dropout delinquent, but instead Rab had encouraged him to do something good, something worthwhile. He had never been exceptional academically but he had a good head on his shoulders and with Rab's help he had discovered a talent for surfing and for passing that passion onto others.

As he wandered around the house he had called home for so long he knew that, at some point, he would need to go through all the paperwork and personal possessions. The solicitor already had the most important documents but Mac was going to be faced with a huge decision about the house. Would he move in? Would he sell? A shiver travelled his spine at that last thought – *okay, so I won't be selling*. But still, he would have to address these matters at some point soon. But for now, he needed to clear his head.

He left the house, locked the door and went for a jog along the beach, pounding the sand with heavy footsteps as The LaFontaines' music filled his mind. There was nothing he could do to prepare for the inevitable Seth Guthrie shit storm looming on the horizon. He would simply bide his time and deal with whatever came, *when* it came. At least he knew it would come and that was something. He felt sure that a man like him would seek some kind of revenge. There would be a court case or an attempt at blackmail. He chuckled when he realised his train of thought. *Coldingham, Mac. You teach surfing and live in Coldingham. Blackmail isn't exactly rife around these parts.*

As he jogged, he wondered if Cassie was okay. Had Guthrie visited her after he'd left Mac's? Was any of what the snake had said been true? Surely Cassie wasn't so two-faced? If she was then she deserved an Oscar for her performance because she had certainly reeled him in, hook, line and sinker. Although deep down he knew the truth; that she *had* been hurt by Guthrie and that her story about the bastard's ill treatment of her was bona fide. She wasn't a liar. She wasn't manipulative. He knew it in his heart. She was caring and sweet and funny. And God he had it bad for her.

He stopped and rested his hands on his knees, his breath heaving from his chest and his pulse thrumming a fast rhythm through his veins. Realisation hit him. He'd fallen for her. This aching in his chest, this need to be near her, to check in on her, to help her. This was love.

Shit. That's all I need. She comes with too much baggage. Too many complications. I don't have the energy, he told himself, knowing that his inner monologue was futile. Memories of her face highlighted by the candle flames appeared in his mind. Her smile, her scent and the way she glowed when she talked about her father. She loved fiercely – that one thing was clear – but he knew how damaged she was and that the chances of her giving her heart to *him* were infinitesimally small.

His chest tightened and he placed a hand over his heart. *So this is what it feels like, eh? Un-fucking-requited love. Great.*

* * *

Back home again, he showered and dressed in a T-shirt and board shorts before rifling through the fridge to find something to eat. *I really need to do a food shop*, he thought as he assessed the meagre contents therein and pulled out a plate with leftover pizza on it. He placed the plate down on the table and was about to sit when he lifted his head and spotted Cassie walking in through the gate. Her head was low and her arms were hugged around her body as she walked with purpose. Something was wrong.

She knew about the fight.

Shit. He opened the door and greeted her with a forced smile. 'Hey. To what do I owe the pleasure?' She grimaced and stopped just before the steps up to the van. When she didn't speak he continued, 'Are you coming in? I'm just about to eat some cold pizza but you're welcome to share if you've not eaten.'

She lifted her face but struggled to make eye contact. 'I'm not coming in, Mac. I think we need to talk. Can we go to the beach?'

He kept the smile in place even though he wasn't feeling it any more. 'We can talk here if you like?'

She tightened her arms defensively across her chest. 'No, I think we should go for a walk.'

He nodded, trying to act nonchalant. 'Sure thing. Let me grab my trainers.' He walked back into the van and to his bedroom but left his main door open in the hope that she would come in anyway. She was acting weird and he had a feeling he knew why. Guthrie had got to her with more lies.

Once his shoes were on his feet he stepped out of the van. 'Okay, I'm all yours.' He held his hands out to his sides as if to show he was unarmed. Her face remained expressionless and she set off walking.

He followed and they walked in silence down the slope only *this* silence wasn't like the comfortable ones they had shared in the past. There was an edge of hostility to the air and Mac tried to conjure up something to say to lighten the mood. Words failed him and instead he simply followed Cassie down onto the sand until she came to a halt outside the closed down café. She sat on the small wall that edged the building so he followed suit.

'Cassie, are you okay? You said you wanted to talk but haven't said two words to me since we set off.'

'How did you bruise your knuckles, Mac?'

He glanced down to where the fresh purple tinged his tanned skin. 'I'm guessing you know the answer to that question.'

Still without looking him in the eye she continued, 'Why did you hit him?'

Mac closed his eyes for a moment. How did he tell her all the things Seth had insinuated without making her feel cheap and uncomfortable, even though he knew deep down that none of them were true? 'He said some very cruel and unpleasant things and I lost it.'

She turned to face him now, her face pink with anger. 'Oh, and do you hit *every* person who says things you don't like? Is that the kind of person you are?'

'No, Cassie. You know that's not how I am. But... the things he said—'

'What things? Hmm? What things did he say that were *so bad* you had to punch him in the face?' Her voice rose with every word.

He lowered his gaze to the ground. 'I can't... I don't want to repeat...'

'Whatever, Mac. Bloody hell. *You* messed *him* around. *You* rang *him* to say you'd sell and then when he came to pay his respects and to arrange a time to talk to you about the land at *your* convenience you attacked him.' Her voice trembled and he could hear the disappointment in her words. 'I thought I knew you but clearly I don't. I think it's probably better if I find somewhere else to live. And I think you should stay away from me from now on.' She stood to leave.

Mac laughed without a shred of humour to the sound. 'You just can't let him go, can you? After everything he's done to you, you still can't accept that *he's* a manipulative bastard.' His voice began to mirror Cassie's now as it grew louder. 'I've *never* said I'd sell my land to him. It's just more lies, can't you see that? He's trying to play us off against one another and you've fallen for it. He's winning.'

She scrunched her brow. 'But he said that you... and you hit... he said you attacked him for no reason, Mac.' Her voice was small now as realisation clearly began to dawn on her.

He raised his arms and let them fall to his lap. 'I wanted to spare you the details of what he'd said. But if it's what I need to do then I'll spell it out for you, shall I? If you must know, the things he said were about *you*, Cassie. He insinuated that *you* were trying to sleep with *me* to convince me to sell my land to him. And that would make you a whore, wouldn't it? Something I know you're not. He said that you were his little spy, running between us to pass on information. And that every time you had been with *me* you then went home to shag *him*. *That's* why I hit him. Because I knew it was all lies. Every damn word! Unlike you, I trusted the friendship we have— had. Any doubts I had were so fleeting that I didn't even need to acknowledge them. I knew he was making shit up to try and get a rise out of me. But *you*... you'd choose to take the word of that arrogant, stuck-up, self-centred prick over mine and *that* hurts, Cassie. That breaks my fucking heart. I honestly thought you knew me better. *Really* knew me. Turns out I was wrong. And to think I've gone and fallen for you. What the hell was I thinking? I must be absolutely bloody crazy.'

He pushed himself off the wall and began to walk towards the slope but stopped with his back towards her. 'Oh no. Oh no, no, no! Please no!' He cried as he set off running up the hill.

* * *

Cassie

Still reeling from Mac's admission of his true feelings and the fact that she'd fallen for Seth's lies yet again, she watched in disbelief and confusion as he ran towards the slope screaming 'No!' at the top of his lungs. She stood but was frozen to the spot for a moment, struck dumb. What had gotten into him? Why had he run away like that?

It was then that she lifted her gaze and noticed the plumes of acrid, black smoke billowing into the early afternoon sky from the direction of Mac's land.

35

MAC

When Mac reached his van, he was greeted with the horrible sight of a twisted, gnarled, contorted shell of a building. The cloud of smoke initially disguised an awful truth from him, but a gust of wind caused the cloud to shift sideways and to Mac's horror he could see that Rab's house was also engulfed in flames. He let out a blood-curdling scream and ran out of the gate and around to his uncle's house.

The wailing siren of a fire engine gained volume as it approached and with his T-shirt covering his nose, Mac kicked at the front door. After several kicks it flung open and he tried his best to get inside but the heat was so intense that he couldn't make headway. Every memory of his childhood and his parents lay in that house. The plans for his parents' cottage, every single photograph ever taken of them, it was all in the burning building before him.

He was about to leap inside when strong arms grabbed him from behind. 'Come on, sir, come away. You can't save anything now.' He turned and peered at the uniformed man in breathing apparatus but tried to struggle out of his grip.

'No! I need to get in! You don't understand!'

The fire officer gripped him hard by the shoulders. 'Sir, the building is unsafe, please. You must leave the vicinity. We don't want to lose you as well as the house.'

Another officer appeared and took his arm. 'Come on, Mac,' she shouted above the creaking and cracking sounds of the crumbling building. 'Let's get you back over to your friend. She's worried sick.'

'No! I need to get in! Please!' Mac's strained voice sounded alien to his own ears. Hoarse and croaky. He tried to pull away from the woman but her insistent grip on him wouldn't relent.

A crowd had gathered at the end of the lane, a safe distance from the two burning structures and when he reached Cassie he collapsed into her.

'Oh God, Mac. Are you okay? Please say you're okay?'

He began to cough, hacking and holding his stomach as his lungs fought to pull in air and expel the smoke. He gazed up at the tear-stained faced of his friend. Managing to draw breath enough to gasp out a string of words he told her, 'It's all gone. Everything's gone. I've lost everything.'

His head started to spin and he grasped at his throat. The air felt thick and tasted bitter. A sleepy haze began to settle over him and stars danced before his eyes...

Cassie

Cassie watched in horror as the paramedics worked on Mac. He was placed on a stretcher, an oxygen mask fastened over his face and he was carried into the back of the waiting ambulance.

Sally appeared and grabbed her arm. 'Oh God, Cassie, is he okay? Is Tadhg okay?' she asked as tears soaked her cheeks.

Cassie shook her head. 'I... I don't know. They took him. I—he looked...'

'Come on. Derek will take you to the hospital. I'll stay here and speak to the police.'

Cassie scrunched her brow. 'Police?'

Sally nodded. 'It's just a matter of course that's all. With it being unexplained at this point they said that they need to ask a few questions. Don't worry. I'll deal with them just now. You go follow Tadhg. It would be awful for him to be alone when he wakes up.'

Oh God. What if he doesn't wake up? The thought hit Cassie like a jolt to her solar plexus and she grabbed her stomach as nausea hit.

Sally cupped her cheeks in both hands. 'Hey. I know what you're thinking and he *will* wake up. He'll be fine. Okay? Now go! Derek has the car ready.'

The journey to the hospital couldn't have been worse. They got stuck behind every long-load, every learner driver and every tractor on the road. It was as if all the country's slowest vehicles had descended on the Scottish Borders in one fell swoop. Cassie chewed at her nails, willing the road to clear, praying that everyone would just turn off at the next available exit. But, of course, they didn't.

A painful hour and fifteen minutes later they pulled into the car park and Cassie leapt from the car as soon as it came to a halt. 'Derek, I'm sorry I need to get in there!' she shouted over her shoulder and didn't wait for a response. She felt sure that the doctor would totally understand.

Once inside she paused to catch her breath before

approaching the reception desk. She was pointed through some double doors and into a room filled with curtained cubicles.

She asked a nurse for Mac but the man scrunched his brow. 'Oh, I'm sorry we don't have a Mac here just now,' he informed her, glancing down at his clipboard.

A familiar voice came from behind her. 'Jerry, hi, we're looking for Tadhg Mackenzie. Brought in a short while ago after a house fire.'

The nurse looked up and smiled. 'Hi, Derek. Ah right. Yes, Mr Mackenzie is in cubicle four. Very groggy but doing okay.'

Cassie covered her mouth with her hands and a relieved grunt came from her chest. *Thank goodness he's awake. Thank goodness.*

'Go on, Cassie. It's best not to overcrowd him. You go on in and I'll go see what I can find out.' Derek urged her towards the blue curtains and she nodded.

She slipped in through the fabric and gasped when she saw Mac laying there, oxygen mask still in place, drip connected to the back of his hand, his face dirty and his hair filled with ash and soot. She rushed to his side, desperate to hug him but not knowing if he would appreciate that after their last conversation. So instead she pulled a chair up to the bed and sat.

She took his hand and he opened his eyes. 'Oh... hey, Cassie. You came,' he croaked.

She nodded and tried to smile without bursting into floods of tears. 'Of course I came, Tiger.'

He smiled and his eyes drifted open and closed as if in slow motion. 'Tiger...'

'H-how are you feeling?'

He swallowed and scrunched his brow. 'Sore. My chest hurts. Smoke. I've never smoked a cigarette in my life and I definitely won't be doing so anytime soon,' he slurred.

Cassie giggled and a couple of errant tears escaped the corners of her eyes. 'No, I don't blame you.' She squeezed his hand. 'I'm so sorry this has happened, Mac. After everything you've been through and now this. I just can't believe it.'

He closed his eyes and his bottom lip trembled. He lifted his hand to his face and pressed his fingers into his eye corners but moisture escaped and left clean trails down his otherwise dirt-covered face. 'It's all gone. The fire took hold too fast. I've literally lost everything.'

'But you're still alive, Mac. That's the most important thing. Things can be replaced.'

He rolled his head slowly from side to side. 'No. Not all things can be replaced. My whole life was in that house and van. And it's all gone. I might as well have died too.'

Cassie gritted her teeth and stood over him. 'Stop that. I won't listen to that kind of talk, Mac. You're still surrounded by people who love you and care for you. So everything isn't gone. *We're* all still here. Do you hear me?'

He opened his eyes and gazed up at her. 'I'm sorry. And thank you. And I'm sorry for shouting at you earlier. I wasn't very nice and you didn't deserve that.'

She closed her eyes briefly but then fixed him with an earnest expression. 'No, you were right. I've let Seth Guthrie pull the wool over my eyes far too many times now. It won't be happening again. If I see him again I'll tell him in no uncertain terms where to go and if I need to, I'll get that restraining order. You have my word on that. He's manipulated me for the last time.'

Mac smiled weakly. 'That's good. I'm glad.' He squeezed her hand back. 'He doesn't deserve you.'

'Hmm, well, I don't think anyone deserves what he's done to us. But he's out of my life. For good. Now I'm going to let you get some rest and I'll come back tomorrow. Can I get you anything?'

He rolled his eyes downwards and peered at his dirty, torn clothes. 'I think I could do with some clean clothes. But... but it's all gone up in smoke.'

She shook her head. 'Don't worry about that. I'll call and pick something up from the supermarket in Galashiels. I'm sure I can find something there. In the meantime, what will you do?'

He smiled again and wheezed, 'Oh, I'm sure the hospital will supply me with a fetching arseless gown.'

She burst into laughter. Partly from adrenaline and partly from the relief of hearing him crack a joke. After what he'd been through, he could've been forgiven for losing his sense of humour entirely. But it was so good to know that he hadn't.

She leaned forward and planted a kiss on his head. 'See you tomorrow, Tiger. Don't be a pain in the arse for the nurses.'

'The only arse in pain will be mine, dying of embarrassment when it's out there for everyone to see,' he slurred his words with a grin and started coughing.

Just then a nurse came through the curtain and adjusted his oxygen. 'I think you could do with drinking some water, Mr Mackenzie,' she told him as she helped him to sit and held a plastic cup to his lips.

'You know you really should use paper cups, not plastic. It's better for the environment,' he told the nurse. Cassie smiled, knowing that the Mac she had grown so fond of was still there.

* * *

The following day Cassie made a detour via Galashiels to pick up some things for Mac. She bought underwear along with Star Wars lounge wear for him to sleep in and a pair of grey joggers and a navy-blue hoodie and a pair of trainers for him to wear when they discharged him. She had managed to get his shoe size from the ones on the floor beside his hospital bed and had guessed at the other items, erring on the larger side just in case.

When she arrived at the hospital she was informed that Mac had been moved to a side room on a ward on the second floor so she made her way up in the elevator to locate him. When she arrived outside the room, the door was closed so she knocked and waited for a reply, which came from an unfamiliar voice. She walked in to find two uniformed police officers sitting by Mac's bed. Mac was now free of the oxygen mask but a grave expression and a furrowed brow were what greeted her.

'Okay, Mr Mackenzie. We'll be in touch soon. Especially if we have more news. Thanks for your cooperation.'

Mac nodded. 'Thank you for letting me know. Bye, officers.'

The male and female officer both nodded politely at her as they passed and closed the door again behind them.

Cassie walked over to her friend and smiled. 'That all looked very serious.'

Mac, still frowning tilted his face up towards her but didn't mirror her smile. 'You could say that.'

She was desperate to ask questions but also didn't want to pry. So she decided to tell him what she had bought. 'I got you some clothes to put on for now. There are some undies, joggers and I bought pyjamas for you too. Thought we could try and protect your modesty.' She grinned as she nodded towards the pale blue gown he was now wearing.

He briefly glanced at the shopping bag. 'Yeah. Okay. Thanks. You'll have to tell me what I owe you.'

She shook her head. 'Oh no, it's really no bother. So... how are you feeling? Is your chest any better?'

He fixed his gaze on her once more. 'It was arson.'

She widened her eyes. Had she heard him correctly? 'Sorry? What?' She had automatically presumed an electrical fault in the van had started the fire and that the breeze had spread it to Rab's. But arson? The thought had never crossed her mind.

'The fire. It was deliberate. Someone burned down my van and Rab's house on purpose, Cassie.'

'But...' She shook her head in disbelief. 'Are they sure? I mean who would do—'

'Oh, I think the glass bottles and petrol-soaked rags found at the scene were a bit of a giveaway.' His tone was terse and his jaw clenched.

'Oh my word. That's... I don't...' She lowered herself to one of the chairs beside his bed.

'I think it was Guthrie.'

She gasped. Her heart skipped and pounded at her ribs. That had been her immediate thought as soon as the word arson had fallen from his lips but she had shaken it off. Not willing to believe that the Seth she had loved would stoop so low. But the Seth of late with his sinister behaviour and talk of winning was a totally different case. She shook her head and stared at the waffle pattern of the pale orange blanket covering Mac's legs.

She took a deep breath and raised her chin until her eyes met Mac's. 'I don't think he would do such a thing. He's not capable of such evil. I mean... I know he's become quite horrible but I really don't—'

'You don't think he's *capable*? He's made plenty of threats of revenge. But oh, don't worry, Cassie, he wasn't trying to *kill* me. He made sure I was out which is his one saving grace. All he wanted to do was destroy my *life*. That's *all*. Well, I guess he succeeded, eh? But as you pointed out yesterday *I'm* still here.'

He held out his hands and grimaced. Then he lowered his gaze and sighed. 'I think you should go.'

Her chin trembled. 'Mac, don't do this. Please?'

'Cassie, he's a psycho, a sociopath. I can't begin to comprehend what would make one man do this to another. Just because I wouldn't sell my land? And because of some stupid, misguided delusion that I'd stolen "his woman". I guess he figured if *he* couldn't have either then neither could I. Well, he got what he wanted. And as you pointed out once before, he always does.'

36

Unable to settle, Cassie paced the floor after her visit to the hospital. Mac had been so hostile but could she really blame him? If it wasn't for *her* he would no doubt still have his land *and* caravan – well, that's if his suspicions were founded on truth. She needed to know. She needed to look Seth in the eye and ask him outright if he was responsible for this horrific life-changing event that had affected her friend so drastically. The last thing she wanted to do was to see Seth but it seemed to be the only way to really find out.

Glancing at her watch she realised it was only twelve thirty. It would take her just short of two hours to drive to the city of Glasgow. And there was a good chance he wouldn't even be in his office. But she couldn't sit around waiting and wondering. She had to take action. She grabbed her car keys and clipped Cliff's lead on – hopefully Sally would dog-sit for her and failing that, Gordon was always happy to have him in the shop.

Thankfully Sally was happy to take him and Jack was ecstatic to have his furry friend around again. So once Cliff was happily settled, she hugged Sally.

'I really appreciate this, you know. I owe you.'

Sally smiled. 'It's what friends do. But... is everything okay? I called Mac this morning and he said you'd just left. He sounded... odd. But when I pressed him on the matter he rushed me off the phone, saying the police were there again. Why would they be there again? And now you're dashing off somewhere mysteriously.' She folded her arms across her chest; worry was evident in her furrowed brow.

Cassie sighed. 'It's all a bit complicated just now. I feel... responsible for what Mac's going through.'

Sally shook her head. 'Cassie that's crazy. You were with him when the fire started so how the heck could you be responsible? I don't understand what's going on between you two but I wish you'd just kiss and get on with it.'

'It's not like that. Well... that is... I mean... Look, there's something I need to do. I promised myself I'd find the truth. And that's what I intend to do. That's all I can say just now. I'm sorry. I really need to go now. Is that okay?'

Sally pulled her in to a tight hug. 'Just be careful, okay? I don't like all this cloak and dagger stuff. I can't help feeling that you're putting yourself in the middle of something that you shouldn't.'

'I promise I'll be fine,' Cassie lied and pulled away to head for the door. She waved goodbye before climbing into her car and setting off.

Thankfully the traffic wasn't too bad, although being in the city she had once called home now sent shivers of displeasure down her spine. Everything looked bigger somehow, busier, noisier. The place that had once been her favourite city was now somewhere she no longer belonged nor wanted to be. She made good time, arriving in the city centre at around two thirty. She parked in the multi-storey close to the location of Guthrie

Developments and dashed across the road to the huge, imposingly modern high-rise on Bath Street. With sweating palms and shaking limbs she took the lift to the fourth floor and exited as soon as the door opened.

Marjorie, the long-standing receptionist greeted her with a warm yet confused smile. 'Miss Montgomery, how lovely to see you. B-but you don't have an appointment, do you?'

'No, it's fine, Madge, I'll just go through.' She turned left and headed towards Seth's office.

The receptionist called after her, 'But Miss Montgomery, Mr Guthrie isn't to be disturbed!'

Yeah, well, that's probably 'cause he's disturbed enough already, Cassie thought as she carried on walking. She didn't knock; instead she opened the door and strode inside.

Seth jumped and looked up from the pile of papers on his desk; his eyes widened. 'Cassie? What are you—'

She stomped over and slammed her hands on his desk. 'What the hell have you done? Hmm? I'm presuming it *was* you. Or your associates.'

Seth smiled. 'I'm sure I have no idea what you're talking about, poppet. Would you like a coffee?'

'No, I wouldn't like a bloody coffee. What I'd like is an explanation.' She glanced at his hand, which was bandaged. 'What have you done? *Burned* yourself?' she asked with a tilt of her head.

He glanced at his hand and immediately moved it out of sight as his cheeks flared red. 'I cut myself making dinner. Not that it's any of your business.'

She straightened and folded her arms across her chest. 'Show me.'

He scowled. 'I'll do no such thing. If you've got something to say, Cassandra, just say it.'

'Did you burn down Mac's house?'

Seth smirked. 'I thought Mr Mackenzie lived in a rather delightful *caravan*?'

'Stop being a pedantic shit and answer me. Was it you?'

He leaned back nonchalantly in his huge, black leather swivel chair. 'I assure you I haven't the faintest idea what you're talking about.'

At that moment, the office door opened and a man barged in and blurted in a panicked voice, 'Mr Guthrie, the Coldingham —' The familiar-looking bald-headed man stopped talking as soon as he realised Seth wasn't alone.

Cassie swung around and glared at the man. 'You! *You* were there. In the village. I saw you.' She turned back to face Seth. 'It *was* you, wasn't it? You arranged for Mac's home to be burned down. You couldn't have the land and so you figured neither could he.' She heard the utter disbelief in her own voice and her heart sank. She hadn't wanted it to be true. However, that wasn't because she wanted to believe better of Seth. It was simply because she knew that if it *had* been arranged by him there was a good chance that her friendship with Mac – and everyone else in Coldingham – was ruined. Seth had killed the one good thing that had happened to her since he had cheated on her.

Seth shrugged. 'If it *was* me you couldn't prove it. Not that it was, of course. But I suggest you take your ridiculous, neurotic allegations and leave. Otherwise, I will sue you for defamation.'

She snorted. 'It's not defamation if it's *true*. You sick, evil-minded bastard.' Anger and hate knotted at her insides and she shook more violently now. 'You couldn't just let me leave, could you? You couldn't just let me be happy. You had to destroy my life and that of those I've grown to care about. That's just the kind of vermin you are. Well, I *will* prove it was you, if it's the last thing I do, I *will* make sure you pay for what you've done to that poor innocent man. He didn't deserve this. Your fight, such as it was, was with *me*, not Mac. He's a sweet, kind, wonderful man and you've just ruined his life!' she shouted at the top of her voice, hoping that everyone in the building could hear her.

Seth stood up and slammed his fists on the desk now; rage radiating from his very core and his cheeks bright cerise as though his head may explode. 'He stole you from me! No one takes what's mine! He deserved everything he got and wants to think himself lucky he wasn't *in* the damned place when we torched it!'

Her jaw fell open. He'd just admitted it.

As if realising he had made a colossal mistake he smoothed down his tie and plastered a fake smile on his face. 'That is, when *it* was torched. I mean, I'd like to shake the hand of the genius who did it though. That land is useless to him now. And it will have reduced nicely in price. I might just give him a call with a lower offer.' He sniggered.

'You really *are* sick, aren't you?' she whispered. 'How I ever loved you I'll never know. How I didn't see through you for what you really are is beyond me. But I'm so grateful that I see it now.' She shook her head in disdain and turned to walk towards the office door but the bald man stepped in her way.

He glanced at Seth questioningly. 'Mr Guthrie?'

Seth shook his head. 'Oh, just let her go, Frank. She can't prove anything.'

The man glanced shiftily between Cassie and Seth. 'Erm... that's what I came to see you about, sir. My wallet—'

Seth's eyes widened. 'Do not utter another word,' he told the man through clenched teeth. 'Cassie, you can see yourself out. And for what it's worth... I *did* genuinely love you... at first.'

Cassie shook her head. 'Well, lucky me,' she sneered at the man whom she had adored for so very long and then back to the other man who eventually stepped aside like a dog obeying its master, allowing her to walk out and slam the door behind her.

The moment the office door was closed, adrenaline kicked in and she realised she may very well be in danger now she knew the truth. She ran along the corridor to the elevator, not stopping to say goodbye to Madge. Her heart was almost in her mouth and terror caused her whole body to shake. She glanced back over her shoulder as the elevator opened. Thankfully, she was still alone.

I've got to go to the police. And I need to get there before he sends Frank or someone else to finish me off.

* * *

The interview room at the police station was cold and stark and Cassie tried to convince herself *that* was the reason she was shaking vigorously from head to toe. One of the detectives had gone to get her a cup of sweet tea seeing as she was pale and couldn't quite get her words out when she had arrived at the station.

The man returned and placed the white plastic cup in front of her and she smiled, in spite of the current situation, as she thought of Mac's comment at the hospital. 'So, Miss Montgomery, you think that there may be evidence *at* the scene which proves the involvement of Mr Guthrie?'

Cassie nodded. 'Y-yes. The man... his associate... he hinted as such when I was at his office this afternoon. S-said something about a wallet.'

'You do realise you did a very dangerous thing, don't you, Miss Montgomery? If Mr Guthrie *was* instrumental in the perpetration of the arson attack, you could have put yourself in grave danger by confronting him.'

Oh God, he's right. What the hell was I thinking? I'm an idiot.

The detective leaned forward. 'I have to say though, between you and me, you've got balls.' He grinned. 'There's not many women... or men for that matter, who'd do what you did in pursuit of the truth. Just don't go doing it again. All right?'

She nodded vehemently. 'Don't worry. I most certainly won't.'

She decided to make another attempt to speak to Mac and although she was completely exhausted and felt like all she had done was drive around all day she made the journey to the hospital again. There was around ten minutes left of visiting time and she thought perhaps that was a good thing. Maybe if time was a factor he would listen. She wouldn't mention anything about her detective work though. Mac would no doubt hit the roof if he knew what she'd done.

She nervously walked into his room. He was lying on the top of the sheets, eyes closed and wearing the Star Wars pyjamas she had brought. He looked ridiculously cute and she smiled to herself, feeling a little spark of hope that maybe he didn't hate her after all.

She cleared her throat and he opened his eyes. 'Oh... hi, Pebble. It's good to see you.'

On hearing him use the nickname he'd adopted for her, her eyes began to sting and the urge to throw her arms around him bubbled up from deep inside and almost overwhelmed her. But instead she smiled and nodded – it was all she could manage.

He sat up. 'Oh, hey, come on, don't cry. I'm sorry for how I was earlier. Come here,' he said in a soft voice, which pushed her over the edge.

She rushed to his bedside and into his open arms. 'I'm so sorry, Mac. All this happened because of me. I know you must want me out of your life and I totally understand that. I promise I'll find somewhere else to live. I'm just so sorry,' she sobbed.

He stroked her hair. 'You'll do no such bloody thing. I'm an arse. You're lovely. Can you forgive me?'

She lifted her face and gazed into eyes filled with sincerity. 'There's nothing to forgive, Tiger.'

He grinned and placed a hand on her cheek, wiping away her tears with his thumb. 'Cassie, none of this is your fault. I don't blame you. I really do mean that. It's him. Guthrie. He's a nutter. Neither of us deserves him.'

'You don't... you don't hate me?' she asked weakly.

He shook his head. 'Not in the slightest, Pebble. But... I have something I really need to ask you.'

She nodded, smiling widely and inside a little flutter sparked to life. An errant thought jumped into her mind that took her by surprise. *Yes, you can kiss me.* 'Anything,' she whispered breathlessly.

'Can I move in to Rose Brae when they discharge me? I don't have anywhere else to go.'

Oh. Of course that was it. Silly me. 'Of... of course you can. It's your house after all. I should move out—'

He shook his head and rested his forehead on hers. 'Nah. From now on, it's besties – Pebble and Tiger – against the world, eh?'

A little disappointment tugged inside her but she smiled and nodded. *Besties. Of course...*

37

MAC

Luckily for Mac, Cassie had agreed to collect him from the hospital the day after he asked if he could stay with her. He was keen to leave the smell of disinfectant behind so when she arrived he was ready to go and wearing the clothes she'd bought him – surprised at how perfectly they fit. A flutter of excitement tripped around his belly at the thought of being close to Cassie twenty-four seven. But he had to continually remind himself that it was both a temporary *and* platonic arrangement. He could buy a new caravan once he knew that the site was ready and that the insurance had been dealt with. He would just need to check how long that would actually be.

Cassie smiled nervously as she walked into his room. 'We'll have to stop meeting like this.' She giggled as her cheeks flushed pink.

'Aye, we're one-all for the hospital pick-ups now. Let's try not to need any more, eh? Deal?'

She laughed. 'Deal.'

He was relieved to be leaving the hospital but knew that there was so much to sort out at home – or what was left of it anyway. He'd had a call from the solicitor to tell him there were letters and documents pertaining to his uncle that he needed to collect but he presumed they were just the will copies so didn't rush to make an appointment.

They arrived back at Rose Brae and walked in through the door. It was a peculiar feeling, knowing that it would be his home for a while. Cliff was as excitable as ever to see him and he immediately lowered to the floor to greet the dog properly. Cliff jumped up and licked his face, almost climbing onto his shoulders and Cassie looked on laughing. Once the dog had calmed Mac stood awkwardly wondering what to do now.

Cassie pointed towards the downstairs bedroom. 'I've put clean bedding on in there for you. And you know where everything else is so... treat the place like your own.' Then she cringed. 'Which technically it *is*.'

He nodded and gazed at her with what he hoped came across as sincerity. 'Thank you again, Cassie. I really do appreciate you letting me invade your privacy like this. I promise you won't know I'm here. And I'll pay my way, food-wise, bills and such.'

She shook her head. 'Honestly, it's absolutely fine. Make yourself at home.'

'I'm going to need to take a trip into Gala or Edinburgh at some point. I can't live in the one outfit I have.' He cringed hoping he hadn't caused offence and he smooth down the sweatshirt. 'As much as I love it. You did good. I'm impressed.'

She blushed again and nibbled at her lip, which immediately drew his attention there. 'I'm so glad they fit. I really wasn't sure what sizes to buy so I went for the easiest option.'

He held his arms out to his sides. 'Well, as you can see, they're perfect. Maybe I should get you to do all my clothes shopping.'

She laughed. 'Oh no. I don't want *that* job thanks very much. Once is enough. I'm more adept at buying designer shirts and ties these days. So if you go to a wedding I'm your girl... if you catch my drift.' She tucked her hair behind her ears as her face coloured a stronger shade of pink.

He found her embarrassment endearing. 'I'll bear that in mind. Now, what do you fancy for dinner? Luckily I have my wallet so I can go get us whatever you fancy.'

She tapped her chin and glanced up at the ceiling. 'I think Chinese.'

'Consider it done. I'll just go stick my bag in my room and I'll go pick it up.'

There was a loud banging on the door and Mac's skin prickled. Cassie jumped and turned quickly to face the door. Clearly they both had the same thought.

Guthrie.

'I'll go,' Mac said insistently as he walked towards it. He yanked it open and sighed with relief. 'Oh, hi officers. What can we do you for?'

'May we come in, Mr Mackenzie? We have news.'

'Sure.' He glanced over at Cassie as he stepped aside and she showed them to the couch. They both sat and Cassie and Mac followed suit.

'Are either of you familiar with a Francis Coutts?'

Mac scrunched his brow. 'Nah. Not me. Cassie?'

She shook her head. 'Never heard of him. Should we have?'

The officers shared a concerned glance. 'There was a wallet discovered at the scene of the arson attack. There wasn't much inside it apart from what looks like a company credit card in the name of Francis Coutts.'

Cassie sat up straight suddenly. 'Frank is short for Francis.'

The male office tilted his head to one side. 'Well yes, we know that but it doesn't exactly help.'

Cassie gasped. 'Frank was that bald guy who was at Seth's office when I went to confront him!'

Mac swung around to face her. 'You did *what*?'

She paled and turned towards him. 'Mac, we don't have time to argue about that now.' She turned her attention back to the police officers, one of whom now had a notepad and pen at the ready. 'There was a man who came bursting in when I was in Seth's office. Seth referred to him as Frank. And the guy had started telling Seth that there was a reason they could be tied to the fire! He got so far as mentioning a wallet but Seth made him stop talking. And I had seen the same man in the village when I was on the way back from the beach. He was in a big black car. I had presumed it was someone from the funeral.' Her words came out in an excited rush.

Mac rubbed his chin. 'Hang on. I remember seeing a bald guy in a black car. I thought it was odd too but... didn't put two and two together.'

The male officer was frantically making notes and the female officer informed them, 'There were receipts for petrol and a petrol canister in the wallet. And the credit card used was a Guthrie Developments credit card. Bingo!' She clapped her hands together, a look of glee in her eyes. 'Looks like Mr Coutts is our main suspect then.'

Cassie shook her head. 'But it was *Guthrie* who instigated it. Surely, he can be arrested too?' she asked with a fear-tinged voice.

The officer shrugged. 'In all likelihood, Miss Montgomery, Mr Guthrie will insist that Coutts acted alone. We don't have any *proof* that Guthrie was connected.'

Cassie leaned forwards and rested her head in her hands. 'He can't get away with it. He pretty much *admitted* it to me.'

The female officer replied in a sympathetic tone. 'Unfortunately, that won't be admissible in court. It's just hearsay. And you and Mr Guthrie have a history, which will make this look like sour grapes. I'm so sorry. But unless we can find proof that Mr Guthrie is definitely connected then we can only go after Coutts. We can interview Guthrie, but knowing the type of clout he has in the business world, he'll more than likely be lawyered-up to the hilt. He has plenty of cash *and* connections. He can get the best backing money can buy.'

The officers stood and the male one spoke. 'We'll be in touch. In the meantime, please do *not* attempt to visit Mr Guthrie again. You'll only complicate matters and potentially put yourself in danger.'

Cassie lifted her chin and nodded despondently. Mac showed the two officers out and once the door was closed firmly behind them he stormed back through to the lounge area.

Through gritted teeth he shouted, 'Are you bloody insane?'

'Not now, Mac. Please.' She stood to walk away but he blocked her path.

'Oh no, you don't. Do you realise how dangerous that was? Have you forgotten what a twisted sicko that man is? Jesus, Cassie. If something were to have happened to you. If he'd hurt you. If... I just...' He gripped the shaggy strands of his unkempt hair and stared at her.

She walked over and cupped his cheek tenderly. 'I appreciate you worrying about me, Mac. But I'm fine. He didn't do anything. So you can calm down now.'

Without thinking he pulled her into his arms and held her close to his chest. 'You're a daft wee mare, you know that? But if anything had happened to you...' He couldn't find the words to finish the sentence without expressing his true feelings so he fell silent and just held her.

Cassie

The food was delicious. They ate sitting on the rug in front of the fire as Cliff drooled between them. Mac opened a bottle of wine and once they had finished eating they both sat staring into the flames, watching them dance and flicker. Cassie found herself observing Mac in her peripheral vision as discreetly as possible. He was such a handsome man. There was something almost sculptural about his features. He didn't have to *try* to look good. It just happened effortlessly. And she hated the fact that she was becoming more and more attracted to him. He had once made it clear that he was attracted to her, too, but after she rebuffed him so forcefully she doubted that he would ever dare to cross the line of friendship she had drawn in invisible ink between them. She regretted it now, finding him more and more appealing as she got to know him better. *But*, she reminded herself, *I'm not looking for more heartache. I don't want a relationship. They only lead to ruin and hurt and sadness. Plus, I love living here. If Mac and I got together and then split, I'd have to leave. And I really don't want to do that.*

No... friendship was good. But she had found herself playing the memory of the passionate exchange they had shared over and over again in her mind, trying to recapture the feeling of his lips against hers, the fresh scent of him infiltrating her senses; the way her body had so willingly betrayed her. But finding someone physically and sexually attractive wasn't enough. He was of the same species as the one who trampled all over her heart. She couldn't go through all that again.

She wouldn't allow it.

As they watched the flames licking at the crackling logs in the fire grate and the companionable silence enveloped them, they listened to the playlist chosen by Mac. He had such eclectic taste and she guessed that many of the bands he loved had been influenced by his carefree, sea-loving parents. The Beach Boys featured heavily and she couldn't help but smile and wonder if perhaps he had been born in the wrong era.

'So... what will you do now, Mac?' she blurted before thinking.

He turned towards her. 'With regards to what?' A look of confusion crumpled his brow.

She rested her head on her hand and eyed him cautiously. She didn't want it to sound like she was trying to get rid of him when he had literally *just* moved in. 'You know, with everything that's happened? Don't you feel like it's time to make a fresh start somehow?'

His furrowed brow deepened and she regretted prying but after a few silent moments he shrugged. 'I suppose so. Finding somewhere to live I guess is the main priority. You won't want me here until time immemorial.'

She leaned across and squeezed his forearm. 'Hey, that's not what I meant. You know you can stay as long as you want. It's *your* house after all.'

He stared into space for a while before speaking again. 'You know... I did have this ridiculous dream at one time...' The corners of his mouth twitched as his words trailed off.

Her intrigue spiked. 'Go on?'

He rolled his eyes and scratched his head, grinning with

what appeared to be embarrassment. 'You'll think I'm a wee daftie.'

She smiled and gave him a gentle, friendly shove. 'Oh, come on. You can't dangle a carrot and then whip it away like that. Spill it, *Tiger*.'

He pursed his lips and narrowed his eyes. 'Aye, all right.' He wagged a finger at her. 'But if you laugh...' He took a deep breath. 'So... you know the shack on the beach that's all boarded up?'

She nodded slowly. 'Yeees?'

'Well...' He shook his head and grinned. She couldn't tell because of the dim lighting but felt sure he was probably blushing at what he was about to admit. 'It's been for sale for ages and I've considered putting an offer in for it a couple of times.'

Cassie straightened her back and widened her eyes. 'Really? But what would you use it for?'

He scrunched his eyes tightly for a moment and cringed when he opened them. 'Okay... you really *will* think I'm a total *bawbag*. But... I fancied opening a wee café like it was before. You know, maybe running surf lessons from there too.'

Cassie clapped her hands. 'Oh God, you have to do it! That would be amazing! The beach is crying out for something like that!' her voice rose with her giddiness.

He grinned, clearly loving her enthusiasm. 'You really think so?'

She nodded eagerly. 'Oh, absolutely.'

Appearing boosted by her encouragement he laughed. 'I even had a name picked out and everything.'

She clapped her hands excitedly. 'Go on, then. What is it?'

He spread his fingers out and gestured in the air. 'Imagine this then… it's a café and a place for surf lessons… so… the name would be… "Surf Sup."' He nodded at her with wide eyes as if begging for her agreement. 'You know, *surf* for the lessons and *sup* for the drinks all the while being a play on words. You get it? Surf's up? *Surf… Sup?*'

She laughed out loud. 'Of course, I get it, you numpty. Good grief you must think I'm thick.'

He guffawed along with her waving his hands defensively. 'Nah… nah I *didnae* say that. I just wasn't sure if it was clear, you know?'

She nudged him playfully again. 'Of course, it's clear. And I think it's bloody *genius!*'

He shuffled around to face her properly. 'You do? You *really* do? I mean… you're not taking the pish?'

'I'm absolutely not *taking the pish*. I think you *have* to do it. I'll help anyway I can. What a great way to use your inheritance and create something of your own.' She really meant it. 'I'm telling you, Mac, Rab would be so, so proud.'

He briefly lowered his head at the mention of his beloved uncle. 'You think so?' His voice came out as a whisper.

She reached over again, keen for any form of physical contact, and gently squeezed his arm. 'I *know* so.'

38

MAC

Mac walked into the solicitor's office with more than a little trepidation. He remembered the same experience when his parents had been killed. And again for the reading of his uncle's will and his stomach churned at the painful, unwelcome memories.

Mr Durant, the kindly, grey-haired gentleman Mac had become all too familiar with, stood and held out his hand. 'Mr Mackenzie, good to see you. How are you holding up?'

Mac nodded. 'Yeah... erm... okay, thanks. Still not really sure it's all sunk in to be honest.'

The solicitor's brow furrowed in sympathy. 'Yes, indeed. You've had rather a lot to deal with lately what with your uncle's death and the subsequent fire. But... I hope I have something that may ease the burden of it all.'

Mac sat in the leather chair opposite and pursed his lips briefly. 'I thought I'd had everything there was to be given after Rab's death?'

Reaching for a thick file on his desk the suited gentleman shook his head. 'No, no. In this file are some things, which I presume you thought lost forever in the fire. I'm not entirely sure why Rab put them in my care, but I had strict instructions that in the event of his death they were to be handed over after his funeral. Obviously with the fire this was somewhat delayed and I do hope you can look past that fact. I surmised from the accompanying letter to me that he wanted you to be of sound mind and prepared for what was in the file and I, therefore, felt it best to wait. Well... now, it's yours. I'll leave you to peruse the contents.' He stood from the desk and handed the file to Mac before patting his shoulder and leaving the room.

Mac took a deep shaking breath and with trembling fingers he opened the file. Inside were blueprints for a house and confusion initially clouded his mind as he tried to figure out why these were being given to him. On closer inspection, he realised it was *the* house his parents had planned to build on the land beside Rab's. He gasped and his eyes welled with tears as he spotted his father's handwriting on notes regarding the resources needed to construct their family home. Flicking further, he let out a sob. There was a thick batch of photographs tied together with ribbon. Photographs of Mac with his parents, with Rab, with his grandparents. Photographs that had adorned the walls of Rab's house... *but how...* He untied the ribbon and lifted each photograph up to examine it more closely through tear-fogged eyes. These were the originals. He could tell by the aged appearance of some. Rab must have framed copies and kept the originals safely for him. *Bless his heart.*

Aware that tears were now unabashedly streaming down his face, he continued to gaze at each and every image with the fondest of memories, yet simultaneously a soul-searing sadness that gripped his insides and made his heart ache. Everything had been lost until now. *Now* he had the memories in physical form. And he only wished he could hug his uncle and thank him for this truly wonderful gift.

Right at the back of the file was an envelope. With shaking hands and barely contained emotions, Mac opened the envelope and lifted out the letter.

Hello, Son,

I know this is all a bit depressing but if you're reading this, I'm no longer with you. I've had heart trouble for a while now, see. But I didn't want to worry you. You'd already lost your mum and dad and I hate that I'm writing this, knowing that when you read it, you'll be without me too. But anyway, I suppose death is just a fact of life, eh?

On to my reason for leaving you a cryptic letter from the great beyond. As you've no doubt seen, I kept all the photos that belonged to your mum and dad. I wanted to make sure they were in safe hands until I was gone. They're the originals of the rogue's gallery I created on my walls. Dust gatherers yes, but ones that I wouldn't have removed for the world. Anyway, these are yours now.

And there's something else I need to tell you. You've inherited my house and my estate, but you'll already know that. What you don't know is that you've also inherited that café on the beach. Don't be cross but I saw you eyeing it up in the property pages when it came up for sale so I bought it for you when I knew I was ill. I could've given it to you back then but I figured grief is something that needs a focus. So this is your project, son. Make that wooden heap into something amazing. Do with it what you will. But do something that makes you happy; something that makes your heart sing and your soul calm. Do it in my memory and know that you were the best son any father could've wished for. I may not

have been your biological dad – my brother was irreplace-
able, I know that – but I looked on you as a son all the same.
And I loved you.

Be happy Tadhg,

Much love, Uncle Rab

* * *

Armed with a head full of new and surprising information, Mac
returned to Rose Brae. Exhaustion had set in and when he
walked in through the door he was ready to climb in to bed in
spite of the early afternoon hour.

Cassie greeted him with a hug and a high-pitched squeak
that screamed of a burden to be shared. 'Mac! Oh thank goodness you're here... wait what's wrong? What's happened? You
look like shit.'

He forced a smile. 'Gee thanks. It's a pretty long story and to
be honest I don't have the energy just now.'

She stepped back and knotted her hands in front of her.
'Oh... okay... not to worry. Can I get you a drink of coffee or tea
or some food or—'

Mac placed a reassuring hand on Cassie's arm. 'You're doing
that stressy thing you do. What's up?'

Cassie shook her head. 'No... no, you're tired. It can— It'll
wait.'

With a sigh, he gently tugged her behind him to the couch
and regarded her with narrowed eyes. 'Spill it, Pebble.'

She closed her eyes and inhaled noisily before huffing out.
'He's in prison.'

Mac scrunched his brow at the old news. 'Coutts? Yeah, I
already know that.'

'Seth!' she blurted. 'Seth is in prison too.'

Mac widened his eyes. 'Fuck! Really? But how...'

Cassie wrung her hands in her lap and bounced her knee as nervous energy evidently coursed through her body. 'Coutts sang like the proverbial canary. Told the police everything. How Seth paid him to torch your van *and* Rab's home. And then how Seth went along for the ride when Coutts decided it was too big a job for one man.' She stared at him with a horror-filled gaze; her cheeks had drained of colour. 'He could've killed you, Mac. If you'd been in there...' Her eyes were wide and they welled with tears as she spoke in a shaky, pain-tinged voice as if what she was saying was just dawning on her like some horrific, new realisation. She gripped the straggly strands of her hair and stared at the carpet. 'It would've been so easy. Then you'd be dead and it'd all be my fault and I wouldn't have been able to live with myself.' She lifted her gaze and locked it on him once more. 'How could I go on? I couldn't... I couldn't carry on, Tiger. I couldn't stand it. I wouldn't survive without you. I *need* you. You mean the world to me.' Her emotion-filled words fell from her lips in a dramatic rush and her chest heaved.

Mac reached up and stroked her cheek. 'Hey, shhh. He didn't kill me. I'm fine so please stop this. Calm down, okay and...' The weight of what she had just said landed on his heart like a falling wave and he gasped. 'Whoa. Hang on. You... wouldn't *survive* without me? I mean *the world* to you?' His heart picked up a pace and pounded at the cartilage of his ribs. Had he heard right? Or had he maybe imagined it? Wishful thinking was a powerful and cruel thing. Or perhaps he'd read in between the lines and discovered imagined meaning there?

Her cheeks flamed and she pulled her bottom lip in between her teeth before she spoke. 'Did I... Did I just say all that out loud?'

He nodded slowly. 'Y-you did. But... what did it all mean, Cassie?' His voice was a throaty, confused whisper.

She fell silent. Her eyes now filled with a different kind of fear. She was frozen in place and Mac had to fight the urge to laugh at her inadvertent impression of a rabbit in headlights. But this really was no laughing matter.

He reached over and squeezed her arm in the hope it would bring her back to earth. 'Hey, it's okay. Just say it. Whatever it is. Good... or... or *bad*. If what I've heard wasn't what you actually meant... just... say it, *please*?'

She swallowed and fixed her soft gaze on him now. 'I'm sorry, Mac. I know that things have been strange between us. Everything started off wrong. From the way we ended up meeting, to you rescuing me from the road, to that kiss outside the cottage...'

His heart sank. He'd misunderstood. His hope faded rapidly and he lowered his head.

She spoke again. 'But the thing is... I said I wanted to be friends and I *meant* it—'

Unwilling to allow the inevitable humiliation to ensue, he stood and forced a wide smile. 'Hey, no worries. That's fine. Shall I put the kettle on now?'

She quickly rose to her feet to join him and as he turned away she grabbed his arm. 'But... that was *then*. I meant it *then*, Mac.'

He turned to face her, his knees weakened with fear and hope. 'And... *now?*'

She closed her eyes. 'That's the problem. My feelings. The ones I didn't have for you...'

God, she was so damned frustrating! He was totally confused as to where the conversation was going and whatever the hell she was trying to say she was doing it backwards. He lifted his chin and locked his attention on her, willing her to just spit it the hell out.

She smiled weakly. 'It turns out I actually *did* have them. Feelings, I mean. For *you*.'

His heart tripped over itself and he rubbed his hand over his shaggy hair. 'You *had* feelings for me?' Should he be happy? Sad? Indifferent? 'Had?' It *was* past tense, after all.

She nodded: a slight, almost unnoticeable movement of her head. 'Have,' she whispered. 'I *have* feelings for you. I'm sorry.'

What's she sorry for?

A loud grunt of relief, or emotion, or whatever the hell it was, left his body and before he questioned for too long where the heck it had come from he swept her into his arms and covered her mouth with his like he had been desperate to do each time he saw her since the last time he'd tasted her lips.

39

CASSIE

The relief of finally getting the truth out in the open flooded her body and she allowed herself to be swept along in a wave of passion as Mac kissed the breath from her. A light-headed sensation of delight replaced the knot of fear in her stomach as she kissed him back with just as much fervour. The feeling of his tongue dancing a heated tango with hers, sent shivers of pleasure through every nerve ending and the heat of desire warmed her core. Her fingers tangled in his tousled hair whilst the stubble of his chin grazed at hers reminding her that this was real.

She was finally in his arms.

He pulled away without warning, his panted breaths coming fast and his brow crumpled in confusion.

He cupped her cheeks and smoothed his thumbs over the flushed skin there. 'Is this real? Because I want this to be real so badly, but I'm also not known for my tact and I don't want to mess this up.'

She allowed a sweet smile to grace her lips and she nodded.

'It's very real. I... I think...' She stopped, afraid of saying too much too soon.

He slipped his hands into her hair and ran his nose down hers. 'You think what? Just say it because the real probability is that I'm thinking the same thing.'

Spurred on by his admission she bravely told him, 'I think I'm in love with you, Mac.'

His responding grin lifted her heart and he breathed, 'You took the words right out of my mouth.'

She crushed her lips to his again, desperate to feel every inch of his body against hers and berated herself for not admitting her feelings sooner. She'd been so cagey about trusting him. But after everything that had come to light about Seth she could see there was no comparison. Where Seth was possessive, jealous and controlling, Mac was genuine, kind, loving and caring. He didn't have a materialistic bone in his body and he had fallen for her after seeing her in her lowest, heartbroken state. After she had, quite frankly, been a bitch of epic proportions. *And* after her ex had done his best to ruin his life.

Mac pulled away once more and rested his forehead on hers. 'Can you do me one thing, Pebble?' She nodded, willing to do anything at that precise moment. 'Will you set the pace here? Because I don't want to mess this up and I just know that I will if I do what I want to do right now. So... just tell me how you want this to go. I'll wait if you want to before we go any further. We can take it slow, see how things go. I *so* don't want to mess this up.' He closed his eyes briefly, emphasising his point.

With her arms around his broad shoulders and his encircling her completely, she felt safe. This felt right.

Without hesitation she gazed up into his eyes. 'What is it that you want to do right now? Just say it, because the real probability is that I'm thinking the same thing.' She smiled; secretly excited by the opportunity to use his words back at him.

He inhaled slowly as if to calm himself before speaking. 'I want to take you to bed, undress you slowly and make love to you for the rest of the evening.'

Her heart skipped and her body tingled at his words. 'Funny... I was thinking I'd like that very much too.'

* * *

Several hours later as they lay in her bed, wrapped in each other's nakedness, Cassie couldn't help the smile on her lips. In the lamplight, she propped her head up on her hand and gazed down at the sculpted chest of the handsome man beside her. Her fears of being intimate with another man had been completely quashed. Tadhg Mackenzie had been both gentle and passionate; taking control of her body and delivering sensations of pleasure with his own that sent her soaring in ecstasy.

'What are you smiling about?' he asked as he tucked a strand of hair behind her ear.

She sighed. 'I think I know now what I've been missing all these years.'

He raised his eyebrows and chuckled. 'Seth not a whizz between the sheets then?'

She felt her cheeks heat with embarrassment. 'It's not that... He was... I don't know... satisfactory, I suppose.'

In an instant Mac scooped her up and climbed between her thighs again. She squealed and then giggled as he nibbled at the sensitive flesh of her neck.

'Well, I hope to goodness I was more than bloody satisfactory. Jeez. No woman should have to put up with satisfactory.'

He moved his mouth downwards until his tongue teased her

nipple and she sighed. 'You were definitely more than satisfactory.' She could feel his arousal against her thigh and it dawned on her that this would be the fourth time of the evening. That had never happened with Seth. He was always quick to jump from the bed and shower after sex, as if the smell of her was one to be washed from his skin immediately. Quite insulting, in fact. Mac, on the other hand, kissed and caressed every inch of her skin again as if feasting on the most delicious dessert he had ever tasted.

'God, Cassie you really are the most beautiful woman I've ever laid eyes on,' he moaned, his mouth full of her breast. 'The feel of you beneath me... God, there really aren't enough words in my vocabulary to describe how much I want you.'

Her eyelids fluttered closed and her lips parted as he continued to devour her. 'You're doing a great job without words, believe me,' she gasped as his fingers drifted lower... lower...

* * *

Mac

Sated once more Mac scooped Cassie into his arms and she rested her head on his chest as he stroked her hair. The scent of her coconut shampoo had been one that he'd loved from the first time he'd been close enough to smell it. Now, he closed his eyes and inhaled freely, relishing the fact that he could.

So, this was what it was meant to be like? This had been making love. He'd always thought the phrase was clichéd and *so* overused but now... *Now* he got it. Now he understood what it meant to put someone's pleasure before his own. To delight in watching a woman's expression tighten and release as her orgasm took hold and to want to keep experiencing that over and over.

The noises of desire and enjoyment she'd made had turned him on so much more than those of any other woman he'd been with. And the way she'd clung to him as he'd reached his own climax, as if it really meant something to her, had solidified the truth he already knew. That he was meant to be hers; that in some strange, miraculous way she had arrived in the village at the right time; that the things he'd endured since her arrival hadn't happened because of her but he'd *survived* them all because of her.

He felt her breath slow as the heat of it caressed his naked chest and he held her tighter. Unwilling to let the night be over just yet. A quick glance at the clock told him that dinnertime had been well and truly bypassed. Yet, even though his stomach growled, he was reluctant to release Cassie from his embrace.

Eventually after the third hungry rumble occurred Cassie giggled. 'I think your belly needs food, Mr Mackenzie.'

He laughed and rested his arm across his eyes to hide his embarrassment. 'Shit, Yeah, that one was really loud, eh?'

She sat upright, revealing the creamy mounds of her breasts to him once again and he couldn't help his attention being drawn there. She really was gorgeous.

She slapped him playfully as she climbed from the crumpled sheets. 'Oi, Tiger. I'm up here. I'll go make some scrambled eggs on toast and open a bottle of red wine. You jump in the shower and come and join me when you're ready.'

He clambered from the bed and tugged her into his arms again. 'I don't want to shower yet. I like wearing your scent on my body,' he told her as he slipped his hands down and squeezed her bottom. Her cheeks flushed. He wasn't sure if what he'd just said had disgusted her and he stuttered an apology. 'God, I didn't mean that to sound... I mean, I didn't...'

She pulled his face down and stopped his words with her mouth. When she pulled away she lightly grazed his chest with her nails. 'You've no idea how good that makes me feel.' She smiled sexily before turning away, grabbing her satin robe and heading for the bedroom door.

40

CASSIE

Once down in the kitchen, Cassie let Cliff out into the darkness of the cottage garden and then located the music app on her phone. She thumbed through to find a Beach Boys tracklist and hit play. As she let her furry companion back into the house, the haunting, sultry opening to 'Good Vibrations' filled the room. As the chorus kicked in, the chill of the tiles beneath her feet lessened as she began to dance around the kitchen, preparing the simple meal for her new man. She sang in to the whisk as Cliff looked on with his head tilted to one side and little tail wagging frantically. No doubt he thought his human had totally lost her marbles.

The tracklist was suddenly interrupted by the ringing of her mobile phone and she reached across the counter top to grab it as she continued to whisk the eggs in her white plastic jug.

'Hello?' she answered breezily in a sing-song tone, unable and unwilling to hide the happiness from her voice.

'Hi, poppet. It's me. It's Seth.'

The smile disappeared from her lips and she felt the blood drain from her skin. Her whisking hand froze and she gulped.

She considered cutting him off but was somehow stone-like, unable to take action. 'W-what do you want?'

A deep sigh travelled across the airwaves and caused a shiver of unease to traverse her spine. 'I want to see you. It's been too long. There are things we need to discuss.'

Ignoring the imploring tone to his voice she closed her eyes and shook her head. 'How did you get this number?'

He chuckled. 'Oh come on, poppet. You know me well enough to have no need for such questions. So... when are you coming to see me?'

Her nostrils flared and as bile rose in her throat she gritted her teeth. 'In *prison*?' she hissed. 'When am I coming to see you *in prison* after you tried to kill my friend?'

'Hey, don't forget I haven't been convicted, darling. Don't be the judge and jury, eh? It's all lies and you know it.' He sighed again. 'I just want to see you. To talk.'

She slammed the whisk down, sending globules of the opaque yellow egg mixture flying across the wooden counter top. 'How are you even allowed to use the phone? And isn't there some kind of rule that says you can't contact me?'

'Cassandra, please, just listen to me. I pulled in a favour and I only have a limited amount of time. I need to see you. There are so many loose ends. *Please.* I just want to talk. I promise you that's all I want.'

Suddenly filled with defiance as she remembered how he'd treated her before the fire had even occurred, she decided to stand firm. 'No. I won't come, Seth and I'd rather you didn't contact me again. I'm hanging up now.'

'Cassie, please.' He insisted as his voice wavered. 'I'm going crazy in here. I just need to see a friendly face. I'm begging you. Please? I know you must hate me right now and I don't blame you for that but please... if you ever really loved me, come and see me. Just five minutes is all I ask. *Please*?'

How could he sound so much like the old Seth now? Had prison really had such an impact on him? Maybe he was truly remorseful. But she couldn't risk it. 'No. Sorry, Seth but I'm moving on and so should you.'

'I think you'll want to hear what I have to say. It's... it's about your mother's death.'

Her heart plummeted as if she was on a fairground ride, only without the fun. 'What are you talking about?'

'You need to come and see me. I'm not prepared to say things over the phone. Let's just say that I've had some interesting conversations in here.'

She was unwilling to believe him. 'My mother was very ill when she died. What could you possibly have to tell me about it?'

'Like I said, I can't talk over the phone. You need to come and see me. But don't tell anyone. This has to be just between you and me, Cassie. Only you and me, okay?' he whispered down the line.

Fear gripped her stomach and she didn't know what to do. If there was any chance of foul play connected to her mother's death she needed to know. 'How do I know you're not just making this up to get me to come and see you?'

'Fine, Cassie, don't come. But you'll forever be wondering. And I would hate that for you. There are people in here who know things. Awful things...' His voice trailed off.

'I'll think about it. But I won't promise anything. I don't even know if I should legally be visiting you.'

'Like I said, no one must know. *No one*, Cassie. I'm putting myself in danger telling you any of this as it is.'

'I'm hanging up now,' she informed him as tersely as

possible and hit the 'end call' button. Her heart pounded and her palms were sweating. What the hell could he possibly know? And why had her dad never mentioned this? So many questions rattled around her head. She had absolutely no clue how to deal with this latest revelation, but deep down she knew she couldn't settle if she didn't find out.

Hands came about her waist and she almost jumped out of her skin. Mac stepped to the side of her so she could clearly see his face. 'Hey, it's only me. Is everything okay?'

She pondered telling him about the call but decided not to spoil the mood they had been sharing. She forced a laugh. 'Ugh, I'm fine. Just so engrossed in cooking, I suppose.'

He nodded to her phone. 'So have I converted you?'

The Beach Boys were singing 'Good Vibrations' again and she tiptoed and planted a tender kiss on his cheek. 'You might just have. I especially love "God Only Knows" but I put it on shuffle and this came up first.'

'I can certainly agree with you on that particular track.' He stepped closer and slipped his arm around her waist again as his other hand caressed her face. 'It'll always remind me of you.'

41

Cassie shook uncontrollably as the prison officer frisked her. She had already walked through a metal detector and been required to hand in her bag. A stern-faced woman with hair scraped back into a ponytail had informed her that her visit was limited to thirty minutes but, in all honesty, she wanted to be out in five. The place was very clean but the fact it was a prison gave her the heebie-jeebies. Never in a *million years* did she expect to have cause to set foot inside one, never mind that it would be to visit Seth Guthrie of all people.

Once inside the waiting area, she glanced around at the other visitors. Some were chatting amongst themselves like this was just any normal day but others, like her, looked uncomfortable and afraid. Once the officers were ready to accept her group of fellow visitors they were shown through to a room with chairs and tables set out as if ready for interviews. They were all asked to be seated and await the arrival of their particular inmate. *Inmate.* Another word she never thought would be associated with Seth. This was all too surreal for words.

Her stomach roiled as she saw Seth walk through the door.

He looked unkempt and older somehow. His unshaven face was pale and his eyes sunken and circled with grey. But this time it was no ploy for sympathy, that much was very clear. She wouldn't have recognised him out on the street.

He gingerly sat opposite her and reached out to touch her hand where it lay on the table. She swiftly moved her hands to her lap.

'Hi, poppet. You look... you look beautiful.' His voice trembled and his eyes welled. The tears shimmered in the harsh, artificial strip lighting.

'Thank you. But please stop calling me poppet. I've always hated it. Now what did you have to tell me that was so important?' she asked dryly.

He gave a light laugh. 'Straight to the point, eh? I guess my influence on you continues.'

She snorted. 'Don't flatter yourself, Seth. You have no influence over me. Not any more. Now why did you ask me to come here?'

He sneered and leaned forwards slightly. 'Your boyfriend waiting for you outside, is he?'

Before thinking it through she snapped, 'You said not to tell anyone, so he doesn't even know I'm here.' She immediately closed her eyes and clamped her teeth down on her lips.

He laughed again. 'Tut, tut. Little Cassie's keeping secrets from her new man already? I didn't expect you to go through with that part. What *will* he think when he finds out?'

She opened her eyes and stood. 'Clearly your reason for requesting a visit was simply to wind me up. I won't stay and listen to it, Seth. Goodbye.' She turned to head for the door.

'Wait! I'm sorry. Please don't go.'

She sighed and turned to see his stature had shrunken and he suddenly resembled a lost puppy. But she was unwilling to fall for his mind games. She wanted to know what he had to tell her about her mother's death then wanted to get the hell out of there. She reluctantly turned and took her seat once more. 'Then explain why I'm here so I can get home.'

'I wanted to apologise. I treated you so badly. You didn't really deserve it.'

Angered by his use of the unnecessary adverb she jutted out her jaw and folded her arms across her chest. 'I certainly didn't deserve any of it. And neither did Mac. I can't believe you would sink so low as to ruin a man's life like that. A man you didn't even know.'

'I haven't been convicted,' he stated plainly, his eyes once again ice-cold and emotionless. God he could turn it on and off like flicking a switch. Devious bastard.

'Oh, cut the bullshit, Seth. You were jealous. You wanted something you couldn't have and so you destroyed it. It's what you do. I just never realised it until now. And your half-arsed apology is of no use to me. It won't bring back Mac's home. You caused that poor man so much pain. He could've died and thanks to my connection to *you* I would've forever felt responsible. So you could have ruined *two* lives. And you supposedly loved me once. Although, I really don't see that, looking back. You wanted a possession. Something you could own and control.' She leaned towards him and spoke through clenched teeth. 'Well, I have news for you. We're fighting back. You can't touch us any more. You can't touch *me* any more. It's over Seth. You lose. You're just a pathetic, spoiled mummy's boy. You deserve to rot in here. Now tell me what you wanted to tell me, so I can go!'

He placed his head in his hands and his shoulders shuddered. For a second, she almost felt guilty for making him cry but when he lifted his head he had a huge grin on his face. She gasped at the incredulity of it all. He was laughing at her!

He rubbed his eyes and shook his head. 'Do you know you're incredibly sexy when you're feisty. I don't know anything about your mother. But it worked, didn't it? You're here, behind your stupid surfer's back. Poor little poppet. Your mummy died through illness, of course. Believe me the naughty boys in here don't even look at me, let alone tell me anything juicy.'

All hope of him genuinely asking for forgiveness or telling her anything of importance faded. 'You callous bastard. How the hell did I ever love you?' The question was rhetorical but he appeared to be about to answer so she spoke first, 'Stop. Just stop, Seth. I don't want to hear any more.'

He held up his hands in surrender. 'You're right. I wanted you back and you were making it difficult. I don't like to lose, simple as that. No one walks out on me and gets away with it. I tried every which way to do things the nice way until you left me no choice. So if you think about it you *are* kind of responsible. If you'd come back to me none of this would've happened. I own you. You're mine. I don't let go of my possessions lightly.' He shrugged as if his explanation was the most natural thing in the world. 'But I did love you, Cassie. I may have a twisted way of showing it, yes. But the fact remains, no one will ever compare to you. And I would do anything to get you back. *Anything.*'

Shaking her head, she stood one last time. 'Oh, Seth, there's absolutely nothing you could *ever* do now to make me love you again. You killed what we had the first time you slept with that woman in our bed. And you continually put nails in the coffin each time it happened after that. But what buried us was when you involved an innocent bystander in the shitty debacle that was our relationship collapse. And then you drag my mother into the mix. You really do need help. I feel sorry for you. Sorry that you have to lie, cheat and manipulate to get what you want. We're over. Done. Have a nice life, Seth Guthrie. I'm sure you'll make some lovely new friends in here.'

Feeling buoyed by her newfound courage she walked away without looking back.

* * *

Mac

Cliff lay on the rug in front of the roaring fire watching as Mac paced up and down the room. Anger prickled at his skin and a sense of betrayal knotted his stomach. *Where the hell was she?* The call had come two hours ago. Perhaps his worst fears had been realised and she'd left?

The door opened and he stopped in his tracks to glare at the new arrival. 'Where the *fuck* have you been? I've been worried sick.'

Cassie halted in the doorway and widened her eyes, clearly shocked by his use of expletives. 'Out,' she stated plainly.

Mac shook his head and smiled sadly. 'Out?'

She nodded and removed her coat, hanging it on the hook by the door. 'That's what I said.' She made her way into the kitchen and flicked on the kettle.

Mac followed and stood behind her, arms folded across his chest where he could feel the angry thud of his heart beat. 'So, how was he?'

Cassie stopped moving and without turning to face him, asked, 'How's who?'

'Come on, Cassie, there's no point lying. I know you went to see Seth.'

She turned with an air of defiance. 'Well, you're wrong. Why the hell would I go visit that psycho?'

Mac raised his arms and let them flop loudly to his sides. 'Jesus. The fact that you went without telling me is bad enough, but now that you're lying about it hurts, Cassie. It really hurts.'

Her eyes darted towards the wall-mounted phone. Mac followed her line of sight. 'Yeah, not only does he have your mobile number, but apparently he has the house line too. I wonder where he got them from, hmm?'

Cassie closed her eyes and lowered her head as she whispered, 'He called when I'd gone. Of course, he called.'

'Oh, *he* called. He couldn't wait to tell me all about your secret little rendezvous. How you've forgiven him now and that you're going to remain good friends. All total and utter bullshit, no doubt, but after everything he's done to us you couldn't keep away from him? He called and you went running? I just don't get it, Cassie. And what I can't get my head around is that you didn't even tell me he'd called you, let alone the fact that you were actually going to visit the bastard. You kept it all quiet. I thought we had something special. A trust between us?'

Tears spilled over from Cassie's eyes and her lip trembled. 'We *do* have that. All of it. I love you, Mac. I love you very much but he said he knew things about my mother's death. He said people in the prison had been talking and that he had things he needed to tell me face to face. I know it was stupid but I had to know if there was the smallest possibility that her death wasn't as I'd been told. He manipulated me. Told me I couldn't tell anyone and that he was putting himself in danger by even calling me. I was stupid to go. I know that now. I can't believe I fell for it. But I honestly didn't think even *he* could be so cruel. But he is. He'd lied just to get me there. Just so he could try and split us up. He's an evil, sick man, Mac. And I'm so sorry. I wanted to believe that our history meant something to him but I was wrong. I know that now. A leopard doesn't change his spots.'

'And you should've known he's the biggest damned leopard that ever lived, Cassie. Seriously, how naïve could you possibly have been?' She hugged her arms around her body and tears streamed down her face. Mac fought the urge to comfort her, knowing what the devious bastard had done and how much it must have hurt her.

She couldn't seem to make eye contact now. 'I was too scared to tell you I was going. Especially with what he'd said. And I knew you'd be angry. I knew you'd disapprove.'

'Damn fucking right, I disapprove! You think I want you anywhere *near* him after what he's already done?' His body shook violently but deep down he knew he wasn't angry with Cassie. He was angry with Seth and his manipulating ways; his unwillingness to let her go. But he also knew that she was a hard woman to let go of. And sadly, he knew that if she had trusted him she would've told him about Seth's call, regardless of the arrogant arse's insistence that she didn't. And after everything they'd been through trust was a necessary foundation for their relationship.

A sad and heavy weight pressed him down and he shook his head; the fight was gone from him. 'Look, I know I can't stop you from doing whatever the hell you want to do, Cassie. We're adults and you're very much your own person – a fact I wouldn't want to change even if I could. But we *have* to be able to trust each other, to not deceive each other. But that doesn't seem to be the case for you. And without trust... without trust we don't even have an us.'

42

CASSIE

After Mac's parting words that had cut her to the core, he disappeared for a couple of hours. *Without trust we don't even have an us.* As easy as that it was ruined. She knew he would be down at the beach but she couldn't bring herself to follow him. He was right. Everything he'd said had been true. She *had* deceived him. She had gone behind his back and done the *one thing* she knew he would hate. And all for what? To discover that her original opinion of the Seth Guthrie she had chosen to leave was right all along. He was still the same manipulative, controlling, arrogant pig he had always been, only now he'd sunk to even more wicked depths. And she had fallen for his games yet again. What kind of an idiot did that make her? One that was undeserving of Mac's love that was for sure. How could he want her now? At times like this she wished Vina hadn't been Seth's sister. She really needed advice but how could she ask it of the one person who loved Seth as much as she had? *Blood is thicker than water*, Cassie reminded herself. Vina had stood by her when the break-up happened, but since Seth had gone to prison she had stopped texting and there had been no calls or emails with details of her wonderful relationship with Harry. The radio silence was deafening. Cassie had thought about contacting her but every time she had picked up her phone to do so she had reminded herself that Seth was in prison because of her when it came down to the truth. How could Vina be her friend now?

She finished putting clothes in her holdall and carried her heavy bag down the stairs with an even heavier heart. Cliff wagged his tail at the sight of her and his hopeful expression broke her heart. He thought they were going for a walk.

But what they were really doing was leaving.

Several hours later and after listening to the Beach Boys on repeat knowing it would probably be the last time she could cope with it, Cassie's dad opened the door and she immediately leapt into his arms as the emotion of the past few hours finally broke her.

'Cassie, darling, whatever's wrong?' her dad asked as he stroked her hair and manoeuvred her inside the cottage as Patch and Cliff skipped around each other excitedly like long lost friends.

'I've ruined it all, Dad. Like I always do. I took the one good thing in my life since Seth and I stamped on it. Why am I so stupid? Why am I so bloody gullible?' she shouted, anger at herself spilling over along with myriad tears from her eyes.

Her father took her hand. 'Come on and sit down. I'll make a pot of tea and you can tell me all about it, eh?'

Another hour later and all cried out, Cassie sat clutching the mug of cold tea that had once been hot and tempting. She'd told her dad everything and sat there awaiting his response. She deserved to be told what an idiot she'd been for throwing away such a wonderful relationship, budding as it was.

But her dad reached out and squeezed her arm instead. 'That mongrel hit you where it hurt the most. I would've done the same. You had to find out. I just wished you had phoned me first, sweetheart. You made an ill-informed mistake. We've all done it. But it doesn't define who we are going to be from now. It simply helps us to realise what our priorities are. And that's what's happened here. You *now* know for sure that Seth Guthrie doesn't even feature on your list. And that Mac is at the top of it. But you can't run away at the first sign of problems. You can't presume that one little bump in the road means it's over. You have to fight for what you know is right for you. And Mac is that thing. He deserves to know where you are and why you ran. He'll be worried sick.'

Cassie placed her mug on the coffee table and covered her face with her hands. 'He's better off without me, Dad. Look at the shit storm I brought to his life. None of this would have happened if it wasn't for me.'

'His uncle would still have died, Pebble. And then he wouldn't have had you there to support him. And in any case, there's no point living on 'what if'. The facts are what's important here. And the fact is he loves you. And you love him. Surely, that's not something you want to lose? Just because Seth was an arse doesn't mean Mac won't be good to you. The two are like chalk and cheese. I think you know that. Did he actually say it was over between you?'

She thought back once again to the heart wrenching words he had left her with. 'He said that without trust there is no us. It sounded pretty final to me.'

Her dad sighed. 'Why are you so pessimistic, Pebble? It doesn't sound final to me. It sounds like he's upset and needed to cool off and think. He didn't ask you to leave. And he wasn't the one who packed his bags now, was he?'

Her dad was making sense. But in her heart, she knew *she* was right. Mac didn't need to pack his bags. Rose Brae belongs to him and he could be happy there without her. He didn't need her around. She just caused trouble. Made him sad and angry. He'd be glad to see the back of her, surely?

Cassie's phone rang and she stared in the direction of it where it sat on the table. She was too far away to see the screen but too upset to answer it anyway. Her dad patted her arm and nodded once as he stood to go answer it for her. He walked into the hallway as he greeted the caller, presumably in case it was someone she really didn't want to speak to. She couldn't hear what was being said but when her father returned she lifted her gaze hopefully, her heart skipping in her chest.

'W-was it him?' she asked as she twisted her fingers in her lap.

Her dad's face crumpled in sympathy and he shook his head. 'Sorry, love. No, it was Sally Cairns. She said she'd bumped into Mac and he'd told her you'd gone. He looked bereft by all accounts.'

She lowered her gaze to the two little dogs nuzzling at her legs, vying for attention. 'But he didn't call. So I'm probably right after all.' She wiped the moisture from her eyes and glanced at the clock. It was almost midnight and she was drained. 'Is the spare bed made up, dad?'

He nodded. 'It's your bed, sweetheart, and it's always made up ready for you whenever you need it.'

She stood and kissed his cheek. 'I think I'll turn in, if you don't mind. I'm shattered.'

'Okay, love. I'll sort Cliff out. You just get some rest. Love you.' He kissed her forehead and she headed for the stairs.

* * *

Once inside the cosy surroundings of her bedroom she closed the striped, blue curtains and lowered herself to the single bed that sat in the centre of the room. The pale blue flowery bedspread still looked pristine and the walls still held the posters from her teenage years. *Oh, to be a teenager again*, she thought. *Only the worries of crushes and exams to concern me back then.*

She undressed and grabbed an old T-shirt and her toiletries from her bag before making her way to the bathroom next door. Once she had washed the tear stains from her face and brushed her teeth she went back to her room to find Cliff curled up in a ball at the bottom of the bed. She bent to nuzzle his fur and he stretched and pawed at her.

'You're such a sweetie, Cliff. What would I do without you?' He wearily wagged his tail and curled back into a ball. Once in bed she flicked off the lamp and lay there in the darkness going over everything that had happened with Seth and then every special moment she had shared with Mac. She swiped at the tears trickling down her face and into her hair and closed her eyes, doing her best to fight the images of Mac, bare-chested in bed, staring at her with that love-filled gaze of his. But it was futile. He was etched in her mind and on her heart forever. And it was something she would have to learn to live with.

* * *

Mac

Hi Mac,

I want to apologise for all the pain I've caused you. It

seems that I've brought nothing but trouble into your life since I arrived. I really hoped we had a future but I see now that you are better off without me. It seems that Seth will do his utmost to ruin my life and the lives of those around me too. Perhaps I just need to be where he can't do this. Far away from you and the others I love. I will send for the rest of my things soon. But please know that I truly love you and never intended to lie to you or hurt you. I wouldn't do that for all the salt in the ocean. Please don't hate me. Be happy.

With more love than I can express on paper,

Pebble

Mac shook his head and scrunched the paper up in his fist. He yelled out as he threw it across the kitchen and didn't bother to watch where it landed.

'Oh no, Seth Guthrie. You don't get to ruin us. You don't get to win this time,' he said aloud to the empty room before grabbing his car keys and leaving the cottage. As he switched on the engine a text pinged though to his phone. In a desperate hope that it was Cassie he scrambled around the passenger seat until he picked it up and stared at the screen.

> She's gone to her dad's. I will send the address
> and phone number. I hope you're okay. Sally x

43

CASSIE

Cassie awoke with a start as a loud banging noise vibrated up through the walls and floors from downstairs. The noise eventually registered as someone pounding on the front door. Both dogs barked in alarm and her immediate thought was that Seth had somehow been released and had come to look for her. Her heart hammered at her ribs and her breathing rate increased as adrenalin surged through her veins. She heard her dad jogging down the stairs yelling at whoever it was to keep their hair on.

'Dad! No!' Cassie yelled, terrified as she leapt from the comfort of her bed and ran for the door. But when she arrived at the top of the stairs, she could see Mac standing in the open doorway and a combination of relief and trepidation flooded her mind.

Mac was running his hands over his hair. 'I'm so sorry, Mr Montgomery. I didn't mean to scare you. It was stupid. I should've called first but, in all honesty, it couldn't wait.'

'You'd better come in, Mac, Cassie's sleeping but—'

'It's okay, Dad. I'm here,' Cassie interrupted as she made her way down the stairs to the door.

Mac's eyes lit up when he saw her but his excitement was quickly replaced by a glare of anger. 'Can we talk?' he asked tersely. She nodded and gestured towards the lounge.

Her dad placed his hand on her arm. 'Will you be okay, sweetheart? I can stay if...' he shrugged and glanced across at Mac.

She smiled warmly. 'No, no it's fine, Dad. You go on back to bed.'

He nodded and turned to Mac. 'Whatever you've come to say, go easy on my girl, you hear me?'

Mac's icy demeanour melted a little and he smiled. 'She's safe with me, Mr M. I promise you that.'

Once her dad was gone she closed the living room door behind them and glanced around the homely familiar surroundings. The room was small and tired but clean. Embers still glowed in the fireplace and above it on the mantel sat photos of Cassie at various ages throughout her life. Mac would be seeing it all; from the plump-faced toddler in pigtails to the brace-mouthed, spotty teenager.

She took a deep breath and turned to face Mac. 'Can I get you a drink? Some food? We've got coffee, water... We do have wine but I'm guessing you drove here so—'

'You're doing that stressy thing again. I'm fine. Let's just sit, eh?' He had softened much more and so Cassie sat, pulling her old tatty robe from her room tight around her.

'It's three in the morning Mac, what couldn't wait?'

Mac huffed and shook his head. 'A fucking "Dear John" letter. You did a runner and left me a "Dear John" letter.'

She pulled at a thread in her lap and shrugged. 'I didn't know what else to do. You said we were over. So I left.'

'Erm, no. What I *actually* said was that without *trust* there's no us. I never once said we were over. But you chose to read between the lines, Cassie. You heard something I never said. Yes, I was angry. And I was hurt. And if I'm honest I thought *you* were ready for us to be over seeing as you went to see *him*. But I didn't want to hear it so I went for a walk to clear my head. I never expected to find you'd gone when I returned.' She listened intently and suddenly felt very foolish. 'And when I found that letter I had to come and find you. I'm not ready to give up on us. If we've hit a hurdle we figure out a way around it. We don't quit.' There was a long pause and he pleaded at her with his eyes. 'Unless... unless *you* want to quit?'

She slowly shook her head as the sting of tears prickled at her eyes. 'I don't want to quit,' she whispered.

He stood and walked around the coffee table to sit beside her. 'That's so good to hear.' His voice cracked as he spoke. 'Because I really don't want to lose you.'

Her lip trembled as she saw her own emotion mirrored in his eyes. 'You haven't lost me. I'm so sorry for what I did. So very sorry. I wish I could go back and change things.'

He reached up and cupped her cheek in his large rough palm. 'Let's just forget it, okay? What's done is done. We can't let him spoil things for us any more. He has to be in the past now. For both our sakes. Okay?'

She nodded as tears left damp trails down her cheeks. 'Okay.'

'We've got so much to look forward to, Cassie. And I... I have something I want to tell you.'

Unable to manage any more words she simply nodded in encouragement and he wiped at his own cheeks. 'I've decided I want to build a house on the land. Thanks to my uncle Rab, I have the original plans for the house my folks wanted to build and I want to go ahead and fulfil their dream. And... And I want you to live in it with me.'

She gasped. 'Really? But what about Rose Brae?'

He laughed. 'Well, we can't live in two places at once, can we? But we'll stay there until the house is built and then... well then, maybe we'll rent it out. It'll make someone a lovely home.'

She gave herself a moment for the news to sink in. 'I can't believe you'd let me have a room in your brand-new house. That's so kind.'

He scrunched his face. 'Hang on. I don't think you're getting this. I'm not renting you a room, you daft wee mare. I'm asking you to live with me. With me in *our* home and in *our* bedroom.'

She widened her eyes as his words actually sank in this time. 'Oh God, I'm so stupid. I didn't realise you meant... And that I'd... Oh, Mac!' She flung her arms around his neck and crushed her lips to his as his arms came about her and he returned the kiss with as much passion and desperation.

He pulled away and smoothed her hair back from her face. 'So, you'll come home?'

She ran her nose the length of his. 'I'll come home.'

44

MAC

Cassie had been home for a few days but Mac still grinned like an idiot every time he looked over and saw her sitting there on the couch. It didn't matter that she was make-up-free, in her joggers and a T-shirt with her legs tucked under her, a mug of coffee in one hand and a romance novel in the other.

To him she couldn't be more perfect.

'Tiger, you're staring again,' she smiled as she spoke. He loved that she had taken to calling him by the silly pet name all the time and he responded in kind with hers.

'That's because you're bloody gorgeous, Pebble.'

The day after she returned to Coldingham, he had spread out the plans for the house and explained each and every aspect of their home-to-be. He loved how enthusiastic she was about it all and how she got excited about the prospect of choosing wall-papers, paint colours and carpets. He knew she had a good eye for such things and couldn't help being equally as giddy about seeing the house when she'd worked her magic. From what she'd said about Seth's apartment, it had been a stark, white pristine palace of a place and she was staunchly against their new home being in any way similar. There would be colour and local artwork along with antique pieces and second-hand furniture. It would quirky and eclectic. And *theirs.*

Cassie had agreed to take the afternoon off work to go to the café with him seeing as he hadn't visited since bringing the keys home from the solicitor's office. He wanted to wait until she could go with him and that day had arrived. She was working at the kitchen table and Mac tried his best to keep himself occupied. He'd waxed both his surfboards. Tidied the garden, walked Cliff *and* been for a jog. But no matter how many things he did the time seemed to tick by slower and slower.

'Good grief, you're like a kid on Christmas Eve!' Cassie said on the fifth time he had poked his head around to see if she was nearly done. 'Come on! Let's just go. This boiler manual I'm proofing can wait.'

'Really?' he asked, sitting opposite her and resting his head on his hand feigning interest. 'Because it sounds riveting.'

She threw a balled-up piece of notepaper at him and he ducked, guffawing loudly.

* * *

Cassie

Cassie had to almost jog to keep up with Mac as they headed down the slope towards the beach and she was quite out of breath when they finally reached the sand. It was a bright but chilly autumn day and the beach was alive with surfers and people in kayaks making the most of the waves created by the east coast breeze.

She paused to take in the picturesque scene and to catch her breath. The sun was low in the sky casting an almost golden glow all around and glinting on anything with a shiny surface. The waves rolled towards the sand but there was nothing ferocious about them as they darted to greet the visitors on the shore. The whole scene was one of serenity and Cassie inhaled deeply as a smile played upon her lips.

Impatient, Mac was soon tugging at her arm. 'Come ooooon. Let's gooooooo.' *Yup, kid at Christmas time.* She rolled her eyes but couldn't stop the grin that accompanied the gesture.

Mac was already at the door jiggling the key in the padlock until it released. He turned and gave a thumbs-up to Cassie. Then his brow creased and he tapped his chin. 'Should I carry you over the threshold?'

'It's a café not a house so it doesn't count. And anyway, we're not married, you wally.' *Yes, Montgomery, that latter point should have been the first thing that struck you.* Suddenly the prospect of being someone's wife didn't seem so abhorrent. Her last experience at planning nuptials had been a disaster but she knew it would be totally different with Mac. She shook her head to eradicate the mental intrusion; after all there had been no mention of weddings. *Good grief, calm down, Cassie.*

Mac playfully chuntered, 'Spoilsport,' as he tugged the door open wide.

They were greeted by a cloud of dust motes dancing in the light that filtered in through the cracks in the shutters and the place smelled damp and dirty through lack of use but Mac didn't seem to notice as he opened each shutter in turn and allowed the daylight to flood in.

He held out his arms and grinned at her. 'See, it's perfect! It needs a lick of paint and a bit of TLC but that's all. I can have that done in a weekend.' He walked over to her and slipped his arms around her as they took in their surroundings. 'I can't believe it's actually ours.' He sighed and rested his chin atop her head.

'Well, it's *yours,* technically,' she reminded him.

He lowered his lips to her ear and whispered, '*Ours.*' A shiver of excitement and lust flitted over her skin.

The walls were whitewashed but in need of a repaint. The tables and chairs were all laid out as if it was just closed for the day and all were in remarkably good condition – nothing that a wipe down with disinfectant wouldn't fix. The floor was made up of orange terracotta tiles, some of which were cracked but in all honesty, it gave the place a bit of character.

He took her by the hand and she followed Mac as he walked behind the counter to the kitchen area. It was large enough to produce anything from cakes to full-blown meals and she knew it was ideal for what he had in mind. Seeing his face light up made her heart soar. After everything he had been through it was so good to know things were improving.

'So how long before you want to be up and running?' she asked as he opened and closed cupboards.

He shrugged. 'Couple of weeks tops.'

Rather taken aback by his timescale she tripped over her own tongue. 'But... I mean... how? You don't know the first thing about running a café how on earth can you be ready so quickly?'

He tapped his nose. 'I have a friend in the village who worked here many years ago and she's offered to go through things with me. And her son is looking for a part-time job to fit in with his studies so I won't be doing it alone. I've seen these metal signs online that I think will look awesome on the walls. Kind of old surfing ads. And some bright wipeable table cloths too. Aww, Cassie, it's going to be fantastic.'

Well, he had certainly got it all set in his mind. And to say she was proud was the biggest understatement. She simply couldn't wait to go along for the ride with him as he realised his dream.

Back at home later he showed her all the things he had seen to brighten the café up and he clicked to order them. Large rustic-looking tin signs with images of beaches and surfers would be adorning the walls in no time at all. His ideas were going to make it the place to be that was for sure. Then there was a brief phone call to a friend of his who was a sign painter and the new 'Surf Sup' sign was in the pipeline.

45

The days were getting shorter as winter approached and Mac had been spending most of his time at the beach café. Cassie had expected business to be incredibly slow on account of the time of year but it turned out that the surfers of Coldingham Bay were nothing if not diehard. Every night since opening Surf Sup he came home with a huge grin on his face and full of stories about his day and the characters he'd encountered. He was buzzing with excitement.

There had been news of a date for the trial too and things were really gearing up. Cassie couldn't wait to put the whole affair behind her and move on with Mac and their wonderful new life together. But it would still take time.

She was sitting drinking coffee on the sofa with Cliff and waiting for Mac to arrive home so they could head out to dinner at Sally and Derek's when there was a knock at the front door.

Cassie scratched Cliff's head. 'Silly dad's forgotten his key again,' she told him as she opened it with a smile.

'H-hi, Cassie. Before you slam the door in my face I wondered if you'd hear me out?'

'Vina! What the heck are you doing here? And *why*? I mean, I don't hear from you in ages and then you show up here?' Cassie didn't try to hide her incredulity.

Vina looked pale and downtrodden in her black leggings and plain grey hoodie. Her hair was pinned up in a messy bun, which really wasn't her usual style. It was the first time Cassie had ever seen her dressed so casually outside of the house and without a full face of make-up. 'Please could I come in? I just want to talk to you.'

'Of course, come in.' She stepped aside.

Vina walked through into the kitchen and smiled at her surroundings. 'This place is lovely, Cassie. So... you. Not like that Glasgow apartment. You were never really right there.'

Cassie huffed. 'Gee, thanks.'

Vina held up her hand. 'No, no, you misunderstand. I don't mean it in a negative way. That place was too stark for you. Too soulless. And you're not soulless, Cassie. You're one of the best people I know.'

Now she was inside and under the LED lights in the kitchen, Cassie could see that Vina's cheekbones were sharper than usual meaning she'd lost weight and from the dark circles around her eyes she clearly hadn't been sleeping. She was unsure what to say.

But Vina spoke again. 'He lied to us all, you know? Seth, I mean. When I went to visit him in prison the week he went in, he told me that you'd cheated on him first. That you'd bad-mouthed me and the rest of the family. That you'd admitted you were only with him for the family fortune. He's my brother so... so, I believed him. That's why I've kept away.' She lowered her gaze and twisted her hands in front of her. 'I know now that he was lying. I know our friendship can never be repaired, Cassie, but... I wanted to at least apologise for that fact. You were the best friend I'd ever had. You were so genuine. No agendas.' She frowned and glanced away. 'I can't actually believe I took his word over yours. But I suppose family loyalty can do that. But anyway, I wanted to say that I wish you well. And that Seth deserves everything he gets. I'm... I'm ashamed to be related to him if the truth be told. I suppose I'll always love him in a way but I don't like him. Not one bit. I can't believe what he's done to you and to your boyfriend.' She lifted her gaze and locked watery, red-rimmed eyes on Cassie. 'I mean it, Cassie, I'm so sorry. And I hope that one day you'll forgive me.' She wiped at her eyes and turned towards the door.

Overcome with compassion, as she was wont to be, Cassie grabbed Vina's arm. 'Hey, you've come all this way; the least I can do is make you a cup of tea. What do you say?'

Vina turned to face her and sobbed as she flung her arms around her. 'Oh, yes, please. That would be lovely. Thank you so much.'

Vina stayed for an hour and the former friends talked at length about what had happened to Seth and how he'd changed. Vina informed her that his penthouse flat had been sold and some of his business interests had been signed over to their father. What was harder to hear was that their parents had been struggling with the knowledge of the depths their son had sunk to in order to try and get what he wanted. They were horrified and there had been a spell in hospital for Vina's mother as a result of the whole situation. Cassie's heart ached for them. They had always been so good to her. They didn't deserve to go through this either.

When she was about to leave, Vina hugged Cassie tight. 'I'm so glad you found someone who treats you right and puts you first. No one should have to put up with what you endured from Seth. And I can only apologise again for what he's put you all through. And for the fact that I introduced you. I just... I guess I never really knew him. I don't know if I'll be in touch again. This is all taking its toll on the family as you can imagine. We're having to build a lot of bridges just now. Harry and I... Well, this whole thing took its toll on us too. I think we're over.' Tears trickled down her cheeks. 'He doesn't want it to be, but I can't put him through all the bad publicity. Anyway, I just wanted to make sure you were okay. My parents were very concerned too but obviously didn't feel they had a right to turn up on your doorstep. They thought a lot of you, Cassie. They *think* a lot of you and wouldn't ever want you to suffer at the hands of my brother, I hope you know that.'

Cassie smiled through tear-fogged eyes. 'Thank you. I think this has been good for both of us. I suppose I've got the answers to the questions I had about where things went wrong between *us*. And if you want to stay in touch... well, that's fine with me. We've known each other a long time and it'd be a shame to lose that friendship. But I also understand that you may need to move on. I know I have to in many ways.'

Vina smiled sadly as she hugged her. 'Be happy, Cassie. Always be happy.' And with a kiss to her cheek Vina walked away into the night to wherever she had parked her car.

A short while later, Cassie was relieved when Mac dashed in through the door, filled with his usual excitable energy. 'Hi, Pebble, wait 'til you hear who I've been chatting to on the phone today at work. Ooh, are you okay? Have you been crying?'

She nodded as he folded her in his warm, familiar embrace. 'I had a visit from Vina today.'

'Seth's sister? What the hell?'

She gazed up at him and kissed the stubble of his chin. 'It's fine. She didn't come to cause trouble. She looked awful. Completely heartbroken by this whole thing. I really felt for her. He'd strung her a line too. And his parents. I think the shock of finding out who he really is has caused irreparable damage to far too many people.'

Mac sighed as he cuddled her close to him. 'Nasty piece of work that poor excuse for a man. Who does that to their parents? I know both you and I would give anything to see ours again.' She nodded into his chest. 'Speaking of which, I've had an amazing idea.'

Excited to hear something good she smiled up at him. 'Really? Has this got something to do with whomever you were talking to on the phone today?'

He tugged her to the couch. 'Yup. I called your dad to see how he was doing and to ask his advice about... something. Anyway, he was saying how much he misses you. And how he wished he lived closer. So...'

She scrunched her brow but grinned; eager to hear what hare-brained scheme he had come up with. 'So?'

'He should move into Rose Brae. He should sell his cottage and move here. The house will be empty once we move into the new place. The builders will be breaking ground at the first sign of spring and these guys work fast once they get going. So, it won't be too long before the house is free for him.'

Cassie opened and closed her mouth. A lump of emotion lodged itself in her throat and her eyes misted over. 'First of all... you called my dad to see how he was? How sweet are you? And second... you want him to come and live here?'

Mac shrugged as if it was the most sensible and obvious idea he'd ever had. 'Makes total sense. Don't you think?'

She lurched herself at him and kissed every inch of his face. 'Have I told you how much I love you?'

He tugged her into his lap and returned her kisses. 'Yeah, but I never tire of hearing it.'

'And you'd be okay with my dad living so close?'

He brushed her hair away from her face. 'Cassie, I would give anything to have my mum and dad close by again. And Rab too. Family is everything. Your dad's great. He treats me like a son and I can't think of anyone I would rather have living in Rose Brae. Although, you can tell him we won't accept rent. As far as I'm concerned, it'll be his house. We won't accept a penny from him.'

She sighed and shook her head. 'Whatever did I do to deserve someone as wonderful as you?'

He grinned. 'Oh, you must have been very, very good at some point,' he said with a teasing wink. 'In fact, I reckon you should take me upstairs and show me just how good you can be.' He raised his eyebrows and leaned forward to nibble on her bottom lip.

She slid off his lap and took him by the hand. 'You don't have to tell me twice, Tiger.'

He stood and with a playful growl followed her as she led him to their bedroom.

46

EIGHT MONTHS LATER...

Saturday meant a long lie in and Cassie was more than happy to take advantage of the fact that Mac was up and out early. He always wanted to get the café open as quickly as possible throughout the summer holiday season when his first customers would no doubt be those catching the early morning waves. Cliff had been allowed upstairs to snuggle on her bed and he was laying there on his back, legs in the air and tongue lolling out one side of his mouth. She would've slept longer if it hadn't been for the little Border Terrier's snoring. How such a tiny dog could snore so loudly was beyond her.

Eventually she gave up and got out of bed and when she went downstairs to make fresh coffee, Cliff gave an indignant sigh and reluctantly followed. Clearly one of them was enjoying their snooze.

The cottage was a little echoey now that their possessions were gradually being boxed up and relocated to the new house. She felt a pang of sadness at leaving the place she had called home. But she knew that exciting things lay ahead and so thankfully the melancholy was brief.

Mac had left her a note on the kitchen table, telling her to meet him at their beach hut at twelve thirty for lunch and promising he would be all hers with no distractions. She smiled and rolled her eyes on reading that last part. Their lunch dates usually entailed a five-minute break for him in which he would serve up baked goods from Surf Sup and a couple of half empty coffee mugs, the contents of which would have been spilled enroute from the other end of the beach. But regardless of that she wouldn't change their previous lunch and dinner dates for all the salt in the ocean. She relished every single one that had taken place at their hut – it was, after all, their favourite spot and an oasis that they enjoyed together.

Once it was made Cassie sipped on her freshly brewed, fair-trade Arabica coffee and gazed out of the kitchen window at the azure sky above. The sun was high over Coldingham on its cloudless backdrop today, which meant the tourists would be out in force when she arrived at the beach. Their cheerful little hut was a talking point and the envy of everyone who visited the bay – locals and visitors alike. It was the best spot to sit and watch the world go by.

Once she had finished her second cup of coffee she decided on a nice, lengthy, luxurious soak in the tub whilst she read her latest romance novel, aptly named *A Seaside Escape*, and as she lay there immersed in both the water *and* the storyline, time began to slip away from her until her fingers resembled grapes left out in the sun too long. Once she was out of the bath and dried she checked the time and then eagerly dashed up to her room. After tugging on simple white undies she rifled through her wardrobe, looking for the perfect summer dress. The white one with yellow flowers seemed to echo the colour of the sun above and she slipped it on before applying sunscreen to every patch of exposed skin. Mac was a stickler for skin protection.

Knowing that their beach dates usually carried on into the evening once Mac had closed the café, she grabbed her pretty shawl too. Although, she knew that if she got too cold Mac would warm up her up – he had that effect even if it wasn't cold. She sighed at the thought of his strong, muscular arms wrapped around her and his warm breath against her ear sending tingles down her spine as they watched the waves lazily meandering towards the shore.

She clipped Cliff's lead on and pulled the cottage door locked behind her and they set out for the beach. It was so lovely that Mac had taken time off from Surf Sup considering how proud he was of the place. He was still in that heady romantic first love phase with his new business venture and she had teased him about being a control freak where the café and surf shack was concerned – but he openly admitted the fact and usually did so with a sexy grin.

His assistants were more than capable of running the place but she admired him for being the ever-present captain of his newly launched ship. *He must be worn out if he's handed control over even for a lunch break*, she surmised. But nevertheless she was grateful and excited at the prospect of a Saturday where she got to see his legs. They were usually hidden behind the counter as he dealt amiably with customers wanting to hire surfboards, book lessons or order lunch. He had finally achieved his dream and Cassie was so happy to be tagging along for the ride.

The village was surprisingly quiet and as she reached the slope that lead to the beach she stopped and turned to admire their new home in all its glory. She crouched to give Cliff a scratch behind the ears as she gazed upon the newly built structure. It was hard to believe that not so long ago so much sadness and drama had occurred on that very plot. But they would soon be moving in and then her dad would arrive to move into Rose

Brae, meaning he would be a permanent fixture in both the village *and* their lives. She couldn't wait.

But how things had changed. And how fast it had all happened. The beautiful little house they'd built on the scorched plot was exactly as Mac's parents had planned it all those years ago. Small but just right for them. Neither Mac nor Cassie was materialistic and this house meant so much more to them. It was the legacy left to him by his parents and Cassie was honoured to have been a part of its realisation. The garden was large which meant that there was space for a man cave, which Mac had earmarked for all his surfing gear, Cassie would have an office inside on the ground floor so she could work and close the door at the end of the day and there were four bedrooms upstairs which meant plenty of room to expand – when that time arose. Cassie and Mac had named their new home 'Phoenix Cottage' rather aptly after what had gone before. But just like the mythical bird that rose from the ashes, they were determined not to let anything keep them down – especially not an egotistical maniac who couldn't stand the thought of anyone being happy and having what *he* couldn't. Shaking her head to eradicate thoughts of Seth from her mind she stood and began the descent to the beach.

A couple of seconds later she spotted Morag from the shop and she waved. 'Hi, Morag! Lovely day, isn't it?'

The elderly lady walked towards her and with a warm smile she held out a rose. 'Ah, Cassie. What a lovely dress. Mac always says you brighten the place up and he's right.'

Cassie took the offered rose and felt her cheeks heat. 'Oh, that's so lovely. Thank you.' She brought the rose up and smelled its sweet fragrance as Morag lifted her hand to wave and walked on towards the main street.

A couple of hundred yards later she spotted another of her

friends. 'Hi, Sal! How are you? I was going to pop round later if you'll be in?'

Sally walked towards her and hugged her. She took her hand. 'You look absolutely beautiful. Radiant, in fact. Mac says you're the most beautiful woman he's ever known.' She too handed over a rose, which Cassie took with more than a little confusion at the coincidence. Then Sally squeezed her hand and carried on walking.

Well, this is all a bit odd, she thought as she watched Sally retreating up the slope. *What's gotten into people today?* 'Maybe she's caught too much sun, eh, Cliff?' She answered her own question.

As she walked on the next person she encountered was Gordon from the antiques shop. Now this *was* strange. He never took time off work unless *she* was covering for him. And he rarely visited the beach. 'Oh, it's too sandy for my liking,' he had informed her once when she had invited him to join her at the hut. But there he was standing on the slope in his usual tweed jacket. Maybe Mac's willingness to temporarily relinquish control of his business was contagious?

'Hi, Gordon. Are you out to enjoy the sunshine too?' She shielded her eyes as she smiled over at him.

'Ah, Cassie,' he said as he walked towards her. Once he reached her he stopped and leaned in to kiss both her cheeks. 'Look at you. Beautiful as always. Mac says you have the most heart-stopping smile. He's right, you know.' He placed a hand dramatically over his heart and held out his rose towards her. She took it and he sighed, smiling and shaking his head as he walked by her and slowly made his way up the slope.

Cassie stopped for a moment, her brow scrunched. 'I think I've walked into an episode of the *Twilight Zone,* Cliff.' She laughed at her own paranoia and continued on her journey.

'Hi, Cassie!' Liam, one of Mac's employees shouted to her from further down the slope. He jogged over, a rose in his hand and a rather embarrassed pink tinge to his cheeks. In his strong Scottish accent he informed her, 'Erm… Mac says you drive him bloody mad and you're stubborn as a mule but he still adores you.' He handed her the rose and jogged on past as fast as he could, making minimal eye contact and without giving her a chance to answer.

Ahh… okay, this is Mac's way of giving me flowers, she surmised with a grin. It was different that was for sure. *He's a romantic, after all. I owe him an apology.*

At the bottom of the hill was Doctor Cairns. He made no effort to hide his reasons for being there. Instead he immediately held out his rose for her. 'Mac says that the fact he swept you off your feet on the day you fell, was the start of the best time in his life. And just as he rescued you then, you rescued him right back and he'll be forever grateful to you. He thanks God every day that you came into his life and doesn't know where he'd be now after everything that's happened, if it hadn't been for you.'

She took the rose and cleared her throat to speak but once her tear-blurred vision had cleared the doctor had gone. *But if it wasn't for me he probably wouldn't have gone through it all*, was the thought that niggled at her.

She gazed at the beautiful, fragrant roses as she stepped onto the sand and as she arrived beside the lifeguard station she lifted her chin and stopped in her tracks with a gasp.

'Dad! What are you doing here? You're not due to arrive for a few days yet!'

He walked towards her with a proud, loving smile taking over his handsome, weatherworn features. 'Hi, my little Pebble. I thought I'd come early and surprise you.' He produced a huge bouquet of the same roses from behind his back and then pulled her into an embrace with his free arm. 'It's so good to see you,' he told her as she took the bouquet from him.

Laughing through tears that were now flowing unabashedly she said, 'I knew Mac was up to something. Now I know what it is. He's brought you to surprise me!' She clung to her father as Cliff skipped giddily at their feet. 'So how long are you staying?'

He released her, took hold of Cliff's lead and grinned. 'Well, that's the good bit. I'm here to stay permanently. Mac rang to say that he's managed to arrange for you guys to move into the new place a week early.'

Her eyes widened and she laughed. 'He *has*? The bloody dark horse! Oh, this is fantastic. Wait 'til you see the house now it's finished, Dad. It's just wonderful.'

He linked his arm through hers and tugged at Cliff to follow. 'I can't wait. Anyway, come on, Mac says we've to have a wee stroll on the beach for a while.'

Laughing again she rolled her eyes. 'And here I was thinking he'd *actually* taken some time off work to make me lunch.' She squeezed in to her dad's side. 'Although this is the perfect alternative.' She smiled fondly as he kissed the side of her head.

As they closed in on the beach hut she moved her gaze away from her dad's long enough to glance towards the beach hut. 'What the—?'

Before her was a sight that stunned her into a befuddled silence. Somehow all the people who had handed her roses were now back on the beach with all her other local friends. Music drifted through the air and she immediately recognised the sound of the group she had seen playing on the beach a few times. They were playing the Beach Boys' 'God Only Knows' and her eyes once again began to sting. The lyrics to this song had become the words that epitomised her relationship with

Mac and then, of course, Doctor Cairns had almost quoted the words at her on Mac's behalf only minutes before.

As they approached the gathered crowd she saw that there was a carpet of rose petals matching her bouquet, strewn on the sand leading up to the hut and that a rose arbour had appeared in front. Cassie's heart pounded in her chest as she realised that her surprise wasn't over, after all.

Standing under the rose-covered archway was her handsome surfer. He looked ridiculous and gorgeous all at the same time. He wore a white T-shirt that was designed to look like a dress shirt and bow tie, and underneath that he wore a kilt in the Mackenzie tartan.

Her dad freed her and she walked towards him still holding the bouquet of roses. Just before she reached the top of the stairs, Sally appeared and took the bouquet from her, her eyes were watery and the smile on her face was so wide.

Once she was standing before her shaggy-haired boyfriend he dropped to one knee. And Cassie gasped, covering her heart with her hand.

Mac cleared his throat and swallowed hard. 'Hey, Pebble. Surprise,' he whispered.

She giggled through her emotional state. 'Hey, Tiger.'

He held up a defensive hand. 'Now, I know I promised you lunch, and I swear there's definitely food involved. In fact, there's a fine spread on over at Surf Sup for everyone later.' The gathered crowd – which now included tourists – all cheered. 'But there was something I wanted to ask you first.'

Cassie wiped at the moisture on her face and nodded in encouragement. 'There was?'

He pursed his lips. 'Yes... Cassie... I... erm... wondered if you... would prefer egg mayo or tuna for your sandwiches?' The crowd burst into a mixture of laughter and pantomime boos.

'Okay, okay! So that wasn't the *actual* question,' he informed the throng with a wave of his hand.

Moving his loving gaze back to Cassie he smiled. 'Cassie Montgomery, you're the most frustrating, feisty, beautiful, sexy woman I've ever met. And I...' his voice trembled and he paused to compose himself. He coughed and momentarily glanced at the ground before taking a deep breath and lifting his face towards hers again. 'I want to be with you always. What we have now... it's more than I could ever have dreamed of. And yes, it's been a hard road to get here but... don't they say that if something is worth having it's worth fighting for? Well... this has been our fight. There have been so many times when you could've walked away. You could've upped and gone for good. Sure, it would've been easier for you to do that. But you're so strong, Cassie, so you didn't leave for good. You came back and you stayed. And now you belong here... with me... with all of us.' He swiped an errant tear from his cheek. 'So, I'm hoping you'll stay forever. Because I honestly don't know what I would do without you. Cassie... will you marry me?' He held aloft a little velvet box, which housed a beautiful, elegant and dainty square-cut diamond ring.

The crowd fell silent and all that could be heard besides the shushing of the sea was the strumming of the Beach Boys track on an acoustic guitar. Cassie gazed down at the man she had fallen head over heels for and her heart filled with love. She belonged *because* of him. And she belonged *with* him. He hadn't tried to change her. He loved her in spite of *and* because of every flaw she had.

Without noticing the bated breath of the people surrounding her she smiled down at the glassy-eyed, handsome man before her and her answer was crystal clear.

'Absolutely 100 per cent yes,' she said before launching

herself into his embrace. He stood and his mouth found hers. They kissed as if they were the only two people on the beach. They were certainly the only two that mattered to each other at that precise moment.

Cassie had often wondered what would become of her broken heart. But standing there on the beach in the arms of the man she would marry as soon as possible, and surrounded by friends – some she'd known for a while and some she had yet to meet – she knew that she had finally found her rightful place with her soulmate, Mac, in Coldingham Bay. And she knew without a doubt that what was once broken was now, and would forever be, fully mended.

Tiger and Pebble forever.

ACKNOWLEDGEMENTS

As always, I want to thank my wonderful family for the support they continue to give me. I'm very fortunate to have you all in my life. And I apologise profusely for every lovingly made cup of tea that I forgot to drink whilst engrossed in writing this story.

Thank you to the team at Boldwood, especially Caroline, for putting up with my neurotic ways. You've been so understanding and I continue to learn from you all. Thank you as always to Lorella, my agent, for being so supportive and encouraging too.

I'm eternally grateful to the myriad authors who inspire me to continue onwards. I've made some wonderful connections both within the Boldwood family and beyond it and I'm so grateful for all of you!

To every single reader who chooses one of my books to read, thank you from the bottom of my heart. There's no greater feeling for a writer than to know their characters and stories are enjoyed. Long may that continue!

ABOUT THE AUTHOR

Lisa Hobman has written many brilliantly reviewed women's fiction titles – the first of which was shortlisted by the RNA for their debut novel award. In 2012 Lisa relocated her family from Yorkshire to a village in Scotland and this beautiful backdrop now inspires her uplifting and romantic stories.

Sign up to Lisa Hobman's mailing list for news, competitions and updates on future books.

Visit Lisa's website: www.lisajhobman.com

Follow Lisa on social media:

 facebook.com/LisaJHobmanAuthor

instagram.com/lisahobmanauthor

x.com/lisajhobmanauth

ALSO BY LISA HOBMAN

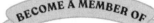

THE SHELF CARE CLUB

The home of Boldwood's
book club reads.

Find uplifting reads,
sunny escapes, cosy romances,
family dramas and more!

Sign up to the newsletter
https://bit.ly/theshelfcareclub

Boldw𝚘𝚘d

Boldwood Books is an award-winning fiction publishing company seeking out the best stories from around the world.

Find out more at www.boldwoodbooks.com

Join our reader community for brilliant books, competitions and offers!

Follow us
@BoldwoodBooks
@TheBoldBookClub

Sign up to our weekly
deals newsletter

https://bit.ly/BoldwoodBNewsletter

Printed in Great Britain
by Amazon

50022293R00205